D1559110

REALM OF EVIL

A Novel

JOHN LYMAN

PRAISE FOR THE GOD'S LIONS SERIES

"Readers who enjoy religious tales filled with symbols and mysteries will find themselves well-supplied."

J.C. Martin, Arizona Daily Star Newspaper

"A thrilling ride through fact and faith. Lyman skillfully blends scientific facts and religious mythology to propel the reader through a marvelous story to a satisfying, if startling conclusion. He paints realistic characters and puts them in terrific binds. Excellent fiction that I waited too long to read!"

Ron Franscell, Bestselling author of "Delivered from Evil"

WHAT READERS ARE SAYING

"Well researched and masterfully woven, this novel will glue you to your seat and have you hanging on with your fingernails."

"Books like this make one think outside of what you think you know about the world."

"I could not put this book down – absolutely unpredictable."

"Simply thrilling! If you read anyone this year, put this author on your short list."

This book is a work of fiction. People, places, events, and situations are the product of the author's imagination. Any resemblance to actual persons, living or dead, or historical events, is purely coincidental.

© 2013John Brooks Lyman

ISBN 9781719829328

All rights reserved.

No part of this book may be reproduced, stored in a retrieval system, or transmitted by any means without the written permission of the author.

Cover art by Steven Morales

johnlymanauthor.com

Once again, I would like to thank my brilliant wife and editor, Leigh Jane Lyman, for her unwavering support and assistance in the writing of this book. Her gentle, guiding nature serves as a model for all that is good in the world.

For Gremlin and Liz

"There is no neutral ground in the universe; every square inch, every split second, is claimed by God and counter-claimed by Satan."

C.S. Lewis

"The proof of the existence of the monster is in its victims."

Zbigniew Herbert

GOD'S LIONS

REALM OF EVIL

JOHN LYMAN

PROLOGUE

HELLSTRAND, NORWAY – 1870

It was almost midnight when the tall priest finally arrived in the tiny Norwegian village and made his way past shuttered windows toward the muted glow of firelight in the town square. Sniffing at an unscented breeze, he felt an unnatural heaviness in the air, and as he moved through the shadowed, empty streets, his senses were heightened by the fact that all the usual nocturnal songs of nature that came from the surrounding forest were strangely absent. The priest hesitated.

The feeling here was strong.

It was a feeling he had experienced before—a long, long time ago after he had been ordained as a young Jesuit priest—when he had accompanied an older and more experienced Jesuit to a troubled village in a distant land, and as the dark memory of what had happened there flashed through his mind, his heart began to race with a panicky urge to flee.

Inhaling sharply, the priest made the sign of the cross and continued on in the direction of the town square where a group of frightened-looking men shivered beneath their heavy coats, their hollow, vacant eyes straining through the tendrils of white smoke that curled from their torches, looking to see if the figure walking toward them was really a man and not something else.

Crossing the cobblestoned square, the priest stopped.

The feeling was stronger now.

He could feel a palpable fear radiating from the group of hollow-eyed men. It was like standing in front of a blazing fire, and as he searched the blank eyes of the men staring back at him, the priest knew that the time for fleeing had passed. Whatever lay in the darkness beyond the flickering light of their torches had already sensed his presence.

No one in the village could recall exactly when it had started, but all agreed that the horrific events had begun occurring right after they had seen the first dark shapes outside their windows at the end of summer, when the days had shortened, and the nights had begun to grow long.

Just past dusk on an unusually warm evening, several people in the village had caught quick, fleeting glimpses of misty dark shapes floating at the edge of a freshly plowed field. All had reported seeing the same thing— foggy apparitions that hovered in the air before drifting off into the blackness of the surrounding forest after they were spotted.

In hindsight, no one had really paid much attention to the first sightings. People had always seen shadowy things at night. Nocturnal sightings were great fodder for the ghostly tales of storytellers who traveled though the rural countryside every summer, exchanging an evening of storytelling for food and lodging before moving on to the next village. But the sightings of the mysterious dark shapes had continued, coming in clusters and occurring more frequently, until finally the first horrifying event had occurred.

On a bright fall day, a young husband and father was working in his field with a scythe to harvest the last of his wheat crop when he stopped for no apparent reason and made his way through the wavering crop to a hand-hewn wooden fence. A neighbor who had witnessed the horrific event stated that the man appeared to be in a daze when he placed the scythe against a fence post and stood back. For several minutes he had stared at the long, curved blade before running headlong toward the sharp point, impaling himself all the way through before his lifeless body fell backward into the reddening stubble of the field.

The senseless act of self-inflicted death had stunned everyone in the village. The young man had been born into a solid family and was loved by his wife and children. He had never taken to drink, worked hard, and had always helped his neighbors when they were in need.

What could possibly have possessed a seemingly normal person to do something like that?

It was then that someone had mentioned the fact that the man had been the first person to spot one of the dark shapes that had recently begun appearing outside their windows, and the word *possession* began to spread throughout the village.

For several weeks after the young man had been laid to rest, life had apparently returned to normal. No dark shapes, no bumps in the night— nothing. And then the second event occurred. A sixteen-year-old girl had returned home from milking cows and had gone straight to bed without eating supper. Later that night the village baker reported seeing a black shape on the road leading from town, and in the early morning hours the village was awakened by screams coming from the girl's house. Fearful of what they might see, many remained inside their homes, while others rushed outside just in time to witness the horrifying sight. The young girl had set herself on fire, and as the flames spiraled around her body, she laughed hysterically and danced in the road until the fire took its toll, leaving behind the smoking remains of what had once been a normal and happy teenage girl.

Three days later, a young couple had awakened to find their young son staring out at the forest from an upstairs window before he was suddenly seized by an unseen force that literally lifted him up into the air before flinging him against the walls of his room. Throughout the day the boy's father and several men from the village had restrained him, but when they heard him growl and saw his eyes turn black they all fell back in fear. Released from their grip, the boy raced from the house screaming profanities, and the next day his limp body was found hanging upside down from a tree at the edge of town.

Then, a week later, the body of an elderly man was found lying just inches beneath the surface of a clear pond with a heavy stone tied around his neck, his eyes bulging and his face frozen in a macabre grin.

For the next month and a half, as authorities and doctors and ministers flocked to the village in an attempt to find some kind of underlying cause behind the bizarre and seemingly self-inflicted deaths, the events continued to occur with startling regularity. It didn't seem to matter if one stayed locked behind closed doors or worked outside in the fields all day, death struck randomly without regard to age or sex, and to add to the horror, the frightened villagers soon found themselves cut off from the rest of the world after local authorities finally resorted to placing a quarantine around the village for fear that some kind of new plague was infecting the minds of the people who lived there.

Soon news of the villagers' plight spread to the coastal town of Bergen, where a group of protestant ministers had gathered to discuss the possibility that the cause behind the events lay within the supernatural realm and not the physical. With only one member of their group abstaining from an otherwise unanimous vote, they decided to consult a Jesuit priest who had recently arrived in Bergen and was said to know about such things.

After listening to their story, the priest withdrew to his small room in the church rectory and prayed before setting off for the village on foot in the dark of night. He knew he had to hurry. The feeling coming from the forest beyond the mountains was strong. He had felt something tugging at him, pulling him toward a shapeless dark horizon, and if he failed to make it in time, whatever was stalking the villagers would surely begin to spread.

Now, as he entered the town square, the frightened villagers peering through the smoke from their torches at the shadowy figure walking toward them were relieved to see a human face when the tall priest stopped and swept a brown woolen hood from a mop of tousled blond hair.

"Who is in charge here?"

Looking up into a pair of startling blue eyes, a middle-aged man stepped forward. "We have no leader, Father. I run the village flour mill. We just received word a few hours ago that you were coming, but there are no Catholics here. We are all Protestants. Why did they send you?"

The enlightened Jesuit's gaze remained steady. "We are all God's children, my son … Catholic and Protestant alike. I'd like to see your cemetery."

"I beg your pardon, Father?"

"The village cemetery. Where is it?"

"It's in the forest … near the ruins."

"Ruins? What kind of ruins?"

"Stone ruins … a circle of giant stones."

The priest felt the hair rise on the back of his neck. "Do you know who built them?"

"No one knows, but they are very old. They were already here when our Viking ancestors settled in this valley over a thousand years ago."

"Are you telling me you bury your dead next to ancient ruins you know nothing about?"

The man could feel the priest's eyes boring in on him. "Why yes, Father. We've always buried our dead there."

"Why do you not bury them next to the village church?"

"We have no church."

"No church?"

"No, Father. It burned down."

"And you never rebuilt it?"

The man glanced nervously at the others. "All of our churches have burned down, Father. It's been happening for years, and the time we spent trying to rebuild them was taking us away from our other work, so we finally gave up and began attending church in the next village."

A physical sense of dread began to claw at the priest's stomach. "Yet you continue to bury your dead in the forest next to old ruins instead of placing them in the sanctified ground of a churchyard?"

"We prefer to keep the remains of our loved ones close by, Father." The man's eyes glazed with the painful memory of a loved one who had recently passed.

"And these stone ruins you speak of … are there any markings on the stones?"

"Yes … quite a few. It looks like some kind of writing, but the language is foreign to us."

"And the people who died recently … all were buried next to these ruins?"

"Of course," snapped an old man standing in the center of the group. "Where else would we bury them? Have we done something wrong? Are you trying to pass some kind of Catholic judgment on us?"

Stepping from the circle of flickering light, the priest stared out at the moonlit outline of a distant ridgeline, his mind filled with thoughts of a time when he had been confronted by other suspicious villagers. "I can assure you that the evil that stalks your village sees no difference between Catholic and Protestant, sir, and I fear it grows stronger by the hour. I need to see where you bury your dead, and I need to see it now."

"Now, Father … in the dark?" The old man's eyes widened as the others shrank back in collective fear.

"I'll take you there, Father." A muscled young man pushed his way to the front of the group. "My brother was the first to die after the dark shapes came to our village. I don't care what's out there. We've suffered enough. It's time to put a stop to this madness."

Waving his torch in the chilled night air, the young man signaled for the others to follow. Emboldened by his words the others quickly fell in behind him, and against the sound of a dog barking in the distance, the dark outline of the village faded behind them as they made their way through monochromatic fields painted blue by the light of the moon filtering through the green of the surrounding forest.

With nothing but flickering torchlight to guide their way, they continued on, until finally the serenity of the blue fields gave way to the anxious blackness of a winding path. Deeper and deeper into the forest they walked, passing a line of ancient Viking burial mounds that had lain undisturbed for centuries. Like the sun and the moon and the stars, the moss-covered mounds had always been a constant to the villagers who lived in the fog-shrouded valleys of Vestlandet—a land of enchanted Norwegian fjords and equally enchanted forests that skirted the rocky coastline along the North Sea all the way from Stavanger to Kristiansund.

Thrusting their torches into the darkness, the villagers pressed deeper into the forest, until finally, like a group of nocturnal swimmers that had reached the opposite shore of a moonlit lake, they stepped out into a fern-covered clearing and stopped. The priest was stunned. There, rising in the distance like a giant shadow, a circle of towering stone monoliths dominated a field filled with lichen-covered headstones that lay tilted precariously in the moist soil.

"Is this the only ruin?" the priest inquired.

"Yes," a man with a gaunt face answered from the darkness.

"And this is where you buried your loved ones?"

"Yes, Father."

Caught up in the dream-like spell cast by the eeriness of the scene, the men stood in silence, their nervous eyes watching the priest.

Why had this priest insisted on seeing the place where they had buried their dead?

The dead were the dead—gone from this world forever. Why were they standing on fog-covered ground filled with the graves of those who were beyond his help?

It was the living who needed him now!

"What are you looking for, Father?" the muscled young man finally asked.

"Where was your brother buried?"

Raising his arm, the man's chin fell against his chest as he pointed to an area of freshly turned earth. "There, Father … his grave is there."

"And where is his headstone?"

"We marked all the recent graves with small wooden crosses while we were waiting for the stone mason to finish the new headstones, but the crosses disappeared."

"The crosses disappeared?" The priest felt a sudden chill pass through his body.

"Yes, right after the burials. We found two of them lying in the forest and one hanging in the branches of a tree. It looked like they had been flung up into the air before falling back to earth. But that's impossible … isn't it, Father?"

The priest could feel his legs growing weak, and his breath began to come in short, shallow gasps as he looked into the faces of the men. "What I'm about to ask you may sound strange … even unholy."

"What is it, Father?" Alarm flooded their eyes. "What is it you want us to do?"

"I need to see the body of the first one to die."

"You mean dig him up!" Flickering shadows crossed the face of the man's brother, highlighting his pained expression.

"I'm sorry, my son, but I'm afraid we must. The bodies of your loved ones have been buried in unsanctified ground, and I must examine the coffin of the first to die after the dark shapes appeared."

Slowly, peering down at the freshly churned earth, the young man nodded, and as the others exchanged furtive glances, the priest made the sign of the cross and doused the black soil with holy water. After bowing his head in prayer, he stepped back and nodded to the men. Quickly, two of them grabbed a pair of shovels that had been left near a fresh gravesite and began digging.

For the next hour the men took turns in their macabre excavation, pausing only briefly while the priest checked for signs of recent tampering, but nothing seemed out of place. The men continued, probing deeper, the smell of musty earth filling the air around them, until finally the inevitable clunk of a shovel against something solid made them stop. Glancing up at the priest, the two diggers in the grave waited as he sprinkled more holy water and nodded for them to continue.

With the cool air wicking the sweat from their dirt-streaked faces, the men quickly set to work removing a layer of flat stones that had been carefully placed on top of a wooden coffin, and when all of the stones had been removed, they began working their shovels down around the sides of the thin wooden box until it was completely exposed on all sides.

Satisfied at last that they had done all that had been asked of them, the two men started to climb from the dark confines of the grave when the priest held up his hand. "Remove the top."

The men shrank back in horror. "You mean … open the coffin!"

"Yes. I need to see what's inside."

"Then you'll have to do it yourself, Father," one of the men called out as they scrambled from the grave's evil embrace. "This is as far as we go."

Grabbing a shovel, the dead man's brother walked to the edge of the grave. "I'll do it."

"No." The priest reached out and gently took the shovel from the young man's hand. "Your friends are right. I should be the one to do it."

With the flickering light from the torches painting the dark earth orange all around him, the priest uttered a silent prayer and climbed down the crumbling sides of the grave. At first he tried to wedge the shovel under the top edge of the coffin, but in the tight space he found that leverage was impossible. Tossing the shovel aside, he bent over and began tugging at the cover with his bare hands, until finally the top separated with a sound that mimicked a stuck boot being lifted from the suction of wet mud, revealing what lay inside.

Reacting with a single, collective gasp, the men lurched away from the edge of the grave, terror coursing through their veins as the scent of fear filled the air. Straddling the open coffin, the priest could feel his head begin to spin. Working to slow his breathing, he quickly made the sign of the cross before climbing from the grave and collapsing on the soft earth.

"Where is he!?" the young man screamed at the priest. "Where's my brother?"

Breathing in the foul air that seemed to be growing fouler by the minute, the priest lifted himself from the moist ground and faced the horrified villagers.

"You must gather your families and leave tonight!" The priest's voice echoed against the silent stone structure that loomed over the field. "Burn it … burn it all!"

"Burn it!?" the men called out in unison. "Burn what … this field … these stones?"

"The village. You must burn everything. Leave nothing behind."

"Burn the village!?" The horrified men gripped their torches as they stared back at the priest.

"What are you talking about!?" a man shouted.

This priest must be mad!

"This is where we live … where our ancestors lived before us," a villager shouted. "This is where we were born … where we grow our food and raise our livestock. It's all we have! We can't just burn it and walk away. That's madness!"

"It will be madness if you stay." The priest stood motionless against the backdrop of a moonlit field full of leaning gravestones that surrounded the towering dark shape that rose in the distance. "Gather your families and leave tonight, and you must mark this area well as a warning to others. Anyone who remains here will soon follow those who have died into a world of darkness that lies beyond the empty grave."

"What's happening, Father?!" the young man pleaded. "Why is my brother's grave empty?"

The priest looked out over all the depressions in the ground. "I'm afraid you'll find that all of the graves here are empty."

"All of them!? The young man's body began to shiver uncontrollably. "Where did they go?"

"Transformed, my son … they've all been transformed."

CHAPTER 1

SOUTHEREN FRANCE – THE PYRENEES

PRESENT DAY

We all love something. For most of us it is another person—a spouse, a child, a lover. Then there are the beloved pets in our lives, the special places in nature we love to go to, the books we love to read, or the art that captures our imaginations and jangles our senses for no apparent reason. But regardless of all the things that bring us joy, our species seems to be searching for the love of something else. We seem to be searching for something that lies beyond the reach of the tactile world we live in … something wonderful that floats unseen in the miasma of our understanding, and it is this kind of love, the love of an invisible presence that is greater than ourselves, that drives us … drives us to be better human beings.

Staring up at the rough-hewn rafters above his bed, Cardinal Leopold Amodeo was thinking of all the things he had once loved but now seemed lost to him forever. With the arrival of spring the heavy snows of winter had passed, replaced instead with all the little budding signs of life that had suddenly appeared in the form of new green leaves and waves of tiny wildflowers that undulated across the alpine meadows below the castle.

But despite the fact that signs of new life were springing up all around him, there was a melancholy sense that the world was still locked in the grayness of winter; that the very essence of life itself was being erased, leaving him with nothing more than a vague recollection of the time he had spent as one of the most powerful cardinals in Catholic Church history.

In the silence of his room he could hear the early morning songs of birds outside his window. It was a stark reminder that innocence still abounded and that many of God's creatures, both human and animal alike, remained blissfully unaware that a great evil had arrived in their world. The dark star was still in the heavens and Adrian Acerbi had been anointed as the Antichrist, and even though the brittle winter landscape was softening to green, Leo feared that the seasonal birth of new life was nothing more than a cruel illusion. Almost overnight the world had been sucked into a black void by an evil presence that had embedded itself within the human race, and things were about to get worse—much worse.

Rising from his bed, he padded to the window and pushed the wooden shutters aside. From his eagle-like perch he gazed down on the misty blue fog that flowed like a hazy river through the valley below, and as his eyes followed the creeping mist, he could see thin shafts of early morning sunlight piercing the thick green canopy of the forest, creating dappled pools of yellow luminosity across a carpet of moist pine needles, like so many searchlights sent to rob the land of its darkness.

Transfixed by nature's beauty, Leo found himself embraced by a selfish wish that he and his friends could all just go on living their lives in their mountaintop sanctuary forever—as if nothing had happened. But something had happened, and just like the blue fog that was swirling through the valley, the unchecked evil that was spreading like a plague across the earth would soon be at their doorstep.

As a concept, Leo knew that evil itself was not something one could strike out against. Evil was a force. It ebbed and flowed through the very fabric of life, and as any student of physics will tell you, a force is not something that can be seen. Thus, we can see the apple fall from the tree but not the force of gravity that pulls it to the ground. Like the invisible dark matter that fills the universe, a force can only be observed by the effect it has on the physical world around it, and in the case of evil, it usually comes cloaked behind a pair of human eyes that stare back at you from the depths of a very black soul.

Evil was a fact of life. It was the human dichotomy. Throughout history the good had always come with the bad in an endless, season-like rotation. To Leo it seemed as if humanity had taken root in manic soil, producing a species that had hopped aboard a genetic roller coaster ride filled with unimaginable highs and stomach-churning lows. But now, with the arrival of the Antichrist, the threat to humanity had risen to a new level.

The world had fallen under the spell of a man who wasn't a man—a creature of sin disguised as a savior, and people had willingly grabbed free tickets to his ride. They were lining up to take their seats on his dark roller coaster, for they had no idea that the man with his hand on the controls would be taking their souls on a ride from which there would be no return.

"Good morning, Cardinal."

Shaken from his philosophic reverie, Leo turned to see Bishop Anthony Morelli standing in the open doorway, his unblinking brown eyes taking in the details of Leo's unkempt room.

"Sorry to disturb you, Leo. I guess you didn't hear me knock. Julian asked me to tell you he's holding a breakfast meeting in his room."

"A breakfast meeting? What's up?"

"I have no idea, but apparently it's important."

"Meet you there in twenty minutes. I need to shower first."

Morelli lingered in the doorway. "Are you sure you're feeling alright, Leo? I mean ..."

"Go ahead, Anthony. Spit it out."

"Well, to tell you the truth, you've been acting a little down lately."

"That obvious, huh?"

"Maybe not to others, but I think I've known you long enough to know when something's bothering you. Maybe it's the isolation. We've been hiding from Acerbi's forces on top of this mountain for months now, and I think it's beginning to affect everyone ... especially the Israelis who aren't used to the long, cold winters in this part of France. Now that spring is finally here maybe our moods will begin to improve."

"I'm afraid the change of seasons won't do much to end our isolation, Anthony, especially given the fact that we're still surrounded by Acerbi's forces. If anything, we've become even more isolated. I used to think I loved the solitude of the mountains, but now I find myself missing the excitement of the city. The sights and smells of Rome, the warm summer rain, the sidewalk cafes and the shouts from the people when I ride past on my little red motor scooter ... it feels like something is calling me home. Believe it or not, I'm even starting to miss the politics at the Vatican."

"Vatican politics, eh?" Morelli adopted a look of mock concern. "You're even worse off than I thought. Maybe I should stir up some behind-the-scenes intrigue around the castle so you'll feel more at home. I'll ask Evita to help."

Glancing up at the mischievous grin spreading across Morelli's face, Leo forced a tight smile.

What would he ever do without his good friend Morelli? The man had always been able to snap him out of his occasional moods of dark introspection just when he needed it the most.

The message was clear. *Get up, Leo. Walk outside and feel the sunshine on your face … go see the woman you love. Life is what you make of it, and there's no sense in dwelling on the past.*

"Have you seen her this morning?" Leo asked.

Morelli's voice echoed as he stepped into the arched hallway. "I heard she was taking a group of children on a field trip to the sacred caves behind the waterfall. You'll probably be able to catch her after your meeting with Julian."

Left alone once again with his thoughts, Leo found himself wondering about the timing of his approaching marriage to Evita Vargas. They had planned to marry on the day of the summer solstice, a date meant to symbolize a long life together, and both had agreed on a simple outdoor ceremony where everyone could stretch out on the grassy banks of the small lake in front of the castle and watch them exchange their vows on the wooden bridge that arched across the water—another symbolic gesture to demonstrate their willingness to always meet halfway when it came to matters of faith and making life decisions together.

With the sun's rays now inching into his room, Leo blinked hard as a bird suddenly darted outside his window, blotting out the light and causing his stomach to tighten. *Something was wrong.* He could feel it. Like the fleeting shadow of the bird, he could sense another dark shape approaching. It felt as though an invisible force beyond the castle walls was calling out to him … whispering his name and telling him to get his house in order. Something was coming, and whatever it was he knew he had to be ready—both mentally and spiritually.

Arching his back in a cat-like stretch, Leo headed for the shower, and when he was done he wrapped a towel around his waist and rubbed the steamy moisture from the mirror. Staring back at him was a face he barely recognized. He hadn't shaved for days, and the crow's feet spreading from the corners of his green eyes seemed to be growing deeper, highlighting the blunted nose and scared left eyelid, reminders of his days as a boxer in high school.

Once again, his stomach tightened as an unreasoning fear welled up inside him.

Something was coming!

4

CHAPTER 2

THE NORTH ATLANTIC

Ice-cold seawater swirled around the steel hull of the *HMS Ambush*, wrapping the British submarine in a frigid embrace as she dove beneath the thermocline and headed for the dark crystalline depths of the North Atlantic. Bathed in red battle lighting, the men inside the sub's control room stared into their computer screens and listened. They were being hunted, and all ninety-seven crewmembers on board knew that the only thing that stood between them and a nameless grave at the bottom of the sea was their captain's ability to outwit those who were chasing them in a game of hide-and-seek beneath the storm-tossed waves.

Standing on the rubber-coated deck over a lighted map table, Commander Colin Moss glanced sideways at his executive officer, Lieutenant Commander Pete Herndon. "What's our position now?"

"We're a hundred miles south of the Icelandic coast at a depth of twelve-hundred feet, sir. There are two other subs in the area that we know of ... an American Seawolf class attack sub and a Russian boomer."

"How far?"

"The Russian is seven miles behind us ... riding close to the surface, but the American disappeared ten minutes ago."

"Where was she?"

"A mile in front of us and three hundred feet from the surface. She was hovering in the warmer water above the thermocline before she disappeared."

"Surface ships?"

"Three destroyers and two aircraft circling the area."

"Bloody hell! They've got us."

"Maybe not, sir." Herndon traced his finger along an undersea ridge line displayed on a multi-colored digital map. "We're sitting between two parallel ridges that run along the bottom. If we didn't give ourselves away in the dive, we might still be invisible to them."

"Not likely." Moss began to pace. "If the American sub followed us into the colder water beneath the thermocline he probably has our position. It appears we're up against a man who knows his business."

Ever since Moss and his crew had seemingly gone rogue several months earlier and had fired four of their nuclear-tipped tomahawk missiles at sites known to contain some of the Acerbi Corporation's quantum computers, they had been hunted by the combined forces of the new world order. As the new leader of the world, Adrian Acerbi had placed the rogue British sub at the top of the list of threats he wanted eliminated, and he was pulling out all the stops to send her to the bottom of the sea.

Referred to as a seven-thousand-ton Swiss watch by the five thousand men and women who had built her, the three-hundred-foot sub was equal to the space shuttle in its complexity. With over a million separate parts and over two hundred and fifty thousand miles of cable running throughout the boat, she was powered by a top-secret nuclear reactor that could power her for the next twenty-five years, and her new passive sonar was so sensitive that she could hear a boat cruising in New York harbor from her homeport of Devonport, England, the largest naval base in Western Europe.

But it was the mind of her skipper that made the HMS Ambush such a lethal killing machine. A recipient of the Order of the British Empire, otherwise known as the OBE, Moss had been called a prodigy within naval circles for his knowledge of tactics—and his opponents were treading carefully.

"Captain … faint sonar contact eight hundred feet directly above us!"

"It's the American," Moss replied calmly. "He's lying in wait … time to go on the offensive. Sound battle stations. We'll fire a spearfish torpedo straight at his underside and then send up some *bubblers* to confuse his sonar while we make our ascent."

"Fire on him, sir?"

"I know what you're thinking, Pete, but judging from his actions so far I believe the American captain will react accordingly. As soon as he begins evasive maneuvers take us back up and level off just below the surface."

"The surface, Captain? We'll be sitting ducks!"

"That may be true, but our only hope of survival depends on our ability to hold their cities hostage, and they know we can't fire our cruise missiles from this depth. As soon as we reach firing depth, we'll send out a broadcast over an open communications channel telling them that if we sense an attack we'll fire all of our missiles. We have twenty-six nuclear-tipped missiles left, and I want to put Acerbi on notice that we're capable of reducing the cities of his new world order into glowing piles of ashes if his forces continue to hunt us."

"But that's madness, Captain! If we do something like that we're no better than he is."

Moss stopped pacing and looked back at his executive officer with a blend of determination and understanding. "I would think by now that you of all people would know my true intentions, Pete. I would never give the order to fire our missiles on innocent civilians, but Acerbi's forces don't know that. Right now, all they know is that we have disobeyed direct orders to return to base and have gone rogue. They have no idea what state of mind we're in, and that's our trump card. They'll be forced to back off while they try to figure out a way to stop us, and while they're doing that we'll slip away and disappear."

Moss removed his braided captain's hat and wiped his brow. "Remember, the American and Russian subs are now Acerbi Corporation subs. They may still be manned by crews from their former countries, but they take their orders from the new one world government now, which means that we're the only ones left with any power to stand up to this new totalitarian regime run by a madman. If we're destroyed the world will have nothing left to fight him with."

"What about the GPS network, sir? All of our targeting data is dependent on satellites controlled by Acerbi's massive computer network."

"We can still pre-program coordinates into the warheads like they did in the old days. They won't be as accurate, but if we're forced to give him a demonstration of our capability, we can land one of our missiles close enough to the target to make him think twice before he tries to hunt us down again."

Herndon smiled back at his captain with a newfound sense of respect. The man knew his business, that was a given, and like a master poker player, he had sized up his opponents and was preparing to make the biggest bluff of his life.

"Give me a fire control solution for the American sub!" Moss's voice boomed through the control room.

7

The weapons engineering officer glanced up at the captain before returning his attention to the targeting screen. "Aye, sir. Target acquired and torpedo ready."

"Fire!" Moss commanded.

"Torpedo away, sir!"

"Release the *bubblers* and head for the surface."

"Aye, sir!" the exec shouted. "Blowing tanks and releasing *bubblers*! Twenty degrees up on the bow planes."

The British sub shot toward the surface, releasing six spinning objects the size of soccer balls that left a thick trail of very noisy bubbles in their wake as they began a zigzag race through the water in all directions.

On board the American sub, alarm bells were going off as men rushed to their battle stations. The noise from the British sub's countermeasure devices had momentarily confused the American sonar operators, but as they adjusted their filters they could hear the unmistakable sound of an armed torpedo racing up from the depths, and it was headed straight for their underbelly. Up until now they had just been involved in a tedious game of hide-and-seek, but the captain of the British sub had just upped the ante. He had caught them completely off guard with his sudden and unprovoked attack.

"What the hell!" the American skipper shouted. "Flank speed! Release countermeasures and take us down behind that ridge off our starboard side. Do we have a lock on the British sub?"

"No, sir," the weapons officer replied. "We can't get a solid lock while his *bubblers* are still making noise in the water."

"What about the torpedo he just fired?"

"Closing in, sir!" The man's face turned pale. "It has a lock on us. Impact in 45 seconds!"

"Damn! Has Moss totally lost his mind!?"

In the ensuing silence the Americans could hear the sonar pings from the British torpedo reaching up from the abyss as it homed in on their hull.

With sweat running down the side of his face, the American skipper looked to his sonar operator. "How far to the undersea ridge?"

"Still over a thousand yards away, sir."

"Too far. We'll never make it."

Suddenly the pinging from the torpedo stopped.

"Captain … incoming radio message!" the radio operator shouted. "Sounds like the British captain."

"Put him on speaker."

After a brief burst of static the voice of the British captain reverberated from the speakers throughout the American sub. "This message is for the two submarines that are hunting the *HMS Ambush*. In a few seconds you will hear the sound of an explosion in the water. This will be a sign that the torpedo we just fired at the American sub has self-destructed on my command. As former allies we have no desire to engage you in undersea warfare, but by the time you hear the explosion we will have arrived just beneath the surface in a position to fire all of our nuclear-tipped missiles."

Moss paused to let his words sink in. "We will be departing the area and are not to be followed. If we detect any attempt to track our movements, we'll retaliate by destroying two major cities on both sides of the Atlantic. We urge both of you, American and Russian alike, to join us in our fight against a madman who has taken control of our world. If you still have any loyalty at all left for your former countries, let us unite and hold this man at bay until the people of the world can find a way to remove him from power.

"I need not remind you that I have fired my missiles at Acerbi targets before and will not hesitate to fire them again, so please, do not follow us. We are on your side, and even though you may not realize that fact yet, I fear you will soon learn that the world is now facing the greatest evil in recorded history. I wish you all good luck in the weeks and months ahead, but do not test me again."

In the silence of the control room, the men of the *Ambush* listened.

"Sonar … anything?" Moss asked.

"Just the sound of our *bubblers* fading away, sir. The American and Russian subs appear to be holding their positions."

"Let's get out of here. Take us south."

"Aye, sir … course one-eight-zero."

Nodding to his executive officer, Moss led the way down a narrow, metal-sheathed hallway to the officer's mess. After pouring two cups of steaming hot coffee, he handed one to Herndon before both men took facing seats on the green padding of a booth-like table.

"I don't know how long we can keep this up," Moss said. "Our nuclear power plant can keep us going for years, but we're still limited by the amount of food we can carry. Sooner or later we'll be forced to resupply."

"As soon as we show ourselves we'll be dead, sir. Acerbi's forces are undoubtedly pouring every asset they have into their search for us, and now that two of their subs have made contact with us, it's only a matter of time. Even if we do manage to escape satellite detection when we surface, some of the men are talking about deserting the boat as soon as we make landfall to resupply. They're starting to worry about their families, and sooner or later their love of home will outweigh any loyalty they may have for the boat."

"What are you suggesting? Are you saying we should just give in … surrender?"

"I think you know as well as I do that the time for surrender has passed, Captain. From what we're hearing about this Acerbi fellow, he's taking no prisoners when it comes to those who have resisted him. Do you really think he's the …?"

"The what, Pete? The Antichrist? To tell you the truth I don't have a clue what he is, but I can tell you this … the man is evil incarnate. You can label him any way you want to, but no matter what you call him the threat to the world is still the same, and we seem to be the only ones holding him back."

"But the men," Herndon said. "They have their own ideas about what's happening back in the world, and different camps are already beginning to form right here on board. At this point I'd say sixty percent of the men believe Acerbi is the Antichrist. The rest think he could be the answer to all the world's problems."

"What about the other ten percent?"

"Undecided. But even though some of the men are beginning to doubt the validity of what we're doing, they all seem to have one thing in common."

"And what would that be?"

"They all agree that they don't especially like seeing another flag flying over our country."

Moss rolled his coffee cup in his hands as he leaned back in his seat. "Good. That gives us some time."

"Time for what, sir?"

"Time to see if the rebel group in France can locate Acerbi and use their burst transmitter to send us real-time coordinates of his position. If they can do that we might just be able to take him out and end all of this. Put us on a course for the North Sea."

"What if he's in a city?"

"That's a bridge we'll have to cross when we come to it. Until then, let's just hope we can stay alive long enough to help bring an end to this madness. As far as we know the Israeli sub *Tekuma* is the only other sub armed with nuclear weapons that hasn't been absorbed into the new world government. We need to find a place to hide … somewhere they'll never think to look … and hope our Israeli friends are doing the same thing."

CHAPTER 3

Windswept rain blowing in off the storm-tossed Irish Sea distorted the view from the streaked windows of the 18th century English manor house as Adrian Acerbi paced the creaky wooden floors. The gray skies outside mirrored the tense atmosphere inside, and no one dared to speak, for Adrian was in one of his *moods*.

Things were not going well, or at least not as planned. He had just been informed that several countries were still refusing to join his one world government, and now, with two rogue subs hiding beneath the waves and threatening to unleash a nuclear conflagration against the countries that were cooperating with him, Acerbi's quest for world domination had been brought to a screeching halt.

Clearly something had to be done. It wasn't supposed to be like this. The war between heaven and hell was reaching its zenith, and the thing inhabiting Adrian Acerbi's body planned to take full advantage of the ongoing conflict between good and evil. He had embarked on a path that had been preordained by a dark revelation since before the dawn of man. *This was his time!* Mankind's destiny had been marked by an unbreachable covenant made before the first ooze of humanity had slithered from its primordial soup, and the time had come for him to claim his master's prize.

Ever since Adrian had been claimed by a dark entity cloaked in the image of his satanic master, the heavens had remained strangely quiet. God may have given these creatures life, but Adrian's master had released him to weave his way into the fabric of their lives and tempt them away from the embrace of their creator. *Who were these humans who dared to oppose his dark rule?* Surely they weren't counting on their God to deliver them? His time had come and gone!

After all, what did it matter if a few people knew that the entity posing as Adrian was nothing more than a satanic errand boy? Those who had studied God's word and knew what was coming would undoubtedly cling to their beliefs and continue to pray for deliverance, and he would be forced to deal with them in due time, but for now they mattered little. In the grand scheme of things, the world had welcomed him with open arms. He was now free to wander the unlocked corridors of their souls, and soon he would take from them that which was most precious.

Suddenly Adrian stopped pacing. His head swiveled toward the center of the towering stone room and his dark eyes bored in on the group of people seated at a long table. "Has everyone arrived?"

Stepping forward, a balding man looked down at his open leather notebook. "Yes, sir. They are all here."

"Then why do I still see some empty seats?"

"Those are reserved for your corporate division heads, sir. They weren't asked to attend."

Adrian's nostrils flared. "And why not?"

"Um … according to the agenda, only military leaders were invited to this particular meeting."

Like a chilled piece of fruit placed on a warm summer table, beads of sweat began to drip from the man's forehead. "Would you like me to summon your corporate leaders as well, sir?"

"Why? So, I can pace this room another day while I wait for them to arrive?" Adrian's dark eyes forced the man to shrink back. "When I said I wanted to speak to all of my leaders, I meant *all of my leaders*. Arrange for them to meet with me tomorrow at my new headquarters … and find the person responsible for drafting the request for this meeting. I have a very limited amount of time to achieve my goals, and more meetings cost more time. The person responsible for this mistake will soon learn a lesson in the meaning of *limited* time."

Bending forward from the waist like a chastened servant, the horrified man closed his notebook and scurried off as Adrian's eyes roamed the faces along both sides of the long table. "I'd like to start with the intelligence briefing. What's happening with our continuing efforts to locate the Catholic cardinal and his friends?" Adrian folded his hands behind his back as his voice rose for effect. "And please … feel free to take note of my choice of words when I said *continuing efforts,* because the search for these people has dragged on for far too long."

A uniformed general with short blond hair and streaked ruddy cheeks pushed away from the table and stood facing Acerbi. Unlike the others, the large man seemed unfazed by the dressing down the previous officer had endured. "One of the main reasons our forces have failed to locate them, sir, is the fact that nothing's been heard from them since the massive ground and air attack we launched against their position in France last year. We've heard rumors that a great many of them survived and are hiding somewhere in the Pyrenees, but for all practical purposes they appear to have scattered on the wind."

The edges of Adrian's mouth lifted in a menacing smile. "Scattered on the wind, General? Do you really believe that I want to stand here and listen to poetic platitudes about our enemies being scattered on the wind? If anything's been scattered on the wind it's our own forces. Can you even tell me just who exactly we're looking for?"

"Yes, sir. I've compiled a complete dossier on the cardinal and his followers, and I've disseminated copies to all of our field commanders."

"I'm well acquainted with the cardinal but read it to me anyway."

"All of it, sir?"

"No … just part of it. I enjoy being kept in the dark while my field commanders have all the facts."

Stung by Acerbi's sarcasm, the general's thick fingers fumbled with the folder in his hands. "Of course, sir … I just meant that the dossier is quite lengthy."

Adrian looked up at the ceiling and exhaled in resignation. "Fine. Give us the condensed version and leave a complete copy with my assistant so I can read it in its entirety after I leave this dreary place."

"Yes, sir." Opening the folder, the general cleared his throat. "The group that attacked our forces last year in the *Field of the Burned* appears to be centered on a charismatic Jesuit cardinal by the name of Leopold Amodeo. Three years ago, before he became a cardinal, Amodeo was a professor of history at Boston College. He was summoned to Rome by his friend and former classmate, Bishop Anthony Morelli, the Vatican's chief archaeologist. They were joined by a young seminarian by the name of John Lowe, and their immediate superior was another Jesuit cardinal by the name of Marcus Lundahl, who went on to become the late Pope Michael. At the time, Morelli was also working with an Israeli mathematician by the name of Lev Wasserman. Wasserman is the man who discovered the mysterious code in the Old Testament that led them to the secret chapel under the Vatican. Many believe this code holds clues to our future and is proof that the Bible was divinely inspired."

With the mention of the word *Bible,* Adrian's vision began to dim. He wanted to lash out … to scream. He wanted the people in this room to hear his real name before he turned them into ashes, but he knew he had to hold back.

I can't reveal my true intentions just yet. He was a deceiver and a destroyer, and he sensed his dark father was watching … waiting.

Slowly, as if he were awakening from a dream, Adrian realized he was shaking. The general's voice seemed far off as his words echoed along the walls.

"Would you like me to continue, sir?"

"Yes … I'm listening." As everyone at the table cast cautious glances in his direction, Adrian struggled to keep his thoughts from drifting off into the dark realm that ruled his every waking moment. His emotions were becoming harder and harder to control, and he had to be constantly on guard to keep them from revealing his true intentions.

Over the past few weeks, Adrian had heard that some of his officers had been discussing his sudden breaks with reality, and that sometimes it appeared as if he had been transported to a world only he could see. Gripping his fists into a tight ball, Adrian could feel his fingernails digging so deeply into his palms that blood began to flow. *At least he bled like these humans.* Looking down at the sticky red liquid dripping from his hands, he vowed never to let his guard down again.

"Wasserman is also quite wealthy," the shaken general continued as he watched the blood drip from Acerbi's hands, staining the aged wooden floor. "Apparently, sir, he inherited his wealth from his industrialist father, which allowed him to pursue his academic interests. He's a full professor at the Hebrew University in Jerusalem and is an expert in group theory, a field of mathematics that underlies quantum mechanics. Interestingly enough, he also holds a PhD in archaeology."

"So, a Catholic cardinal and a Jewish millionaire …"

"He's a Christian, sir."

"What?"

"Professor Wasserman is a Christian … a Protestant Christian, but we've also learned there are several Jews and possibly even some Muslims embedded within their group. What we've uncovered is a mish-mash of people from varying religious backgrounds who have joined together in a common cause."

"And just what would that common cause be, General?"

The general shifted uncomfortably on his feet. "Your destruction, sir."

Adrian felt the room sway. The very cornerstone of his plan was centered on the fact that the world's religions would continue to war

16

against one another—as they had always done, yet here was a group that had come together in a unified effort aimed at preventing evil from washing over the world.

No one had seen this coming!

"What size group are we talking about here, General?"

"We're not exactly sure, sir. There could be hundreds of them. Wasserman himself fled from Israel aboard his yacht last fall with a large group of Israeli citizens."

"I know. I confiscated the boat after they abandoned it in a Spanish harbor."

"Yes, sir. I read the report. They undoubtedly headed into the mountains and were able to link up with Cardinal Amodeo on the French side of the border. We still haven't figured out how the cardinal escaped from New York and made it to France, but we know he and Wasserman were behind the attack on our forces in the *Field of the Burned* last year. The cardinal's girlfriend is a Cathar, as are some of the Spanish members of his group, and a large number of Cathars disappeared from some of the nearby towns around the same time, which gives us reason to believe there's a Cathar stronghold somewhere in the vicinity."

"Cathars." Adrian laughed. "Why doesn't that surprise me? Several members of my own family have been linked to that religious sect for almost seven hundred years, including Eduardo Acerbi and his wife, Colette … the people who raised me. Did you know Eduardo murdered his other adopted son, Rene?"

The general looked down at his hands. "Um … no, sir. I wasn't aware of the connection."

"The old man thought Rene was a monster, so he killed him." Adrian's eyes took on a glassy look. "But he tried to protect me …"

Like a twisting, lethal parasite, something raged inside him, cutting off his words. What little remained of his human side had just received a vision of the adoptive parents who had loved and protected him before his transformation—*into what?* What had he just remembered? He felt like a surfer who had just been pushed underwater by a giant wave. The harder he tried to free himself from its swirling grip the more furious the thing inside him became—pushing him farther away from the light that was trying to penetrate the murky green surface of his subconscious.

What was happening to him?

"But enough about my family life," Adrian continued with a disarming smile that made everyone at the table breathe a sigh of relief. "I believe we were discussing the possibility of a Cathar stronghold. Why haven't we located it yet?"

The general's eyes swiveled from Acerbi as he aimed a green laser pointer at the gigantic flat screen on the wall behind him. "As you can see by this map of the area, they've isolated themselves in a very mountainous part of the world, sir. It's extremely rugged terrain, and the entire area is honeycombed with caves. The Pyrenees have thwarted armies since before Roman times, and this past winter saw some of the heaviest snowfall in years. We're hoping the spring melt will bring them out of hiding. For that reason, we've kept our forces to a minimum to give them a false sense of security. Instead of a massive show of force, we've begun setting up hidden cameras along all the highways leading into and out of the area. These are plugged into our vast computer network that employs facial recognition software and monitors every security camera in the world. If they're foolish enough to show themselves, they'll be arrested on sight. We've pretty much chased them back to the Stone Age, sir. The area is completely surrounded by our troops, and we believe they've been reduced to living in caves at this point. No one is getting in or out of there without us knowing about it."

"That's all very well and good, General, but we shouldn't confuse the word surrounded with the word captured. Stay on top of them and keep me posted on your progress."

"Yes, sir."

Rubbing his temples, Adrian scanned the table. "I'd like to hear a report from my air commander."

Still dressed in her olive-green flight suit, Samantha Jennings blew a wisp of red hair from her forehead before rising from her seat at the end of the table. "The skies are ours, sir. Nothing moves through the air without our permission."

"What about the countries that haven't joined us yet?" Adrian asked, walking toward her.

"Their air defenses have been neutralized by our computers. So far they've been smart enough to realize that if any of their fighters leave the ground their only path back to earth will be in the form of smoking debris falling from the sky. We also have total control of all communication and intelligence gathering satellites circling the globe."

By now Acerbi was standing directly in front of her, his black eyes inches from hers. "Then why haven't they joined us yet?"

Jennings felt her knees begin to grow weak as she tried to maintain eye contact, but the black orbs staring back at her made it impossible. She felt dizzy, unable to concentrate. She had finally been called into the presence of a man she had come to admire and respect; a man who had captured the world through what she believed was the sheer will of his charismatic wisdom and intellect, yet she couldn't bring herself to look into his eyes. Born with a mental toughness that bordered on obsession, she had never shied away from looking anyone in the eye before, but this was something different.

"I asked you a question, Commander."

Jennings' eyes fluttered involuntarily as her vision dimmed and her head began to spin. Like a moth that had just flown too close to a flame, she began to feel a sense of impending doom, and when she was finally able to focus again, she saw that Acerbi had moved away and was pacing again. Released from his otherworldly stare, she regained her composure and continued. "I believe the question of why others haven't joined us yet falls under the umbrella of international diplomacy, sir. As your air commander I only follow military orders."

"Then what's your best guess?"

"I can only assume that the continued threats from the rogue British and Israeli subs have emboldened those sovereign nations that have failed to join us. Their captains have already let it be known that if we try to take any military action against them they will begin taking out our major cities, and if that happens all bets are off. We must show the citizens of the new one world government that we can protect them, otherwise we'll appear weak and our coalition will begin to crumble."

A thin smile returned to the corners of Acerbi's mouth. "And there you have it." Adrian turned his attention back to the general. "Is there any indication that these rogue subs are somehow connected to the Catholic cardinal and his group in France?"

"None that we know of, sir."

"Then we must make every effort to find out before we make our next move. Increase our forces and begin moving them into the Pyrenees. I want this cardinal and his friends flushed from their hiding place. Once we're finished with them we'll focus on the two rogue subs. It's time to call their bluff and show the world what happens to those who oppose us."

CHAPTER 4

The atmosphere inside Julian Wehling's room was subdued when Leo entered and found him sitting all alone, munching on a piece of toast and peering through a tiny pair of wire-rimmed glasses at a pile of yellowed papers scattered across his desk.

"Good morning, Cardinal," Julian said without looking up. "Would you care for some coffee?"

"I'd love some."

Leo waited as Julian continued to squint at the faint Latin script on a scroll that was obviously very old. Absorbed in his work, the Cathar leader was the embodiment of the stereotypical cloistered professor of medieval history he had once been at Cambridge.

"Bishop Morelli told me you were holding some kind of meeting here this morning," Leo continued. "Am I early or late?"

"Let's just say you're the first to arrive." Wehling reached for an earthen pot and filled Leo's cup full of steaming coffee. "I wanted to speak with you alone before the others showed up."

"What's on your mind?"

"Several things, Cardinal. Walk with me." Rising from his high-backed wooden chair, Julian led Leo beneath the stone arches that separated his room from the long terrace that ran along the outside wall of the castle. "How are your wedding plans coming along?"

"Well, speaking as a man who's never even considered the possibility of marriage, I'm assuming everything is progressing as planned. Evita seems pleased."

"Good. Glad to hear it."

Leo detected a brief flash of urgency in Julian's clipped responses.

"But you didn't ask me here to talk about my upcoming wedding plans, did you, Julian?"

"No, you're quite right, Cardinal … I didn't. Right now our knowledge of what's going on in the outside world remains limited, but suffice it to say that we know Acerbi's efforts to dominate the world under the umbrella of his one world government are beginning to take hold. North and South America, plus all of Asia and large swaths of Africa and the Middle East have decided to join, and it's a foregone conclusion that those who haven't will soon follow."

"What about Europe?" Leo looked out at a line of distant mountaintops piercing the horizon. "I was under the impression that the entire continent had fallen under his control."

"Not all of them. We received word late last night that Switzerland has just joined. Apparently, they tried to hold out by claiming that their neutral status exempted them from joining, but after the flow of money in and out of their country was stopped by Acerbi's computers they were finally forced to give in."

"So which countries are still holding out?"

"Not many, which brings me to the point of our meeting. At four o'clock this morning we received a burst transmission that originated from somewhere north of here … very far north, and whoever sent it knows you're here. The person who sent it claimed that they have information that will help us in our cause, and they want to speak with you … alone and in person."

"Why me?"

"No reason was given, Cardinal, but like it or not, you've become a symbol of the resistance against Acerbi. They're sending a private jet for you that will be landing at an abandoned air force base in Spain five days from now. The pilots have instructions to wait on the ground for an hour. If you fail to show up they'll leave without you."

Leo could feel the invisible dark tug reaching out to him from beyond the castle walls. "How does anyone even know I'm here?"

"We don't know yet," a familiar voice called out behind him.

Leo turned to see Professor Lev Wasserman and his son-in-law, John Lowe, standing in the shade cast by the stone pillars separating Julian's room from the terrace outside.

"Lev. You know about this?"

"Yes, and we've been trying to find out who sent it, but they didn't leave much of a digital trail to follow."

"Any ideas yet?"

"None … but whoever sent it obviously has a burst transmitter and the secret codes needed to send an encrypted message to our burst receiver. At first we thought it had to be coming from a sub. The *HMS Ambush* is still out there somewhere … and so is the *Tekuma*, but the transmission didn't originate from the sea. It came from land."

"But it has to be coming from some kind of military source," John added. "I mean, a burst transmitter is a top-secret device that no one outside a few select military circles has access to … right?"

"In theory," Lev responded, "but you have to ask yourself why a military force would be trying to contact Leo, and only a few trusted sources have the secret encrypted codes that would allow them to access our burst receiver. Without the correct codes the message would have been marked as a fake and would have never reached our receiver. The entire system is built around a failsafe protocol used to prevent someone from sending false commands to nuclear subs."

"I don't like it," John said. "Acerbi's quantum computers are capable of quickly breaking any code. This has all the hallmarks of a trap."

Lev peered up at his son-in-law through a hanging tuft of curly gray hair. "Normally I would agree with you, John, but whoever sent the message knows that Acerbi's computers have been lagging behind in their ability to intercept messages sent by burst transmitters, but more importantly, they also know that Leo is here. If Acerbi knew that Leo was here I doubt we'd be having this conversation right now. I believe the message is genuine even though the source remains a mystery. As far as we know, the only other person who has the codes to our burst transmitter is Daniel in Israel."

Leo felt a tingling sensation at the back of his neck. "Has anyone tried to contact him?"

"Yes," Julian said. "*He's not answering.*"

CHAPTER 5

Working in the vineyards, Daniel and Sarah Meir were reveling in the sunshine reflecting off the sand dunes separating the rows of grapevines from the beach, and from their vantage point, they could see Lev Wasserman's shimmering white villa facing a section of the Mediterranean coastline that had come to be known as the Israeli Riviera.

It had been eight months since Acerbi's one-world government had absorbed Israel into its global fold and Lev and the others had escaped to France aboard the Carmela, the yacht named after Lev's late wife, but Daniel and Sarah had never regretted their decision to remain behind to watch over the villa and tend to the fields.

Aside from missing their friends, they loved their life by the sea, and as long as Acerbi's men were unaware that one of the world's premier cryptologists was living right under their noses, they would continue to fly under the radar, living their lives in relative peace along with a handful of other academics that had chosen to remain behind with them.

At least that was the plan. But plans have a way of unraveling when you least expect them to, and as Sarah clipped a bunch of grapes and dropped them into her basket, the stillness of the afternoon was shattered when a dozen Humvees sporting the colors of the new world police force sped through the villa's front gate and headed up the gravel driveway. Judging from the sudden arrival of so many police vehicles, it was obvious that the day they had dreaded for so long had finally arrived. Somehow, Acerbi's forces had just discovered Daniel's true identity.

It was time to flee.

Running for a small white car loaded with supplies for just such an eventuality, they jumped in and drove unobserved down one of the grassy vineyard roads before bouncing up onto the coastal highway and speeding away to the north. It had been their plan all along that if the villa was ever raided they would head north, following the coast through the former countries of Lebanon and Turkey in an effort to reach their friends in France. But despite their well-laid plans, they both knew they still faced some unavoidable obstacles. They would be forced to pass through the numerous checkpoints that had sprung up on all the roads that lined this section of the Fertile Crescent, and they were approaching the first one now.

Reaching into a hidden compartment beneath the rear seat that concealed automatic weapons and two backpacks filled with supplies, Sarah retrieved their fake Acerbi ID cards as Daniel slowed for the checkpoint.

"Good afternoon, sir," the officer said, peering into the car. "Identification cards please."

Handing the man their cards, Daniel gripped the wheel as he watched the guard swipe their cards through a black box attached to his computer terminal and waited. If their ID's were discovered to be fakes, they would be arrested on the spot.

Unbelievably, Sarah turned up the volume on their CD player and uncorked a bottle of wine as she placed her bare feet on the dash and began singing along with the music.

"What are you doing!?" Daniel's eyes were bulging.

Casting a wink in his direction, Sarah continued rocking her head in motion with the music. Approaching the vehicle, an irritated-looking guard rapped on her window. Blinking up at him, she rolled the window half-way down. "Did you need something, officer?"

"Could you please turn the volume down, ma'am … and there's no drinking allowed at the checkpoints. Has your boyfriend been drinking?"

"He's my husband, and no, he doesn't drink. Give him one of those breath tests if you don't believe me."

The guard wiped the sweat from his forehead and looked at the line of cars forming behind them. "That's exactly what I'm going to do."

Walking around to Daniel's side of the car, the guard shoved a small plastic device through the open window. "Please blow into the mouthpiece, sir."

Casting an angry glance back at Sarah, Daniel did as he was instructed and waited as the guard holding their ID cards walked back over to the car. "Their ID's check out. No previous arrests for drunk driving on his record. What's the breathalyzer say?"

"Looks like 0.0." The unsmiling guard took the ID cards and shoved them through the open window into Daniel's shaking hands. "You're good to go, sir. There's been some rebel activity in the area, so if you notice anything suspicious please give us a call … oh, and I'd keep that bottle of wine corked while you're on the road. No open alcoholic containers are allowed in a moving vehicle."

"Will do," Daniel said, tossing the cards into the glove box. "Thanks." Slowly, he drove away from the checkpoint before glaring across the seat at Sarah. "What was that all about?"

"Call it a diversion. I gave them something else to focus on while they checked our ID's."

"But you made them suspicious."

"Suspicious of you being a drunk driver, which kept their minds off anything else … like searching the car for weapons. It worked, didn't it?"

"I'm not sure." Daniel checked the rear-view mirror. "It looks like a black SUV just pulled out onto the road behind us."

"Probably nothing to worry about. If they had discovered who we were they would have detained us at the checkpoint." Sarah glanced back over the front seat. "I'll keep an eye on them."

Inhaling the musty aroma of freshly turned earth that drifted through their open windows, the two continued on, speeding past grove after grove of olive and pistachio trees that dotted the Lebanese countryside while keeping their eyes on the mysterious black vehicle following behind at a discreet distance. Topping a rise in the road, they slowed when they saw that the valley below was streaked with drifting smoke.

"Where do you think all of this is coming from?" Sarah asked.

"I have no idea." Daniel glanced nervously in his side mirror. "Where did that SUV go?"

"I don't see them. It looks like they turned off. It's hard to tell with all this dust and smoke."

"Does it look like any other vehicles turned onto the road after they disappeared?"

"There's nothing behind us. Why don't we pull over and stop for a minute to see if they pass?"

"No, we need to keep going. We'll know soon enough if they're following us."

The sudden whine of an artillery shell flying overhead caused both of them to duck just as a yellow flash preceded an explosion in the field off to their right.

"That was an artillery shell!" Daniel shouted, watching a ribbon of thick black smoke curl into a bleached springtime sky. "Someone is shelling these fields for some reason."

"The guard back there said there was some rebel activity in the area." Sarah twisted in her seat to scan the distant hills. "Maybe Acerbi's forces are just laying down a field of fire hoping they'll hit something."

"How far is it to the next checkpoint?"

"I don't know. They're not marked on the map." Glancing up, Sarah watched a dot on the horizon materialize into the shape of a helicopter. "I think I know why that SUV suddenly stopped following us. That chopper is headed straight for us!" Digging her fingers into Daniel's shoulder, she pointed to a distant building. "There's a barn or something on the other side of this olive grove. It's the only cover for miles."

Slamming on the brakes, Daniel swerved off the roadway and hurtled over an embankment before bringing the car to a stop between a row of trees. The steady thump from the helicopter's spinning blades was growing louder, echoing across the field like the distant drumbeat of an advancing army. With no time left, they grabbed their rifles and backpacks from the hidden compartment under the back seat and took off running in the direction of a leaning wooden barn at the far end of the grove.

Running as fast as they could, they glanced back over their shoulders and stopped. The chopper was hovering just behind their car.

"If he spots us we'll never make it!" Sarah shouted.

The two locked eyes before diving into a pile of leaves just as their little white car disappeared in a shattering explosion that rippled the ground beneath their prone bodies. Jagged pieces of red-hot metal sliced through the air, snapping overhead branches and embedding themselves in the gnarled trunks of thousand-year-old olive trees just as the dark earth that had been lifted into the sky by the explosion began raining down all around them.

Like a giant bird of prey, the chopper continued to hover, rising up and edging sideways over the tops of the trees in a predator-like hunt for signs of life. Satisfied at last that no one on the ground remained alive, it made a slow, pirouette-like turn and flew away, disappearing just as quickly as it had appeared to wherever it had come from.

Picking themselves up, Daniel and Sarah brushed the dirt from their clothes and looked around. In the aftermath of the attack, a thick cloud of black smoke marked the spot where their car had once stood.

"I wonder if they discovered that our ID cards were fakes or if they're just attacking anything that moves on this highway?" Sarah whispered hoarsely.

Reaching out, Daniel rubbed a smear of black soot from her forehead as he tried to mentally retrace their movements.

Had they done something that had given them away?

Now, standing in the middle of an ancient olive grove with their only means of transportation going up in flames, Daniel looked back toward the road and froze.

The black SUV was back!

It had just pulled to the side of the road next to their burning car, and two men with guns were climbing from the vehicle.

Kneeling behind a tree, Daniel tried to think. If their true identity had been discovered after they left the last checkpoint, these were probably the men who had just called in the airstrike. There was no way they were going to let one of the world's premier code-breakers get away and use his talents against them, and the attack by the helicopter had made it clear that they weren't interested in taking prisoners. They wanted him and his wife dead, and the two men now entering the olive grove with assault rifles had probably been sent to make sure they hadn't escaped.

Looking around for a way out, Daniel knew they had to make it out of there alive, because if they didn't, Leo and the others would never know what he had just discovered in the Bible code twenty-four hours earlier.

CHAPTER 6

The fine mist spreading from the base of the waterfall felt cool against Leo's upturned face as he waited for Evita to emerge from the sacred caves behind the curtain of water. The news he had come to deliver wasn't exactly the kind of news any groom would be anxious to share with his prospective bride, especially one who had waited so patiently. In less than twenty-four hours he would be leaving, which meant their wedding plans would have to be put on hold until he returned.

Through the liquid veil of falling water, Leo finally saw her wavering image materialize from the cave entrance, leading a group of school children along the slippery ledge and through the mist until they reached the grassy bank at the water's edge. "OK, children … off to school with you," she cooed. "And don't dawdle. Your teachers will be waiting for you."

"Thank you for taking us to the caves, Miss Evita," a small girl said, twirling a blond ringlet with her finger. "It was kind of scary, but fun."

"There's nothing scary about the sacred caves, little ones. They are places of refuge. If you are ever in danger they will protect you, but you must never go there alone. You must always have permission from your parents, and you can only enter with an adult who knows the way out. Now go," Evita giggled. "Your teachers are waiting."

Straightening to her full height, Evita watched the children disappear across the sloping lawn in front of the castle before she turned away and walked toward Leo. With her floor-length red velvet dress skimming the tops of the moist grass, she tossed her long black hair back over her shoulders and fixed Leo with a look that made him melt inside.

She's making this impossible!

Against the roar of falling water pounding in his ears, Leo reached out to her, but before he could take her in his arms she pushed away.

"So … when are you leaving?" Her large brown eyes blinked back at him, searching his face for the reaction she knew was coming.

"What?"

"You heard me, Leo. When are you leaving?"

"How did you know?"

"I used to work for Spanish intelligence … remember? Old habits die hard. Javier told me about the mysterious burst transmission before I left for the caves with the children this morning."

"Mendoza told you?"

"He was part of the group trying to locate the source of the transmission last night."

"But he should have waited …"

"There are only three Spanish members of the Bible Code Team, my love. There's me, Javier Mendoza, and Dr. Diaz, who seems to be avoiding everyone lately. We're the only three Cathars on the team, which means we kind of have to stick together, especially when one of us is planning a wedding."

Leo glanced down at Evita's folded hands. "You know I have to go."

"Even if you don't know where you're going … or who will be waiting for you when you step off the plane? You know as well as I do that you could be walking into a very clever trap."

For a lingering moment two pairs of unblinking eyes met in mutual understanding. Both knew the risk Leo was taking, and both knew that as soon as he flew off into the unknown five days from now it could very well be the last time any of them would ever see him again. It was a terrible gamble, but it was a gamble Leo knew he had to take.

"Did Javier tell you why I'm going?" Leo asked.

"Not all of it … just that whoever sent the message wanted to speak to you in person … alone."

"I'm afraid there's more to it than that." Leo took her in his arms and held her close. "Whoever sent the message said they possessed information that could help our cause, which means they might know how we can stop Adrian Acerbi from taking over the world."

"But Adrian is the Antichrist … right?" Evita arched her back and stared up at the sky, her body language telegraphing the frustration she felt inside. "I mean … if he is who we think he is, then any attempt to stop him would be impossible … wouldn't it?"

Leo's green eyes followed Evita's gaze to the top of the waterfall. "I'm afraid that trying to stop the Antichrist would be like trying to stop a force of nature, but whoever sent that message knows where we are and how to contact us. That one fact alone makes it imperative that I get on that plane and see what our mysterious friend has to say."

CHAPTER 7

By now the activity in the castle had reached a fever pitch following the strange burst transmission from the north. Five days was hardly enough time to plan Leo's trek across the Pyrenees to an abandoned airfield in Spain, and the men tasked to accompany him had gathered to discuss the possibility that they were all heading into a well-laid trap.

Staring at a wall of paper maps, an elite squad of Israeli commandos known as Team 5 had crowded into a cramped room near the front gate of the castle with the group of crossbow-wielding Cathar fighters who had brought their families to this mountaintop sanctuary after Acerbi had risen to power.

It had been eight months since Acerbi's network of powerful quantum computers had seized the internet, paralyzing the infrastructures of practically every country on earth. Everything from military command systems to food and fuel distribution networks—even the ability for individuals to purchase the necessities of everyday life—Acerbi controlled it all, and the message had been clear.

Cooperate or wither on the vine and die.

It had been the mantra of a new age. In his speech delivered at the United Nations, Adrian Acerbi had promised a new era of cooperation among nations under the banner of a one world government. He had offered up a vision of a world that would be forever free from the specter of war, famine, and disease, and he had been welcomed by almost all with open arms.

Of course, none of his promises had been real. He was a wolf in sheep's clothing come to cull a wayward herd that had wandered too far from its shepherd. Those who had failed to read the signs were about to be led to the slaughter by the embodiment of evil. They were about to

35

surrender their souls in exchange for the treasured conveniences of modern-day life, and only those who had been able to see what was about to happen had fled into the countryside in an attempt to escape the totalitarian regime that was now spreading across the world.

Live to fight another day had become the mantra of the eclectic group of people that Leo and the others had decided to join in a modern-day version of a castle hidden on the top of a mountain, and the decision to flee into the wilderness ahead of Acerbi's advancing army had never been a question.

They were a strange mixture indeed. Over a hundred Cathar families who had built the castle had been joined by a group known as the Bible Code Team. Comprised of top-notch scientists and military men led by a Catholic cardinal and a world-renowned Israeli mathematician who had discovered a hidden code in the Old Testament, there were Catholics, Protestants, Jews, and Muslims, and they had all come together with one unifying goal—to fight back against the evil that was now spreading across the globe.

Now, waiting to hear the details of the mission they all knew was coming, a dozen Cathar fighters and six members from Team 5 waited as the former head of the Mossad stood at the front of the room and smoothed a wisp of thinning gray hair back over his scalp.

"Good morning, gentlemen," Danny Zamir said. "We need get started. This morning we received two additional burst transmissions. In the first transmission, we were informed that there would be no satellite coverage of the abandoned airfield in Spain while the jet is on the ground. Whether that's true or not remains to be seen. The second transmission contained a warning."

The room became deathly quiet.

"If Leo fails to show up at the airfield at the appointed time, there will be no further communication from the person who sent the transmission."

The silence in the room shifted to a soft murmur.

"Now," Zamir continued, pressing his fists against the table and leaning forward on a pair of thick forearms. "You will be leaving the castle tonight under the cover of darkness. Our scouting parties have reported back to us that Acerbi's forces in the area seem to be going about their business as usual. Most of them are former French police officers who have been absorbed into Acerbi's world police force. As we all know, the French are a very proud people. They're fiercely protective of everything French, and from what we've heard most of them aren't too happy with the fact that they've been forced to give up their national identity."

"Neither are we!" a voice at the back of the room called out.

Zamir smiled patiently. "I believe this explains why we're beginning to see that the French aren't being too aggressive when it comes to seeking out those who oppose the idea of joining a one world government. That being said, we can't afford to let our guard down, because most of their upper echelon officer corps are all hard line Acerbi followers."

"What about the motion sensors we discovered on the paths in the forest below the castle?" Gael asked. "They're impacting our ability to patrol the surrounding area."

Zamir bit his lower lip in a familiar gesture that indicated he was thinking. "I think it's probably best for now to leave them in place. If we remove them we'll be waving a red flag to Acerbi's forces that some kind of military force is operating in this area of the forest. We'll simply stay off the paths and continue to use the underbrush for cover. As far as our mission tonight is concerned, you'll be heading south through the hidden pass that leads through the mountains. No sensors have been located there, so we should be OK."

Zamir's son Ben raised his hand. "What about drones?" the young commander of Team 5 asked. "They have night vision capability, and they can spot our heat signatures from the air no matter how thick the forest canopy is."

"Acerbi's forces have only two drones operating in this area, and the men who maintain them at the local base in Foix have informed us that both drones will have mechanical problems tonight." The elder Zamir winked. "Now ... get some rest. The cardinal will be ready to go at 1900 hours."

CHAPTER 8

The men preparing to leave for the abandoned airfield in Spain had gathered in the castle's great hall with those who had come to see them off. Everyone who knew about the unfolding mission was acutely aware that this was no ordinary scouting patrol around the base of the mountain. This was a full-on military foray into thick forest that was bordered by steeply-rising mountains on both sides, and the possibility that they were all heading into a trap was very much on everyone's mind.

In the flickering candlelight, shadows played against the towering stone walls and danced across the rows of wooden tables filled with heaping platters of sumptuous vegetarian fare. Dressed in homespun clothing with their crossbows at their sides, it seemed to Leo as if he was looking at a medieval tableau frozen in time as he watched the Cathar fighters dining with their wives and children.

"How long until you leave?" Evita asked, squeezing Leo's hand under the table.

"Thirty minutes."

Leo noticed that the food on her plate remained untouched, and as he looked across the table at Lev Wasserman sitting next to his daughter, Ariella, and her husband, John Lowe, he noticed that John was silently picking at his food, indicating that he too had lost interest in eating.

"What's the matter, John?" Leo grinned. "I don't think I've ever seen you so quiet before … except maybe on your wedding day."

John set his fork on the plate before glancing up at Leo. "I just don't understand why you have to go flying off alone for a meeting with a total stranger!"

"It's a calculated risk, John. I'll admit to that, but I have to trust my instincts on this one. As Lev mentioned earlier, if Adrian is behind this it would mean he knows where I am … which means he knows where all of us are, and if that were true we probably wouldn't be sitting here having this conversation right now. Bottom line, I have no choice but to get on that plane. We can't stay locked up behind these stone walls forever. Our continued survival depends on making contacts in the outside world with others who feel as we do, and this is the best opportunity we've had so far to do just that."

John sighed as he continued to pick at his food. "How will we know if you've arrived safely at your destination?"

"The person who contacted us obviously has a burst transmitter. I'll see if I can use it to send back a coded message."

An uncomfortable silence followed as the entire Bible Code Team cast darting glances at one another. Leo had been a unifying father figure to most of them, and his impending departure had filled them with the same anxiety faced by countless military families throughout history who had watched their loved ones heading off to questionable wars in places that were totally foreign to them.

Sitting beside Leo, Alon Lavi, the hulking former Israeli commando, was sulking next to his fiancé, Nava. Both had given up their military careers to join the Bible Code Team and work full time for Lev Wasserman, and their moods reflected their frustration at having to remain behind as Leo trudged off into the unknown without their protection.

Peering through a mass of candles that had melted to the top of the hand-hewn table, Bishop Anthony Morelli munched absent-mindedly on an apple as he talked with a man wearing a bright orange fly-fishing shirt. He was speaking with Moshe Ze´ev, the former Israeli general, and his wife, Hadar, the famed chef from Tel Aviv.

Except for Daniel and Sarah, this was the core group of the Bible Code Team that had come together two years before in Lev's Mediterranean villa on the coast of Israel. Together, utilizing a code uncovered in the Old Testament, this close-knit group of Christians soon discovered that they had all been enlisted in a fight against evil—*chosen ones* drafted for a holy mission they barely understood themselves. Along the way they had been joined by three Spanish Cathars—Evita Vargas, Javier Mendoza and Dr. Raul Diaz, who were all eminent scientists in their own right.

"What about a tracking device?" Alon asked. "We could conceal it in your clothing."

"I have a feeling the man who's sending the jet for me will have already thought of that," Leo replied, watching the pin-points of candlelight bouncing off the swirling red wine in his glass. "I understand that there will be a total of eighteen men going with me to Spain … six from Team 5 and a dozen of Gael's Cathar fighters."

"Yes," Alon said. "We figured that was the optimal size force for a mission of this type. I wish we could send more, but we have castle security to consider. We barely have enough men to keep a twenty-four lookout from the walls as it is."

Leo brushed the comment aside with a quick wave of his hand and took a final sip of wine before setting his empty glass down on the table. "Actually, I was getting ready to say that I think I should go alone. There's no need to risk other lives babysitting me on a walk through the woods."

"You and I both know that's not going to happen, Leo." Alon's eyes narrowed. "You'll be crossing back through the same mountain pass we used when Gael brought us all to the castle last fall. If you remember, that was no walk in the park, and it's definitely not babysitting. We want to make sure you have a tactical advantage when you get to that airfield in case you're walking into a trap. We protect our own, Cardinal. We always have and we always will. Like it or not, those eighteen soldiers are going with you."

Sitting quietly, Lev saw Evita fighting back tears as she listened to Leo discussing his security concerns with Alon. Holding his glass high he stood and cleared his throat, cueing the others at the table to raise theirs. "A final toast before you leave, Leo."

Lev put on his biggest smile. "May your journey take you safely into the warm embrace of friendship … and bring you back into the waiting arms of the friends who let you go."

CHAPTER 9

A metallic *clink* echoed in the stillness when the six Israeli commandos and a dozen Cathar fighters exited the tunnel at the base of the mountain.

"Everyone stop!" Captain Ben Zamir's whisper sounded almost like a shout in the muted, leafy quiet of the surrounding forest. "We need to secure any loose gear right now. This isn't summer camp. You men need to tighten up!"

The Israeli soldiers exchanged sheepish grins with their Cathar teammates as a small, black and white goat with a tiny bell tied around its neck emerged from the underbrush and wandered by, bleating at the heavily-armed men.

"I don't think he got the memo about keeping his equipment quiet, sir," Sergeant Efron quipped, grinning at his ruffled-looking commander as the little goat disappeared behind a tree.

"Maybe we should buy some goats of our own and let them loose in the forest," Efron continued. "All those tiny little bells would really screw up Acerbi's listening devices."

Ben found it impossible not to grin back at the seasoned veteran. "That's actually not such a bad idea, Sergeant. Where's the cardinal?"

"Here." A hand shot up from the middle of a group of soldiers.

"You look good in an Israeli uniform, Cardinal," Ben grinned. "I'm assigning you to Sergeant Efron. Your job is to stay in his shadow all the way through the pass. From here on out we'll only be using hand signals … no voice communications unless we're forced to use our radios. Is that understood?"

With only the whites of their eyes shining out from the camouflage paint on their faces, the men nodded back in unison before they disappeared into the misty blue glow of the moonlit forest and headed off into the pass that wound its way through the Pyrenees.

For the next four days the men moved silently over familiar ground, stopping occasionally for quick cat-naps and breaks for cold meals along the way. Thankfully, the terrain they had to cross was relatively flat, making their progress over the spongy forest floor much easier.

Although Leo had tried to maintain a regular exercise regimen, he had recently begun to feel every one of sixty-two years and was grateful for the frequent rest stops the young men had planned along the way. With mountains rising all around them, the weather changed frequently as rising air currents poured over the surrounding peaks and cascaded down into the pass, making it rainy and windy one moment, then calm and dry the next.

Even when things were calm and the sun's warmth penetrated the leafy canopy over the shadowed path through the valley, it seemed to Leo like their clothing never fully dried out before the sky turned dark again and the next rainstorm swept down from the mountains, drenching them in a swirling mist that found its way through even the tiniest opening in their green ponchos before working its way into the woolen clothing beneath.

On the final day of their trek through the forest, Leo found himself trudging along behind Sergeant Efron, staring at the back of the man's head as they slogged up a muddy incline to the base of a massive boulder. On the other side Leo could hear voices, and after they circled around, they saw Ben Zamir standing at the top of a rise and pointing down at something.

The light seemed brighter here.

Inching his way around Efron, Leo climbed up beside Ben and squinted in the bright sunshine. The valley had opened up. They had made it through the pass, and below them, stretching toward the horizon, a broad panorama of green trees stopped at the edge of a large swath of dry Catalan grassland that stretched as far as the eye could see. Their view extended for at least a hundred miles, ending on their left in a blue haze that could mean only one thing. The sea was just beyond the horizon. They were now in Spain.

Quickly, Ben climbed the boulder and pulled out his binoculars to scan a flat expanse of grassland off to their left. "It looks like the abandoned base is right at the base of this mountain."

"Strange place to put an airbase," Efron observed. "I mean, I can understand wanting it close to the border, but these mountains can quickly

44

turn into a death trap for low-flying aircraft, especially in bad weather. The crosswinds in this area must be fearsome."

"Maybe that's why they abandoned it." Ben slid down the side of the boulder. "Come on, let's keep moving. The faster we can get to that base and scout the area around it the quicker we can find a place to dry out and catch some sleep before the jet arrives. I want the perimeter locked down and secured with a two mile buffer zone. No one gets near that base while the jet is on the ground, is that clear?"

"What about threats from the air?" Gael Wehling asked. His Cathar fighters nodded. "We should have no problem securing the perimeter from ground threats, but the surface-to-air weapons we brought have limited altitude capability if we're attacked from the air."

"If we encounter a full-blown assault from the air it means we've walked into a trap," Ben answered. "The mission will be over right then and there, because there'll be no point in waiting around for a jet that was probably never going to show up in the first place. Our only option will be to retreat back into the mountains and meet up at our predetermined rendezvous point before we head back to the castle."

Slinging his rifle over his shoulder, Sergeant Efron glanced back at Leo. "Remember, Cardinal … stay close to me."

"I appreciate your concern, Sergeant, but I've been looking after myself for 62 years now. This isn't exactly my first rodeo, you know."

"I realize that, Cardinal," Efron said, a mischievous grin spreading across his face. "But if you get yourself killed I could lose my stripes."

The two men laughed out loud, eliciting a withering glare from Ben Zamir. "We're not there yet. This is where things really start to get hairy. Time to split up." Ben nodded to Gael, and within seconds he and his band of Cathar fighters had disappeared down through the forest and out into the grassland at the base of the mountain.

"Let's move out," Ben said. "While Gael sets up a defensive perimeter we'll be going in through the main gate."

CHAPTER 10

The sun was just setting over the far reach of the western horizon when Team 5 arrived at the graffiti-covered main gate. Finding it deserted with all the windows broken out, they moved cautiously across a weed-covered expanse of concrete, entering an artificial canyon created by two long rows of facing aircraft hangars streaked with rust.

Whistling through the cracks of the cavernous buildings, a mournful wind whispered the same melancholy tune that seemed to be attached to all abandoned places, making the men feel even more isolated from a world they had been forced to hide from. Leo pointed to a tall cinderblock tower topped with green-tinted, wrap-around windows and painted with a garish motif of alternating orange and white blocks. "Looks like they definitely wanted that building to stand out for some reason."

"That's the old control tower," Ben said, studying the red brick building that extended out from the base of the tower. "That's where the jet will probably park after it lands. Visiting pilots usually head for the main building beneath the control tower."

Dropping to one knee, Ben began issuing a series of hand signals to the men behind him. Instantly, two commandos ran ahead and entered the building while Sergeant Efron and the others jogged off to scout the row of ghostly hangars behind them.

"Come on, Cardinal." Ben's teeth gleamed as he smiled through the caked camouflage paint on his face. "Let's get you inside that building. Who knows, some of us might even get some uninterrupted sleep tonight."

* * *

The anticipated night of uninterrupted sleep had evaded Leo as he tossed and turned in his sleeping bag on the hard linoleum floor of the old terminal building. Sleep had initially come to him quickly, but his dreams had been filled with fast-moving, collage-like images from his past. He had dreamt about his mother and father and their tiny wooden house in a small Pennsylvania coal mining town. He had seen Evita wearing a flowing white gown, welcoming him home from the doorway of a mountaintop cabin before the scene suddenly changed to a place in the Israeli desert that he would rather forget. He had seen the waterfall behind the castle, and Saint Peter's Basilica rising majestically over Vatican City, where Pope Michael and Eduardo Acerbi had been talking to him as if they were both still alive. With the real world lying just beyond his conscious thoughts his dreams had become life, while his waking life had become the dream.

Awakening with a start, Leo looked up at the rain-streaked windows and heard the wind rattle the glass along the front of the darkened building. "What time is it?" he asked Sergeant Efron.

"The sun's just coming up, Cardinal. It won't be long now." Efron opened a can of camouflage paint. "And smear some more of this on your face."

For the next hour the men sipped lukewarm coffee and took turns looking through the windows, until finally one of the men called out. Jumping to their feet they all peered into the gloom just in time to catch a glimpse of the small white jet emerging from a line of dark, low-lying clouds—giving the pilots just seconds to correct for wind drift before the jet's tires squeaked against the rubber-scarred end of the concrete runway.

Turning onto a weed-choked taxiway, the jet's bright landing lights swept the front of the long brick building, momentarily blinding the camouflaged men inside as the plane rolled to a stop. Inside the cockpit, the two pilots stared out at an apparently deserted airfield.

They had been told to expect this reception by the man who had sent them.

Exchanging glances, the pilots opened the cabin door and descended the air stairs into a gray drizzle.

"Just follow my lead, Cardinal," Ben said. "You and I are going to walk out to that jet and tell the pilots that we're making a preliminary check to make sure the plane is secure before we bring the *cardinal* out. Dressed

48

like that they won't know who you are until you reveal your true identity once we're on board."

Leo adjusted the heavy Kevlar helmet. "I really don't see the need for all of this, Ben. I doubt they'll try anything on the ground. If they're here to kidnap me they'll simply wait until we're in the air and lock the cockpit door before flying me straight to Acerbi."

"That's a very real possibility, Leo, but right now I'm more worried about a sniper in the area. Acerbi has proven to be a very crafty tactician. He doesn't need a big force on the ground. The arrival of this jet could be a ruse to draw you out into the open so he can be done with you here and now. If that's his plan, those two pilots standing out there are nothing more than collateral damage to him. They're expendable, because if Acerbi is involved, he knows you're not alone and that the men he sent won't be returning if anything happens to you here on the ground."

"You guys really do think of everything."

"Not everything, Cardinal. Like you said, once the door to that jet slams shut your fate is out of our hands. If you want to change your mind then now is the time. Personally, I think this whole set-up stinks."

The dark green camouflage paint accentuated the whites of Leo's eyes as he peered out at the two pilots standing in the drizzle. "I really don't have much choice. Whoever sent that jet could very well hold the key to our survival, which means the fate of everyone we love depends on me walking out to that plane."

"That's just the kind of guilt trip Acerbi would lay on you if he was trying to draw you out," Ben said, his eyes scanning the tree line in the distance.

Leo hefted his backpack. "Well, guilt trip or not, it's time to go. Besides, I've been dying to show everyone my imitation of an Israeli commando."

Grinning back at the tall cardinal, Ben made a final check of the area before the two men walked through the door to meet with the pilots. From his position high in the tower, Sergeant Efron scanned the surrounding rooftops through his rifle scope before extending his search to the tall brown grass that lined the perimeter of the airfield. Although he couldn't see them, he knew Gael and his men were out there somewhere.

If anyone was foolish enough to approach the field on the ground they were in for a big surprise.

Focusing his attention back on the concrete tarmac below, he saw that Ben and Leo had already climbed the air stairs with the two pilots and were ducking into the sleek Gulfstream jet. They were now out of eyesight, and all he could do was wait.

Inside the aircraft, the captain welcomed the two men aboard. "As you can see, gentlemen, we are the only ones here. I can promise you the cardinal will be safe. Between the two of us we have over twenty thousand hours of flight time in jets, and our boss is a stickler when it comes to maintaining his aircraft."

"And does this boss of yours have a name?" Ben prodded.

The two pilots smiled at the expected question. "I'm afraid that's something we're not permitted to discuss," said the captain, "but I can assure you that we are all on the same team. The cardinal's safety is our top priority, and we'll be returning him to this same airfield two days from now."

Ben's voice suddenly matched his icy expression. "We'll be waiting."

The captain continued to smile. "If everything is in order, we'd like you to bring the cardinal on board as soon as possible. We're playing a very dangerous game with air traffic control right now. They think we've dipped down below their mountain radar coverage due to the bad weather, and if we don't pop back up on their screens in the next few minutes they'll start to wonder where we've gone."

Removing his helmet, Leo stepped forward, startling the two surprised pilots. "I'm already on board." Turning to Ben, he clasped him on the shoulder. "It's time for me to go. Be sure to thank the others for me, and I'll see you back here in two days."

CHAPTER 11

As soon as the jet lifted off the runway and entered the clouds, Leo knew that he probably wouldn't be seeing the ground again anytime soon.

They could be flying anywhere!

Reclining his chair, he unwrapped a deli sandwich provided by the crew and sipped the first hot coffee he had tasted in five days. Picking up a remote control, he turned on the flat screen TV at the front of the cabin. As soon as the picture sprang to life, he was filled with a sudden realization.

It had been eight long months since he had watched television!

From the looks of things, the news programs had remained unchanged. Against a digital headlines and the never-ending banners that ran continuously across the bottom of the screen, the overly-excited stream of chatter that came from the talking heads only added to the sensory overload crammed into one screen.

But now, in addition to the competing messages, there was something new. At the bottom of the screen, below the pretty face of the female newscaster, the Acerbi Corporation logo jumped out at him. This wasn't CBS or NBC, or CNN. He quickly switched to a new channel where an old movie was playing. Again, the Acerbi corporate logo was prominently displayed at the bottom of the screen. Leo began rapidly surfing the channels, and every time he paused the same logo popped up again and again in the lower right-hand corner. ABC, FOX, even the BBC—they had all disappeared. This was obviously a new kind of television that more closely resembled the state-sponsored programming he had been forced to endure on his trips to countries that were controlled by totalitarian regimes, but in this case, a worldwide audience was being bombarded by a totalitarian *corporate* regime.

Of course! Leo marveled at his own surprise. *Adrian Acerbi now controlled all the media!*

The jet bounced through a trough of rough air, forcing Leo against his seatbelt as he leaned his head into the aisle and saw that the cockpit door had been left open. The two pilots seemed to be chatting pleasantly, letting the autopilot do the tedious work of keeping the aircraft on the correct heading.

Unbuckling his seatbelt, Leo stood and stretched. They had been flying for two hours and he thought he would stroll forward to see if the pilots were in a talkative mood. The jet bounced again, forcing Leo to brace himself in the aisle between two seatbacks.

"Are you OK back there, Cardinal?" the co-pilot asked, glancing back over his shoulder. "Maybe you should sit back down and buckle up until we're out of this turbulence."

"How much longer until we land?" Leo asked, continuing to inch his way toward the cockpit.

"Another hour and ten minutes," the captain answered in a low baritone. Leaning forward, he tapped his finger against a glass screen displaying a color-coded digital navigation map. "The total flight time from Spain to Oslo is three hours and ten minutes."

Oslo! They're flying me to Norway! "Why didn't you let me know where you were taking me before we took off?" Leo asked, finally making it to the cockpit door.

The captain flicked a toggle switch over his head and swiveled in his seat. "Sorry, Cardinal, but we had strict orders not to let anyone know where we were headed in case any of your friends back on the ground in Spain were captured by Acerbi's forces after we left. Believe me, I felt bad about not letting them know. I could see the concern on their faces, but we had strict orders not to discuss our destination with anyone on the ground." The pilot pointed to the door jam. "There's a little fold-out seat by your knee. Why don't you join us?"

The sudden openness from the pilots made Leo breathe a little easier. Lowering the small padded seat, he settled in and leaned forward to peer at the opaque grayness outside the cockpit windows as the jet hurtled through the wet sky. "Will the weather be like this all the way to Norway?"

"We should be starting our descent into Oslo in about thirty minutes, Cardinal," the co-pilot answered. "Once we're out of the clouds you'll be able to see the Norwegian coastline."

Taking a chance, Leo decided to prod some more. "As long as we're being open about things now, can you tell me who you're taking me to see?"

"Sorry, Cardinal, but I'm afraid that part of the puzzle will have to remain a mystery until after we arrive, but I think you'll be pleasantly surprised. Until then, sit back and enjoy the ride."

For the next thirty minutes the jet continued to rise and fall in the turbulence of a confused sky, until finally, little glimpses of color began appearing through breaks in the gray overcast of a storm system that had swept in from the North Sea and enveloped most of the European continent.

Breaking through the clouds, the jet's wings rocked in a rhythmic dance with the frosty air as the plane descended over a wind-whipped ocean and crossed a jagged green coastline before finally landing at Oslo's Gardermoen airport just north of the city.

Bypassing the main terminal, the jet turned off the end of the runway and taxied directly into an isolated hangar on the opposite side of the field. As the engines whined down, Leo felt a rush of cold air when the co-pilot opened the cabin door and a plain, four-door sedan with dark tinted windows pulled up next to the jet and stopped. Climbing from the driver's seat, a large man with broad shoulders and thinning hair opened the rear passenger door and waited. Dressed in a blue, pin-striped suit with a red tie and gold tie clasp that matched his cufflinks, the driver looked like a man who would be more at home in a boardroom instead of chauffeuring others around in a car.

"You'll be traveling overland from here, Cardinal," the co-pilot told Leo, nodding toward the driver. "I think you'll find your stay most enlightening. We'll see you back here in a couple of days."

Feeling like a first-grader stepping off the school bus on his first day of school, Leo shook hands with the pilots and descended the stairs to the concrete floor of the hangar. Without a word, the driver motioned Leo into the back seat of the car and closed the door before walking around and squeezing into the driver's seat.

"I'm afraid I must ask you to duck down in your seat until we're clear of the airport, sir."

"Duck down?"

"Yes. Just in case. I'll let you know when we're clear."

Just in case? Leo could feel his heart rate increase slightly as he leaned his tall frame across the back seat. The car lurched forward, and from his horizontal position he could tell by the sound of the car's engine that the driver was speeding.

After the car swept through a few leaning curves, the driver finally turned his head and called out to Leo. "You can sit up now, Cardinal."

Peering outside, Leo was greeted with a blurred view of the rural expanse of green pastureland that stretched along the sides of the E16 highway leading north away from Oslo. "What time is it here?" he asked, watching the airport fade behind them.

The man smiled up into the rearview mirror. "Norway is in the same time zone as Spain … Central European Standard Time. You won't have to reset your watch, if that's what you're asking. Please, Cardinal, allow me to introduce myself. My name is Gunnar Neilson. I apologize for not introducing myself to you sooner, but I was busy listening to the driver in the lead security vehicle up ahead."

Leo's eyes zeroed in on the small curled wire snaking from the man's right ear and down into his collar. "Security vehicle?"

"Yes. Actually, there are two of them. There's an SUV full of armed men about a kilometer ahead of us and another following behind. The boss wants to make sure nothing happens to you while you're in Norway."

"That's very considerate of him … whoever he is," Leo said. "This just keeps getting more intriguing by the minute. I was under the impression we would be going into Oslo."

"Acerbi's people are everywhere now, Cardinal … especially in the cities." The driver studied Leo's clothes. "Besides, walking around Oslo wearing an Israeli Special Forces uniform might raise a few eyebrows. We're keeping your visit as low profile as possible. If we do our job right no one will ever know you were here."

"It's good to know I'm being looked after so well." Leo watched the man's eyes in the rear-view mirror for any hint of emotion. "My friends think I'm walking into a trap."

"You took a chance, Cardinal … I'll give you that." The driver kept his eyes fixed on the road ahead. "We figured the odds of you showing up were 50-50 at best."

"I'd say that's a pretty close assumption. How much farther do we have to go?"

"Once we clear the tunnel ahead we'll be in the mountains. It shouldn't take more than an hour to get where we're going." Gunnar reached down into the seat beside him and tossed a thick, fur-collared parka into the back seat. "Here … you'll be needing that."

54

CHAPTER 12

Commander Samantha Jennings held her head in her hands and stared down at the stack of intelligence briefs lying on her desk. The weather had cleared over the English coast and the blue sky beckoned. She wanted to be outside—to be flying, but as the air commander for Adrian Acerbi's European theater of operations, she found that her increasing duties kept her chained to her desk reading intelligence briefs and enduring an endless stream of seemingly pointless meetings.

For the most part her job was pretty straightforward. The absorption of so many countries into Acerbi's one world government had been met with very little resistance, and the need for military intervention had dropped to an all time low after the Acerbi Corporation had decided to name the new geographical districts around the world after the former countries that had existed there before, thus giving the appearance of sameness to those who now lived under the banner of a single flag.

The British Isles were still referred to as the United Kingdom, the district in Europe that had once been France was still called France, and the three new North American districts were still referred to as Canada, the United States, and Mexico.

Acerbi had proven to be a master manipulator by creating the false illusion that the former nations of the world still retained some semblance of a national identity, making it far easier for people to accept the fact that the very essence of who they were as individuals was slowly being erased as they lined up in droves to accept their shiny new government ID cards.

For those who had embraced the new order of things, life had become easier. By becoming citizens of the new world government, billions of people had been given access to a material world filled with endless possibilities, but for those who had refused to join, life had become more difficult—a lot more difficult.

No surprise there. Jennings smiled to herself.

Those who had continued to hold out by refusing to accept Acerbi as their new savior found themselves struggling to make ends meet or had given up altogether, fleeing into the countryside to eke out a hardscrabble existence from the land. Around the world many had formed pockets of resistance that had coalesced into formidable rebel uprisings led by men and women the new government quickly labeled as paranoid conspiracy theorists or so-called religious zealots. Their pictures were flashed over the internet, and the neighbors who turned them in to Acerbi's forces were generously rewarded.

What fools! Jennings thought to herself. *Couldn't they see what the man was trying to do?* International borders were disappearing all over the world, and former enemies were rapidly becoming united under a single banner. *What was wrong with that?*

Jennings actually felt sorry for them, but regardless of how she felt her boss wanted the rebels stopped, and it was the job of the forces under her command to take charge of the air and root the malcontents out of hiding so they could be offered a final chance at citizenship or—or what? Jennings had heard rumors of *indoctrination* camps springing up in isolated locations around the world, but she had never actually seen one of them.

What went on there?

It might be interesting to find out, but right now she had other things on her mind. The stack of folders marked *Top Secret* on her desk was making her head throb. Gulping down her third cup of coffee, she reached for a folder and began to read.

Attention: Wing commander – Acerbi European Base of Operations
Subject: Rebel activity in vicinity of UK airfields

… *Military police have reported the theft of several dozen shoulder-fired stinger missiles from a secure weapons depot in the northern section of the district. All low-flying government aircraft approaching and departing UK airfields in the district are considered to be potential targets. Please adjust perimeter security as necessary.*

Samantha tossed the folder aside and made a mental note to talk to the base security chief as she reached for the next folder.

Attention: Wing commander – Acerbi European Base of Operations

56

On 6 June, a Gulfstream jet on a flight from Oslo, Norway to Barcelona, Spain requested a diversion from its assigned cruising altitude to avoid wind turbulence over the Pyrenees. The aircraft descended to a lower altitude and disappeared from radar for twenty-two minutes on the Spanish side of the border in the vicinity of an abandoned Spanish Air Force base before suddenly reappearing on a climbing reverse course for Norway. Subsequently, the pilots stated that they wished to return to Oslo and cancelled their flight plan into Barcelona. When questioned by air traffic control, the pilot in command stated that they had been on a training flight and had decided to cut the flight short due to the deteriorating weather in the area. Upon further investigation, weather in the Barcelona area at the time of the flight was found to be within acceptable limits, and other aircraft in the area were arriving and departing from the airport without any reported problems. Aircraft in question was a G5 Gulfstream jet, number LN50218 registered to the Norwegian Jet Group, a company that leases executive business jets to individuals and companies on a fractional ownership basis.

Probably some corporate weenies who didn't want to bend their company's new jet, Jennings mused. Yet the missing twenty-two minutes did seem odd. Biting her lower lip, she placed the folder in a separate basket for further evaluation.

Glancing out her second story window, Jennings sat bolt upright in her seat. Driving across the tarmac, a motorcade containing Acerbi's distinctive dark blue limo was headed for his private hangar. As wing commander, why hadn't she been notified of his arrival on the airfield?

Grabbing her smart phone, Samantha called the front gate and rushed downstairs.

"Front gate," a male voice answered. "Corporal Blythe speaking. How may I assist you?"

"This is Commander Jennings. Why wasn't I informed that Mr. Acerbi just entered the base?"

"Oh … Commander … I thought you knew."

"And just how would I know if no one bothered to call me?"

"I'm sorry, ma'am. Mr. Acerbi said you were expecting him."

Jennings froze. "What did he look like?"

"I beg your pardon, Commander?"

"I asked you what Mr. Acerbi looked like. You did see him, didn't you?"

"He looked like Mr. Acerbi, ma'am."

"Did you check his ID?"

"No, ma'am. We never check his ID. He's Mr. Acerbi, and the transponder codes for the security vehicles escorting him onto the base checked out. I recognized most of the men driving them."

"Well, for your information I had no idea he was coming, and no one bothered to notify me. I want you to place the base on orange alert until I find out just what's going on!"

"Orange alert, ma'am!?"

"That's what I said. Do it now!"

"Yes, ma'am … right away, I …"

"And stop calling me ma'am. I'm your commander, not your mother!" Jennings punched the off button on her phone and jumped into her personal command vehicle. Switching on the flashing blue strobe lights she hit the gas and sped off across the field before coming to a screeching halt next to an unmarked C-17 cargo plane surrounded by Acerbi's security men. Exiting the limo parked behind the plane, Acerbi stepped into the sunshine.

Breathing hard, Jennings leaned forward and stared through the windshield.

That's not Acerbi!

The dark-haired man looked remarkably like him, but he was at least two inches shorter, and unlike Adrian, who walked with an air of authority, this man stepped almost hesitantly, as if he wasn't sure of where he should go.

Clicking the safety of her pistol to the off position, Jennings stepped from the car and headed directly for the man. As soon as she reached him a tall, dark-suited security man stepped between them.

"I'm sorry, Commander, but Mr. Acerbi is in a hurry."

"Too much of a hurry to say hello to his air commander?" Jennings brushed past the security officer and caught up with the Acerbi look-alike. "Who are you?"

The man recoiled without answering.

"You're not Adrian Acerbi!" Jennings placed her hand on her gun and stepped closer just as a dozen security men reached for their weapons.

"What's going on here!?" A burly sergeant asked, his eyes moving between Acerbi and his hot-tempered commander.

"This man isn't Adrian Acerbi!" Samantha shouted.

From inside the limo behind them, a familiar voice called out. "Stand down, Commander. Get inside and close the door."

Samantha could feel the hair rise on the back of her neck as she leaned down and peered into the back seat of the long blue limo. Reclining in his seat, Adrian Acerbi smiled up at her. "I said get in, Commander."

What in the world was going on?

"Uh … yes, sir." Right away Samantha could see that she was talking to the real Adrian Acerbi as she crawled into the back seat and closed the door.

"You certainly are a fireball, Commander Jennings."

"I believe that's why you hired me, sir." Samantha exhaled as she looked through the tinted glass and watched the man pretending to be Acerbi ascend the ramp at the back of the waiting aircraft. "Do you mind telling me what's going on here?"

"I usually don't make a habit of explaining my actions, Commander." Acerbi's dark eyes were studying Samantha's profile. "But since I admire your tenacity and the way you go about your job, I'll indulge your curiosity just this once. The man you see entering that aircraft is one of my body doubles. I often send doubles on missions of little importance, so I can focus on more important matters. How did you know he wasn't me?"

"Well, for one thing, sir, your double is almost two inches shorter than you are, and our security was breached the moment you drove onto the airfield without prior notification. I just happened to see your motorcade and called the front gate. When the guard said he was told that I was expecting you, I knew right away that something was wrong."

"Very impressive, Commander. Would you care for a glass of wine?"

Samantha felt her face flush. She was sitting in the back of a limo with the most powerful man in the world, and he had just complimented her work and asked her if she wanted a glass of wine.

"No, thank you, sir, but I'm on duty."

"Of course. You would say that." Acerbi reached into a walnut cabinet next to his seat and poured a glass of wine as he watched the jet taxi into position for takeoff. For a moment all conversation was lost as the big plane thundered down the runway and lifted into the air.

"Do you fly, Commander?" Adrian asked.

"Yes, sir. Ever since I was a little girl …" Samantha froze. Like a broken hologram that had suddenly lost its power, Adrian Acerbi's image had blurred for just a moment into something else.

"Please continue, Commander." Acerbi's eyes probed her face as she pressed her fingers to her temples.

Was she seeing things?

"Oh … sorry, sir," she blurted out, avoiding Adrian's dark gaze. "I just felt a little dizzy for a second. I've been doing a lot of reading this morning. As I was just saying, I've loved flying since I was a little girl. I used to wash airplanes to earn money to pay for flying lessons at the local airfield outside the small town I grew up in. I earned my pilots license the year I graduated from high school, and after college I …"

A bright flash of light suddenly erupted from a nearby hillside, followed by a trail of white smoke that twisted in a corkscrew-like arc toward the climbing jet before streaking into the back of one of the engines. Like a time lapse image of a flower opening to the rays of the sun, an orange ball of death-tinted flame blossomed in the sky with the sound of rolling thunder.

Witnesses on the ground had seen the blast before they had heard it, and as they braced themselves against the shockwave, they watched as flaming pieces of metal fluttered toward the ground like dry fall leaves while the main section of the fuselage cartwheeled into the trees at the end of the runway with a sickening thud that shook the earth beneath their feet.

Instantly Samantha Jennings was out of the car and running across the field toward the rising cloud of black smoke. Although her brain was telling her there was nothing she could do, her body was telling her to run. Keeping to the edge of the runway she stopped and cupped her hands over her eyes to see if anything was moving in the acrid, billowing smoke, while behind her, the wail of sirens filled the air as a boxy yellow fire truck screamed past and disappeared through the wall of smoke.

Breathing hard, she bent forward and propped her hands against her knees, letting the hot wind twist strands of her dangling red hair around her face as she took in a few deep breaths. In her peripheral vision, she saw the outline of the long blue limo slowly pull up beside her.

"There's nothing you can do, Commander," Acerbi said through the open window. His voice sounded disconnected in the dark interior of the limo. "Get in. We'll take you back to your car."

Slowly, Samantha opened the door and lowered herself into the seat next to Adrian. "You could have been on that plane, Mr. Acerbi!"

"But I wasn't. I'm sure by now you've read the security briefs concerning the recent increase of rebel activity in the area. I believe this was a rather spectacular display of their capability. Not only do they possess the weapons necessary to take down one of our aircraft, but they also appear to have an intelligence gathering capability that allows them to coordinate their attacks. Someone thought I was on that aircraft, and they were able to communicate that knowledge to whoever shot it down."

Samantha's eyes grew cold as she stared back at Acerbi.

He had purposely allowed one of her aircraft to be shot out of the sky as a test!

"You knew someone was trying to kill you, didn't you, Mr. Acerbi?"

"Of course. Why do you think I brought my double along?"

"But what about the people on board, Mr. Acerbi?! If you would have included me and my security team in on this, we could have employed our countermeasures to divert the missile that just killed everyone on that plane. Those people were loyal to you, sir, and they all had families! Why didn't you tell me you were testing our defenses? We could have achieved the same goal without any unnecessary loss of life."

"Calm yourself, Commander. Where's that iron will of yours that I've come to admire? I've accomplished exactly what I wanted to accomplish. The rebels now believe I'm dead ... at least for now, and while they celebrate I'll be flying off on a different aircraft to my real destination."

"Are you telling me this was a diversion, sir?"

Acerbi's eyes flashed. "That's exactly what I'm telling you, Commander." The limo rolled to a stop next to Samantha's car. "I believe this is where you get off."

"Yes, sir." Samantha looked out through the tinted glass at the smoke rising in the distance. "Thank you for the ride, Mr. Acerbi. It's been most enlightening."

With that she stepped from the limo and closed the door behind her.

This is exactly where I'm getting off, she told herself, walking toward her car. *I've had enough of this psychopath!*

Driving back to her office, she ran upstairs and gathered all the security folders from her desk. Sweeping them into a nylon briefcase, she walked back outside and slid into the front seat of her car. Driving slowly, she approached the front gate and stopped. The guard on duty saluted smartly and approached the driver's side window. "Afternoon, Commander." He hesitated, looking off in the direction of the rising column of black smoke. "I've never seen a plane go down before. Do you want us to remain on orange alert?"

Samantha thought for a minute as a helicopter gunship swooped overhead, heading for the hill the missile had been fired from. "No, go to green and call off the dogs. The rebels are long gone by now."

"Yes, ma'am ... er, I mean, Commander."

Samantha smiled. "Ma'am will do just fine from now on, Corporal."

After today no one will be calling me Commander again.

"Oh, and Corporal, I need you to do me a favor. My cell phone battery just died and I need you to tell the duty officer that I won't be in tomorrow. I'll call him later."

"Yes, ma'am." The corporal saluted. "Have a good evening."

Taking her foot off the brake, Samantha pulled away from the gate, her eyes squinting at the road ahead.

She wouldn't be in tomorrow… or any day after that for that matter.

Samantha Jennings was about to disappear, for she had just been allowed a glimpse into a future she wanted no part of. The rumors about Adrian Acerbi were true, and somehow, she had to find a way to connect with the people who had just tried to kill him without getting herself killed in the process.

CHAPTER 13

Winding through the Norwegian countryside, Leo was surprised to see that the main road between Oslo and the North Sea coast was only two lanes wide. "Not much traffic today," he said to the driver.

Gunnar waved his hand at the mountains rising all around them. "Most Norwegians fly between cities, Cardinal ... especially when traveling between the north and south. Geographically, Norway may be long and thin, but it's one of the largest countries in Europe and the tall mountain ranges and deep fjords make point-to-point travel by road difficult. In the past few years the government has tried to connect the country with an ambitious road building program that involves lots of tunneling ... and we're about to enter the longest road tunnel in the world ... the *Laerdal* Tunnel."

Looking ahead, Leo saw that they were approaching an uninspired tunnel entrance at the base of a small mountain. "The entrance is a little anticlimactic, don't you think?" Leo smiled. "I guess I was expecting to see some kind of grand flashing sign alerting people to the fact that they were about to enter the world's longest tunnel."

"Norwegians don't like to brag, Cardinal." Gunnar winked up into the rear-view mirror. Seconds later the sedan sped through the tunnel's plain curved entrance, trading bright sunlight for a subterranean world illuminated from above by a line of white lights that seemed to run into infinity along the top of an arched ceiling carved from solid gray rock. "Hope you don't suffer from claustrophobia, Cardinal."

Leo winced. Even though he had worked in a Pennsylvania coal mine alongside his father and uncles the summer before college, he hated tight spaces. "Just how long is this thing?"

"A little over 24 kilometers. That's fifteen miles for you Americans."

"Fifteen miles!" Leaning back in his seat, Leo closed his eyes and tried to picture wide open spaces as the halogen lights whizzed overhead. When he opened them again, he was startled to see that the car had entered an immense, hollowed-out cavern bathed in a diffuse, bluish light.

Leo marveled at the unexpected sight. "What's this?"

"Oh … the blue caves." Gunnar smiled proudly. "This is the first of three large caverns created by the tunnel engineers to relieve drivers of the mental strain of having to drive through such a long-enclosed space. They even thought to place little yellow lights around the base to create the impression of driving into a sunrise. It's very soothing, don't you think?"

"It's quite beautiful actually," Leo said. He was just beginning to enjoy their new surroundings when they were suddenly thrust back into another long stretch of claustrophobic grayness, eventually passing through two additional blue caverns before finally speeding through the tunnel exit and returning to the world of sunlight and fresh air.

From this point on the road began to climb, skirting small running creeks and steep drop-offs as it twisted beneath the snow-capped mountains. After following the climbing road another twenty miles, Gunnar turned off onto a paved side road that twisted through a dark primal forest. Ten minutes later the car finally came to a stop in front of an immense timbered lodge set back among some of the tallest trees Leo had ever seen.

"We're here, Cardinal. The man you've come to see is waiting for you inside."

Stepping from the car, Leo saw a group of armed men exiting a black SUV that had just pulled in ahead of them.

Gunnar wasn't kidding about the security vehicles shadowing them.

Looking around at the silent armed men who were facing the forest, Leo hesitated as he blinked up at the tall mountains ringing their position and shivered in the cold, pine-scented air.

Gunnar motioned to a carved wooden door beyond a stone archway. "Go ahead, Cardinal. He's just inside. He's waiting for you."

No turning back now.

Taking a deep breath, Leo opened the door and stepped inside. To his right he saw a long, traditionally-furnished great room painted by the flickering firelight in an oversized fireplace made from rounded river rock, and sitting in an overstuffed chair with his back to the door, a gray-haired man was reading a book.

Slowly, the man laid the book on a side table and stood to face Leo.

For a moment Leo just stood there—transfixed. He was frozen in place, unable to move as a flood of emotions overcame his ability to think. He had prepared himself for almost anything—but not this. Reaching out he tried to steady himself against the wall, for he was staring into the piercing blue eyes of Pope Michael.

"*Marcus?*"

"Please, Cardinal … sit." The man took an urgent step forward and guided a shaken Leo toward a facing blue and gold wing chair. "I'm not Marcus … I'm his brother … Steig Lundahl. I'm afraid it's a common mistake."

Marcus had a twin brother!?

Leo's ears started to ring as he felt for the arm rests of the chair and continued to stare up into a pair of striking blue eyes set in a weathered face. "You're Pope Michael's twin brother?"

"Brother, yes … twin, no."

The man even sounded like Pope Michael.

"Most people always assumed we were twins when we were together, and I admit the resemblance is remarkable, but on closer inspection I think you'll see that I'm quite a few years older than my late brother … although our difference in age matters little now that he's gone."

Lundahl's face slowly melted into a mask of sadness. "Unfortunately, my brother will never know what it felt like to grow old like me."

Leo clasped his hands together to keep them from visibly shaking. "I'm afraid you'll have to forgive my reaction, Mr. Lundahl. It's just that Marcus never told me he had a brother."

"Is it really so surprising, Cardinal? As his close friend and confidant, you knew that my brother was a very private man. We also have a sister. She's a well-known artist who lives in the coastal town of Stavanger. At least she did until Acerbi came to power. She and her husband now live in a small village in the northern part of the country. I sincerely apologize for not being able to prepare you in advance. I know how close you and my brother were. I should have anticipated your shock, but my security people advised me not to reveal my identity in case our transmission was somehow intercepted by Acerbi's people. A mistake like that could have been disastrous for everyone concerned."

Leo continued to stare. "Marcus was always very introspective, so I guess I never really found it that unusual that he avoided discussing personal issues, but the fact that he never told me he had a brother and sister defies reason. Frankly, I'm surprised no one in the press ever mentioned it when he was being vetted in the court of public opinion after he became pope. I guess the only thing any of us ever really knew about his family was the fact that his father was a wealthy Norwegian industrialist."

"That's true, Cardinal. In fact, as you probably already know, our father did business with another wealthy industrialist … Eduardo Acerbi, the man who ended up adopting Adrian Acerbi and his brother Rene."

"Yes, your brother told me about that. I knew Eduardo well." Fond memories of the frail old man came rushing back to Leo. "In fact, we became close friends. He saved the world you know."

"I've heard that story. He made one of the most difficult decisions a man could ever make. I remember him and my father discussing business in this very room when Marcus and I were still just children. Although my father tried to hide it, we could tell he was very upset when he was forced to break off all ties with the Acerbi Corporation after Eduardo disappeared and Rene eventually took over."

The elder Lundahl crossed the room to a large plate-glass window and gazed out at the surrounding mountains. "It feels strange to gaze out on a world that looks so unchanged when you know that it is slowly being robbed of its humanity." Lundahl glanced back over his shoulder at Leo. "I imagine that's what people thought when World War II broke out. One moment farmers were plowing their fields, milking cows and talking with their neighbors, and the next, the sky was filled with the drifting silk of Nazi paratroopers landing in their fields. Like a man who decides to build his house near the edge of an eroding cliff, the existence of our species seems poised to crumble into oblivion in the blink of an eye if it fails to recognize the erosion of the spiritual world around us."

Leo shifted uncomfortably in his seat as Lundahl turned away from the window with the vacant look of one who had just seen something that had left him feeling lost. The resemblance to Pope Michael was uncanny but the differences were clear. Unlike Marcus, with his penchant for short hair and a clean-shaven face, the elder Lundahl sported a beard and long gray hair that hung down over his collar. His nose was a little longer and his face a little more drawn, and running just below the right eye, a jagged scar creased his cheek. But the eyes! They were Lundahl eyes. There was no difference there.

This was going to take some getting used to.

"Would you care for some coffee or tea before you change out of those clothes, Cardinal?"

Lundahl's voice sounded far away, and Leo found himself drifting off in the warmth from the fire. "Excuse me … what did you say, Mr. Lundahl?"

"We've readied a room for you upstairs. I wanted to know if you would like some coffee or tea before you take a bath and change into some clean clothes for dinner."

For the first time all day Leo realized how he must look to others, or worse, how he must smell after his five-day trek through the Pyrenees without a bath or change of clothes. "If you don't mind, Mr. Lundahl, I think I'll skip the coffee and go straight to my room."

"Not at all, Cardinal, but before you go I'd like to tell you how pleased I am to meet a man who was such a loyal friend to my brother. It's like getting a little piece of him back. We have a lot to discuss in the next twenty-four hours, and I fear that time is growing short. If we are to have any chance at all of stopping Adrian Acerbi from doing what he was sent here to do we must begin right away."

For a moment Leo thought he had misunderstood Lundahl's last statement. "I beg your pardon?"

"I was saying that if we are to stop Acerbi we need to act swiftly."

Leaning back in his chair, Leo studied the room's intricately-carved paneling. Apparently, he had heard the man correctly.

Did Pope Michael's brother actually believe that he could stop the unstoppable?

"I don't mean to appear skeptical, Mr. Lundahl, but …"

"Of course you're skeptical, Cardinal. I'd be skeptical too if someone told me they believed they could stop the Antichrist, especially if that person was the brother of the late pope. You'll be interested to know that my brother and I shared some of the same views on a lot of things … including religion, but you should also know that if some of my brother's beliefs had ever been made public, many would have considered them to be extremely controversial … even heretical."

Heretical? Lundahl's choice of words surprised Leo. It was true that Marcus had possessed a biting wit that was sometimes tinged with sarcasm, and many people who didn't know him well occasionally misinterpreted the true meaning of his words, but in all the time Leo had known him he had never heard him make a single statement that could be even remotely interpreted as veering away from the core beliefs of his faith.

"What exactly are you referring to, Mr. Lundahl?"

"Did the two of you ever discuss the Book of Revelation?"

Leo smiled. "Only to the extent that we both found it a little confusing, as do most theologians."

67

"I believe my brother found it a little more than confusing, Cardinal. In fact, you might find it surprising to hear that he had begun to question any attempts to portray the book in a literal sense. I mean, let's face it. If any book in the Bible is open to interpretation, that one would be right at the top of the list."

The old man turned to look back outside, his breath fogging the window as he waited for Leo to reply, but the cardinal remained silent ... listening.

"I'm afraid you'll find that I'm nowhere near as religious as my brother was," Lundahl continued. "But that doesn't mean I've joined the fashionable secular crowd made up of those who find fault with practically everything they read in the Bible. Unlike the growing cadre of agnostics and atheists springing up around the world I still believe the Bible is a sacred text inspired by God, but I also believe there's room for interpretation, and so did my brother, especially when it came to Revelation ... a book that's filled with mystical symbology that, despite claims to the contrary, no one has really ever understood."

Turning from the window, Lundahl met Leo's questioning gaze with a steady stare. "What I'm trying to say, Cardinal, is that the Book of Revelation is just as much a mystery today as it was when it was written almost two thousand years ago. No one has any idea what that book is trying to tell us, and I'd be very suspicious of the motives of anyone who claims with any certainty that they know what any of it really means."

Leo leaned forward in his chair. "Is that why you sent for me, sir ... to discuss the meaning of Revelation?"

"You're getting warm, Cardinal. Why don't we talk later after you've had a chance to rest?"

CHAPTER 14

After making his way upstairs to his room, Leo stripped off the filthy military uniform he had been wearing for the past five days and headed for the shower. Glimpsing the reflection of his bearded, paint-smeared face in the mirror, he stepped into the shower, and for the next twenty minutes he alternated between lathering up and letting the steaming water rinse the caked dirt from his pores into soapy ringlets of brownish water that circled down the drain.

Stepping out, he wrapped a towel around his waist and shaved. After his long trek through the Pyrenees and the prolonged stress of wondering if he was being led into a trap, a wave of exhaustion swept over him. He felt as if every ounce of adrenalin had been purged from his system, making even the smallest movement feel like a workout. Stretching out on the bed his eyes drifted shut, and a few seconds later he was fast asleep.

The next morning, he awoke to find that he was still wrapped in a towel with a thick comforter draped over his body. He had slept through the night, and judging from the angle of the sun outside his window, it was now early morning.

Instantly he thought of Steig Lundahl and their conversation the day before. The man had proven to be a welcoming host, but beneath the disarming charm Leo had sensed the deep sadness of a lonely man who had been cast adrift in a world that was changing before his eyes.

Sifting through a stack of clothes, Leo found a clean white dress shirt and pair of jeans that seemed to fit and quickly dressed. The looming question of why Steig Lundahl had gone to all the trouble to bring him to Norway was still hanging in the air, and the man was still an enigma to him. There was something about him—something in the eyes—Lundahl eyes, and just like Marcus, Steig's gaze seemed to take in everything around him with a slow deliberate movement. He was a lot like his brother in many ways, but there was still an undeniable difference.

Descending the stairs to the first floor, Leo found himself standing in a paneled hallway filled with stuffed animal heads mounted over a gallery of family photographs. Starting at one end of the wall, it was obvious from the clothing worn by the people in the black and white photos that the first section of pictures had been taken sometime in the 1920's, and as Leo continued along the wall of photos, he saw that they changed from black and white to the Kotachrome colors of the 1950's, eventually morphing into the vibrant digital images that appeared in the newer photographs. But there was one thing that hadn't changed since the first color pictures had begun to appear, and that was the stark blue eyes of the Lundahl clan as they gazed back at the camera.

The Lundahls were obviously a close family that enjoyed being together. The pictures had been taken indoors and out, day and night, summer and winter. There were scenes of family members gathered together in the snow in front of the timbered lodge or seated at long, candle-lit tables piled high with food, along with the more informal photos of them lounging by a lake in a summery setting, roasting marshmallows over an open fire, but all along the wall of photos that spanned several generations a central theme seemed to emerge. Mixed in with pictures of a family at play were also pictures of smiling men and women holding guns as they stood over freshly killed wildlife that lay bleeding on the ground.

These people were all hunters.

They had probably always been hunters, Leo thought, leaning forward to study a picture taken of Marcus and Steig when they were young. The family's evolution into hunting had probably been a natural progression. After all this was Norway, and the Lundahl bloodline ran all the way back to Viking times, when hunting had been a necessary part of their survival skill set. Still, Leo found it odd that a family that had produced a man like Marcus Lundahl—a man who abhorred killing anything, had collectively perpetuated a culture rooted in hunting. Not only had they embraced it, but judging from the pictures, they celebrated it.

"Ah, Cardinal. I see you're awake."

Leo turned to see Lundahl's tall figure standing behind him.

"How do you like our little wall of fame?" Lundahl's face glowed proudly as he looked up at the photos.

"It's a wonderful collection," Leo said, "but I can't help wondering why Pope Michael never mentioned having such a large family."

"We're not only a large family, Cardinal, but a very private one as well. Come … breakfast is almost ready. You must be famished." Lundahl turned and led Leo down the hallway toward the back of the house, entering a large kitchen with beamed ceilings and a belching cast-iron stove that was fiercely guarded by a stout woman who didn't bother to look up when the men entered.

"I hope you enjoy good home-cooked food, Cardinal," Lundahl said, nodding his head toward the cook. "Hildie there doesn't tolerate any of the artificial frozen stuff that passes for real food in the restaurants nowadays. You're in for a real treat."

The sizzling aroma of seasoned meat cooking on the grill wafted through the air as the two men seated themselves at a long kitchen table.

"Is that beef I smell?" Leo asked.

"Venison, Cardinal. I have it every morning for breakfast. Do you enjoy eating wild game?"

"I grew up in a Pennsylvania mining town," Leo said, looking past Lundahl into the smoky kitchen with fond memories of his past. "We ate a lot of deer meat, but I've been sticking pretty much to vegetables lately."

"Oh, that's right. Cathars are vegetarians."

This man knew exactly where Leo had been living!

Lundahl reached across the table and filled Leo's glass with orange juice. "I can tell by your expression that you're probably wondering how I knew where you've been hiding all this time."

"The thought had crossed my mind."

"Well, let me set your mind at ease. Ever since he left home Marcus and I had kept in close contact with one another, and I was well aware that you were one of his most valued and trusted friends. I also knew all about Adrian Acerbi and the dark star … about your Israeli and Cathar friends, and the mountain cabins in the Pyrenees. After Marcus died and we heard that you were still alive and had been spotted in France, it didn't take a genius to figure out that you were hiding somewhere in the mountains along the French border. I figured your Israeli friends had a burst transmitter, so I simply called you."

"How did you get your hands on something like a burst transmitter?"

"We invented them, Cardinal. In fact, our company manufactures every burst transmitter used in the world today."

Leo's eyes narrowed. "But someone had to give you the correct encrypted code or you wouldn't have been able to access our receiver."

"Let's just say we have ways of making our little machines *call home* in case we want to know where they are," Lundahl smiled. "It's called a back

71

door … a little secret we usually don't share with outsiders. At the turn of the last century my great grandfather started a company that manufactured industrial tools. When the North Sea oil fields opened up we turned our attention to building large oil rigs. Our once-small tool company grew into a vast, multinational corporation, and after our father took over he realized that oil was a finite commodity and began investing in high tech enterprises like satellite communications and the new cell phone technology that was just coming online. I've continued the tradition by branching out into things like nanotechnology and genetic-based pharmaceutical research, and the Lundahl clan is still considered to be one of the wealthiest families in Norway, if not the world … at least until Acerbi took over."

Leo stared back … speechless. Why hadn't he known any of this?

"Don't look so betrayed, Cardinal. It's obvious to me that you're still wondering why one of your closest friends never discussed his rich family with you over a glass of wine."

"Something like that," Leo blurted out. "I don't mean to sound skeptical, or even worse, disrespectful, but if the Lundahl family is really as wealthy as you say it is I would have thought their standing in the world's financial community would have been common knowledge. As the Vatican's Secretary of State, it was my job to know which families had joined the wealthy elite across the globe, and your company wasn't even listed among the Fortune 500. From what I'm hearing now, your family's right up there with the Rothschilds."

"As I said before, Cardinal, we are a very private family. My grandfather developed quite an intricate plan to keep our business holdings camouflaged beneath a layer of shell companies that couldn't be traced back to the family. I've always compared it to a giant spider web, and the spiders who built it were hiding in the shadows to protect their young. My father and grandfather were both very wise men. In addition to the obvious tax advantages of such a scheme, they also wanted their children to feel safe walking down the street. They wanted us to be free to enjoy life to the fullest without the pressures that came from other people knowing how wealthy we really were."

The conversation broke when Hildie marched to the table with two steaming metal platters piled high with grilled venison steaks, scrambled eggs, and freshly baked bread. Staring down at the first hot food he had seen in five days, Leo hesitated.

"Please, Cardinal," Lundahl said. "Eat. Have you lost your taste for meat living in that Cathar castle?"

72

"No, it looks delicious, but I've been traveling for days now, Mr. Lundahl, and I still don't know why I'm here. I think it's time we talk about that."

"Of course. I've obviously kept you in the dark for far too long, but I felt it was important that you got some rest first." Lundahl leaned forward and drained his glass of juice as his eyes searched Leo's face. "Earlier, Cardinal, I mentioned that my brother had begun to re-examine his interpretation of Revelation, and like you, he assumed that Adrian Acerbi was the prophesied Antichrist, but in the last days of his life he had come to believe that Acerbi was something entirely different."

"Different?" Leo felt his appetite disappearing. "Different in what way?"

"There's no doubt that Adrian is evil incarnate, Cardinal, but he's not the Antichrist."

Was this man serious?

"And just how exactly did Marcus arrive at that conclusion?" Leo asked.

"That's what we're here to discuss, Cardinal. It's the main reason I sent for you. I can tell by the look in your eyes that you're beginning to think I'm quite mad, but after you hear what I have to say I believe you'll see that my brother's reasoning was solid."

"I'm always open to new lines of thinking, Mr. Lundahl ... as long as they don't cross the theological line into the realm of pop religion, but a lot of very learned people, including your brother, spent a great deal of time sifting through a considerable amount of evidence, and we've all reached the same conclusion. Personally, I find it hard to believe that Pope Michael suddenly changed his mind about Adrian Acerbi's true identity without mentioning it to me, so I'd be very interested to hear what you have to say on the matter. If Adrian Acerbi isn't the Antichrist, then who is he?"

Lundahl's unblinking blue eyes continued to stare across the table. "He's a world-class demon, Cardinal, and like all demons, my brother believed he could be expelled. I sent for you because you are the only one who can open the door that will send that *thing* back to wherever it came from."

CHAPTER 15

Crouching behind a gnarled olive tree, Daniel and Sarah watched a tall, muscular man step from the SUV, followed by a shorter, bearded man. Carrying Israeli assault rifles and wearing desert-camouflaged shirts wrapped in body armor, both men cautiously descended the embankment next to the road and stopped to inspect the burning car. For a long moment they just stood there, staring down through the smoke at the twisted wreckage before advancing through the trees toward Daniel and Sarah's hiding place.

Every second the men were getting closer. Daniel and Sarah's only chance was to run, but the olive grove was surrounded on all sides by open fields. The only cover for miles around was the old wooden barn they had spotted from the road earlier. They could try to make it there, but as soon as they took off running they would surely be spotted.

Stay or run?

Either way, in a matter of minutes their deadly game of hide-and-seek would be over.

With all of their options running out, Daniel and Sarah readied their weapons with the knowledge that they would probably be forced to fight their way out.

"They probably think we're hiding in the barn," Daniel whispered. Slowly, he moved his hand to the firing selector switch on his rifle and flicked it to *full auto*. "At least we'll have the element of surprise on our side. Just point and shoot."

Sarah gripped her rifle. "I know how to shoot, Daniel … remember?"

Peering around the tree, they could see the men moving closer. They were only twenty feet away, when suddenly they stopped and did the unthinkable. They laid their weapons on the ground and began shouting Daniel's name.

"Daniel … Daniel Meir!" Both men thrust their hands into the air and slowly turned in a circle. "We are friends."

Daniel and Sarah exchanged puzzled glances. There were only two options. Either these men were really on their side, as they claimed to be, or they were very good at what they did.

Killers or friends? Daniel weighed the odds.

"Mr. Meir!" the tall man called out. "Please … we don't have much time."

"What do you think?" Sarah whispered, her pulse rising.

Daniel sat up and flattened his back against the tree. "We really don't have much of a choice. They know we're somewhere in this grove and it looks like they'd rather talk than shoot. I'll stand up while you cover me."

Sarah let out a long slow breath as she stared back at her husband. "OK, but those guys look like they know what they're doing. Have them keep their hands in the air just in case they have pistols hidden in their waistbands. If they make a move I'll point and squeeze … just like you said."

Kissing her on the forehead, Daniel took a deep breath and stepped from behind the tree with his rifle shouldered at eye level. "Who are you?"

The taller man started to lower his hands. "Keep your hands in the air!" Sarah shouted, stepping out next to her husband.

The man quickly jerked his hands back into the air as Daniel's finger tightened on the trigger.

"I asked you a question." Daniel said, moving closer. "You've been following us for miles. Who are you?"

"We're Israelis!" the bearded man shouted.

"Soldiers?"

"Yes … Israeli Defense Force."

Daniel blinked hard. "Why would IDF soldiers be following us?"

"Professor Wasserman has been trying to contact you but he hasn't been able to get through," the tall man replied. "Ben Zamir sent a burst message to our headquarters asking us to check up on you. We drove past the villa just after Acerbi's forces entered the compound and spotted your car ahead of us on the highway. We've been following you ever since, but with Acerbi's forces in the area we had to wait for the right moment to approach you."

The man's face erupted into a grin as he jerked his thumb back at the burning car. "We figured this was probably a good time to make contact."

Daniel kept his rifle pointed at the man's head. He wasn't about to let a quick smile lull him into a false sense of security. "How do you know Ben Zamir?"

"We work for him. Not all of Team 5 left Israel."

"Are you telling me you're members of Team 5?"

"We're more like support personnel, sir, but we all belong to the same family. We're part of the security team that remained behind to look after a few select people, and you're one of them."

"Then you should know the code word." Daniel's finger tightened on the trigger.

"Oh, right," the short man blurted out. "The code word is *cardinal*. We also have the secret access code to your burst transmitter if that helps." The man rattled off a series of letters and numbers Daniel had committed to memory. Both codes were correct.

"They must be who they say they are," Daniel said, glancing sideways at his wife. He could see the lingering doubt in her eyes as she kept her rifle pointed at the men.

"Look." The taller man's voice sounded impatient as he glanced back toward the highway. "I can understand how you two must feel right now, but if you want to make it out of here alive you're going to have to start trusting us. I don't know what else we can say to convince you. If you want to stay here and take your chances it's up to you, but Acerbi's forces are all over this area and it looks like they've figured out who you are. They're probably headed this way right now to confirm that you're both dead after the chopper took out your car. We have to leave now … with or without you."

With reluctant nods Daniel and Sarah slowly lowered their rifles.

"Where exactly are we going?" Daniel asked. His finger was still on the trigger as he watched the two men lower their hands and reach for their weapons on the ground.

"We have to make it to the Lebanese coast." The bearded soldier slung his rifle over his shoulder and cast a nervous glance at the sky. "We have a very short window of opportunity to make it to our rendezvous point. Do you still have the burst transmitter?"

Daniel nodded to his backpack.

"Thank God you didn't leave it in the car," the man said. "We'll need it to contact the boat."

"The boat?" Sarah asked. "What boat?"

"The one that will be taking all of us to join your friends in France, but we have to hurry. If we don't make it to the rendezvous point on time they'll leave without us, which means we'll be on our own surrounded by Acerbi's forces and a lot of other people in this area who don't especially like us."

CHAPTER 16

Lundahl's words still echoed in Leo's mind after the two men finished breakfast and moved into the large great room at the front of the lodge. Although it was technically springtime, a light snowfall had begun to dust the ground around the timbered lodge as Lundahl walked across an ancient Persian carpet to the large expanse of glass at the far end of the room. "I never seem to tire of looking out at the forest when it snows, Cardinal, but after a long winter stuck in the Pyrenees I suppose you've probably grown tired of it by now."

It was obvious that Lundahl was in no hurry to discuss his brother's sudden change of heart concerning Adrian Acerbi's true identity, but Leo knew an explanation was coming as he continued to indulge the illusion of small talk and left the comforting glow of the fireplace to join Lundahl by the window. "Actually, I enjoy the quiet and solitude of the mountains, but you're right; it has been a long winter, and I do miss my occasional trips to the beach. There's something healing about the ocean and the feel of the sun warming your skin. I guess I'm one of those people who feel divided in my need for the closeness of a mountain forest and the openness of the sea, but Evita and I will probably end up living somewhere near the water after we're married. Over time I've learned that my fiancé is definitely a beach person."

"Fiancé … hmm." Lundahl emphasized the word *fiancé* as he continued looking out the window. "Now that's not a word you hear every day coming from a Roman Catholic cardinal. What did Marcus have to say about that?"

Leo smiled. "Well, despite his outward display of conservatism he was very much in favor of bringing the institution of marriage into the priesthood. Your brother was a very forward-looking man, and I believe he saw many things within the Church that had to change if our faith is to survive going into the new millennium. Allowing priests to marry was one of those much-needed changes."

"And what about the Church now, Cardinal? Do you still think it will survive?"

Leo's features hardened. "The Church will always survive, Mr. Lundahl. It will be here long after you and I are both gone."

The time for small talk was over.

"If you don't mind, sir, I'd like to get right to the point. That was quite a statement you made earlier when you said that Marcus was starting to wonder if Adrian was really the Antichrist in spite of some pretty overwhelming evidence. You obviously agree. Why is that?"

"I'll answer that question in due time, Cardinal, but first I'd like to talk about what's happening around the world right now." Lundahl paused to watch a deer walk from the forest and stop to nuzzle the grass beneath the thin coating of frost on the ground. "Are you still the Vatican's Secretary of State?"

Leo found himself caught off guard by the question. "To be honest, I have no idea what's going on within the walls of Vatican City right now. As a matter of fact, I'm not sure the title of cardinal even applies to me anymore."

"We'll get to titles later," Lundahl said, "but for now I think we should take a look back in time. We need to examine the past so that we can see what's about to happen again in the future if we fail to act. My brother and I held lengthy conversations about his fears concerning the future of the world and the Church in general, and I know that he intended to discuss these things with you after you returned to Rome from your trip to the United Nations."

Leo could feel his pulse begin to rise with the memory of his brush with death at the airport in New York before he had escaped to France.

"As a former professor of history," Lundahl continued, "I'm sure you know the answer to the question I'm about to ask, but please, Cardinal … indulge me for a moment. In all of human history, what single century stands above the rest in terms of lives lost and man's inhumanity to man?"

"The last century," Leo said without having to think. "The 20th century was by far the most horrific and deadly century in the history of mankind."

"And just why do you think that was?"

"I suppose I'd have to say technology; the ability to wage war on an industrial scale using weapons of mass destruction that no one had even imagined before."

"Exactly. Needless to say, modern technology has given humanity the ability to destroy the world many times over, and it doesn't take a rocket scientist to see that things are only going to get worse while we all sit back and wait for it to happen. We're also seeing the emergence of new kinds of diseases … a disturbing trend that seems to be following us into the new millennium. But I'm afraid that's just the tip of the iceberg. Today, using things like genetic engineering and biotechnology, a single individual with the right knowledge has the power to initiate a doomsday scenario from which we might never recover. You yourself were engaged in a battle with just such an individual a couple of years ago. Power like that has never existed before. Now I ask you … just what effect do you think all of this is having on people all over the planet?"

"I guess I would have to say it's making them more afraid."

"Right again. And what happens when people are afraid?"

"They look for a way out. They look for a … a savior."

"Bravo, Cardinal! My brother had come to believe that the world was being prepped."

"Prepped?"

"Yes … prepped. Prepped by fear, Cardinal, and once people become afraid their instinct for survival opens the door for someone who looks like they have all the answers to their problems, and the world believes that person has already arrived in the form of Adrian Acerbi."

"The very person you deny is the Antichrist," Leo added.

"Yes," Lundahl answered. "But despite the evidence to the contrary he's not who you think he is."

Silence filled the room as the two men continued their forest vigil through the window.

"I'm afraid this is where you and I disagree, Mr. Lundahl," Leo said, breaking nature's spell. "I believe Adrian Acerbi is exactly who he appears to be. The evidence is overwhelming, and I'm not just talking about the arrival of a man who has suddenly appeared on the world stage with the power to bend others to his will. There have been many such men throughout history, but none of them have been accompanied by the supernatural evidence your brother and I both observed with Adrian's rise to power, and we weren't the only ones to see it. Many top experts from various fields of study came to the same conclusion when the evidence was presented to them. The Antichrist is here now, and the signs all point to the fact that he walks among us in the very human form of Adrian Acerbi."

"And just what evidence have you observed?" Lundahl asked. "Enlighten me."

"Where is all this heading, Mr. Lundahl?"

"Please, Cardinal … indulge me for just a little while longer. What evidence have you seen?"

"I think you're well aware of the evidence," Leo said, "which is why I'm beginning to wonder why you continue to question it. You undoubtedly know that the code we discovered in the Old Testament contains multiple encoded passages that predicted a dark star would herald the arrival of the Antichrist, and that in the days preceding Adrian's rise to power astronomers discovered a dark star that had never been observed before, lying at the outer reaches of our own solar system. It actually traveled to Earth and touched our atmosphere at the exact same moment of Adrian's reported transformation from a boy into something else in Turkey. The astronomers who witnessed this miraculous event unanimously agreed that the dark star's behavior violated all known laws of physics, leading us all to the conclusion that we were dealing with a supernatural force from another realm."

"Yes, that's true, Cardinal … another realm … a realm of evil! The evil realm you speak of most certainly exists. In fact, you've had brushes with it in the past in your battles with demons in the Negev Desert and in the chapel under the Vatican. A realm of evil has existed since before humans even walked the earth, but to say that this current manifestation of evil is the embodiment of the Antichrist is a rush to judgment."

"I would hardly call it a rush to judgment," Leo said, suddenly struck by the contrast between the tranquil snowfall outside and the gravity of the discussion the two men were having in the warmth of a cozy Norwegian lodge. Just like the window that separated them from the weather outside, a thin veil existed in the universe separating good from evil, and just like the glass, he knew that humanity's illusion of safety could be shattered in the blink of an eye.

Shaking loose from his brief philosophical reverie, Leo continued. "I think it's important that you know that we were all very self-critical and that we took our time and examined all the evidence before we jumped to any conclusions concerning Acerbi's identity."

Lundahl nodded his head as he looked past the falling snow at an invisible point in the distance. "I'm sure you were all very thorough in your observations, but shortly before my brother died he called to tell me that something was bothering him … that maybe he had missed something, and it had to do with biblical prophecy … namely the Book of Revelation. He told me that he was beginning to think that the arrival of the dark star and Adrian Acerbi was some kind of cosmic sleight of hand … something to divert our attention away from something else that was happening."

"Marcus called you?" Leo asked. "We talked just hours before he died, and he never mentioned any of this to me."

Without answering, Lundahl turned away from the window and returned to his place in front of the fireplace. Tiring of the constant guessing games, Leo followed and took a seat in one of two facing wing chairs. The time had come for him to voice the lingering doubts about Lundahl's theory that had been edging at the back of his mind.

"You'll have to pardon my cautious nature, Mr. Lundahl, but it's obvious from your previous statements concerning the Book of Revelation that you doubt the word of Scripture, so I have to ask … are these really Pope Michael's thoughts, or are they tinged with your own beliefs? Do you even believe in an Antichrist, or do you think this is all some big fairy tale concocted by a bunch of super elders to explain what's happening in the world right now?"

Lundahl's blue eyes seemed to glow brighter. "Oh … I definitely believe in the Antichrist, and so did my brother, although our views on the reality of just who and what he is may tend to differ from traditional interpretations. That being said, I can say without a shadow of a doubt that Adrian Acerbi is most certainly not the Antichrist that everyone has been expecting."

Lundahl stretched his weathered hands toward the fire in an effort to relieve the pain in his arthritic joints. "As to my previous statements concerning Revelation, I'm glad you brought that up, because the book itself proves my point."

Leo's mind was flooding with doubts. "How can a book you claim is filled with confused and mystic symbology prove any point, Mr. Lundahl? You can't have it both ways!" Leo could hear his voice rising. He was beginning to wish he had never come to Norway. Lundahl's theological musings seemed to ring with the usual arguments he had faced every fall with each new incoming class of college freshmen who felt compelled to expound on their own interpretations concerning the meaning of biblical passages.

Lundahl breathed in deeply. "I can see that your patience is wearing thin, Cardinal, so I'll come straight to the point. The last time Marcus and I spoke he told me he had been reading and rereading Revelation in an effort to gain some kind of insight into what was really happening in the world. That statement alone goes to show that he believed the book was divinely inspired and that it contained something he was missing. Let's be clear on this. My brother never doubted Scripture. His only doubt stemmed from the many interpretations given to the word of God by men who brought their own agendas to the table of religious teaching. You might say he was a purist. He wanted to know what God was trying to tell us without all the noise of a thousand other voices shouting that they and they alone knew the true meaning of His words."

Leo watched the fire's light cast a glow around the older man as he spoke. He had probably been the last person to speak with Pope Michael before he died, and Leo desperately wanted to hear what the two brothers had spoken about.

"As you know," Lundahl continued, "there are literally thousands of differing interpretations of Revelation floating around out there. It's no wonder that people are so confused, so let's just agree for the sake of brevity that there are three main theological camps when it comes to trying to decipher what it all means.

"First, we have the *postmillennial* camp … the one that ascribes to the theory that the Antichrist has already come and gone, and that things will get better and better until Christ returns. I think we can safely rule that interpretation out, especially considering current world events and the fact that society seems headed in the other direction with things like mega churches for atheists being built around the world.

"Then we have the *amillennial* camp that doesn't believe in a literal Antichrist at all. They believe that any mention of him is figurative and represents wickedness in general … that the Book of Revelation is merely a colorful analogy of events that have already passed. This means that those who ascribe to the amillennial theory scoff at the idea of things like the rapture, the seven-year period of tribulation that follows it, or even the promised millennial kingdom of Christ yet to come.

"This brings us to the third and fastest growing camp—the *premillennialists* … or as some prefer to call them, the *pre-tribulation* group. They are the only ones who believe in a literal Antichrist. The premillennialists interpret the Old and New Testaments literally and believe in a coming rapture and seven-year tribulation in which the Antichrist will rule over the earth before Christ's return. If you happen to be a part of the premillennialist camp, then you automatically have to rule out the possibility that Adrian Acerbi is the Antichrist."

"Why is that?" Leo asked.

"Because, Cardinal," Lundahl continued. "Everyone's still here. The faithful haven't disappeared from the face of the earth in some kind of magical event the premillennialists call the *Rapture*. Although it proves my point about Acerbi, it will probably shock you to hear that I find the whole idea of a physical ascent into the heavens by millions of living human beings to be utterly ludicrous. The word rapture isn't even mentioned in the Bible. From everything I've read, the first time it appeared was in some religious pamphlet printed a few hundred years ago."

"I'm well acquainted with those arguments, Mr. Lundahl. I believe we're discussing 1 Thessalonians 4:17, which refers to a time when the *'dead in Christ'* and *'we who are alive and remain'* will be *'caught up in the clouds'* to meet with *'the Lord in the air'*. The pre-tribulation rapture theology you speak of first appeared in the 1830's after being developed by John Darby and the Plymouth Brethren. The theory was later popularized in the early 20th century with the appearance of the Scofield Bible, causing many to believe that a great number of people would be left behind on earth for an extended period of tribulation after those who have accepted Christ into their lives are literally taken up into the air to be with the Lord."

As he talked, Leo could feel himself slipping back into his former role of *teacher*. "The word rapture derives from the Latin *raptus*, meaning *to carry off*, and many theologians today believe that the concept of a rapture more closely describes the final resurrection of each individual soul. As a Catholic cardinal my beliefs tend to fall in line with the individual resurrection theory, but everyone is entitled to their own beliefs, and we as Christians must respect those beliefs. I have a feeling we'll all find out which camp is right soon enough, but I take it from your comments that you don't ascribe to any of these end-time scenarios."

"And you would be right, Cardinal. I warned you from the very start that my faith is not as strong as yours or that of my brother, and that some of my own personal views might tend to lean a little to the left of the traditional religious worldview, but I can assure you that my intentions are pure. Take the doctrinal history of the rapture as an example. Since the 1700's, countless men considered themselves to be imminent theologians and invented all kinds of theories on the subject. And each put their own spin on things, including one who actually said, with a straight face, mind you, that the first ones to be lifted up to heaven before the tribulation would be a group of women he called the *Wise Virgins*. I believe that theory alone brings home my point. All of these fanciful theories came from the minds of men, Cardinal … not God, which is why we were given a warning about the arrival of false prophets in the end times … a warning I take to heart every time I read a new interpretation of Scripture written by someone who claims to know the *real* meaning of God's words."

"And you are wise to do that, Mr. Lundahl, but I wouldn't be so quick to shake off the idea that the faithful could disappear in the blink of an eye. In the same section of the book of Matthew that warns of false prophets it was Christ himself who said, *'No one knows about that day or hour, not even the angels in heaven, nor the Son, but only the Father'*. I believe that one single quote captures the very essence of the mystery of faith. It's a very personal journey for all of us, and His words have always meant different things to different people, but only God knows what's really in store for us."

"But that's exactly my point, Cardinal. People can quote Scripture all day long to bolster their own beliefs, but I want you to try to keep an open mind for a moment."

Lundahl paused, caught in the hypnotic lure of watching the flames curl around the new logs he had just placed on the fire. "What if we aren't living in the last days? I mean, what if God is sitting back and allowing all of this to happen as a warning to the people of the world … a kind of message to us all that we've been drifting away from a God-centered existence. This could be our final chance to return to Christ-like ways before it's too late."

Leo sat bolt upright in his chair. All of his life he had felt like he was being pulled along by an invisible current, as if he had been tossed into a great river that flowed to a destination that had been waiting for him all along. Now, listening to Pope Michael's brother, something inside him clicked, but he needed to hear more. "What did Marcus have to say about your theory?"

"It's not my theory, Cardinal … it was my brother's theory. That's why I had to speak with you in person … so you could look me in the eye and know I was telling you the truth when I told you that my brother had come to believe that we weren't living in the last days … that all of this was just a test. He believed that God's silence was really more of a shout. God is watching … waiting to see if mankind will keep to their self-centered ways or open their eyes to the truth that awaits them. The war between heaven and hell has begun, and the dark star has anointed Satan's most powerful demon … a demon that mimics the Antichrist to demonstrate his power to get people to accept an evil savior in exchange for comfort and material wealth."

Unable to remain seated, Leo stood and began pacing the floor. "Your brother always did have a very unique way of looking at things. It was one of the things I admired about him the most, but if what you're saying is true, it means that your brother's voice was silenced by someone or something before he had a chance to share his views with the rest of the world." Leo paused for a moment to think. "You'll have to excuse me, Mr. Lundahl, but it's going to take me some time to digest all of this."

Lundahl pivoted away from the fire with such force that it caused the burning embers to swirl upward and fly against the metal screen. "Listen carefully, Cardinal, because I'm about to shine a brighter light on the reason you are here. As far as I'm concerned you can take all the time you need to digest the things we're discussing, but remember, I'm just the messenger, and time is growing short. I brought you here not only out of a sense of duty to my brother, but because the world is sick right now. Our planet needs time to heal, both physically and spiritually, and you are the key."

"But I ..."

"Please, Cardinal ... let me finish, because you need to hear this while we still have time. There's a reason my brother's beliefs had suddenly taken a radical departure, and he dared not share them with anyone else ... even you ... a man of superior faith and intelligence that he trusted to the end. Do you know why Marcus became a priest?"

Leo was taken aback by the question. "Hopefully, for the same reason anyone would choose the religious life ... to serve."

"Yes, of course ... that's part of it, but there is another reason. It has to do with our family history and a religious lineage that stretches all the way back to the Middle Ages. Like all ancient Scandinavians, our ancestors, the early Norwegians known as the Sámi, were adherents of Norse paganism. After the arrival of Christian missionaries, our people became Christianized. At that time most of the population was Catholic, but following the Lutheran Reformation of 1536, there was a shift in the religious makeup of the country."

"I know," Leo said. "Pope Michael and I had several discussions on the subject. A lot of people found it strange that the College of Cardinals chose a Jesuit Cardinal from Norway to be their next pope, especially since Catholicism was banned in Norway for almost three hundred years."

"That same split between religions mirrors the differences within our own family, Cardinal. Only a small percentage of the Lundahl clan maintained their Catholic ties after the Reformation, but we are all Christians just the same. The point I'm trying to make is that we all sprang from a country once steeped in paganism. There are signs of it everywhere ... from markings found carved in stones along the fjords to ancient burial grounds scattered deep in the forests … and it was a brush with something from our ancient past that kindled a desire in my brother to enter the priesthood."

Leo could feel the hair suddenly rise on the back of his neck, as if a long-dead breeze from a bygone era had followed an unseen presence into the room. "What do you mean when you say he had a brush with the past?"

"I'm talking about his infatuation with something that happened hundreds of years ago, Cardinal … when one of our ancestors faced a terrible evil deep in the forest."

"Evil? What kind of evil?"

"The worst kind, Cardinal … the worst kind. Back in the late nineteenth century, one of our distant ancestors lived in the coastal town of Bergen. His name was Jonas Lundahl and he was a Jesuit, like you. At the time, Catholicism was just returning to Norway and Jonas was one of the first Norwegians to return from Catholic seminary to begin spreading the faith to the people of Bergen. It was said that he was very pious and seemed overly stern at times, and over the years he had become known as a famous exorcist. That probably explains why he was asked to go to a small village on the other side of the mountains that had become the scene of several unexplained deaths. People in neighboring villages had begun to attribute the events to demonic possession, and what Jonas found there after he arrived confirmed their worst suspicions."

Lundahl retrieved a bound leather book from a shelf next to the fireplace and handed it to Leo. "These are some of his notes written after he returned from that village."

Opening the worn book, Leo retrieved his glasses and began to read. The writing was in English, not Latin as Leo had expected from a Jesuit priest who had attended seminary in the nineteenth century. For the next several minutes, he scanned through the brittle vellum pages, until finally his eyes settled on the last page that described some of the priest's final moments in the village before the narrative abruptly ended.

Removing his glasses, Leo could feel his pulse begin to rise as he laid the book in his lap. "Is any of this really true?"

"Marcus believed it was. Legend has it that the villagers led Jonas to an ancient circle of stone in the forest surrounded by a pagan burial ground the local populace had been using to bury their dead. After he performed the rite of exorcism, he ordered the people to burn their homes to the ground and never return. When Marcus and I were growing up he heard the story from one of our aunts who gave him that book of handwritten notes. He was captivated by the story. Our distant priestly relative became a hero to him. When he was only fifteen, Marcus hitchhiked to Bergen and spent the entire day searching the library for anything he could find on the subject, and later that year when we were on our way to summer camp, he got off the train at a station along the way and walked to the site where the village had once stood. He even hiked out into the surrounding forest to see the circle of stone but was warned to stay away by a young couple who lived nearby. You might say he had become obsessed with the subject, and I believe it was that obsession that led my brother to the priesthood."

"Have you read this, Mr. Lundahl?"

"Yes, but as a former professor of history I thought it would make more sense to you. I see you're on the page where he describes the circle of stone ... the place he called the *demon hatchery*."

Leo felt a vague prickling at the back of his neck. "Is the stone ruin still there?"

"Oh yes, it's still there alright, although no one in their right mind would go anywhere near the place. Marcus told me he could feel the evil ... that the air was thick with it."

"I'm afraid both Jonas and Marcus were right, Mr. Lundahl. I've seen this type of ruin before, and that's exactly what it is ... a place where demons enter the earth plane. Do you know what happened to Jonas after the exorcism? Did he leave any other notes?"

"Accounts vary, but I've been told they were locked away in a room below Saint Paul's Catholic Church in Bergen after his death. Apparently, Jonas retreated to the church rectory after he returned from that village and never came out again. He died a year later. He had succeeded in stopping whatever was happening to the people in that village, but it had taken a great toll on him. His final request was to be buried in consecrated land, and after he died the people from the village erected a bronze statue of him over his grave in a little garden area between the church and the rectory."

Leo reached out to the table beside him and picked up a framed picture showing a solitary Marcus Lundahl standing in front of the weathered bronze statue of a priest holding a cross to the sky. "I'm afraid whatever Jonas discovered out there in the forest is just sleeping, Mr. Lundahl. According to his notes, Jonas theorized that the newly-buried dead of the village were being transformed into demons. That's why all the new graves they opened were empty. He believed the ruin was somehow connected to the underworld, and that the mysterious ring of stone was some kind of demonic generator. It needed more fuel to keep running, and the people of the village had become that fuel until Jonas arrived and broke the cycle with God's help."

"You'll be interested to hear that Marcus agreed with your assertion that whatever is out there is probably sleeping, Cardinal. He also told me about the ruin in Turkey … the one where Adrian Acerbi was transformed. On the day Marcus called to tell me he had come to believe that Adrian was really a demon and not the prophesied Antichrist, he also told me that he believed the world was about to be enveloped by a realm of evil … that whatever was sleeping within the ruin would soon awaken and envelop the world like a maelstrom, and Adrian Acerbi is the key."

"So, if I'm hearing you correctly, you're saying that Marcus theorized that this demon was sent here to prep the world before he unlocks some kind of cosmic underworld door."

"At least that's my interpretation of what my brother was trying to say. What you do with the information is up to you, but I would trust my brother's instincts with my life. In fact, that's exactly what I am doing. Now that my brother is gone I'm handing over the fate of my family and every other family in the world to you. Your place is back in Rome, Cardinal, because you hold the key to a different door. Marcus told me that he knew there had to be more clues to what was happening hidden somewhere in the Secret Chapel below the Vatican, and he was preparing to send you and Bishop Morelli back down there to find them. I wish I could tell you more, but unfortunately all phone service with the Vatican was suddenly interrupted before my brother and I finished our last conversation."

Breaking the stillness of the room, the sound of voices in the hallway outside preceded the rustle of footsteps as the well-dressed man who had driven Leo from the airport rushed into the room. "Excuse me, Mr. Lundahl," Gunnar said. "But they're coming. We have to go."

"Are you sure they're headed here?"

"Yes, sir. They're about twenty minutes out."

Unfolding his weathered hands, Lundahl rose from his chair. "I'm afraid our time here has come to an end, Cardinal. I had hoped that we would have had more time to continue our discussion, but it appears that Acerbi's men have discovered our little family hideaway. Unfortunately, time has been our enemy, for it was only a matter of time before his quantum computers were able to break the codes and trace the origin of our transmissions to this location."

"What about the jet!?" Leo asked. He could feel his heart pounding as a sudden vision of Evita flashed through his mind. "My return trip to

France! I need to warn my friends. If Acerbi's men have the codes for the transmitters, then everyone in the castle could be in danger!"

"We sent them a warning before we shut everything down," Gunnar said. "But it's possible that our transmission was jammed. As far as your return trip to France is concerned, Acerbi's men just raided the hangar and arrested everyone there. We can't go back to the airport."

Handing Leo his coat, Lundahl faced him with sympathetic eyes. "Let's go, Cardinal. You'll be safe as long as you're with us. I'm sure we can find a way to get you back to your friends in a few weeks."

"That's not good enough!" Leo was practically shouting. "There are people waiting for me … people I care deeply about, and they're probably totally unaware that their transmitter codes have been compromised. I need to get to Oslo and find a way back to France as soon as possible."

"I'm afraid that's out of the question, Cardinal. Now that Acerbi's people have broken the codes to our transmitters it's highly probable that they also know you're in Norway now. There are cameras on every street corner in Oslo, and it would only be a matter of time before they got their hands on you. The city is the last place you should go."

"I'm hoping Acerbi's people will be thinking the same thing," Leo said. "I appreciate your concern, Mr. Lundahl, but I have to get back to my friends. I'm going into the city, with or without your help."

Lundahl's shoulders visibly slumped. "Very well then. If you refuse to come with us I'll have Gunnar drive you to my townhouse in Oslo until we can figure out a way to get you back to France sooner. Once you get to the city stay inside and don't go out for anything. We'll come to you." Lundahl's gaze returned to the forest outside. "We're being hunted now, Cardinal. There are predators waiting in the shadows, and we must all tread lightly from this moment forward."

Spoken like a true hunter, Leo thought. But there was one thing Lundahl had forgotten.

In order to stop a predator, the hunted must become the hunter.

CHAPTER 17

Samantha Jennings was monitoring the two-way voice traffic on the tactical radio in her car as she sped through the front gate of the airbase and headed for her small apartment. Except for the radio chatter focused on the search for those who had brought the plane down, all other communications seemed normal.

So far so good.

If things went according to plan, her absence from the base wouldn't be eyed with suspicion for at least another twenty-four hours.

Twenty-four hours. That's how long she would have to shed her identity and disappear into the shadowy underworld of those who had unplugged themselves from Acerbi's one world government. For a moment a panicky sense of loss took hold; the result of doubt and fear and her sudden decision to leave based solely on a gut reaction. As for a plan, she had none.

Spur of the moment decisions were always a bad idea! Samantha told herself. And they were especially bad for someone like her; a career military officer who had dedicated her adult life to the rigors of a military command structure that had always stressed the fact that planning equaled success. Ever since she had joined the Air Force she had viewed the world through the prism of a military tactician, where methodical planning could mean the difference between life and death, but then again, so too was the ability to think on one's feet and adapt to a constantly evolving battlefield environment.

She could do this!

As a well-known member of Acerbi's inner circle, she knew her face would be recognized wherever she went, but right now none of that mattered. All she knew for sure was that she had to put as much distance between herself and him as possible before somehow trying to make contact with the people who had just tried to kill him.

Watching the front gate of the airbase fade in her rear-view mirror, she placed her odds at 50-50. Even if she managed to make contact with the rebels they would probably view the sudden defection of a high-ranking member of Acerbi's forces with suspicion and treat her accordingly ... or worse.

Whatever the outcome she had to try, because whatever she had seen in the back seat of Acerbi's limo had frightened her. For a split second, his image had blurred. She had seen something inexplicable. Something horrible. And whatever it was, it had become a part of Adrian Acerbi, a man who had just proven to her that he possessed a world-class capacity for Machiavellian deceit along with a willingness to sacrifice the lives of innocent people in the blink of an unsympathetic eye.

Pulling into the assigned parking space at her apartment, she left her military-issued cell phone lying under the seat of the car and locked the doors before charging through the front door of her small, one-bedroom apartment. After peeking back outside in a paranoid check to make sure she hadn't been followed, she walked into her neat bedroom and quickly shed her olive-drab flight suit before grabbing a pair of jeans and slipping on a pale blue T-shirt and a pair of running shoes.

Running shoes. How appropriate, she thought. For the first time in hours, Samantha Jennings smiled as she stuffed a few belongings into a backpack and grabbed the keys to her personal car before heading back out the door.

Parked next to her government-issued military vehicle, her green 1974 MG Midget looked dusty and forlorn. She never had time to drive it, and aside from a few personal items in her apartment, the little green car was one of the few non-military things she owned.

Scrunching down into the low-slung seat, she started the engine and took a wistful look back at the geraniums she had planted in little pots on the balcony of her apartment.

This was no time to become sentimental!

Shoving the stick shift into reverse, she backed out and drove away. A few minutes later, Samantha Jennings was speeding toward London on a multi-lane expressway.

CHAPTER 18

The plain black sedan sped past a line of military vehicles headed up the mountain in the opposite direction as Gunnar and Leo peered through the patches of mountain fog for signs of a roadblock ahead.

"That would be Acerbi's men headed for the lodge," Gunnar said, watching the vehicles that had just passed them disappear in his mirror. "At least this low cloud cover kept them from launching their choppers."

"What about Steig and the others?" Leo asked.

"I wouldn't worry too much about Mr. Lundahl, sir. He's long gone by now."

"What about you, Gunnar?"

"I'll join Mr. Lundahl and the others later. Right now my job is to keep you safe, which means I won't be taking you to the townhouse."

"You think Acerbi's people will be watching it?"

"I'd bet a year's salary on it, Cardinal. Mr. Lundahl probably thought it was safe because the property is listed under another name, but Acerbi has some of the best security people in the business working for him, and sooner or later they'll make the connection."

In the sweeping descent down the mountain road, Leo could feel his ears pop. "Why don't you just drop me off at a coffee house or something? It's still early in the day, and I'm pretty good at disappearing into a crowd."

"That's not going to happen, sir. I'm not about to drop you off on some street corner in the middle of a strange city and leave you to fend for yourself. I have a better idea. I'm taking you to a little bed and breakfast I know of."

Was this guy serious?

"Did you just say you're taking me to a bed and breakfast?"

"Yes. Don't be alarmed, Cardinal. The house belongs to some friends of mine … an American couple who moved here a few years ago. He was in the U.S. Air Force … analyzed satellite photos or something … and she was a nurse. Their neighbors are used to seeing strangers come and go at all hours of the day and night, so it will be the perfect place for you to wait while we try to figure out how to get you back home."

Gunnar reached into the glove box and pulled out a baseball cap and a generic pair of sunglasses. "Here, Cardinal … put these on. We're entering the city now, and there are cameras everywhere."

With the mountain snow and drizzle behind them, patches of blue sky began to appear as Gunnar turned off the Trondheimsveien highway and took a circuitous route through narrow backstreets before pulling onto a wide boulevard that fronted Oslo's largest park—the *Vigelandsparken*. Also known as the *sculpture park*, it was named after the famous Norwegian sculptor Gustav Vigeland.

From his massive stone sculpture of intertwined human figures in the center of the park, over two hundred additional bronze and stone sculptures depicting humanity in all of its forms radiated out over the landscaped grounds where families picnicked and lovers strolled during the short summer months. Considered by all Norwegians to be a national treasure, it was one of the most breathtaking parks in all the world.

Driving past a row of tour buses parked near the park's front entrance, Gunnar squinted at the street signs until he found the one he was looking for—*Nordraaks Gate*. Trading the crowds along the boulevard for a quiet neighborhood, they drove down a leafy street lined with parked cars on both sides before finally stopping in front of a white, two-story house with a blue awning over the front door.

Gunnar pulled to the curb and let the car idle, waiting to see if anyone had followed them, but the street behind remained empty. "OK, Cardinal, let's go."

The two men quickly exited the vehicle and walked up to the front door. After one knock, a thin woman with long, gray-streaked hair opened the door. "Gunnar! What a pleasant surprise!"

"Hello, Kathy. Is Edgar here?"

"Why yes," she said, glancing up at the tall man standing beside him. "But if your friend here is looking for a room I'm afraid we're all booked up."

"We're not looking for a room." Gunnar winked. "This man is a friend of ours."

The woman visibly stiffened as she leaned her head outside and looked up and down the street. "Better come in then." With no pretense of small talk, the woman ushered the two men back to their private quarters where a middle-aged man wearing a flannel shirt was just hanging up the phone. "Gunnar!" the man exclaimed, standing. "It's good to see you, old friend. Would either of you care for some coffee?"

"I'm afraid we don't have time, Edgar," Gunnar said quickly. "This is Cardinal Leopold Amodeo, and he needs our help."

"Did you say … Cardinal Amodeo … as in *the* Cardinal Amodeo?"

"Yes … in the flesh." Gunnar turned to Leo. "Cardinal, I'd like to introduce you to Edgar and Kathy Stiles. They're part of a group here in Oslo that feel the same way we do about Acerbi's one-world government."

Removing his cap and sunglasses, Leo extended his hand. "Sorry to barge in on you like this. It's a pleasure to meet you both. I hope I'm not being too much of a bother."

Edgar and Kathy traded astonished looks.

"Uh, no bother at all, Cardinal," Edgar finally managed to say. "In fact, we're honored. How can we help you?"

"The cardinal just came from a meeting with Mr. Lundahl," Gunnar said. "We promised to fly him back to France tomorrow, but Acerbi's people finally traced the origin of our burst transmissions and raided both the lodge and the hangar at the airport early this morning. With your connections, I thought you might know of a way we could get the cardinal back to his friends in France a little sooner."

"All I really need is a car," Leo said quickly. "I don't want to put anyone else in danger."

"You wouldn't even make it out of Oslo, Cardinal," Edgar said. "Without one of the new ID cards and the facial recognition cameras at all the checkpoints, Acerbi's people would have you in custody before the sun went down. You're welcome to stay here with us." The man winked. "We always keep a spare room available for *friends* who are trying to evade the glare of Acerbi's attention."

"I'm afraid you don't understand, Mr. Stiles," Leo said. "There are a lot of innocent people in France who are unaware of the fact that Acerbi's forces may already know where they are hiding, and I have to warn them before it's too late!"

Stiles began to pace. "What about Lundahl's jet?"

"It's probably still in the hangar," Gunnar said, "but Acerbi's people arrested everyone there and I'm sure they're watching the place waiting for us to make a move."

"Was there a flight scheduled today?"

"No. The mechanics were doing routine maintenance. We were planning on flying the cardinal out tomorrow morning."

"Then it's possible the pilots weren't there," Edgar said. "Do you know where they live?"

"Yes, but Acerbi's security forces have probably already …" A look of sudden realization crossed Gunnar's face. "They won't find them!"

"What?"

"The pilots were going fly fishing today!"

"Fly fishing?" Edgar grabbed his coat. "It's still early. Do you know where they fish?"

"Of course. I've gone fishing with them dozens of times. We usually go to the same spot."

Edgar kissed his wife and swept his car keys from the table. "We'll take my car. Let's hope the fish are biting today and that those two pilots are still there. We've got to get to them before Acerbi's people do."

With the lengthening days of summer, the sun was already high in the Norwegian sky, but the thick cloud cover prevented its warming rays from reaching the ground as Edgar guided his twenty-year-old Volvo out of the city and up a paved road that skirted the vertical cliffs bordering a deep blue fjord. The slight drizzle that had returned to the city had given way to a freezing rain that sheeted against the windshield, and the longer they drove the more concerned the three men inside grew. With the weather worsening it was likely the pilots had given up on fishing for the day and returned home, where Acerbi's men would surely be waiting for them.

Leo glanced out at the stormy clouds hovering just above the road. "How much farther is it, Gunnar?"

"We're almost there, Cardinal."

For another ten minutes they continued up the winding highway until finally Gunnar spotted a side road bordered by tall brush. "Turn in here!"

Leaving the paved highway behind, the Volvo bumped along a rutted forest road that ended at a shallow stream bubbling over a smooth rock bottom. There was no one in sight.

"No car." Gunnar pounded on the dash. "They're not here. Turn around and head back to town! Maybe we can catch them."

Without answering Edgar spun the wheel and bounced back up onto the paved highway, pushing his old car to the limit as they sped back down toward the city.

"Stop!" Gunnar shouted. "Back up!"

"What is it?"

"Their car … it's parked in front of that roadside inn we just passed. They must have stopped to warm up and grab a bite to eat."

Leo fingered the rosary in his pocket. *Thank you, Lord!*

"Wait here." Gunnar opened his door. "Someone in there might recognize the cardinal, so I'll go in alone." Looking around, he stepped out and crossed the graveled parking lot before disappearing through the inn's weathered door. Once inside, he spotted the two pilots sitting across the red-carpeted dining room at a table next to a roaring fireplace.

"Gunnar!" the captain waved him over. "Come … join us."

Taking a quick look at the other diners, Gunnar motioned to the two men before stepping back outside.

"What's up with Gunnar?" the co-pilot asked.

The captain set his coffee mug on the table. "I don't know, but it looks like something's got him spooked. Leave some money on the table and let's find out what's going on."

As soon as they stepped out onto the inn's covered porch, Gunnar took the captain by the arm and pointed to the Volvo. "Acerbi's men raided the hangar this morning. They arrested everyone there. You need to leave your car here and come with us … now."

Trading surprised looks, the two pilots quickly followed Gunnar across the parking lot and squeezed into the back seat of the ancient Volvo.

"In case you didn't catch their names earlier, Cardinal, this is Captain Luke Bell and his co-pilot, Robert Poole." Gunnar looked back at the two pilots. "Do either of you have any family members staying in your apartments?"

"Not me," Bell said. "Robert has a girlfriend, but she's visiting relatives in Sweden right now. She won't be back for a couple of weeks."

"Good. Don't call her."

"She'll freak out if I don't call her." Robert's face turned pale. "She'll think I'm seeing someone else!"

"Acerbi's computers will trace the call. I'll get a message to her. Do you have your cell phones?"

"We left them in the car," Bell said. "The coverage where we fish is kind of spotty."

"That's probably why Acerbi's people haven't found you yet."

The words were barely out of Gunnar's mouth when two international police cars sped by on the highway with their lights flashing.

Bell twisted his large frame and looked back through the rear window. "Looks like you found us just in time. Where are we headed?"

"The airport."

CHAPTER 19

The old Volvo rolled to a stop a block away from the hangar where Lundahl's jet was parked. While Leo and the others remained in the car, Gunnar and Bell jumped out and walked behind the hangar next door. Cautiously, they peered around the side of the tall metal building. Parked in the grass between the two hangars, they spotted a single police car with two officers sitting inside—watching, and off to the side, behind a glass door near the front of the hangar, Gunnar could see the shadowy outline of a man standing just inside the entrance.

"Looks like two, maybe three men guarding the jet," Gunnar said. "There's no way we can get to it now."

"What about a diversion?"

"Even if we got rid of the guards somehow, as soon as we fired up the engines and taxied out of the hangar air traffic control would be all over us." Gunnar's face took on a hard edge. "It doesn't look like that jet is going anywhere."

"That's right," Bell grinned. "That jet isn't going anywhere, but another one is."

"What are you talking about?"

"There's an old Lear 25 for sale. It's parked inside another hangar at the end of the street."

"Is it flyable?"

"It'll get the job done. Robert and I flew it a few weeks ago. We were thinking of taking out a loan so we could buy it and start our own air ambulance company. There's big money in private medivac flights. The interior is a little rough, but the engines were just overhauled and the airframe's in good shape. The owner wants to buy a new Cessna Citation and he's getting desperate to sell the older plane. If I tell him I'm bringing some investors by to check out the jet we can probably wrangle another test flight out of him, which means we won't raise any eyebrows with the guys over at air traffic control when we take off."

"You think it's still for sale?"

"Only one way to find out. If it is we'll fly you and the cardinal out of here today right under Acerbi's nose."

Gunnar's expression clouded. "I'm afraid I won't be going with you."

"What? You can't stay here, Gunnar. Acerbi's men know who you work for, and they smell blood in the water. You have to get on that plane."

"I can't. My place is here in Norway. I've worked for Mr. Lundahl for fifteen years now, and I've kind of grown fond of the old man and his family. This will be a one-way flight for the cardinal."

Bell bit his lower lip as he glanced up at the threatening sky. "Sounds like a one-way flight for us too."

"I'm afraid that's a decision you and your co-pilot will have to make together. If you both agree you'll have to ditch the jet and disappear for awhile, because you won't be able to come back here."

Bell actually laughed. "Either way we're out of a job, but I'm up for it … and I'm pretty sure Robert will go along too, but if the computers at air traffic control catch even a whiff that something's not right we'll never make it off the ground."

Gunnar's face turned rigid "We have to get the cardinal back home. We promised him, and according to Mr. Lundahl, he may be the only one who can stop what's happening in the world right now."

Bell's eyes bulged. "You're kidding! The cardinal?"

"That's what I said. He's probably the most important passenger you'll ever have, so make sure he arrives safely."

Memories of his days as a young military pilot always willing to take on the most dangerous missions flooded Bell's mind as he looked back at the tall, silent figure sitting in the back seat of the Volvo. "Let's go."

Returning to the car, Gunnar instructed Edgar to wait while he and the others walked to the Lear hangar down the street. In the front office, a lone mechanic sat reading a magazine with his feet propped up on the desk.

"Help you gentlemen?"

"Hi … remember me?" Bell asked.

The mechanic adopted a blank stare.

"I was here a few weeks ago. My partner and I took that old Lear for a spin." Bell nodded toward Leo and Gunnar. "These two gentlemen are our investors. They want to make sure the old bird will still fly before they loan us the money."

"Oh, she can fly alright," the mechanic said. "I just can't give you permission to fly her."

"Can you call the owner?"

"I can try, but he hasn't been answering his phone this morning." The mechanic grinned. "He just got married."

"Oh, I see." Bell peered off into space as if he was thinking. "That's OK. There's another plane we need to take a look at anyway. It's a little newer than your Lear and ..."

"Hold on." The mechanic jerked his feet off the desk and grabbed his cell phone. "The boss really wants to sell that plane. Let me try again." After listening to a few unanswered rings the mechanic's face lit up. "Ah, there you are, sir. I hate to bother you right now but I have some good news. The pilot who flew your plane a few weeks ago is back, and he brought his investors along with him. He wants to take her back up for a final test flight." The mechanic paused, listening. "Ok, I'll tell them." He laid his phone on the desk and stood. "My boss said you can have it for an hour, but he wants to be reimbursed for the fuel this time."

"No problem," Bell smiled. "We'll top her off when we get back."

"You'll have to top her off now, sir. She's almost empty, and the fuel truck will want the money up front."

Bell exchanged looks with Gunnar. If any of them tried to use their credit cards the hangar would be swarming with Acerbi's men in a matter of minutes.

"No problem." Reaching into his coat pocket, Gunnar pulled out a roll of cash. "I'll take care of this."

The mechanic eyed the roll of paper bills like a bass watching a worm wiggle on the end of a hook. "Cash? You don't see many people using that anymore."

"You might want to start, young man." Gunnar winked. "Cut up your plastic and start using cash. When you have it you have it, and when you don't you don't. It's a lesson I learned from my father. Only bankers get rich from people who live on credit."

The mechanic eyed Gunnar's impeccable blue suit and gold cufflinks.

"Can you ask the fuel guys to hurry it up?" Gunnar asked, handing the man a wad of cash with an impatient flourish. "We'll wait in the pilot's lounge while you roll her out."

"I'll call the fuel truck right now, sir."

While the mechanic called the fuel truck, the four men walked down a nondescript hallway through a metal door and stepped into a windowless room tainted with the aroma of oil and jet fuel. Leaning against a wall, a thread-bare couch faced a small kitchen area that contained a grease-stained table and an old coffee maker that held a glass pot ringed at the bottom with a brownish, hard-baked goo.

"I hope this guy takes better care of his plane than he does his hangar," Gunnar said, looking at Bell.

"Don't worry. We checked the maintenance logs the last time we flew it. I wouldn't go back up in the thing if we had spotted a problem."

The mechanic opened the door and stuck his head in. "The fuel truck is busy fueling a big charter jet across the field, but we're next in line … shouldn't be too long. Just make yourselves at home. Want some coffee?"

Gunnar eyed the goo at the bottom of the pot. "No thanks. We'll just wait."

"Suit yourselves. I'll call you when the jet is ready."

Unable to remain seated in a windowless room with nothing to do, Leo decided to walk out into the hangar. The steady drizzle had stopped, but the gray skies still held the promise of more rain to come as he watched the mechanic hook the jet up to a small tractor and pull it out onto the tarmac for fueling.

"I hope I see you again someday, Cardinal."

Leo turned to see Gunnar standing behind him, looking through the open hangar doors at the distant mountains. "I wish you the best of luck in whatever it is you have to do."

"Thank you, Gunnar," Leo said. "None of this would have been possible without your help."

"Don't thank me yet, Cardinal. You still have to make it to France. I only wish I was going along for the ride, because I have a feeling it will be an exciting one."

Leo's eyes narrowed as he watched the fuel truck pulling up next to the jet. "So do I, Gunnar. So do I."

CHAPTER 20

Parked beneath the faded image of a turquoise seahorse that smiled down at them from the concrete wall of an abandoned beach hotel, Daniel and Sarah looked out over the blue expanse of the sea beyond the Lebanese coast through the salt-fogged windows of the SUV.

"It's time to call the boat," said the soldier sitting in the front passenger seat. He pointed to Daniel's backpack. "Would you mind, sir? They'll only answer if I use my code."

Glancing at Sarah, Daniel handed his backpack across the seat.

Peering inside, the soldier pulled out a thin, brown-colored device that resembled a small laptop computer. After plugging it into a short antenna with a magnetic base, he reached out and stuck the antenna to the roof of the SUV, then entered his operator code and typed in a brief message. A few seconds later a cryptic reply materialized on the screen.

Hold your present position.

"That's strange," the soldier said, pulling at the ends of his beard. "They didn't give us the time or coordinates for the rendezvous."

"Let me see that." Daniel leaned over the front seat. "Ask them for their present position."

The soldier typed again and waited.

Nothing. There was no reply.

Daniel stared at the green letters flashing on the screen. "What boat did you just call?"

"The *Tekuma*. She's supposed to be submerged just offshore."

"A sub. That could account for the delay. Ask them for a coded ID check."

The soldier typed. Again, there was no reply.

A ring of sweat began spreading on Daniel's collar. "Something's not right. We need to get away from here … now!" Grabbing the transmitter from the puzzled soldier, he jumped from the vehicle and jerked the antenna off the roof. Looking around, he ran up a set of steps littered with chunks of fallen concrete and entered the shell of an old five-story hotel that had once welcomed thousands of happy beachgoers over the years. Working quickly, he set the antenna in an empty window frame and used his own code to type in a message to the *Tekuma*.

Leaving the transmitter behind, he ran back outside and threw himself into the back seat of the SUV. "Go!"

An expression of fierce intensity crossed the faces of the two soldiers as the SUV bounced up onto the highway and headed north. "What happened, sir?" The tall soldier asked.

"I think Acerbi's computers may have broken the codes to our burst transmitters, which means they can track our movements if we send out a message. I just sent a coded abort message to the *Tekuma* alerting them to the fact that our communications might have been compromised. If I'm right we're about to have a lot of company in the next few minutes."

"What about the *Ambush* … the British sub?" The tall soldier asked.

"We don't have their codes," Daniel replied. "It's a fail-safe mechanism instituted to keep the information compartmentalized so that no one person would have the codes to both transmitters. Both subs should be safe as long as they don't transmit."

With the sun just beginning to set in the west, Daniel looked off at a dusty orange haze following a tractor plowing a nearby field.

"There!" Sarah shouted, pointing over his shoulder. The jagged outline of a small hill town stood out against the setting sun. "We're sitting ducks driving past all these open fields. We need to drive to that town."

"There's a farmhouse a few miles back," the driver said, staring off at the distant hill. "It's a lot closer."

"No!" Daniel's eyes searched the empty sky. "Sarah's right. We need to get as far away from this highway as fast as we can. That hilltop town will provide us with cover, and we'll be able to watch the area for miles around."

"They're right," the other soldier said. "Step on it."

Turning off the highway they headed through olive groves, driving past weathered mud houses that looked like they had grown from the soil rather than having been built on top of it. Reaching the base of the hill, they climbed a series of switch-backs until they reached the top and entered a cobblestoned square surrounded by more mud-built dwellings whitewashed to reflect the burning rays of the sun over the long summer months.

Driving past a few curious villagers, the driver headed for a space between two buildings and stopped. Quickly they all got out and walked to the edge of town where they were greeted with an unobstructed vista that stretched all the way to the sea. Except for a few cars on the highway and the lone tractor in the field below, there was no other sign of activity.

"I know you're the computer expert, Mr. Meir," the tall soldier said, "but I sure hope you know what you're doing. That sub was our only way out of here."

"All I can tell you is that the message we received wasn't coming from the sub. Whoever sent it was probably trying to …"

Daniel's voice was drowned out by the thunderous roar of three fighter jets streaking by overhead with their afterburners engaged. Within seconds the jets had covered the distance between the hillside town and the beach. The foursome watching from the hillside town barely had time to blink before a roiling ball of orange flame erupted in a straight line along the distant coastline, completely enveloping the old hotel. A split second later the sound of the rolling explosion reached their ears, followed by a shockwave that rocked the village.

"Whoa!" The bearded soldier took a step backward and whistled through his teeth. "You were right, sir. They were just waiting for us to call and give our position away!"

Awestruck by the sight of such swift and total destruction, Sarah watched the sea breeze carry the smoke away from the beach and over the surrounding fields. "Look! The old hotel … it's gone!"

From the north, a big, low-flying jet appeared over the horizon and began circling over the Mediterranean just off the coast.

"That's a sub hunter," Daniel said solemnly. "They know the *Tekuma* is out there somewhere."

Together the group winced as huge plumes of seawater erupted into the air; a signal that the plane was dropping explosive charges in an attempt to send the *Tekuma* and her crew to the bottom of the sea.

At the same time, a flight of six Sikorsky MH-53 *Pave Low* helicopters appeared from the south following a curved arc of sand past the smoking ruins of a building once dedicated to the art of play. For several minutes the large military choppers circled the smoking foundation of the old hotel, the wash from their rotors stirring the sand and exposing the scattered remnants of a painted turquoise seahorse, until finally they swerved away and continued up the coast, leaving the lone sub hunter aircraft crisscrossing the ocean in a widening search pattern before it angled off and flew away.

In the violent aftermath of the attack, the stillness of the peaceful hilltop village served as a surreal contrast to the brutal display of firepower they had just witnessed.

"Now what?" Sarah mumbled.

"I'm running out of ideas," Daniel said. He looked to the two soldiers. "Do you guys have cell phones?"

"Yeah," the tall one said. "Who do you want to call?"

"No one. Remove the batteries and throw them away. Then we'll drive back to the beach and burn the SUV so Acerbi's people think it was destroyed in the attack."

"But their helicopters already swept the area," the soldier said. "They probably already know we got away."

"Not necessarily. The shell of that old hotel was five stories high and there's a lot of concrete lying around. Since it's starting to get dark, they'll probably send in a ground team tomorrow morning to search the area for the remains of the vehicle."

"What about bodies?"

"All we can do is hope they think we're buried under one of those heaping piles of concrete and call it a day."

"Then what?"

"One step at a time," Daniel said, watching the sun disappear in a yellow sliver along the darkening horizon. "We've got all night to figure that out."

Slowly, the group returned to the SUV and drove down the narrow hillside road before crossing the highway and returning to the beach. Stepping out into the offshore breeze, Sarah took off her shoes and let the soft sand squish through her toes as she walked toward the water.

"What's she doing?" the bearded soldier asked.

Daniel's smile glistened in the moonlight. "I think she's just trying to pretend for a moment that we aren't running for our lives."

Sarah's scream erased the smile from the three men's faces as they took off running toward her. Standing with her back to them, she was facing four dark figures that had just emerged from the surf and were walking up onto the beach.

Instantly the two soldiers flattened themselves on the sand and aimed their weapons, but for Daniel the choice wasn't so easy. That was his wife standing out there, and he was determined to reach her before she could be captured … or worse.

By now Sarah was walking backward, keeping her eyes focused on the advancing dark shapes as she backed into the comforting embrace of her husband.

If they were going to die, at least they would be together. They had given it their best shot, but in the end it seemed that Acerbi's men had finally outsmarted them.

"Daniel!" a dark figure shouted. "Daniel Meir!"

Standing in front of Sarah, Daniel gripped his weapon as the light from the moon highlighted the faces of the armed men walking toward them.

"I'll go peacefully!" Daniel shouted over the roar of the surf, "but if you do anything to my wife the men in the dunes behind us will make sure you never leave this beach alive."

The dark figures froze. "Easy there, boy," a voice called out from the darkness. "We're from the *Tekuma*."

"The *Tekuma*!" Sarah gasped. "But the sub hunter … the explosions in the water!"

Sweeping a neoprene hood from his head, a serious-looking man lowered his weapon and walked closer. "Obviously we survived."

"We were told you wouldn't wait," Daniel said, watching the other three men drag a black rubber boat up onto the beach.

"Our captain wasn't leaving without you. He chose this area for a reason. The sea floor along this area of the coast drops into a deep sea canyon a few hundred yards from shore, and we've been hiding down there waiting for Acerbi's forces to leave the area." The man's eyes searched the darkness behind Daniel. "Why don't you give your friends in the dunes a shout? We're a little anxious to get all of you on board as soon as possible."

"We need to torch our vehicle first," Daniel said.

"Leave it." The man looked amused. "I don't think a blazing fire on the beach would be a good idea right now. Besides, the abandoned vehicle will give Acerbi's men something to do. Once they find it they'll think you're all still on the run here in Lebanon and flood the area with troops. Too bad we can't hang around to watch the fun, but we have orders to get you guys to France as soon as possible."

CHAPTER 21

The takeoff was really more of a whoosh than a roar as Leo settled into the plush leather seat and watched the green countryside disappear as the jet climbed through an opaque mist that quickly blocked the view through his window. Left with nothing outside to look at, Leo leaned back and closed his eyes.

The pilots had told him the flight time back to Spain would take longer than usual. Instead of taking a direct southerly course, they would be following a flight plan that would take them west out over the North Sea for a supposed hour-long test flight that would presumably terminate back at the airport of origin—but in this case things would go horribly wrong. The little red and white Lear jet would never be returning to Oslo.

As soon as the jet broke out into the sun and reached its assigned cruising altitude of 33,000 feet over the North Sea, the co-pilot's head appeared in the cockpit doorway. "Better tighten your seatbelt, Cardinal. We're getting ready to put her into a dive. It might seem a little scary but don't worry … we practice this sort of thing all the time when we're simulating a loss in cabin pressure. Just hang on and pretend you're on a roller coaster."

Great, Leo thought, gripping his armrests. He had been in an aircraft that had hurtled toward the ocean before, and it was nothing like a roller coaster ride. A few seconds later he heard the roar of the engines drop as the pilots came back off the power and the nose dipped, pushing him into the back of his seat when the jet plunged at a 45-degree angle toward the clouds below. Tilting his head, he could see the pilots talking but their words were drowned out by the slipstream shrieking over the cabin, tearing at the flexing wings with a wind speed that surpassed any storm found in nature.

Taking a quick look out his window, Leo could see the long fuel tank bouncing up and down at the tip of the wing in a rapid blur that was amplified by the harmonic vibration from the high-speed dive. Leo braced himself. Any moment now the airframe would be stretched beyond its structural limits and the wings would finally snap, leaving them strapped inside an aluminum tube hurtling toward the cold water of the North Sea without any hope of recovery.

Yes, this was much worse than any roller coaster.

Piercing the cloud cover, the jet continued its dive, pressing Leo deeper into his seat and making it impossible for him to lift his arms as they reached the bottom of the dive and leveled off. The awful vibration that had threatened to tear them apart was now gone, replaced instead with the smooth push from the engines as they sped over a storm-tossed sea only fifty feet below their wings.

"Are you OK back there, Cardinal?" Bell asked, grinning back into the cabin.

"Fine ... thank you. I'm just glad the wings stayed on."

"This jet has the same type of wings as those used on fighter planes. It would take a lot more than a dive like the one we just made to pull the wings off."

"LN485 Papa ... this is Oslo center ... do you read?"

"Sounds like air traffic control is already looking for us," Bell said, turning his attention back inside the cockpit. "Did you turn off our transponder?"

The co-pilot glanced off to his right as they streaked by an offshore oil platform at eye level. "I switched it off just before we pulled out of the dive. Right now, the folks sitting in front of their radar screens back in Oslo are thinking we just crashed into the ocean."

"Make sure you kill the radios and navigation computers too. For the next few hours we need to become a black hole in the sky."

Turning south, the jet streaked low over the dark, swirling waters of the North Sea in an effort to keep from becoming a blip on coastal radar. With their radios turned off they were forced to resort to the old dead reckoning method of air navigation used by Charles Lindbergh when he crossed the Atlantic in 1927. It was an iffy way to navigate over open water then, but even iffier flying a modern jet traveling at almost five hundred miles an hour. At that speed, the slightest miscalculation could place them hundreds of miles off course.

For the next two hours they skimmed through the tight air corridor between the UK and the European mainland. Looking at his watch, Bell inched the control yoke over and began a slow arc to the east, until finally the Atlantic edge of the Pyrenees came into view. They had hit their intended target right on the money.

"You're almost home, Cardinal," Bell shouted into the back of the cabin. "We should be landing in twenty minutes."

Leo quickly made his way up to the cockpit and leaned between the two pilots to take in the panoramic view of the rising curvature of the mountains outside the frosty windows. "Any chance we can fly over the castle on the French side of the mountains before we land in Spain?"

"That's cutting it pretty close, Cardinal. We're running low on fuel, plus the old airbase in Spain doesn't have functioning runway lights and it will be getting dark soon."

Leo's eyes drifted to the green peaks off to the north. "I really need to check on them, Luke. After we land at the old airbase it will be another four days before I make it back through the forest to the castle. Just a quick look … that's all I need."

The captain checked the fuel gauge and nodded. "One quick flyby, and then we have to land."

"Thanks." Leo patted Bell on the shoulder and made his way back to his seat as the pilots guided the jet over a valley and threaded their way through a tight mountain pass before streaking directly over the castle.

Pressing his face against the glass, Leo's fingers literally clawed at the window as an anguished cry escaped from his lips. Below them, black smoke rose from the mountain top as flames billowed from a solitary window in the only portion of the castle that still remained standing, and the park-like setting was now a treeless expanse of gray, pock-marked craters surrounded by the unmistakable sight of bodies lying on the smoking ground among scattered piles of rubble.

Behind the blackened remains of the still-burning castle, the waterfall was the only recognizable feature in a landscape that now looked almost alien, and the small lake that had graced the entrance to the castle was slowly disappearing as the water flowed through a bombed-out cut in the shattered remains of one of the tall walls that had surrounded the once beautiful grounds.

Nothing man-made was recognizable. It was all gone—senselessly destroyed. Leo twisted in his seat in a final desperate effort to spot any signs of life through the tiny window until the jet leveled off and turned to the south. With tears streaming down his face, he collapsed into his seat and stared blankly out the window, watching the castle fade from view as the jet streaked back into the safety of a mountain pass.

113

They were gone! All gone!

Slowly, he grasped his rosary and held a shaking hand over his eyes to avoid the horrified looks from the pilots staring back at him from the cockpit.

For several minutes Leo prayed silently, but when the co-pilot saw him look up, he noticed that the cardinal's eyes had taken on a cold, lifeless stare.

"Should we say something to him?" he asked the captain.

"No. There's nothing we can say to him that would change the way he feels right now. Leave him alone."

"Yeah, you're probably right." The co-pilot gazed back out his window at the smoke rising from the mountain behind them. "I can tell you one thing, though. From the look in his eyes, I wouldn't want to be the one he's thinking about right now."

CHAPTER 22

Driving into central London's crowded streets, Samantha Jennings was having a hard time making up her mind as she passed through the heart of a city festooned with cameras protruding from every imaginable location. She needed time to think—to plan out her next move, and she needed coffee and something sweet to eat.

Cut off from everything familiar, the fear of being totally alone made her wince as she looked for somewhere to stop. *Maybe she should just turn around.*

Even though she had left word with the duty officer that she was taking the day off, it was still possible that her actions would be viewed as suspicious. In fact, everything Acerbi's officers did seemed to be filtered through the prism of suspicion, and an overachieving wing commander who had suddenly stopped answering her phone certainly fell under the heading of suspicious activity.

Samantha bit her lower lip as she approached Covent Garden and turned onto King Street. After squeezing the little MG into a rare parking spot across from St. Paul's Church, she walked aimlessly along Bedford Street for a few minutes before crossing over to New Row where she found a small coffee shop named after the street.

To her, the shop seemed to sparkle. She hadn't been to a little coffee shop alone since college, and the sight of the pub-like, black painted wood exterior and the smiling people sitting behind the large panes of spotless glass almost brought tears to her eyes.

So this was how people outside Acerbi's war machine still lived.

The few tables inside were taken, so after purchasing coffee and a thin wedge of some kind of brown cake with green nuts in it, she walked back outside and sat on a wooden bench. Sipping her coffee, she watched the people walking by, seemingly oblivious to one of the ever-present security cameras silently watching them from the top of a street lamp. Suddenly she felt nervous again. The idyllic but brief memories of her life before she had joined the military no longer seemed relevant, and she had no way of knowing if her colleagues back at the base were already looking for her. Any moment now a car full of security men could pull to the curb and take her away, leaving only a half-full cup of coffee and a piece of cake lying on the bench—the only reminders to the world that she had ever existed.

It was time to go.

Walking back to her car, she slid behind the wheel and headed up Bedford Street. Driving slowly, she coughed in the exhaust from a double-decker bus in front of her as she crossed the bridge over the Thames and approached the modernistic Waterloo Station; the main terminal for trains departing for France via the Chunnel.

Quickly realizing that she had just entered one of the most camera-encrusted areas of the city, she turned onto York Road. Crowds of people seemed to appear from out of nowhere, and as she glanced off to her right, she spied the London Eye surrounded by gawking tourists lined up to ride the giant Ferris wheel.

As she zoomed up Albert Embankment and headed toward Vauxhall Bridge, she saw a building off to her right that resembled an upside-down wedding cake. It was the SIS building, more commonly referred to as MI6 headquarters, where the camera coverage would be even more unbelievably thick. No matter where she turned she seemed to be heading into the teeth of the tiger.

Samantha was suddenly seized by the thought that she had no idea what she was doing. She had come to London with some ill-conceived plan to make contact with those who were opposed to Acerbi and his new world order, but she had no clue where to start.

This had been a crazy idea!

Fear began to take hold as she drove by the looming SIS building, but just as she was almost past, she remembered something one of Acerbi's intelligence people had told her. He had been upset that, despite the fact it was rumored MI6 was still loaded with people just waiting for the chance to strike back and take him down, Acerbi had decided to leave the previous intelligence community intact due to their vast experience.

Better to leave those buzzing little spies concentrated in a single nest, Acerbi had told his own intelligence officers before instructing them to place some of their own people on the inside to keep an eye on things. *When the old guard has served their usefulness, we'll know exactly which ones to eliminate first.*

Slowly a plan began to form in Samantha's mind. It was a risky plan, but at this point she knew her options were running out. Already she could feel the noose tightening. If she turned around and tried to leave the country by boarding the Chunnel train to France, Acerbi's computers would flag her and she would be arrested as soon as she stepped off the train in Paris, and if she returned to her base there would be questions— lots of questions. Looking back over her shoulder, she pulled to the curb outside the SIS building and remained sitting in her car.

A creeping sensation inched up her back, for she knew that at this very moment dozens of eyes were already on her, watching her every move. From the obvious uniformed guards at the entrance to the not so obvious gray-haired gentleman reading a paper on a nearby park bench, dozens of people were suddenly interested in the girl who had just parked her car in a no-parking zone in front of one of the most recognizable intelligence buildings in the world.

Needless to say, the people inside were still a little nervous after someone had fired a Russian-built RPG-22 anti-tank missile at the building back in 2000, and they were still considered to be a prime target for various militant groups and the occasional nut job or secret agent wannabe.

This was, after all, the home of the fictional James Bond, but fiction or no fiction, a real intelligence officer inside the building was already uploading her photo and license plate number into the computer, and in a matter of seconds they would know that Adrian Acerbi's air wing commander was parked in front of their building for some reason when she was scheduled for duty at the air base.

It's only a matter of time now, Samantha thought. Thinking back to the quaint little coffee house she had just left, she leaned back with memories of a carefree youth that had ended the day she had signed on the dotted line and was shipped off to a spartan military base for basic training. It had all seemed so exciting at the time, but with a growing feeling that she had left behind a youth she could never recover, the excitement of her new career had begun to fade over time.

Who would be coming for her? She wondered, glancing up at the building. *Would it even matter?* Would she be approached by an officer from Her Majesty's Secret Service, or would it be one of Acerbi's goons who had been alerted to her presence?

Her question was answered when a yellow and blue police cruiser known to the locals as a *panda* car pulled up behind her with its blue lights flashing.

That didn't take long, she thought.

Stepping from his vehicle, a young police officer walked up to the driver's side of the car and smiled down at her. "Good evening, miss. You're parked in a no-parking zone. Be a good girl now and move along please."

"Did you just tell me to be a good girl?"

The officer's smile faded. "No offense miss … it's just my way of bein' friendly … kind of like I was talkin' to my sister, if you know what I mean."

"Well, I'm not your sister, and I'm not going anywhere until I speak to someone inside that building."

The officer glanced at up at the building's blue tinted glass and shrugged his shoulders before holding his hand to the concealed earpiece in his left ear, making it obvious that someone was speaking to him. After listening to the voice on the other end, his bearing changed dramatically. "Your escort will be along presently. Please remain in your car." His cockney accent had suddenly disappeared.

Seconds later, a pleasant-looking man in a gray suit emerged from the building, followed by a dark-haired woman dressed in a white blouse, a black, knee-length skirt, and high heels. Together the pair walked directly to the car.

"Good evening, Commander Jennings," the man said. "What brings you to our neighborhood?"

Samantha twirled a strand of red hair with her fingers. "I was thinking of making a career change. I've always been interested in intelligence work."

"Well, you certainly have an interesting way of submitting your application." The man's face remained neutral, but his eyes were probing. "My name is Stephen Yates, and this is Gwyneth Hastings. We're both officers in Her Majesty's Secret Service. Why don't you come inside and we'll have a little chat over some tea?"

CHAPTER 23

The Lear jet circled down for a landing at the abandoned Spanish airbase and taxied up to the old tower building. After shutting down the engines the pilots peered back into the cabin at their silent passenger. Still clutching his rosary, Leo was staring out the window, seemingly oblivious to the fact that they were on the ground.

"What now?" the co-pilot asked.

"We barely have enough fuel to make it to Barcelona," Bell replied, looking out at a pair of rusting fuel tanks across the field. "Unless we can find some jet fuel lying around, this is the end of the line."

Behind them they heard the unmistakable click of the cabin door being unlocked, followed by a rush of humidity. Looking back, they saw that Leo was already exiting the aircraft. Rushing to meet him, a group of Israeli soldiers came flooding from the brick building.

"Cardinal!" Ben Zamir shouted. "We weren't sure if it was you or not. You're in a different plane." Ben paused. Right away he could tell something was very wrong. Leo's face was drained of color, and his eyes had taken on a hollow, vacant look. "What is it, Leo ... what's happened?"

"You don't know yet, do you, Ben?"

"Know what?"

"The castle. It's been attacked ... there's nothing left but smoking ruins."

Ben took an involuntary step backward. "My God! Are you sure?"

"We just flew over it. There's nothing left but total devastation."

"Any sign of survivors?"

Leo hesitated. "I saw a few bodies, but that was all."

"Just bodies!" Ben's mind was running a hundred miles an hour as he tried to process what he was hearing. "My father ... Lev ... Evita?"

"I don't know. We only had time for a short flyover, but it didn't look good. Have you heard anything at all?"

"No. We were ordered to maintain strict radio silence for fear of giving away our position."

Leo felt a hand on his shoulder and glanced around to see Sergeant Efron and the other soldiers forming a tight circle around him. "Are you sure you didn't see any survivors?"

"It was hard to tell … the castle was still burning." Leo's eyes drifted off to toward the distant mountains. "It looked like the attack just happened."

By now Ben's knuckles had turned white from gripping his rifle. Like all Israelis, the possibility of a surprise attack on their homeland had been instilled in him since childhood, but this was different. Somehow this seemed more personal and he could feel a cold anger rising up inside him, making it hard for him to think clearly. Like a tiger cornered by a group of mindless hunters looking to turn his skin into a trophy, he wanted to strike out at something—anything. There had to be a way out of this, and he was determined to find it.

"Signal Gael and his men," Ben said. "We're leaving for the castle … now!"

Efron stared back before reaching into his backpack and retrieving a small aluminum tube that looked like a small flashlight. Pointing it in the direction of the old fence line, a bright green laser beam shot from the end and danced along the tall weeds at the edge of the runway. A few seconds later, his signal was returned by a single red flash as Gael and a dozen Cathar fighters emerged from the underbrush and began walking toward the tower.

"Those men all had families living in the castle," Ben said, looking down at his boots. "It was supposed to be a place of refuge!" Looking back at Bell standing next to the jet, he charged past Efron and grabbed the captain's shirt. "Who are you guys really working for?" he screamed.

"Easy, Ben!" Through a cloud of swirling anger, Ben heard Leo's voice behind him. "These two men just risked their own lives to save mine, and now they're just as hunted as we are."

Ben released his grip. "Where did they take you, Cardinal?"

"Norway. We have a lot to discuss, Ben, but it's going to have to wait. Right now, we need to focus all of our attention on getting back to the castle and looking for survivors."

While Ben continued to eye the pilots suspiciously, Leo walked across the concrete to meet the group of Cathar fighters and deliver the devastating news, but instead of anguished cries or shouts of anger, the Israelis saw the Cathars nodding back silently in a stoic display of acceptance.

"They don't seem to be too upset," Efron whispered to Ben.

"I think the Cathars look at things a little differently than we do, Sarge. They also had a pretty extensive escape plan, so they might know something we don't."

Efron shouldered his rifle and pulled out his night vision goggles. "Let's move out … and you all better prepare yourselves. We won't be doing much resting or sleeping for the next few days."

By now darkness was beginning to envelop the airfield, and the distinct greenery of the mountains had been transformed into nothing more than shapeless black humps that blotted the stars behind them.

"We need to take a different route through the mountains," Gael said to Ben. "By now there are probably hundreds of Acerbi's troops searching the area around the castle for anyone who escaped. To go back the way we came would be suicide." He pointed to the dark shape of a tall mountain in the distance. "We must follow the path of the *Pure Ones* and enter the caves of the *Sabarthés*. If there are any survivors, we'll find them there."

Efron nudged Ben. "What's he talking about?"

"I don't have a clue."

"The waterfall!" Leo shouted. "The entrance to the sacred caves beneath the mountain!" With his thoughts beginning to clear, the color returned to his face. "Evita always told the children to go there if there was ever any trouble because it was a place of safety. That's where they would have gone when the castle was attacked."

With the look of a man who had just sensed the naiveté of a hopeless wish, Ben turned to Leo. "I'm not trying to crush anyone's hopes, Cardinal, but Gael is right. Acerbi's men are probably swarming over the area now and have already discovered the cave behind the waterfall. They're probably searching it right now."

"They probably are," Gael agreed. "But the cave system within the Pyrenees has been a place of sanctuary for our people for over a thousand years. It extends for hundreds of square miles and hides secret caverns that no one will ever find without a Cathar guide."

Gael's eyes reflected the starlight as he studied the outline of the distant mountains. "The tallest mountain overlooking the valley is *Saint Bartholomew's Peak*. We refer to it as the *Mount of Transfiguration*, or the *Tabor*. It has been our plan all along that we would go there if the castle was ever discovered, and that is where we will find them. The valley that lies below is called the valley of the elm trees, or the *Olmés*. There is a secret pathway that leads from the *Olmés* to the caves of the *Sabarthés*. That is the path of the Cathars … the path of the *Pure Ones*, and that is where we must go."

Leo had suddenly become re-energized with a new sense of hope—hope that Evita had escaped into the labyrinth of caves behind the waterfall. *A place of safety*! That's what she had told the children, and that's where she would have led them when the castle was attacked.

She must have made it!

"What about the jet?" The soldiers turned to see Luke Bell standing behind them.

"What about it?" Ben asked.

"We should move it into one of the hangars."

"So now you're giving orders?"

Like two angry bulls enclosed in a small pasture, the two men locked eyes. A seasoned Israeli commando, Ben Zamir was not someone any sane person wanted to pick a fight with, unless of course that person was a man like Luke Bell, a former fighter pilot who had also been the captain of his college football team and had single-handedly overpowered three armed captors after being shot down over Iraq in the second Gulf War.

"This doesn't look good," Efron said, taking a step toward the two men.

"Wait." Leo extended his arm. "Those two dogs just need to sniff a little while longer."

"As I was saying," Bell continued, "we need to move the jet into a hangar. By now Acerbi's people in Norway have interviewed the ground crew at the airport in Oslo and know the cardinal was on board. Even though we made it look like we crashed into the North Sea, as soon as it gets light tomorrow the first satellite that passes overhead will snap a picture of the missing jet parked out in the open at an abandoned airbase."

Ben blinked at Bell before stepping back. "They think you're all dead?"

"That was our goal, but if they find the jet they'll know the cardinal is still alive and is somewhere in this area."

Feeling a little foolish, Ben cast a sheepish look back at Bell before glancing at Efron. "Why don't we help these two gentlemen push their jet into one of the hangars, Sergeant … and find them some weapons. We're moving out in twenty minutes."

"We won't be needing any weapons," Bell said. "We're staying here."

"Staying?" A confused Leo brushed past Ben. "There's nothing here but empty buildings, Luke. I think the two of you might be better off coming with us."

"No offense, Cardinal, but we also have people we need to return to. We thought we might head into Barcelona and see if we can find a way to contact them."

Leo paused, silently studying the resolve in the eyes of the two pilots before finally reaching out to shake their hands. "Thank you for bringing me home. I only wish there was some way I could repay you both for the sacrifice you've just made."

"Just take care of that Acerbi guy, Cardinal," Bell said, glancing off in the direction of the burning castle they had just flown over. "If you can do that, I have a feeling we'll all be safe."

CHAPTER 24

All through the night they walked, stopping only to refill their hydration backpacks from fast-moving mountain streams before moving off into the soft blue glow of the moonlit forest.

This was a magical place, Leo thought, listening to the sound of the wind moving through the branches over his head as they moved silently in the pine-scented air. The whispering breeze was like the voice of a faceless messenger telling him that Evita was still alive. He could almost feel her life force reaching out to him; her sweet hand brushing against his face. She was out there somewhere, and no matter how long it took he would find her, and the broken fragments of their lives would become whole again.

"The path forks up ahead," Gael said, peering at the dark outline of the trail. "The fork to the left leads to the castle, but the one that breaks to the right will take us to the *Tabor*."

"Don't you think we should reconsider and check the area around the castle first?" Leo huffed as they reached the fork and began climbing the steeper path that led off to their right.

"I know what you're thinking, Cardinal, but as I said earlier, these mountains have served as a sanctuary for our people for over a thousand years, and if anyone made it into the caves beneath the mountain they're safe for now. The caves of the Sabarthés are as numerous as the stars, and they are protected by secrets known only to us. Once an outsider enters the labyrinth beneath the mountains there are many paths they can take, but if you fail to follow the right one, you could find yourself facing a raging underground river or staring down into a black abyss that drops off into the depths of the earth. Over the centuries many have tried … and many have failed."

"Then why do so many people continue to explore them?"

"Legends abound here, Cardinal, and the area we are headed to holds some of the greatest mysteries of them all. Some say that the Cathars who lowered themselves over the walls of *Montsegur Castle* the night before it fell to the Crusaders carried the Holy Grail itself, and many believe it is still hidden somewhere within the labyrinth of the *Tabor*. Others say they carried with them *Le Trésor Cathar*, better known as the sacred scrolls, but the strangest story of them all is the legend of the lake."

"The legend of the lake?"

"Yes. It is one of our more ancient legends ... one that goes all the way back to Druid times. The Druids were here before we were, and evidence of their legacy can be found everywhere if you know where to look. In fact, many believe we are descended from them. You'll have a chance to see the lake when we begin our ascent up the path of the *Pure Ones* that runs between *Montségur* and the *Tabor*. The water is dark, and it's surrounded on three sides by steep cliffs. Our ancestors called it the *Lac des Druides* ... the Lake of the Druids."

Gael paused to study the stars before continuing up the steep path. "The story of the lake goes back almost two thousand years, when the people who lived in the valley at the base of the mountain suddenly began dying of a mysterious illness. A person could be well in the morning and fall over dead that same night. The Druids who lived in the forest advised them that they must rid themselves of all material wealth ... that they should throw all of their gold, silver, and precious stones into the waters of the lake. For days the people of the valley hauled cartloads of gold and other riches up the mountain and dumped the contents into the lake's still waters. Soon thereafter the water turned black and the people of the village were cured of their affliction, but the Druids left us with a warning. If anyone touched the gold and silver that was dumped into the lake they would die of the same illness. To this day the waters of the lake remain black, while all of the other mountain lakes around the *Tabor* are crystal clear."

"Is that the reason your people continue to shun material wealth today?"

"The legend is part of the reason, Cardinal, but our decision to forego material wealth stems from our Christian beliefs. You know ... the part where it says that it is easier for a camel to pass through the eye of a needle than it is for a rich man to enter the kingdom of heaven."

"It seems the world has forgotten those words," Leo said. "I'm afraid the majority of people don't want to hear the truth anymore. They want to

126

continue living with the illusion of well-being, even if they know the illusion could crumble at any moment."

"Maybe that's why you're here, Cardinal. You started out as a teacher. Maybe you will be a teacher again someday … but first you must gather your students."

Leo was struck by the constant reminders from others that there was some kind of unfulfilled destiny awaiting him, an undiscovered truth lying just beyond his reach, and all he had to do was open his eyes and look in the right direction. Were they really reminders, or were they merely a string of unrelated statements that had been zinging at his subconscious in the wake of his discussion with Steig Lundahl?

Only you can send that thing back to wherever it came from, Cardinal!

The words tugged at the back of Leo's mind, causing him to wonder if the answers to his questions were lying out in the open like a bright flower waiting to be picked—or were they lying concealed, like some mythical treasure beneath the black waters of a mysterious mountain lake?

For the next several hours they skirted the rocky foothills of the *Tabor*. Below they could see the dark ruins of *Montsegur Castle* rising above the *Field of the Burned* as a pale yellow line along the eastern horizon announced that dawn was fast approaching, and as the soft orange rays of early morning sunlight reached down into the valley and began to paint the castle's time-ravaged walls, the ancient fortress began to glow like a blazing ember that had been thrust into the sky by a giant, uplifted hand for all the world to see.

"We're almost there, Cardinal," Gael said. "This trail intersects the path of the *Pure Ones* that leads to an opening near the top of the mountain."

Leo grunted in the thin air. His legs were aching from the steep climb, but thoughts of finding Evita gave him the strength he needed to push through the pain and exhaustion.

That is where we will find them!

Gael's words came tumbling back to him as they reached the storied path of the *Pure Ones* and continued up the mountain, taking one agonizing step at a time. Onward and upward they climbed, skirting the mysterious black-watered lake Gael had told them about to a shaded glen at the end of a narrow canyon. Glancing over his shoulder, Gael smiled back at the others before plunging into a narrow opening behind a thin stand of quaking aspens.

Inside the cave, the sound of dripping water blended with their footsteps as they followed a pathway that wound past prehistoric stone monoliths to an amazing subterranean cavern that rose almost four hundred feet above their heads. Glistening white stalactites stood like sentinels in front of gold-streaked marble walls covered with crystals of every imaginable color, and as they all paused to take in the beauty of the space, Gael pointed to ancient images of the sun and the moon carved into a large boulder.

"This space is known as the *Cathedral of Lombrives*, and the images of the sun and the moon are reminders from our ancestors that all of this beauty was created by the great artist who lives beyond the stars. Come, we must hurry."

Crossing the space, they squeezed through a fissure in the rock and followed a natural passage deeper into the mountain. They continued on, barely speaking as they walked, until finally they entered another majestic space, but instead of gold-streaked walls they saw that this cavern was made up of gray rock that arched over a black abyss that plunged thousands of feet into the darkness of eternal night.

Dropping his backpack on the floor, Ben walked up next to Leo and Gael and peered over the edge. "Now what?"

With the touch of one hand, Gael pushed against a section of rock wall that swung inward, revealing yet another seemingly endless passageway that stretched into infinity.

"You've got to be kidding," Leo exhaled, shining his light into the darkness. "Another passageway?"

"Yes," Gael said. "Another passage, but I think you'll like where this one leads."

As soon as they stepped through the opening, Ben held up his hand and stopped when he thought he heard the faint murmur of voices ahead.

"Is that …?"

"Yes … it is." Gael's smile broadened into a grin. "Turn off your lights."

As soon as all their lights had been extinguished and their eyes adjusted to the darkness, they began to see the faint glow of torchlight flickering against the walls of a small cavern in the distance.

"I told you this is where we would find them."

CHAPTER 25

Samantha Jennings was sitting beneath an air conditioning vent that was spewing cold air over the single metal table and two chairs in the center of a green painted room. The obvious two-way mirror on the wall would have been almost laughable were it not for the fact that she knew someone was probably watching her fidget as she stared at the walls, and as time dragged on she could feel the innate anxiety that had followed her since childhood rising to a whole new level.

Had she made the right decision, or had she just thrown her life away?

She was about to find out.

The door clicked, making her jump as the dark-haired woman and the gray-suited man she had met earlier entered the room.

The man remained standing while the woman took the remaining empty seat across the table from Samantha. "Sorry for making you wait, Commander. Just doing some checking. Do you remember our names?"

"Not really."

"I'm Gwyneth Hastings, and this is Stephen Yates. We're MI6 intelligence officers."

In Samantha's hyper-alert state the woman seemed colder.

Not a good sign.

"To be honest," Hastings continued, "we find your sudden interest in our organization a little puzzling, especially in view of the fact that you already hold a high-ranking position in the military. Do you mind telling us why you felt the need to have this interview conducted in secret?"

Before Samantha could answer the question, a man wearing blue scrubs entered the room with a tray full of syringes and lab tubes.

"What's this?" Samantha asked.

"We need to take a sample of your blood before we run you through the polygraph."

"Take my blood!" Samantha pushed her chair back. "Run me through the polygraph? I thought we were just going to have a friendly little chat!"

"Standard operating procedure," Hastings replied. "First, we check you out, and then we let you check us out. Fair enough?"

Samantha glared up at the man as she held out her arm. "Go ahead, check my blood ... ask me anything."

"We will." Hastings opened the door. "Be back as soon as they're through with the polygraph."

After taking a quick sample of Samantha's blood, the man in scrubs left and a bent-looking man with thick glasses entered the room holding what appeared to be a laptop computer. After attaching a blood pressure cuff to her arm and three electrodes to her chest, he plugged the wires into the device and began going through the usual test questions designed to measure her body's physiological response to simple questioning before probing deeper into the reasons behind her visit.

When he was finished, he quietly disconnected his machine and waddled back out of the room, leaving Samantha scratching her arm and staring at the green walls. Once again, the door clicked and Hastings was back with the gray-suited man.

"Looks like you passed with flying colors," Hastings said.

"Personally, I think a polygraph test is about as useful as a Ouija Board," Samantha snapped back. "How do you know I didn't pop a beta-blocker before I came in here to squash the physiological responses to your questions?"

Hastings smiled across the table. "The toxicology screen we ran on your blood sample revealed no drugs present. Also, the results of the voice stress analysis were normal. The questions we've asked so far appear to have been answered honestly, so we've decided to press on."

"Quite so," the man added. "Now, Commander, if you don't mind, we'd very much like to hear the reason behind your sudden unannounced visit."

"How long have you been an MI6 officer, Mr. Yates? That is your real name, isn't it?"

"Yes ... why do you ask?" Yates looked surprised at the question.

"I simply wanted to know if the two of you were here before Acerbi came to power and absorbed our country into his one world government like a giant sponge."

Yates loosened his tie. "And why would our length of service be of interest to one of Acerbi's high-ranking air commanders?"

"Because, I have a feeling there are still some of us left who just might share some common ground. The polygraph guy asked me if I was here on some kind of undercover mission for Acerbi. Why would he ask me that if you weren't a little worried about undercover operatives being sent in to check on your loyalty to him?"

Hastings smoothed her blouse and leaned forward in her chair. "Is that why you're here, Commander … to see how loyal we are to Adrian Acerbi?"

"No. Believe me … you don't want to talk to those people. I'm sure that as soon as the UK joined Acerbi's happy little family he sent swarms of his own intelligence people here to learn as much as they could about how British intelligence operates, and after that, I'd say that at least half of the original MI6 officers probably left in disgust while the rest of you remained behind out of a sense of loyalty to your country. How did you feel when you looked out the window and saw the Union Jack being lowered outside the SIS building and replaced with one of Acerbi's black and gray flags?"

Hastings remained non-committal. "Sorry, Commander, but I really don't see where all of this is leading. What is it you want from us?"

"Who's behind there?" Samantha asked, looking across the room at the mirror.

"Actually, no one right now," Yates answered.

Samantha turned around and smiled at the two intelligence officers. "Well, as wild and crazy as this idea might seem to someone standing in a small room inside MI6 headquarters, I'll go out on a limb here and say there's a pretty good chance that anything said in this building is being recorded right now."

Hastings exchanged glances with Yates before walking over and standing next to Samantha. "That's why we chose this room for your interview, Commander. It was specially designed to prevent eavesdropping, no matter how sophisticated."

For a moment both women locked eyes.

"You know, Commander," Hastings continued, "before Acerbi took over I conducted a lot of interviews with people seeking political asylum from some very nasty and brutal political regimes around the world, and frankly, you remind me of them. Everything about you, from your choice of words to your demeanor, screams defector. The only question is, just what are you defecting from? You might also want to know that the moment you entered this building your picture was flashed to every Acerbi intelligence office in the world, which means that your boss already knows that you are here and talking to someone inside this building right now. If you have something you want to tell us, you'd better make it quick if you want our help. More than half the people in this building are Acerbi loyalists, and your sudden appearance here has raised all kinds of red flags."

Samantha looked back at the mirror. "I want out."

Hastings could feel the hair rise on the back of her neck. *There it was.* This was gut-check time. The course of their discussion over the next few minutes would decide if they would bring her into the fold or send her back out into the cold to fend for herself.

"You want out of what, Commander?"

"Out of the military … out of Acerbi's government … out of everything!" Samantha had finally said what she had come to say, and from the looks on the faces of the two MI6 officers they had heard her loud and clear. The ball was now in their court.

"Just who do you think we are, Commander?" Yates asked.

"I'm hoping you are both still loyal MI6 officers who want to see our national sovereignty returned to us. Acerbi is a madman. I've watched him up close, and I can guarantee that whatever he's planning for the world won't be pleasant. I've weighed the options and you are my last chance. If I'm arrested for treason, then I'll know I've been talking to the wrong people. But if you are still the people I believe you are and you want to be rid of Acerbi, then I'm your girl. I know how he operates, and if there is some kind of organized resistance against him, I want to be a part of it."

Hastings' eyes became laser-like in their intensity. "We have a better idea, Samantha." For the first time all day, Hastings had referred to Samantha by her first name. "We want you to return to your base as soon as possible."

"Return to my base?! Is that some kind of joke? According to you I'm already under suspicion. I'd be arrested as soon as I entered the front gate and hauled in front of Acerbi to explain why I came here."

"No, you won't. We've already notified your headquarters that you are here looking for more information on an intelligence report that came across your desk a few days ago. I believe one of the base intelligence officers we spoke to referred to you as '*our OCD commander*'." Hastings smiled. "As far as they know you are just being your typical, overzealous self."

"So what are you saying?" Samantha asked. "Are you telling me to go back to work and act as if none of this ever happened?"

"Yes, that's exactly what I'm saying, only now you'll be working for us."

"For MI6?"

"Not exactly." Hastings glanced at her watch. "The old MI6 is gone … gobbled up along with most of the other intelligence services around the world. As you've already guessed, only a few of the original MI6 officers remain, and the Acerbi clowns who've replaced the real professionals have no idea what we really do."

"That's true." Yates folded his arms and huffed. "One of them actually bought a used Aston Martin and was seen drinking martinis in a tuxedo at a private dinner held in the old Russian embassy building."

"Then what exactly am I joining?"

"We've formed a secret group, Samantha … a group of solid MI6 officers who want to see the Union Jack flying over this building again, but we have to be very careful. Acerbi's not foolish enough to believe that everyone has come willingly to the party. He has to know there are still some of us left who liked things the way they were, but he's playing it smart by keeping some of the old hands around. That way we can teach the new people how to be proper spies and he can keep us all grouped together. It's a double-edged sword and a very dangerous game we're playing. We've become moles in our own intelligence service."

Hastings glanced at her watch again. "I'm afraid that's all we have time to tell you right now, but suffice it to say you will be much more valuable to us on the inside than on the outside. As soon as we're finished here we'll give you some routine intelligence paperwork that will help support the reason for your visit when you return to your office. With our help everything you did today will be looked upon as totally above board, so if anyone asks, just tell them exactly where you went and who you talked to. We'll corroborate your story. Also, don't try to contact us directly … we'll contact you. This is a new game for you, Samantha, so let us take the lead. Do exactly as we say, and we'll do our best to keep you safe."

Samantha nodded. "I understand. What do I do after I return to work?"

"That's the hard part, Commander," Yates added. "Being on the inside is always a lot more dangerous than working from the outside. Just be yourself. Don't do anything out of the ordinary or behave in a way that will look out of character. Most people working on the inside give themselves away by allowing their inner feelings to show through. The subconscious is a powerful force, and it can show itself in a hundred different ways if it raises its ugly head at the wrong moment. We find that

133

a little self-delusion usually works in cases like this, but the important thing to remember is to keep acting like the same gung-ho warrior you've always been."

Hastings tossed a dark blue intelligence folder on the table and swept a wayward strand of dangling black hair from her forehead. "This is a three-day-old report on a Gulfstream jet that filed a flight plan from Norway to Barcelona. It disappeared off radar in the vicinity of an old Spanish airfield at the base of the Pyrenees, then suddenly reappeared on a reverse course twenty-two minutes later without going on to Barcelona. When the aircraft was contacted the pilots stated they were returning to Norway without going on to Barcelona due to the deteriorating weather, but the tower in Barcelona reported the sky was improving that day."

"I read it," Jennings said. "Weird."

"Yes … very," Hastings noted. "There's more. Soon after the jet returned to Oslo, Acerbi's quantum computers traced a 0.5 nanosecond burst transmission from Norway to a mountaintop in France. Do you know who Cardinal Leopold Amodeo is?"

"I think we all know who he is," Samantha answered. "Acerbi hates the man."

"And what about you, Commander … what are your feelings about the cardinal?"

"To be honest I don't really know much about him other than the fact that he seems to have a lot of popular support, especially from those who believe that Adrian Acerbi is the Antichrist. Personally, I admire the man. He's a warrior … like me. I led an aerial attack against him last year after he rescued those people in the *Field of the Burned*. His tactics were brilliant."

"I'm glad to hear you're a fan," Hastings said, "because the cardinal is a very important player in all of this. Apparently, the quantum computers have broken all the codes to the previously secure burst transmitters, and they were able to ascertain that the transmission from Norway was addressed to the cardinal and included explicit instructions telling him where to meet a Gulfstream jet at an abandoned Spanish air base."

Samantha's jaw dropped.

"Sound familiar?" Hastings leaned on the table. "After the code was broken it didn't take long for Acerbi's people to identify the man in Norway who sent the message. His name is Steig Lundahl."

"Why does that name seem so familiar?" Samantha wondered out loud.

"Probably because Pope Michael was known as Marcus Lundahl before he became the pope," Hastings observed. "Steig Lundahl is the late

134

pope's brother. We have no idea why the cardinal was meeting with him, but luckily they both escaped before Acerbi's forces arrived at Lundahl's isolated lodge. Acerbi was furious that they got away, but he knew the transmission from Norway was received somewhere in the Pyrenees. He smelled blood in the water and had the satellite surveillance over the area tripled. In a matter of hours they had discovered the camouflaged outline of what appeared to be a castle at the top of a mountain near the French town of Foix."

"The Cathars?" Samantha asked.

"That would be my guess. We know that entire families in the area presumably fled into the mountains and disappeared after Acerbi came to power, and rumors have been swirling for months that the cardinal and some of his Israeli friends are with them."

Samantha's eyes narrowed. "Acerbi's done something to them, hasn't he?"

"Yes." Hastings lowered her eyes. "He ordered a drone strike on the castle early this morning."

"What!" Samantha's entire body felt cold. "That's not possible! I mean, I would have known about such an attack."

"You were gone, Commander." Hastings reached into the blue folder and pulled out some satellite photos that had recorded the aftermath of the attack in vivid color. "Apparently, Acerbi himself ordered the attack. He wanted to give the cardinal a homecoming he would never forget."

"Where's the cardinal now?"

"Intelligence from one of our operatives in Oslo points to the fact that he flew out of Norway in a small jet around the same time as the attack on the castle, but according to air traffic control the plane disappeared from radar over the North Sea shortly after takeoff."

"Crashed?"

Hastings winked. "We believe that's what they wanted everyone to think. Apparently, the people at Acerbi's space intelligence division were also suspicious. They thought to check the satellite images of the abandoned air base in Spain to see if the jet turned up there, but all they saw were empty runways and buildings. After they were through analyzing the digital images they turned them over to us for further evaluation. Of course, being new to their jobs, they failed to look for heat signatures. Take a look at this." Hastings handed a black and white digital photo to Samantha.

"Looks like an infrared photo," Samantha said.

"It was taken with a special thermographic camera inside a so-called *weather* satellite we use from time to time. We still have a lot of toys that Acerbi's people don't know about." Hastings pointed to the photo. "Notice how that hangar behind the tower seems to be glowing white … while all the others are dark?"

Samantha exhaled. "I'm an air commander. I've studied hundreds of satellite photos before. It's pretty obvious that there is some kind of heat source inside that hangar."

"Bingo!" Hastings pointed again. "See those two black objects … the ones that look like giant seed pods spaced about twelve feet apart?"

"Yeah." Samantha squinted as she held up the photo. "What are those things?"

"The source of the heat. You're looking at the heat signatures of two very warm objects inside the hangar. Right away we knew we were looking at two jet engines cooling down, and when we compared their size and location to the placement of the engines at the back of a Lear 25, we came up with an exact match. There is a jet in that hangar … the same kind of jet that disappeared over the North Sea. It looks like the cardinal has returned to the Pyrenees, Commander."

Samantha rubbed her chin as she stared at the photo. "Why are you showing me this?"

"Because we've decided to help him, and you could play a major role in that."

"Help him?" Samantha asked. "I mean, what possible use could he be to us? Why not focus on a military coup instead? We could take Acerbi down from the inside. I know a lot of military men and women who would probably jump at the chance."

"We've already thought of that," Yates said, "but organizing the successful coup within a military organization as large as the one Acerbi commands would prove to be an impossible task. By nature, a military force depends on people following orders without asking questions, and those who don't follow along like good little ducks soon find themselves out of a job. In order to succeed, this revolt must come from the people, and right now the cardinal has become the de facto face of the resistance. This latest atrocity by Acerbi's men against peaceful families will only serve to weaken his popular support. People will start to look for a new hero, and if we throw our support behind the cardinal, we may be able to keep him alive until Acerbi's house of cards comes tumbling down."

Samantha unconsciously clenched her fists into tight balls. "You do know what you're dealing with, right? Adrian Acerbi is a man who is unnervingly single-minded and totally ruthless when it comes to achieving his goals. You don't know him like I do."

"Exactly! We *don't* know him like you do … which is why you will be so valuable to us." Hastings pulled out a cell phone and handed it to Samantha. "I want you to call the duty officer at your base and tell him the battery on your cell phone died. Let him know exactly where you're calling from and tell him you'll be back in your office in the morning. As soon as you're finished speaking, leave that phone on the table and go out the same way you came in. We'll contact you in a few days. For now you'll be dealing only with us. If anyone else tells you they're working with us play stupid and wait for our next contact. If we think they're on to you we'll move you to a safe house."

"But how will you contact me?"

"We want you to sign up for a night course at a local college. Pick something like a foreign language to make it look like you are trying to increase your advancement potential in the military."

"Why?"

"A college campus is one of the best places to meet other people without raising suspicion. The CIA uses them all the time for clandestine meetings. We especially like the library."

Hastings stood erect. For the first time in a long time she felt like she was returning to the job she had been born to do. Through Samantha, she had finally found a way back to the tradecraft of secret meetings made in the shadow of overwhelming power, and if anyone had been born with a genetic predisposition toward becoming a working intelligence officer, MI6 officer Gwyneth Hastings was that person.

"Remember, Samantha," Hastings concluded, "we always try to keep things simple, because in our line of work the simplest plans usually work the best. Trust your instincts. We've heard this Acerbi guy can be a real spooky character, but try not to let him get under your skin. He's just a man … and any man can be broken. Now, don't forget to leave that phone here after you call your base."

Without so much as a handshake, the two intelligence officers opened the door and walked out of the room. After staring blankly at the green walls for a few minutes, Samantha made the call to the duty officer and left the phone on the table before making her way out of the building.

Outside, she could smell the river on a fresh breeze that stirred the leaves along the lighted walkway that led to her car. Once inside, she released the band holding her long red hair and let it flow out over her shoulders.

Spooky.

The word made Samantha smile as she sped away from the building. It was a very fitting word to describe a man like Adrian Acerbi. The intelligence guys had nailed it. They were all dealing with a very *spooky* guy.

CHAPTER 26

As soon as Gael led the men into the torch-lit cavern, Leo spotted a pair of dark brown eyes looking back at him from the center of a huddled group of children. Dropping his backpack, he pushed his way through the damp crowded space and took Evita in his arms, lifting her up and holding her tight.

She was alive! For now that was all that mattered. He felt a renewed strength coursing through his veins, and no matter what happened next, they would be together, for he vowed then and there that he would never leave her behind again.

For some reason, memories of Eduardo Acerbi and his wife Colette filled his thoughts. He had never seen a couple so devoted to one another. For over forty years, after Eduardo had given up a huge fortune and disappeared without a trace to be with the woman he loved, they had lived a quiet and peaceful life together, hidden from the glare of an increasingly intrusive world in a small French farmhouse.

Theirs had been a true love story, and for the first time in his life Leo was able to identify with the unshakeable bond he had observed through the years between couples in love. Now, holding Evita in his arms, he finally understood why Eduardo had abandoned a life of wealth and privilege so that he and Colette could live together in peace, for if a man truly loves a woman he will do whatever he has to do in order to keep her safe.

"I thought I'd never see you again," Evita said, her tear-filled eyes peering up into his.

Leo held her tighter. "What happened?"

"The attack?"

"Yes. How did they find you?"

"We have no idea. It was a beautiful morning. I had just taken a group of children to play by the lake when a missile flew right over our heads and hit the warehouse. The force of the explosion knocked us off our feet, and when I looked up there was smoke everywhere and people were running outside to see what had happened. That's when the second missile hit the castle. After that all I remember is running with the children toward the waterfall."

Evita buried her head in Leo's shoulder and sobbed quietly. "Not everyone made it out."

Looking around the cavern, Leo estimated there were at least a hundred survivors crowded together in the tight space. "Is this everyone?"

Evita's fingers dug into Leo's sleeve as she peered over her shoulder. "I'm not sure. People were running in every direction. By the time the children and I reached the cave behind the waterfall the third missile hit the castle. It was a classic drone attack … with multiple drones firing from different directions. As soon as we saw the castle collapse we moved away from the cave entrance and never looked back."

"Cardinal!" Leo felt a thunderous clap on his back and looked up to see Alon supporting Nava as she limped along at his side.

"Alon … Nava! Thank God you're both safe. What about the others?"

Alon hesitated. "John and Ariella are missing, along with many others."

"Missing? What do you mean, *missing?*"

"I mean they didn't make it into the caves with the rest of us, but that doesn't mean they're dead. We saw several people lowering themselves over the walls to the steep paths that lead down to the base of the mountain, so unless Acerbi's men were waiting for them, it's possible they escaped into the forest."

"Where's Lev?"

Alon's eyes darted to a dark corner. "Over there with Bishop Morelli and Moshe. He's not taking this very well. Ariella was the light of his life. Danny Zamir and Francois Leander are trying to organize a group to go look for them, but the Cathars think it's still too dangerous."

"Where's Julian?"

"Also MIA, along with Colette and the two Muslim families." Alon nodded toward one end of the cave. "Javier Mendoza and Dr. Diaz are in a side tunnel helping with some of the wounded."

Alon lowered Nava to the cave floor and peeled back a jagged tear in her jeans to expose a bloody gash. "Looks like a piece of shrapnel nicked your leg below the knee. Doesn't look too deep. I'll check with the medics to see if they have some antibacterial ointment in their field kits before we put a bandage on it."

With Alon gone, Nava coiled up next to Leo and Evita and watched Lev talking quietly with Morelli. "He's devastated, you know. He's hardly spoken to anyone since the attack. He thought Ariella and John were ahead of him, but once he found out they never made it into the cave, Alon and Moshe had to physically restrain him to keep him from running back outside. I've never seen Lev like that before. He was like a wild man."

"Ever seen a tiger when one of its young are threatened?" Evita asked.

Nava smiled. "I guess I'd probably act the same way."

"No. You'd be much worse," Evita said. "Lev's a man and you're a woman. Mama tigers are much quicker to attack when one of their babies are threatened."

Leo squeezed Evita's arm. "I'm going to go talk to him. I'll be right back."

"Take your time," she said, "He needs his friends around him now."

Leo slowly made his way past huddled groups of people. Some were totally unharmed, while others had sustained injuries ranging from cuts and bruises to broken bones and worse—like the people with gaping head wounds who should have been in the operating room of a trauma center instead of languishing on the damp floor of a cave, their golden hour long past.

In a single day of mindless violence, the lives of the people close to him had been ripped away. Their world of air and light had been replaced by a primitive hand-to-mouth existence in a dark cave that existed on the fringes of a world-wide society that appeared to be thriving under Acerbi's leadership, but just like their ancestors, they had made a conscious decision to walk their own path, even if that path led them to an early death at the hands of those who worshipped a dark god. They had been born in the love of a God of light and they would return to that light, for there was one thing Acerbi would never control, and that was their souls.

"Hello, Lev," Leo said quietly, sitting beside him.

Staring off into space, Lev's curly gray hair hung down in wet rivulets across his forehead—his eyes vacant pools, as if he was listening to an internal dialogue only he could hear. Looking up, he blinked hard. "Leo?"

"How are you doing, my friend?"

"I can't believe you made it back to us."

"I almost didn't. I just heard that Ariella and John are still missing, but we're talking about two of the most resourceful people I know. They're out there somewhere, and we'll find them."

"We've got to go!" Ben eyes were wild as he raced to the back of the cave and reached out to grab Lev by the arm. "Now!"

Lev stumbled to his feet. "What is it?!"

"Our gas detectors are lighting up. I think Acerbi's men are flooding the caves with gas!" Ben cupped his hands around his mouth and shouted. "We need to evacuate back out the same way we came in."

In an instant the cave became a thrashing mass of arms and legs as everyone grabbed what they could and walked, ran, limped, or were carried as they tried to escape the ghostly tendrils of the approaching gas.

"How fast can gas travel underground?" Evita asked Ben as they ran.

"It depends on what kind of gas they're using and where they're injecting it into the cave system. Caves actually breathe. They're like giant lungs, and once a gas is introduced into an underground environment it mixes with the subterranean air currents and gets pulled through the entire system."

Looking down at his gas detector, Ben saw the indicator light flashing yellow. "We need to be breathing fresh air in the next fifteen minutes!"

Ahead, they could see the glimmer from the gold-streaked marble in the towering cathedral-like space near the exit. Together they struggled, the strong helping the weak as they lifted stretchers and passed them from one pair of willing hands to another across small chasms and around subterranean boulders, until finally they reached the cave entrance and came spilling out into the daylight before collapsing along the path that led down to the lake of dark waters.

By now the sun was high overhead and the early morning dew had long since disappeared as Leo and Evita collapsed on the warm grass and filled their lungs with fresh air. But something wasn't right. Leo's thinking had become cloudy, and farther down the path he could hear shouting. His vision was becoming dimmer, and glancing to his left, he saw that Evita appeared to be sleeping on the grass next to him.

Suddenly, like a large bird swooping overhead, a dark shadow blotted out the sun. Struggling to lift his head, Leo knew he must be feeling the effects of the gas as he drifted between the two worlds of reality and dreams.

What is that? He thought. *What's blocking the sun?*

And then he heard the voice.

"Hello, Cardinal. It's so good to finally see you again. Maybe now we can have that nice long chat I've been looking forward to for so long."

Leo strained to make out the shape hovering above him, but the darkness was almost complete as his eyes rolled up into his head and his body slumped against Evita's sleeping shoulder.

Removing a pair of expensive-looking, black leather gloves, Adrian Acerbi looked down on Leo and watched his chest rise and fall.

He didn't want him dead ... at least not yet.

Standing next to Adrian, his ground commander looked out over all the people sprawled along the path leading from the cave. "Looks like we finally got them, sir. What do you want ...?"

The commander's lips froze in mid-sentence. Acerbi's eyes were fixated on the cardinal's gold ring, and as the sun's light glinted against the raised image of the cross, Adrian's entire body seemed to blur into—into *what?*

Unsure of what he had just seen, the shaken commander stepped back. "Are you alright, sir?"

Acerbi quickly looked away. "What did you say?"

"I asked if you were alright, sir."

"Of course." Acerbi eyed the commander for any sign of fear. "Nice job, Commander. Have your men transport these people to the staging area and have the choppers fly them back to our base at Foix. Make sure the wounded get priority at the local hospital. This is supposed to look like a rescue mission, and the more people we save the better we look."

"Yes, sir ... no problem. We'll make sure the prisoners are all well cared for until you decide what you want us to do with them. What about the cardinal? Any special instructions?"

Acerbi paused. "No, just keep them all comfortable. I want the world to see that we went to great lengths to rescue these people even though they opposed the government that just saved them. Let's see how well the cardinal's rhetoric plays out in the court of public opinion now."

143

CHAPTER 27

With no moon to reflect off the white sand bordering the mouth of the Aude River, earth and ocean merged into an inky point in the distance, where only the synchronous roar of the waves crashing against a distant French beach told Daniel and Sarah that their small rubber boat was nearing land.

Behind them, the crew of the *Tekuma* kept a sharp lookout for any approaching boats as the Israeli sub rose and fell in rhythm with the sea a few hundred yards offshore. On her last trip here, she had delivered Israeli Team 5 to the beach, and the plan had been to call them to meet the sub when it arrived, but the plan had changed.

The sudden appearance of Acerbi's forces at the rendezvous point off the coast of Lebanon had confirmed the fact to the *Tekuma's* security officer that their transmitter codes had been compromised, and until they could prove otherwise they weren't about to risk giving away the sub's position.

In other words, there would no call to Team 5 alerting them to the fact that Daniel and Sarah had been delivered to France as ordered. The survival of the sub remained a top priority, meaning the crew would be forced to leave them on a deserted beach at night to search for their friends on their own.

An unseen wave washed across the bow of the small boat just as they heard the sandpaper-like rub of the boat's rubber hull sliding against the wet sand. A following wave pushed them closer to the beach, scattering small fish and hermit crabs that darted off in the shallow water.

Jumping out, a Special Forces soldier wearing a black wetsuit held the boat at the edge of the surf, while Daniel and Sarah slid over the side and walked up onto the dry sand.

"Sorry to leave you two here like this," the soldier said. "To tell you the truth I wish we were going with you to join up with Team 5, but we have orders to remain with the sub. The captain wanted us to hurry things up because we have a pre-planned rendezvous with a tanker offshore in a few hours to take on some diesel fuel, but after that I have no idea where we're headed. Sometimes I think it would be better if we just parked the thing."

Daniel hefted his backpack over his shoulder and looked back at the soldier. "That may actually prove to be a good way to stay hidden."

"What ... park the boat?"

"Well, it's certainly not my place to tell sub captains how to run their boats, but if I was the captain of the *Tekuma* I think I'd give some serious thought to getting as far away from the Mediterranean as possible and looking for a deep river to hide in for a while. The *Tekuma* may be one of the most sophisticated conventional subs ever built, but she still relies on diesel engines to charge her batteries. No matter how quiet you try to be, sooner or later one of Acerbi's nuclear-powered hunter-killer subs will hear you. After that it will only be a matter of time before the rest of the pack closes in."

The soldier frowned back through the dripping salt water running down his face. "I'll be sure to relay that little piece of advice to the executive officer when we get back on board. Right now our biggest problem is our inability to communicate with our home base, and we haven't heard from the British sub for weeks. With the burst transmitters compromised we're totally cut off."

"Tell the security officer to keep your transmitter turned on but only in the passive receive mode. Even if the codes have been compromised there may be a way we can work around Acerbi's computers and start using them again."

The soldier braced for an incoming wave. "How would something like that work?"

"Well for one we could set up an encryption code that mutates in a random pattern that would make it virtually impossible for a computer to unravel because it's constantly changing."

"A code that mutates?"

"Yeah," Daniel said. "It's not really a new concept. The problem is getting the burst transmitters to accept new access codes, which requires a key that would have to be physically delivered to the boats."

The man gave Daniel the same kind of look usually reserved for college students taking their first physics class. "I'm not sure I'm following you, sir."

"Think about shooting at a moving object," Daniel shouted over the roar of the surf. "You don't shoot at the object ... you shoot where you think it will be. That's how a mutating code works ... the key tells you when to pull the trigger. Kind of like putting a key in a lock but waiting for the right signal to open the door."

A dark wave crashed into the small boat as the two soldiers jumped inside. "If you say so, sir," the soldier called out. "Good luck to you and your wife. I'll tell the security officer what you said, so if you get that transmitter thing figured out give us a call."

"Will do," Daniel shouted into the salt spray. "And thanks for the ride."

Walking back up on the beach, he saw Sarah sitting quietly and looking up at the stars. "Well, here we are," he said, throwing himself down on the sand beside her.

"Is this the romantic European vacation you've always promised?" she giggled.

"Hey, at least we're out of Lebanon."

"Yeah ... at least that." Sarah pursed her lips in a mock frown. "Do you speak French?"

"Uh ... no, do you?"

"Not a word."

"Well, that shouldn't be much of a problem here in France." Daniel grinned. "I think by now they've grown pretty used to people tromping around their country who don't speak the language."

"Speaking of people tromping around the country, what about the facial recognition cameras?" Sarah asked. "I mean, they're pretty much everywhere now, especially in public places like train stations and airports."

"We won't be headed for any cities. We'll stick to the small roads and villages and camp in the forest outside of Foix."

"Foix? Do you think that's smart?"

"I think the place is worth scouting out. I know they're living somewhere close by. The only trick is trying to find them without giving ourselves away by asking too many questions." Daniel stood and brushed off the sand. "Come on. Let's get off this beach before the sun comes up."

CHAPTER 28

Leo's back was twisted in an awkward position when he opened his eyes. At first all he could see were colors, but as his vision began to return to normal, the colors became shapes, and the shapes became people.

Curled on one side he found it difficult to move, and when he looked down, he saw the reason why. Surrounded by at least a hundred other people, he was handcuffed to a metal cable that ran along the floor of a large cargo plane, and the muted whine from the turbo prop engines told him they were in the air. Still foggy from the gas, he tried to remember what had happened. He remembered the cave, walking out into the fresh air and feeling dizzy—but there was something else!

Acerbi! His black eyes had been looking down at him when he drifted off. Somehow, he had found them, and now they were all chained to the floor of a cargo plane en route to—where?

Straightening himself to a sitting position, he uttered a quick prayer of thanks when he saw Evita next to him, still sleeping soundly.

Gently, he nudged her. "Evita!"

Slowly she stirred, pulling at her restraints. "Ow! What the ..."

"We're handcuffed."

"Handcuffed? Where are we?"

"I'm guessing we're in one of Acerbi's planes. He must have gassed the entire cave system to flush us out."

Evita blinked to clear her vision. "You mean we're his prisoners?"

"At least for now." Leo winked as he looked down a line of huddled men, women, and children. A man dressed in black fatigues was walking toward them.

"We'll be landing at an airbase north of London in about fifteen minutes," the man announced. "As soon as we land you'll all be taken to a comfortable hotel. I believe they have lunch waiting for you."

"Where's Acerbi?" Leo asked.

The man smiled. "Mr. Acerbi is on a different aircraft, sir. You are all his guests, and I've been told you'll have plenty of time to speak with him later."

Evita held up her arms and wiggled her wrists in the handcuffs. "Funny way to treat guests, don't you think?"

"Oh, those," the man chuckled. "We had to restrain you for your own safety during the flight. We'll get you out of those as soon as we land." Stepping carefully, the man turned away and made his way back along a line of chained *guests* to the front of the aircraft.

"I'd love to know what Acerbi is up to," Evita whispered to Leo. "He could have killed us all in France and no one would have been the wiser. It's obvious he wants us alive for some reason, and that makes me even more nervous."

"Actually, I think all of this fits his twisted personality perfectly," Leo said. "He's still trying to play the role of savior, only this time it won't work. A lot of innocent people died in the attack on the castle. He has blood on his hands now, and no matter how he tries to paint the truth, sooner or later the real story will get out."

"I think you've forgotten that the man paints the truth with a very wide brush," Evita whispered back, "and if I'm right, we're about to become a cog in his propaganda machine."

A jarring thump accompanied by the screech of tires told everyone on board that they had landed. Turning off the active runway, the big cargo plane lumbered past a row of hangars before stopping next to a line of waiting buses. Entering the aircraft through a side door, a group of mostly female soldiers began removing the handcuffs as they handed out bottles of much-needed water with sympathetic nods.

Rubbing his wrists, Alon moved in next to Leo as the main loading ramp at the back of the aircraft was lowered to the ground.

"What do you think they'll do with us?"

"I have no idea." Leo noticed that Alon was flexing his jaw muscles; a sure sign to anyone who knew him that the big Israeli commando was preparing for a fight.

"Let's not do anything to antagonize them just yet," Leo cautioned. "We need to put on our most cooperative faces until we know exactly what they're up to. If the past is any indication of the future it won't be long before Acerbi tires of this game of pretend, and when that happens we'd better have a rock-solid plan for escape."

Standing by the cargo door, the man in black fatigues held up his hand. "We'd like the cardinal to exit the aircraft first."

Leo reached out and took Evita by the hand. "She's coming with me."

The man grinned back like a hungry salesman. "Of course, sir ... as you wish."

Together, Leo and Evita slowly descended the ramp at the back of the aircraft into a fresh breeze. Blinking in the sunlight, they could smell the green of the English countryside as a crush of waiting reporters grappled with their cameras and thrust their microphones ahead like spears as they surged forward, hurling questions at the disoriented survivors.

Accompanied by a squad of soldiers, the smiling man in black fatigues wasn't smiling anymore. "Back off!" he bellowed to the reporters. "This was only supposed to be a photo op. There will be no questions until these people have recovered from their ordeal. Now please, clear a path to the buses."

Ignoring the man's request, a reporter wearing thick black glasses held up a skinny arm. "Cardinal Amodeo! Why did you abandon your church?"

Instantly the reporter was grabbed by two soldiers and muscled into a waiting Humvee. The response by the soldiers seemed out of proportion to the question, but what really grabbed Leo's attention was the reaction of the other reporters. None of them seemed the least bit surprised at their colleague's question or the harsh treatment he received at the hands of Acerbi's soldiers, and in a move that looked almost orchestrated, the rest of them shuffled away without complaint.

These people didn't act like normal reporters.

Of course! They all worked for Acerbi. In the months since he had come to power, the press had been swallowed by his immense corporate machine, and the questioning journalists of old had been quietly shoved into early retirement, while a new breed of Acerbi corporate reporters had been moved into top power positions in every news organization in the world.

To the public at large, it appeared as if nothing had changed. Except for the Acerbi corporate logo at the bottom of their screens, the news they received from their television and computer screens still looked the same. But what they didn't know was that they were all looking at a well-orchestrated illusion, because in truth, the people of the world were now receiving all of their information through the filter of a massive communications empire that controlled every media outlet in the world.

151

The truth had become the lie, and the lie had become the truth. Any story having to do with Acerbi was carefully scrutinized by censors and choreographed to make him look like a benevolent and philanthropic father figure, and anything he did, no matter how questionable it might seem, was always met by his stated philosophy that sometimes the end justified the means, especially when they were dealing with something as important as world peace.

Leo's eyes drifted across the tarmac to the reporter with thick glasses sitting in the back of the Humvee.

He was smiling and joking with the soldiers!

They were being set up!

They had all just become actors in a well-rehearsed show! The so-called rescue in France—the outward display of concern for the survivors in front of the cameras as they were being helped off the plane—the waiting buses that would take them to a *hotel* for some much-needed food and rest. It was all a very convincing act that would soon be showing on television screens all over the world.

People would be able to see with their own eyes that Adrian Acerbi treated even those who opposed him with dignity and respect, and the question asked by the so-called reporter had been cleverly designed to make Leo look like a weak man who had deserted his flock in the eyes of the public.

Acerbi had played out his little charade perfectly. He was systematically destroying everything Leo had ever stood for, and he was winning.

But what exactly was his end game?

"We really need to get moving." The man in black fatigues motioned to Leo and Evita. "Would you two please board the first bus?"

"We'll board after the others," Leo shot back.

Without bothering to reply the man turned away and ushered the others into the buses while Leo and Evita waited patiently. When they were sure no one had been left behind, they stepped up into the air-conditioned hum of the motor coach.

Slowly the bus rolled away from the flight line, but as soon as it rounded the corner of a hangar Leo saw something through his window that caught his attention. Standing next to an official-looking black car that sprouted a small forest of antennas from its roof, he spotted a red-haired woman wearing a flight suit—and she was looking directly at him.

CHAPTER 29

The ground was wet, and John's hands were shaking so badly that he was having a hard time trying to start a fire.

"Want me to try?" Ariella asked.

"I think I can do it." John struck another match against the nest-like bundle of tinder he had gathered, and a few seconds later smoke was stinging his eyes. At last they had fire, and for the first time in two days they began to feel some hope as the leaping flames chased the frigid embrace of the chilled mountain air from their bodies.

The attack on the castle had happened so suddenly that there had been no time for a warning. The day had dawned under a brilliant blue sky, and John and Ariella had been taking their usual morning walk around the small lake in front of the castle when the first missile hit the warehouse.

For a few seconds they had just stood there, mesmerized by the rising column of fire and unable to comprehend what they had just seen. People were running from the castle, and as they gathered outside on the manicured grounds to see what had happened, another missile came streaking overhead and hit the castle, while a second appeared over the horizon from a different direction and struck the opposite side in an apparent coordinated attack.

With nowhere to run, John and Ariella had flattened themselves on the grass until the attack was over, and when they looked up they had seen scattered groups of men, women, and children—all running toward the cave at the base of the waterfall.

Lifting themselves off the ground, they sprinted toward the burning castle to see if they could help, but already the front of the weakened structure had begun to collapse, making any attempt to rescue people trapped inside impossible. Fighting their natural instinct to run, they made their way around to the back of the castle to see if they could help anyone there but were met by a thick wall of smoke billowing from an impenetrable mass of swirling, tornado-like columns of fire that danced inside what had once been the great hall.

It was time to go.

They had made it halfway to the waterfall when they had spotted the first choppers rising up from the valley below. Skimming over the walls, John and Ariella watched them fire rockets into the compound before slowing to a hover as Acerbi's soldiers began rappelling down onto a field of craters that now dotted the park-like area in front of the castle.

For John and Ariella time had run out. They would never make it to the waterfall. In a matter of seconds more soldiers would be swarming over the grounds, blocking any hope of escaping down into the mountain. Their only way out was up, which meant they would have to climb the mountain behind the castle.

For two miserable days and nights following the attack they had clung to life in the shadowed crevices of a heavily-forested area above the smoking remains of the castle. The spring cold front that had descended on the Pyrenees had brought snow to the higher elevations, and with no food and suffering from the biting cold, John knew their options were running out as he looked through the binoculars at the pockmarked grounds below.

The soldiers were gone!

Moving cautiously and fearing a trap, they climbed down from their rocky nest and approached the blackened remains of what had once been their home. Evidence of the short occupation by Acerbi's troops was everywhere in the form of muddy boot prints and other battlefield debris, but the soldiers themselves were gone. Thankfully there were no bodies. Apparently, Acerbi's men had removed the ones they had found lying in the open, but John felt there might still be others buried beneath the collapsed stone walls.

Looking out over the scene of devastation, John began walking toward the castle, but Ariella reached out and stopped him. "I know what you're thinking, John," she said, "but there's no way anyone in there is still alive. The fire consumed everything, and it would take heavy equipment to move all of those gigantic blocks of stone. I promise that if we survive we'll return someday and build a fitting monument to their sacrifice."

Nodding silently, John turned away and walked under one of the few trees that still remained standing in the park-like area. Gathering some dry tree limbs, he started another fire while Ariella scooped up a singed blanket and a few unopened MRE packs left lying around by Acerbi's soldiers.

For a moment John felt the creeping sensation that they were being watched, making him wonder if Acerbi's forces might have left a few hidden cameras behind to see if anyone returned.

Remaining in the area was no longer an option.

They would have to keep moving … down to the warmer air below where they could begin searching the forest for the others … if there were others.

There had to be! Ariella told herself. She had seen at least a hundred people make it into the cave behind the waterfall.

"Should we try the cave?" she asked.

Scooping out the remainder of what appeared to be apple cobbler from an MRE pack, John looked toward the waterfall. "We can take a look, but I'd be surprised if Acerbi's men haven't blown the entrance already. If they haven't it's probably booby trapped."

Ariella rubbed her exposed arms and piled her long brown hair on top of her head before covering it with a knit ski hat she had found lying on the grass. "Let's go, John. This place is giving me the creeps."

"Yeah, it feels different here now. This was such a beautiful place, but it was the people who lived here that made it so special. We need to start looking for the ones who escaped down into the tunnels behind the waterfall. They might have made their way out into the forest by now."

"I saw my father!" Ariella blurted out suddenly.

"What?"

"I saw my father … the day of the attack. He was with Alon and Nava. They were running toward the waterfall with a young woman and some children. Alon had a kid under each arm when he ran into the cave."

John stared back at Ariella without speaking.

Why had she waited until now to tell him?

For the first time he noticed that his wife's eyes had taken on a faraway look, and she seemed quieter than usual. Maybe the food they had just eaten would help, but he didn't like what he was seeing. She seemed exhausted. They both were, but it was obvious Ariella had hit some kind of emotional wall, and the energetic spark that had always driven her seemed to be growing dimmer.

John wrapped his arms around her and drew her close. "That's great news, sweetheart. At least we know he's still alive."

"I tried to look for others," she continued, "but I didn't see anyone else running toward the waterfall after Alon made it through. Israeli Team

5 still hasn't returned from that airfield in Spain with Leo, and Daniel and Sarah seem to have fallen off the face of the earth." Ariella's lips began to tremble as she laid her head on John's shoulder. "We're losing all of our friends, John. Acerbi is winning."

"We don't know that, Ariella. At least we're together, and we'll find the others. We know they're out there somewhere."

"Why don't we go into town?"

"Town! You mean Foix?"

"Yes … that's exactly where I think we should go."

"That's crazy, Ariella. We'd be spotted by the surveillance cameras the moment we entered the city."

"Maybe not. Baseball caps and sunglasses seem to confuse the facial recognition software, and we need supplies. Who knows … some of the others may be there too. It's worth a try."

"I have a better idea," John said. "Why don't we try to link up with Team 5 at that abandoned airbase in Spain?"

"Fine … whatever." She shifted listlessly, but John had seen the first glimmer of fire returning to her eyes. "I think wandering aimlessly through the forest looking for the others would be useless at this point. Our chances of finding our friends anytime soon is probably close to zero, John, and we still need supplies. We need warmer jackets, some sleeping bags, food … plus something to carry it all in."

"Do you have any money?"

"A little." Ariella reached down and pulled a small wad of cash from the back pocket of her jeans.

"I can't believe you still have that."

"I didn't have anywhere to spend it," she smiled.

For a few precious minutes they lingered in front of the warming fire before John finally agreed. "Alright, Ariella … we'll do it your way." Taking a final look around the once-beautiful grounds, he kicked at the dying fire. "Let's go."

* * *

With their baseball caps pulled down low, John and Ariella made their way down a rocky path to the base of the mountain and crossed a muddy field to the highway. The first car they saw stopped.

Driving an aged yellow Citroen, a middle-aged woman waved the pair into her car.

"Thank you for stopping," Ariella said. "Are you headed to Foix?"

"Yes … lived there most of my life," the woman answered in English. "You two been camping or something?"

"We ran out of supplies," Ariella smiled. "We thought we could make it to town and back before it gets dark."

"Well it's a pretty long way if you're walking." The woman glanced out her side window. "My husband said he saw a lot of smoke coming from the mountain a couple of days ago. Any idea what started it?"

"Could have been lightning," John answered quickly, "but our campsite was too far away to see what was burning."

"It's supposed to get colder tonight." The woman eased off the gas and downshifted before entering a tight curve in the road ahead. "Maybe you two should get a hotel. I've never liked camping myself. I don't really see the point when there's a comfortable hotel with dry sheets and hot water just down the road … a fact my husband doesn't seem to grasp. He loves to camp, but I refuse to go. I mean, just look at the two of you. You're still shivering."

John gave the woman a weak smile. "I guess it depends on your comfort level. Sometimes it's good to spend some time out in our natural environment."

"You mean *unnatural* environment!" The woman laughed out loud. "I know right where to take you."

"I beg your pardon?" Ariella asked."

"The best camping store in Foix. A friend of ours owns the place. I'll make sure he gives you a good deal. Are you two on your honeymoon?"

"No … we've been married for a couple of years now." Ariella bit her lower lip as she glanced over at John. *Whose car had they just gotten into?* This woman was a non-stop question machine. Studying the woman's profile, Ariella decided to ask a few questions of her own. "Your English has an American accent to it. Is that where you're from?"

"Yes, but I've lived in Foix since I was a teenager. I guess you never lose the accent. My husband and I …" The woman paused to squint through the windshield. "Oh damn … another roadblock!"

John froze when he saw the flashing blue lights on the road ahead. "What is it?"

"Oh, it's just another bother," the woman grumped. "The military has been setting up roadblocks on the roads around here for the past several weeks. It's a real pain. All this talk from this Acerbi guy about how he wants to simplify things by eliminating borders. If you ask me things have only gotten worse. His soldiers can stop you anytime they want for no reason, and there's nothing you can do about it."

Ariella reached across the seat and grabbed the woman's arm. "Turn around!"

"What?!"

"I said turn around. We lost our ID cards when we were hiking."

"No can do, honey," the woman said. "If I turn around now they'll only come after us for evading one of their checkpoints. I've seen it happen before."

"Maybe you could just pull over and let us out," John said. "We'll walk back to our campsite and look for our ID's."

"Too late for that." The woman tapped nervously on the steering wheel. "They've already got us in their sights. Just tell them what happened. I'm sure they'll understand."

With nowhere to go and their options quickly running out, John and Ariella held their breath as the car slowed to a stop in a sea of flashing blue lights. Turning away from a group of laughing soldiers that were standing in front of a massive armored vehicle, a stern-looking sergeant approached the car.

"ID cards, please."

Rummaging through her purse, the woman finally produced her card. "Here you go. My two friends here were camping in the mountains and lost their cards. I picked them up a few miles back and offered them a ride into town. Can they get new cards in Foix?"

Listening in on the conversation, a young officer walked over to the car. "More hitchhikers?"

"Yes, sir," the sergeant answered. "And they don't have ID's."

"Scan them."

"Yes, sir." The sergeant motioned to John and Ariella. "Please step out of the car."

"Why?" Ariella could feel her whole body shaking. "We haven't done anything wrong."

"Sorry, miss, but since you two don't have ID cards we'll have to scan you. Won't take but a minute. Once you're cleared you can get new cards at our office in Foix. Follow me, please."

With any chance of escape pegged at zero, John and Ariella followed the sergeant into the back of a large truck.

"You'll need to remove your hats and sunglasses for the facial recognition scan," the sergeant said, motioning John to a seat in front of a camera plugged into a computer. "Just look at the camera."

A few seconds later the sergeant's eyes grew wide as he ripped a sheet of paper from the printer and handed it to the officer standing behind him.

"Cuff them and put them in the van with the other two." The officer's command had come in the flat bureaucratic monotone of a man just doing his job.

"Are you arresting us?" John asked

"Yes we are, Mr. Lowe." The officer calmly folded the sheet of paper and shoved it in his shirt pocket. "And please don't try to run. I don't feel like filling out any death forms today."

John and Ariella stared into each other's eyes as the soldiers handcuffed them and led them from the large truck to a waiting van. Fumbling with his keys, a soldier unlocked the back door and pulled it open

Climbing up into the back of the van, John and Ariella were stunned when they saw Daniel and Sarah staring back at them.

"Well, at least we found them," Daniel said, smiling weakly at Sarah.

CHAPTER 30

A thick fog had moved in, obscuring the grounds surrounding the grand hotel where Leo and the others had been taken. Surprisingly, they had been allowed to roam the facility at will, taking their meals in the hotel's dining room and indulging their children with swims in the indoor swimming pool, but despite the outward show of hospitality, the ring of soldiers surrounding the building served as a constant reminder that they had been encased in a gilded cage provided by a man who had already made it obvious that human life held no value.

The swarm of media attention and aura of hype surrounding their arrival had dwindled, replaced instead by a subdued ambiance that matched the thickening fog. Throughout the day members of Acerbi's staff could be seen coming and going, but strangely, Acerbi himself had stayed away; a fact Leo and the others had taken note of.

Pulling aside the rose patterned curtains covering the windows of her room, Evita peered outside. She was tired of living in the shadows and hiding from the world, and she desperately wanted the fog to go away so that she could feel the warm sun on her skin again. Why didn't Acerbi just let them all go, she wondered. After all, he had proven his point.

What harm could they be to him now?

"Wishing won't make it go away," Leo said, watching her stare out at the fog from his chair across the room. "These coastal fogs in England can last for days."

"How do you know we're by the coast?"

"I don't, but I'm pretty sure the weather covering the lowlands outside is drifting in off the English Channel."

Evita turned from the window and fell back onto the bed. "How long is Acerbi going to keep us here? This is insane. We haven't been charged

161

with any crime, but we're not allowed to leave. This may be a comfortable prison he's created for us, but it's still a prison."

Leo crossed the room and sat on the edge of the bed. "The first chance we have to escape we'll take it. Until then we'll just have to play along. No matter how much we feel like standing up to him, we have to consider the children first. For now, we can only sit back and let him parade us around like the happy and cooperative guests he's trying to make us out to be and hope he lowers his guard. We only draw the line if he insists on making us swear allegiance to him in front of the cameras. That's a line I won't cross."

"Do you think that's what he wants?"

"I have no idea what he really wants, but …"

A loud commotion in front of the hotel drew Leo and Evita's attention to the window. Looking down at the circular drive that passed through the portico below, they saw that a line of soldiers had formed around a van that had just arrived.

"Look, Leo!" Evita cried out.

Stepping from the back of the van they saw John and Ariella followed by Daniel and Sarah, and from their perch behind the curtained window, they saw Lev trying to push his way through the soldiers in an effort to reach his daughter.

"I think this explains why Acerbi hasn't made an appearance yet," Leo said. "He's waiting until he has all of us in one location so no one outside can tell the world what really happened up on that mountaintop."

"Well, we're all here now!" Evita pounded her hands on the window sill. "How in the world did he find us?"

"Who knows," Leo said, placing an arm around her shoulders. "Lundahl told me that Acerbi's computers might have traced the last burst transmission from Norway before they shut it down, but we're dealing with a supernatural entity that has a technological advantage, and I'm sure he had other assets focused on the hunt for us." Leo watched their four friends entering the hotel before turning away from the window. "There's something else Lundahl told me. He said that Marcus had come to believe that Adrian isn't the Antichrist."

"What!?"

"I know … strange but true. He told me that Pope Michael had recently come up with a theory that Adrian was possessed by a demon posing as the prophesized Antichrist; that everything that was happening had originated from outside the existing framework given to us in the Book of Revelation. I didn't get to hear all of it, but according to Lundahl we seem to be caught in the middle of an unexpected event that is somehow connected to the continuing war between heaven and hell."

Evita blinked back at him. "But what about the code in the Bible … the references to Adrian Acerbi as the Antichrist? My God, Leo … he controls the entire world. What more proof do you need?"

"I thought the same thing at first, but when I was returning from Norway I remembered something that had been bothering me for quite some time. I always thought it was strange that Satan created a creature like the Antichrist by transforming him from a normal boy like Adrian Acerbi. It didn't make any sense."

"What do you mean?"

"Well, for one, we know that God's timetable and Satan's timetable for the end of days don't exactly coincide. We've always suspected that the Devil's book we discovered in the Negev Desert might have had the power to alter that timetable and give Satan a head start, and we've seen increasing evidence that the world is being seeded with demons right now. According to Pope Michael's theory, Adrian is evil incarnate, but he's not the Antichrist. He's something else. Think about it for a moment. The Antichrist wouldn't need to be transformed from an unwilling human host, which is exactly what happened to Adrian. I have a horrible feeling that we're missing an important piece of the puzzle, and the worst is yet to come."

"We've got to tell the others about this right away, Leo … and then we need to start looking for a way out of here. The world is spiraling toward the brink of extinction, and it's time for the *chosen ones* to begin fighting back."

"I was thinking the same thing," said a voice behind them. The two turned to see Bishop Anthony Morelli standing in the open doorway to the room. "If Marcus's theory about Acerbi is true, then we must know the true identity of the demon before we proceed, or risk being destroyed."

"And just how do you plan on doing that?" Evita asked.

"The chapel," Leo answered for Morelli. "I think I know what my good friend the bishop is trying to tell us. Somehow we've got to find our way back to Rome."

"Aren't you forgetting something?" Evita asked.

"What?"

"We're still Acerbi's prisoners."

163

* * *

On the third floor of the local college library, Gwyneth Hastings looked through an empty space in a long line of books and tapped her watch for the third time. Samantha Jennings was running late, and if she didn't show up in the next sixty seconds operational protocol dictated that Hastings would have to leave.

Looking back up, she saw Samantha's brown eyes peering back at her through a space between two books.

"What kept you?"

Samantha swiveled her head to make sure they were alone. "I wanted to drive my own car."

"Keep driving the military command car," Hastings cautioned. "You should be monitoring the radio chatter from the base security office. Are you ready for this?"

"As ready as I'll ever be. Are we a go?"

"Yes, and it has to be tonight."

"Tonight!?"

"I know this is happening a little faster than we planned, but we just received some fresh intelligence that leads us to believe tomorrow will be too late. We think we can fry the surveillance satellite overhead with a laser, but once your aircraft is out of the local airspace you'll be on your own. Good luck, Commander."

CHAPTER 31

The hotel's Victorian dining room dripped with luxurious touches as the survivors flowed under a latticework archway and brushed past the potted plants to take their seats beneath a spectacular stained-glass dome dominating the ceiling.

Seated at a reserved table topped with perfectly aligned gold-rimmed dinner plates set on a starched linen tablecloth, Leo and Evita traded looks with Lev Wasserman as Ariella and John and Daniel and Sarah took seats across from them.

Off to the side, a group of Acerbi's ever-present public relations people were trying to remain inconspicuous as they circled behind a row of decorative white columns and aimed their cameras at the diners in an attempt to catch a tableful of smiling faces that could be circulated over the internet to show the world how well the survivors were being treated.

As waiters hustled around the tables with overflowing trays of appetizers, it was apparent that Acerbi was pulling out all the stops to put everyone at ease, but a reserved chair next to Leo was having the opposite effect.

"Who do you think that's for?" Evita winked at Leo. "Acerbi?"

"Your guess is as good as mine, but with all these cameras present I can't see him choosing this venue for a meeting with us. He likes to be in total control, and he won't be able to control the chilly reception he's bound to receive if he enters this room."

"It will be a deadly reception if I get my hands on him," Lev mumbled between bites of stuffed olives.

"It doesn't seem like they've increased their security," Evita added, scanning the entrances. "Of course, that could all change in the next few minutes."

Lev leaned in close to Leo. "Daniel just told me that he's found something new in the code."

Looking up quickly, Leo took note of all the hovering waiters. "Maybe we should talk about that later."

A sly smile crossed Lev's face. "Don't worry, Leo," he whispered. "I'm well aware that there are a lot of ears around us right now, and I'm sure the centerpiece on the table is equipped with some very decorative listening devices."

Across the room a pair of children who hadn't seen their father since the attack on the castle burst into sobs, prompting the PR people to quickly swivel their cameras away from their table just as a woman with bright red hair swooped through the entrance with fire in her eyes. "Why don't we get these cameras out of here and let these people eat in peace?"

"I'm sorry, Commander," said a young PR man. "We're just following Mr. Acerbi's orders."

"Fine, film away, but I doubt you'd get a smile from anyone here even if you handed them a winning lottery ticket." Samantha Jennings abruptly turned away and walked to Leo's table before seating herself next to him in the reserved seat.

"Good evening, Cardinal," she said, shaking out her napkin. "My name is Samantha Jennings. I'm the wing commander for Mr. Acerbi's air forces here in Europe. I led the counter attack last year against a group of people led by a man who rescued some of our prisoners in the Field of the Burned. Obviously, I missed my target, because I'm talking to that man right now."

The two locked eyes before Leo answered. "That's quite an introduction, Commander."

"I had a feeling you would be the type of man who respected an honest approach."

Evita's long hair brushed the table as she peered around Leo. "And did you also lead the attack on the castle?"

Samantha cast her eyes down at the table. "No, that was someone else. I had nothing to do with that."

"So, you admit that Acerbi's forces were responsible for attacking innocent women and children."

"Yes, but if you repeat what I just said you'll lose your only way out of here."

Leo and Evita exchanged surprised looks as a bevy of waiters descended on the table with the first course—Beef Wellington.

As soon as they departed with their empty trays, Samantha laid her hand flat on the tablecloth and slid a folded piece of paper under the edge of Leo's plate. "Don't open that until you're alone, Cardinal," she whispered. "And make sure you destroy it after you read it. All I can tell you now is that things aren't what they appear to be. Feel free to talk among yourselves after I leave. I made sure the listening devices at the tables were deactivated before I arrived. We'll talk later."

Caught off guard, Leo maintained a neutral expression.

Who was he really talking to?

He was sitting next to one of Acerbi's top commanders, and the word *trap* entered his mind as he reached under the edge of his plate and palmed the tightly-folded piece of paper.

"What are you really up to, Ms. Jennings?"

"Read the note, Cardinal. Like I said, we'll speak later."

Samantha pushed her chair away from the table and stood as a PR man swiveled his camera to film the scene.

"I'm afraid I can't stay," Samantha announced in an overly loud voice. "Duty calls back at the base. It was nice meeting all of you. If there is anything I can do to make your stay more comfortable please tell one of the staff and they'll get word to me."

Turning away from the table, Samantha inhaled and walked briskly toward the lobby before disappearing through the front doors into the fog outside.

"What was that all about?" Evita asked.

"I'm not sure yet." Leo looked around the table to see if any of the wait staff seemed overly interested in listening to the discussion at their table. "Anyone know where the restrooms are?"

Ariella pointed with her fork. "Down that hallway. They're pretty fancy ... just like the rest of this place."

"Excuse me ... I'll be right back." Tossing his napkin on the table, Leo stood and walked past a bevy of PR people to a wood-paneled men's room filled with gold-plated fixtures. After making sure he was alone, he entered one of the stalls and removed his reading glasses from his shirt pocket before unfolding the note.

Two buses will be arriving at the front entrance at exactly 9PM tonight to take you all away from here. Tell only the leaders in your group. Everyone must appear to be surprised and fearful when they're loaded onto the buses or the soldiers here will become suspicious. If you fail to follow my instructions you and your friends will all be dead before sunset tomorrow.

Leo quickly ripped up the paper and flushed it down the toilet before exiting the stall. Still alone, he walked to one of the sinks below a wall of mirrors and turned on the water. Splashing away the beads of sweat running down his forehead he lingered, staring back at his reflection before scanning the area for cameras and returning to the table.

"We're leaving tonight," he whispered to Evita.

"What's going on?"

Leo looked at his watch. "An hour from now two buses will be arriving at the hotel entrance to take us somewhere."

"How do you know this?"

"The woman who just sat at our table."

"Jennings?! Are you serious? She's one of Acerbi's commanders! Why would you trust anything that came from a woman like that?"

"Call it intuition, but I saw real fear in her eyes. I have no idea what her motive is, but she certainly doesn't have to resort to trickery to make us do what she wants. If she wanted to load all of us on buses tonight she'd simply have her people point their guns at us and tell us to do it. Something else is going on."

"I don't know, Leo … a person like that. What about trying to make an escape on our own?"

"If we tried to make a run for it most of us wouldn't make it past the doors of the hotel. I spotted at least fifty soldiers around the perimeter the day we arrived, and they were all armed with high caliber weapons."

"Did she say where they were taking us?"

"No … she just said we'd talk later."

"And you believe her?"

"I'll admit it's a crap shoot, Evita, but at this point we don't have much choice. I can't get the look in her eyes out of my head. My gut tells me she's trying to help us."

Evita looked back over her shoulder at the armed men standing by the entrance. "And what do you think all the soldiers around the hotel are going to do when we all pile into buses and just drive off into the fog?"

"She's their commander, and whatever is about to happen has obviously been well planned." Clearing his throat, Leo stood and put on his biggest poker smile as he approached the table where Danny Zamir was seated with his son Ben. Leaning over, he spoke softly. "We're leaving tonight."

"What?" The elder Zamir's face remained as placid as a lake, the result of years spent in the artful pursuit of foreign intelligence. "I don't think this is a good place to talk."

"The listening devices at the tables have been deactivated. Two buses will be arriving in front of the hotel at nine o'clock. Tell only the leaders. I hate the fact that we can't tell these people what's happening after all they've been through, but they have to look like they're really afraid when they're loaded onto the buses or the soldiers will become suspicious."

"Does this have anything to do with the red-haired woman who just visited your table?" Zamir asked.

"Yes."

"You do know who she is, don't you, Cardinal?"

"She told me."

"And you're OK with this?"

"Like I told Evita, we don't have much choice."

Zamir closed his eyes as he weighed the options. "At this point I have to agree. They could do whatever they want to us without having to play any games."

"See you in an hour." Turning away from the table, Leo literally bumped into a woman holding a camera.

"Oh, excuse me." Leo grinned. "I'm about to head upstairs to my room and take a shower. Would you like to film that?"

The woman stared back at him with cold eyes and let loose with an exasperated sigh before turning on her heels and marching off toward another table without offering a reply.

OK then, Leo thought, heading for the lobby staircase.

Time to get this show on the road.

CHAPTER 32

The wait staff was still busy clearing dishes from the hotel dining room when the young lieutenant on duty in the front lobby got the call.

"Lieutenant Youngblood here."

"This is Commander Jennings. How's everything going over there, Lieutenant?"

"Pretty quiet here, Commander. Everyone went straight to their rooms after dinner."

"There's been a change of plans. We're moving them out tonight."

"Tonight?"

"That's what I said. There will be two buses pulling up to the main entrance at 2100 hours. That doesn't leave you much time, Lieutenant, so better get moving and make sure they're all down in the lobby and ready to go when the buses arrive."

"Yes, ma'am. We'll take care of it." The lieutenant hit the *off* button and looked to the female corporal standing beside him. "Let's start knocking on doors. They're moving all of these people out of here tonight."

"I thought they weren't leaving until tomorrow. Why the change of plans?"

"How would I know?" His tone reflected a growing impatience. "Of course you're more than welcome to call Commander Jennings and ask her yourself."

The corporal shrank back and turned to a group of soldiers standing by the hotel's main entrance. "OK, people. They're moving the civilians out of here tonight. I want them all down in the lobby in twenty minutes!"

The bored-looking soldiers suddenly came alive and began heading to the rooms upstairs just as the lieutenant's cell phone rang again. Glancing at the small blue screen he could see that the duty officer at the base was calling. *As if I don't already have enough to do.*

"This is Lieutenant Youngblood."

"How are things going, Youngblood?"

"We're moving as fast as we can, sir. We should have everyone downstairs in twenty minutes."

"What in the world are you talking about?"

"The move, sir. Commander Jennings said the buses would be here at 2100 hours."

"What move? What buses? Have you been smoking something, Lieutenant?"

"Uh, no sir. Commander Jennings just called and said we're moving these people out of here tonight."

There was a slight pause on the other end of the line. "Hang tight, Youngblood. I'll call the commander and see what's going on."

"Should we still move them down to the lobby, sir?"

"Yeah, go ahead. She probably just forgot to notify me. I'll get back to you."

* * *

The thickening fog made the bright lights of the hotel appear dimmer, creating the illusion that the building was farther away than it really was as the driver of the lead bus turned off the main highway and glanced back at Gwyneth Hastings.

"Do you think they'll be ready?" he asked.

"They'd better be." Clutching her secure cell phone in her hand, Gwyneth peered through the expansive windows at the front of the bus before glancing back at the MI6 officer posing as a bus driver. "Veering from our schedule by only a few minutes could cause this entire operation to come crashing down all around us."

Approaching a military checkpoint blocking the tree-lined road leading up to the hotel, the two buses came to a full stop. Stepping up into the lead bus, a gruff-looking young soldier scanned the empty seats behind Hastings. "ID cards, please," he said to the driver. "Who's your passenger?"

"I'm from public relations," Hastings said.

The soldier frowned. "Oh, I see … more first-class treatment. Personally, I think these people should all be in jail instead of lounging around in some fancy hotel."

"Does that include the children?"

The soldier was momentarily caught off guard by her aggressive response. "Uh, no ma'am … of course not. I just meant …"

"Look," Hastings shot back. "We're both just following orders, so let me make this easy for you. We're on a strict time schedule, so keep your opinions to yourself and get off the bus before I call Commander Jennings and tell her one of her soldiers is holding things up."

The soldier's face reddened. "I still have to scan your ID cards."

"Go ahead … scan away. We're waiting."

Glaring back at Hastings, the soldier swiped both cards through a small device the size of a cell phone before handing them back. "You're good to go. Pull ahead to the hotel entrance."

He turned to exit the bus, then stopped to glance back at Hastings. "You might want to work on your public relations skills, ma'am … just saying."

Her eyes narrowed. "Do you really think I work for public relations?"

"No, ma'am … I don't. Your ID card says you have a level 4 security clearance."

"That's right, which means if I hear any radio chatter about us being here you'll be facing a very bleak future."

"Mum's the word," he said, quickly stepping off the bus.

As soon as the doors hissed shut, Gwyneth and the driver exhaled.

"It looks like that new Wi-Fi device you hid under the dash actually worked," the driver said.

"Yeah … the tech guys really came through on that one. Apparently, the little bugger intercepts the signal from the devices they use to scan the ID cards before sending back a false clearance, so as far as anyone knows we were never here."

"Why were you so hard on the soldier?"

"I had to put the fear of God in him so he wouldn't say anything over the radio."

"Looks like it worked," the driver said, pulling away from the checkpoint. "He didn't appear to be in a talkative mood after he got off the bus."

Continuing up the tree-lined road, the bus slowed to a stop after they pulled under the portico fronting the hotel's entrance. As soon as the door at the front of the bus hissed open, the female corporal standing by the curb squinted up at the driver. "They're all waiting in the lobby. Want us to bring them out?"

"Yes, please. We need to have them all on board as soon as possible."

"What's the big hurry?"

"Don't know, ma'am. I'm just the driver."

Watching from the lobby, the lieutenant felt his cell phone jangle in his pocket again.

What now? Looking down at the screen, he saw that it was the duty officer calling him back. "Youngblood here," he answered.

"Hello, Youngblood. I just spoke with Commander Jennings. She said the orders to move those people came down from HQ this afternoon, but we can't find them. Go ahead and load um' up while we try to get confirmation."

"Yes, sir. Then what?"

"Don't let those buses leave until you hear from me."

"Will do." The lieutenant clicked off and turned to see Leo standing behind him. "OK, Cardinal. Let's get your people on those buses."

"Do you mind if I ask the young lady in the bus where we're going?" Leo asked.

"Be my guest."

Casting a glance back at Evita, Leo walked out to the bus and climbed on board. "Hello, Ms. Hastings. I believe the last time we saw each other was in Gibraltar. I'm relieved to see that you're a part of this."

"Thank you, Cardinal. It's good to see you again too." A buzzing sound prompted them both to look down at the vibrating cell phone dancing in Hastings' hand.

"Excuse me, Cardinal … I have to take this."

On the other end Hastings could hear Samantha's out-of-breath voice. "Gwyneth … it's Samantha."

"I know. We're already in front of the hotel. I was beginning to panic."

"Sorry," Samantha breathed. "I've been a little busy."

"Have we been cleared through the main gate at the base yet?"

"Yes, but there's a new problem … one I didn't anticipate. The duty officer called me earlier to check on the orders authorizing the move, and now he's calling HQ for confirmation. They're going to hold the buses until he receives a clearance."

The color drained from Hastings' face. "I thought that was all taken care of."

"So did I, but he's playing by the book. I didn't think he'd actually call to check on the orders after I told him it was OK."

"Can you stall him?"

"I'm pulling up in front of his office right now."

"OK. Call me back. They're already boarding." Hastings clicked off and looked down to see two sleepy-eyed children climbing the stairs up into the bus. The little boy in front was dragging a stuffed animal behind him.

"Who are you?" the boy asked, rubbing his eyes.

Always uncomfortable around children, Hastings struggled to smile. "My name is Gwyneth."

"Where are we going, Gwyneth?"

Hastings winked up at the driver. "We're about to take a very exciting ride."

CHAPTER 33

The orange glare from the halogen security lights outside filtered through the blinds, casting zebra stripes of light across the duty officer's desk as Samantha Jennings burst into the office followed by two military police officers.

"What do you think you're doing, Captain?"

The officer quickly stood at attention behind his desk. "I beg your pardon, Commander?"

"Why did you place a hold on those buses … and why are you questioning my orders?"

"Uh … protocol, Commander. According to regulations we're required to verify all computer orders."

"So, my verbal orders weren't sufficient enough for you?"

"No, ma'am … I mean, yes, ma'am. I was just following regulations. There's probably some kind of glitch at HQ."

"There's a glitch alright, but it's not at HQ. Since when does a captain countermand a commander's orders?"

"I just thought we should hold the buses until we …"

"You thought! Is that what you just said, Captain … you thought? I'm placing you under arrest for directly disobeying the verbal order of a superior officer. Who did you speak to at HQ?"

The captain's face paled and his posture began to sag. "I didn't speak to anyone, Commander. I just ran an authentication check through the computer and there was no record of any such order. I was waiting for a call from HQ when you arrived."

"Hook him up and get him out of my sight," Samantha said to the officers. "I'll take care of things from here."

"But Commander!" the captain shouted. "I was just doing what I was trained to do."

"I guess that will be up to the judicial review board to decide, Captain, and if I were you I wouldn't say anything else."

The sweating captain stared down at the floor, his feet dragging as the military police led him from the office. Quickly, Samantha sat in front of his computer and began scrolling through his latest communications with HQ.

There!

The last communication was from an intelligence officer at the London headquarters building.

From: 380th Headquarters Group/ Intelligence section
To: Duty Officer, Acerbi Air Command / European base of operations

Subject: Authentication request

Message: Will check on order and get back to you. Have you notified your commander?

Major I.O. Higgens
Section Chief
Computer records section

Perfect! Samantha had worked with Higgens in the past. She slapped her hand on the desk and picked up the phone. It seemed to ring forever until someone finally answered. "Higgens here."

"Good evening, Major. This is Commander Jennings. I hear you've been having some trouble verifying an order for my duty officer."

"Oh, hello, Jennings. I'm afraid your chap down there is right. We can't seem to find any such order in our system. Are you sure it originated from HQ?"

"Apparently there is no such order." Samantha crossed her fingers. "We just found our duty officer passed out on his desk next to an empty bottle of scotch. The man was drunk as a skunk. I think we can safely disregard that authentication check. At this point we have no idea what was going on in that man's mind."

"Sounds like he's due for a vacation. I'll take care of it on this end, Jennings, but a copy of the request has already gone on to MI6 for review."

Samantha held her breath as she thought. "Oh great. That's just the icing on the cake. Now I have those people to deal with. Do you know what officer at MI6 received the copy?"

"Hang on, Jennings … let me check. Oh, here it is." Samantha heard a chuckle on the other end of the line. "It went to an intelligence officer by the name of Gwyneth Hastings. You'd better watch that one, Commander. I've had dealings with her before. You're in for a real treat."

"I've heard that about her."

"Anything else, Commander?"

"No … thank you. I appreciate your help. Talk to you later, Major."

A visceral sense of relief flowed over Samantha as she clicked off and quickly punched in Gwyneth's number.

"Hastings."

"Our little situation has been taken care of," Samantha said. "They actually sent a copy of the confirmation request to you at MI6 for follow up. Have they loaded everyone on board the buses?"

"Yes, but they're still holding us."

"Let me speak to the officer in charge."

Hastings looked across the aisle and gave Leo a thumbs up before stepping off the bus and handing her phone to the young lieutenant. "It's your commander, Lieutenant, and she'd like to speak to you."

Listening, the young officer's eyes widened. "Yes, Commander … right away!" Handing the phone back to Gwyneth, he began shouting to the soldiers standing in front of the bus. "Stand aside. These buses are leaving … now!"

Climbing back into the bus, Gwyneth held onto the back of the driver's seat and watched the doors hiss shut before the bus began to move away.

"Where to now, Ms. Hastings?" Leo asked from his seat next to Evita.

"The air base."

"The air base!?"

"Yes. We're flying all of you out of here tonight. We decided to put the families from the castle on a cargo plane so we can fly them to that abandoned airfield in Spain. It's away from any populated areas where they might be spotted landing, and we figured they'd be able to blend in with the Catalonian culture of the area without raising any suspicions. We've been told that many of them have strong family ties there."

"And what about us?" Leo asked.

"You and your friends will be boarding another jet flown by Commander Jennings."

"Jennings?"

"Yes, Cardinal. I know it's a lot to take in right now, but you're just going to have to trust me on this one."

"And where will we be flying?"

Hastings smiled back at him. "I thought you already knew the answer to that one, Cardinal. You're going to Rome."

CHAPTER 34

Approaching the main gate to the air base, Hastings tensed as the soldiers waved them through without making them stop. The buses continued on, their drivers nervously watching their rear-view mirrors as they rounded the side of a large white hangar and stopped. Waiting for them, a C-17 cargo plane and a smaller Gulfstream jet sat on the flight line, their strobe lights flashing through the fog.

"Looks like our rides are ready to go," Evita said, nudging a frowning Leo. "What's wrong?"

"I don't like this." He glanced across the aisle at Hastings talking to someone on her phone. "Acerbi may be a lot of things, but he's not stupid. Even if we do manage to make it off the ground the friendly skies will turn ugly real fast if his people find out what's really going on. I have a feeling we're about to kick a hornet's nest."

Evita's eyes searched Leo's face. "Where's your faith, my love? From what you said, if we would have remained behind at that hotel our chances of coming out of this alive were close to zero, and from what I've seen so far it looks like they've planned this operation pretty well."

"But that's exactly my point," Leo said. "There has to be a lot of people working behind the scenes to make all of this happen, and a single wolf in sheep's clothing could bring it all crashing down."

"No one's going to be doing any crashing, Cardinal." Leo turned to see Hastings glaring back at him from her seat across the aisle. "Sorry we weren't able to brief you earlier, but we didn't have time. As you could probably tell from Samantha's note, we discovered that Acerbi had a little trip planned for you and your people tomorrow … one you wouldn't be returning from. Since then we've been working around the clock on a plan to get all of you out of here, and as soon as we're in the air I'll fill you in on the rest of the details."

Standing between the buses and the planes, a group of airmen wearing reflective vests used glowing wands to direct the families to the cargo plane, while Leo and the others made their way up the stairs into the smaller jet. In less than ten minutes the buses were empty and everyone had been loaded aboard both aircraft.

In the back of the large cargo plane, Gael and the Cathar fighters were sticking close to the families, while inside the sleek Gulfstream jet, Leo watched the members of the Bible Code Team file through the door and silently take their seats. The last one to enter was Gwyneth Hastings, who took a final look outside as the door swung shut and Samantha Jennings fired up the engines.

Looking to the side for any sign of ground vehicles headed their way, the red-haired commander turned onto the main runway and shoved the throttles all the way forward, sending the jet hurtling down the rubber-scarred concrete before it streaked into the air. A minute later, the C-17 and its precious cargo of men, women, and children followed them into the sky.

After setting her course, Samantha looked back into the cabin and motioned to Gwyneth. Unbuckling her seatbelt, Hastings made the uphill climb to the cockpit. "Everything OK?"

"I'm not sure. Two fighters took off right after the cargo plane lifted off."

"Don't fighter planes take off all the time from air bases?"

"Usually, but I cancelled all fighter exercises scheduled for tonight so that we'd have the airspace all to ourselves."

Hastings peered out into the darkness. "Damn! Where are they now?"

Samantha pointed to the radar. "One is following the C-17. The other is somewhere behind us. When are your people going to take out that military satellite with the laser?"

"It should have happened already."

Samantha scanned the control panel. "I'm still receiving a signal."

Suddenly the navigational and radar screens went blank. "There it goes." Samantha exhaled. "I can't see the fighters anymore, which means they can't see us either."

"So … are we safe?"

"As long as the fighters don't make visual contact we should be just as invisible to them as they are to us, but I still don't like the fact that someone countermanded my orders and launched those fighters. Something is going on, and I was kept out of the loop for some reason."

A chill ran down Hastings' spine. "That means it had to come from somewhere higher up."

"Exactly." Samantha looked back to scan the dark sky behind them through her side window. "This might be a good time to brief our passengers."

Backing out of the cockpit, Hastings inched her way down the sloping aisle of the climbing jet to Leo's seat. "It's time for that briefing I promised you, Cardinal. The first part of our plan seems to have worked fairly well, but after we left the ground two fighters took off behind us. We've managed to knock out the air defense satellite that covers the airspace around us, so that's keeping us safe for now, but it's only a matter of time before they bring another one online and we light up like a Christmas tree on their radar screens."

"Well, Ms. Hastings, it sounds like you've already lit the fuse. If they're on to us our only alternative is to throw the dynamite."

"What are you talking about, Cardinal?"

"A plan that's been rolling over in my mind since the day I saw the castle burning. I just didn't know how we would be able to pull it off until now."

"Please, Cardinal … there are two fighter planes out there right now, and we don't know their intentions. If you have any ideas that could help us, now is the time."

"Is this aircraft equipped with a burst transmitter?"

"I believe all command aircraft have them, but they're not much use to us now that the codes have been compromised."

"Not necessarily. When I was in Norway, Steig Lundahl told me something very interesting about the transmitters his company manufactured when I asked him how he was able to send a message to us at the castle without having the encrypted code needed to access the Israeli's burst transmitter. Steig said there was a way he could send a message to any burst transmitter without having the code. Something about a back door."

"A back door?"

"Yes. I thought that if we could find a way to contact him he could send a message to the *HMS Ambush* without giving away their position."

"The *Ambush*? And ask them to do what?"

"Take out Acerbi's quantum computers … or at least some of them. That's how he came to power … they control everything. A surprise attack on his computers could release his grip on the world, and with his entire network at risk, we'd have a bargaining chip to use if he moved to counter attack. In other words, Ms. Hastings, we'd be calling the shots for a change."

Hastings was dumbfounded. "I think you picked the wrong profession, Cardinal. It's brilliant. The only problem is we don't have any way of contacting Lundahl right now. After he moved from his lodge to a secure location he cut himself off from all outside communication." Standing in the aisle, she took on the glassy expression of someone lost in thought as she chewed on the end of her cell phone. "We don't need a back door."

"What do you mean?" Leo asked.

"We have the code to the sub's transmitter. We can send a one-way transmission directly to the sub ourselves without compromising their position."

"How would you do that?"

"The subs aren't transmitting, but they're probably listening in passive mode. We just have to re-route our transmission through a satellite not linked to Acerbi's defense network to avoid detection by his computers, but we'll have to be quick about it. Once they move another satellite over the area to replace the one we fried, their computers will be able to lock on to us and anyone we communicate with."

"How long will it take for Acerbi's forces to move another satellite overhead?" Leo asked.

"I don't know. An hour … maybe less."

"But aren't all satellites linked to his computer network?"

"Not the weather satellites. We've recently begun using them to communicate with some of our operatives in the field after we found out Acerbi's computers don't monitor the weather sats for communications traffic. They only download weather information from them. Apparently, the people who programmed the quantum computers didn't realize they could also be used for communications, which left a big chink in their armor. Even if they pick up our transmission they probably won't have time to recognize it for what it is before our message reaches the sub and it launches."

Leo instantly recognized a chink in their own armor. "But if you use the old compromised codes to send a message to the *Ambush*, won't they think Acerbi's people are sending it? They might think they're receiving false coordinates to make them use up their missiles and give away their position."

Leo detected a slight twinkle in Gwyneth's eyes. "The message I send will include a coded message from me to the captain that will validate the authenticity of the coordinates. Right now I'm more worried about those two fighters behind us, because as soon as their targeting computers come back online we're in big trouble."

Like a wild animal that had suddenly been released from its cage, Hastings turned and sprinted back up the aisle before bursting into the cockpit. "We need to send an encrypted message to the *Ambush*!"

Samantha swiveled in her seat. "And just how do you suggest I do that?"

"Use the burst transmitter and route it through the weather satellite."

"Clever. What's the message?"

Hastings pulled out her personal smart phone and scrolled through the menu. "Here, send this." She held the tiny screen up in front of Samantha's face.

"Those are earth coordinates," Samantha said.

"That's right. They're the geographical locations for six of Acerbi's quantum computers that we've been able to locate over the past few months. Tell Captain Moss the time is now, and make sure the message contains the words *strike with extreme prejudice!*"

CHAPTER 35

Adrian Acerbi, or rather, the thing inside Adrian Acerbi, was raging. Someone had just knocked out one of his major communications satellites with a focused laser beam of tremendous power, and now all of his forces in the UK and most of Western Europe were operating in the blind. In addition, his links with every security camera and cell phone tower in the area had also been interrupted, and his plan to finally be rid of the cardinal and his friends looked like it was about to fail. How could this have happened!?

His plan had been perfect!

Ever since he had learned that Samantha Jennings had made contact with MI6 he had become suspicious, and his suspicions had turned out to be well-founded after his intelligence people had followed Gwyneth Hastings and Samantha to a college library and photographed their meetings. In the course of their investigation, his people had also tapped in to the wireless traffic between Hastings and a team of retired MI6 operatives working with her.

In short, he had known all along about Samantha's treachery and Hastings' escape plan for the cardinal and his friends. Both women had been very resourceful, and when he had learned that they would be flying the survivors out of the country, he had decided to hold back and wait. He would use their resourcefulness against them by simply allowing them to escape. After that his fighters would simply shoot them down over the English Channel. It would then be reported to the press the cardinal and his friends had stolen two aircraft from the base before colliding in mid-air over the foggy channel, tragically killing everyone aboard both planes. Once again, Acerbi's forces would be absolved from any wrong-doing.

Pacing the floor of the English manor house, Acerbi continued to rage. His simple plan to be rid of the cardinal had failed. Hastings and her little group of former spies had engineered an end-run by frying his main communications satellite with a laser, and the escaping planes had disappeared off radar.

What were they planning?

The unearthly howls that came from his room frightened even the toughest men assigned to guard him, but luckily for them they were spared the sight of the thing that briefly separated itself from its human host. Its monstrous head moved from side-to-side as its blood-red eyes stared out the window and its screams echoed across the barren windswept landscape that fell away to the storm-tossed sea below the cliffs.

Its fury spent, the demon prepared to retreat back into Adrian's body, but for just a moment, before his eyes grew dark once more, Adrian had been released from the demon's grip. Using his own eyes … his human eyes, the real Adrian Acerbi had caught a glimpse of a world that had been hidden from him since that day in Turkey, when the dark star had descended and he had become … what? What had he become? But even more importantly, how would he return to what he had been before?

The demon immediately sensed a brief awakening of its human host and pushed his soul back down into that dark place where it had been locked away—away from the sight of those who had once loved him.

They would never love him again!

The demon face smiled. The innocent boy had been returned to a place of eternal darkness, and the thing that now inhabited his human shell once again looked out on a world he knew he had always been destined to rule.

Raised voices and running footsteps in the hallway outside preceded a loud knock on the door. Acerbi jerked it open to find two senior officers staring back at him.

"What is it … do we have satellite coverage yet?"

The two officers traded frightened looks before the senior man spoke. "Yes, sir. I think you should come with us."

CHAPTER 36

The rain was coming down in sheets, blotting out the tops of the sheer cliffs that snaked along the edges of the narrow Norwegian fjord below.

Riding on the surface of the deep blue water, the *HMS Ambush* blended in with her dark surroundings.

"I don't like it, Captain," the executive officer said. "If the burst transmitters have been compromised like we suspect, this order could be coming from Acerbi. He could have us launching our missiles into empty farmland for all we know, not to mention the fact that we'd be giving our position away as soon as we fire."

"Is their satellite still dead in the air?" Moss asked.

"Yes, sir, but they're probably moving another one in to replace it as we speak."

"Have the missile room set the coordinates we just received into the targeting computers. We'll use the same weather satellite for GPS guidance and dive the boat right after we fire."

"Are you sure about this, sir?"

"Positive. *Strike with extreme prejudice.* Those are the same code words I gave to my daughter before we left."

"Your daughter, sir?"

"Her name is Gwyneth. She works for MI6. They gave her a cover surname so the bad guys wouldn't know we're related, and right now she's the only one we can trust. She wouldn't ask us to launch unless she had verified the intelligence on the targets first."

Reaching overhead, the captain grabbed a microphone. "This is the captain speaking. We're about to launch six missiles at confirmed Acerbi targets. There should be no civilians at those sites. When the last missile is away we'll dive the boat and make our way back out into the North Sea."

Replacing the microphone, Moss glanced over at his executive officer. "Fire when ready."

* * *

Following the two officers downstairs to a large room that contained a maze of wires linking dozens of computers, Acerbi stood in the doorway and looked at the horrified expressions on the faces of the men and women staring unbelievingly at the scattered bits of data scrolling across their screens.

"What's going on?"

A heavyset general hefted his large frame from his chair and braced himself. "Six of our quantum computer sites have just been taken out by a coordinated missile strike. All of Europe, Africa, and the Middle East are now invisible to us."

Adrian crossed the room and peered at a computer screen blinking on and off as it searched for a signal from a massive computer that was no longer there. He appeared strangely calm, but no one dared to look him in the eye. They had all witnessed his fury before, and no one wanted to be the one to throw the switch.

For a moment he just stood there, stone-like, until finally he turned to the general. "When did this happen?"

"About seven minutes ago, sir. I sent for you right after we received confirmation." The usually unflappable general recoiled when he saw the whites of Adrian's eyes turn completely black.

"Do we know where the attack came from?"

"We detected launch signatures from a fjord in Norway. Probably a sub, sir."

Under Acerbi's dark glare, the tension in the room was becoming almost unbearable to the men and women who were trying to avoid drawing any unwanted attention to themselves. Their new world order had just suffered the greatest defeat in its short history, and as they stole quick glances at Acerbi they all knew they were witnessing the calm before the storm.

Sitting in front of one of the few computer screens still online, a young private swiveled in his chair and motioned to the general. "I have an incoming message for Mr. Acerbi, sir."

"A secure text?"

"No, sir. It's a phone call from an aircraft. It's being routed through a satellite, and the person calling says he wants to speak to Mr. Acerbi."

"I'll take it," the general said.

"The caller said he'd speak only with Mr. Acerbi, sir."

Adrian brushed past the general and grabbed the phone. "Hello, Cardinal!"

"How did you know it was me, Adrian?"

"Who else would be behind this attack on my computer network?"

"I'll make this short," Leo continued. "Your entire military command and control structure for this part of the world has just been decimated, so I suggest you do exactly as I say. First, you will order all of your military forces to stand down, especially the two fighters you sent to intercept us. After that, you will have your media lackeys begin broadcasting the breaking news that your grand experiment to unite the entire world under a single banner has failed, and that you will be stepping down as their leader effective immediately."

"You must be joking, Cardinal. Why would I do something like that?"

"The answer is very simple. Any attempt to deviate from these demands, or any attempt to retaliate against us will result in an immediate attack against your remaining computer centers, which I am ordering you to shut down as soon as we're through speaking. Your new world order is finished, Acerbi."

Leo held his breath. He was playing the biggest poker hand of his life, and he had just bluffed. They had just sent a message to the *Tekuma* telling them to head for the American coast and prepare to strike Acerbi's computer centers there, but they had no way of knowing if their message had gotten through. The command to shut his remaining computers down would have to come from Acerbi himself, because until the *Tekuma* was in a position to strike, he still had the means to retaliate in an Armageddon-like scenario aimed at innocent civilians.

"Why didn't you just attack me personally, Cardinal?" Acerbi's voice was eerily calm. "You obviously know where I am."

"You and I both know that as soon as you sense an attack on your human host you'll simply flee to another hiding spot. No ... I will deal with you later, Adrian ... after the countries you've held hostage have had their sovereignty restored and you see your new world order come crashing down around you."

Leo paused to let his words sink in. "Oh, and one more thing. The man you installed as the new pope is out. We'll be holding a real conclave of cardinals when I return to Rome to name a new pontiff. I know what you are, Adrian, and your time on earth is growing short."

The line went dead in Adrian's hand, and what happened next would be remembered by everyone who witnessed it for the rest of their lives.

Acerbi's entire body began to vibrate. Unable to conceal its identity or control its fury, the human form around the demon began to lose definition as the room filled with rotating points of light that revealed flashes of a hideous, red-eyed apparition that grew in size above the frozen people watching.

Without waiting to see what would happen next, the horrified men and women fled from the room as the demon's high-pitched screams echoed through the building, blasting the sulfur-infused air in an endless stream.

Those who were standing closest to the building thought they heard the demon call out. It sounded like someone screaming underwater.

"Cardinal!"

CHAPTER 37

The sleek Gulfstream jet touched down at Rome's Leonardo da Vinci airport and taxied to an international terminal building reserved for private aircraft. Now that Acerbi's vast network of powerful quantum computers had been taken off line, pre-existing networks began to regain control. Everything from the power grid to satellites to the internet—even traffic lights. The new world order had begun to lose its grip on people's lives, and those who had seen it for what it really was were rejoicing in the streets. Others just stared openmouthed at their television screens. Like lost sheep, they seemed to be blissfully unaware that they had just been rescued by a new shepherd who had chased a predatory wolf away from their pasture and back into its dark hiding place.

Standing in the aisle at the front of the plane, Leo and Lev embraced.

"Congratulations, Cardinal." Lev grinned. "Whatever you said to Acerbi seems to have worked, because we just landed without being blown out of the sky." His grin faded. "Now what?"

"I'll be taking up residence in *Castel Gandolfo* for the next few days while the false pope vacates the papal apartments."

"What was his name?" Lev asked.

Leo frowned. "Acone ... Cardinal Serafino Acone. I was told he chose the name *Innocent* after becoming pope. That's quite a contradiction in terms, especially considering that the man was anything but innocent. Anyway ... he's out. There will be a new dawn over the Eternal City tomorrow when I resume my former position as the Vatican's Secretary of State, and my first order of business will be to call for a new conclave of cardinals to choose a real pope. The doors to Vatican City will be open to the faithful once again."

Lev's expression turned serious. "I wish I could be here to see it."

"But you are here."

"It's time for us to go home, Leo. Commander Jennings has agreed to fly the rest of us on to Israel. We'll be leaving as soon as the jet is refueled."

"Of course. What was I thinking?" Leo embraced the man he had come to love as a brother. "Israel is where you belong."

"This isn't a goodbye, my friend," Lev grinned. "As soon as you get things working again at the Vatican, you and Evita will be coming to the villa for a well-deserved vacation."

Leo cast a wistful look toward the city. "I'm afraid I won't be taking a vacation anytime soon. Acerbi is still out there, and I have a feeling he's not going to give up so easily. I want you to be especially cautious when you return. We can't afford to let our guard down until he's no longer a threat."

"Excuse me, Cardinal."

Leo turned to see Daniel standing in the aisle behind him. "Do you have a moment?"

"Of course."

"We haven't had a chance to speak yet, but Lev just gave me a quick rundown on Pope Michael's theory about Adrian Acerbi, and the day before Sarah and I left Israel I found something in the code that you need to hear before we leave."

"Tell me."

"I've thought long and hard about this, Cardinal, but I know I'm right. While you and the others were in France I went back through all the encoded messages we've discovered so far in the Torah to look for anything that might shed some light on what was happening in the world. I wanted to find out all I could about the dark star and Adrian Acerbi's unparalleled rise to power. That's when I found it … something we all missed earlier."

Leo's stomach tightened.

"Remember when we were all on the yacht in Patmos last year," Daniel went on, "when I showed you the coded messages that led us there in the first place?"

"How could I forget?"

"At the top of one of the pages in Genesis we found the word *Patmos*. Below that was the phrase, *cave of the sign*, which was followed by the geographical coordinates that led us to the cave where we found the scroll depicting the scene of a jackal giving birth to two snakes."

"Go on."

"I believe the image on the scroll was a warning. We also found the words *birthplace, mother of the two,* and *final transition* on the same page. When we saw the image of two snakes and Lev called out the names of Rene and Adrian Acerbi, we naturally assumed we were looking at the representation of a supernatural birth, and that one of the two boys was destined to become the prophesied Antichrist. For a long time I've been wondering about that. I mean, why would Rene be depicted on the scroll along with Adrian? What was his purpose? And then it hit me. We weren't looking at the birth of two human children. We were looking at something entirely different. I started going back over the page in Genesis, and that's when I found it."

"Found what?" Leo asked.

"A single missed word."

Leo stared at Daniel without blinking. "What word?"

"Preceding the word, *birthplace*, the word *demons* appeared!"

"Demons! How did we miss that?"

"I don't know. We're still dealing with the supernatural here, but don't you see what this means? The two snakes we saw depicted on the scroll weren't Rene and Adrian like we first thought. They were demons … or at least one of them was."

Daniel shifted nervously under the intense gaze of the cardinal. "If you look at the proximity of the words *birthplace* and *demons* on the same page, a different picture begins to form. I believe the dark ruin in Turkey is a birthplace—a birthplace for demons, and one of them found its way into Adrian Acerbi."

Steig Lundahl's words came rushing back to Leo. He had called the ruin in Norway a *demon hatchery.*

"But you just said only one of the snakes was a demon," Leo said. "What was the other snake?"

Daniel exhaled slowly. "Also a demon. They arrived together … as if they were just the first wave of an attack."

"An attack?"

"Yes," Daniel continued. "And it matches the theory postulated by Pope Michael and his brother. If I'm right, Adrian Acerbi's so-called transformation was really more of a demonic possession, meaning we have a much better chance of defeating him than we would if he had been the true Antichrist. I believe there's something else going on, Leo, but I have no idea what it is."

Once again, Leo felt the tug of a dark presence circling just beyond their reach, and like the distant drumbeat of an advancing army, he could hear the words in his head.

Something was coming!

CHAPTER 38

Ducking through the jet's narrow doorway into the bright Roman sunshine, Leo inhaled the warm summer air. It was good to be back in Rome, but better still to be out of hiding. The sky seemed bluer and the colors of the flowers planted nearby were more vibrant; their sweet scent rising up to welcome him home. It didn't matter to him that the perfumed welcome was mixed with the smell of jet fuel. It was the smell of freedom, and he was looking out on a world that had just been released from the yoke of a madman.

Squinting in the sunlight, Leo and Evita walked into the small executive jet terminal accompanied by Bishop Morelli, Francois Leander and Gwyneth Hastings.

"Where's Mendoza and Diaz?" Evita asked

"They said they needed some beach time," Hastings quipped. "They're flying on to Israel with Lev and the others. Oh, and while I'm thinking about it, you'll be needing a new encrypted smart phone, Cardinal. Like it or not, word will soon leak out to the public that you are the man behind Acerbi's fall from grace, and world leaders will be looking to you for guidance as Acerbi and his new world order fades into history. I have a feeling you're about to become a very busy man."

"As if he's not busy enough already," Evita said, noticing the exhaustion in Leo's eyes.

"It may look peaceful," Hastings continued, "but the world is still in a state of turmoil. Until the evolving situation is resolved, I'm afraid we're going to have to surround the cardinal with a ring of security. The days of anonymous strolls together through the streets of Rome are over for you two, at least for the time being."

Frowning, Evita locked arms with Leo as the group made their way through the small terminal and through the glass doors to the covered sidewalk in front, where several beaming Swiss Guards stood at attention next to three black SUVs parked along the curb.

Feeling the emotion rising inside him, Francois stared back at the group of loyal men he had feared he would never see again. "How did you know …?" His unfinished question hung in the air when he caught sight of Gwyneth talking on her cell phone.

Of course.

"Where to, Cardinal?" asked a young guardsman holding a door.

Leo had to think for a moment. Things were beginning to happen faster than he had anticipated. "As much as I'd like to sample some real Italian coffee in a quiet café, we need to go straight to *Castel Gandolfo*."

"We assumed you would be returning to the Vatican, Cardinal."

"I think it might be better if I wait for Acone to leave the Holy City before I return."

"Then you can return right now, sir," the soldier said. "He left an hour ago with the soldiers that replaced us after Pope Michael died. We've been told that all of the Swiss Guards that were replaced by the Acerbi Pope are making their way back to Rome as we speak."

"The Acerbi Pope?" Leo asked.

"Yes, sir … that's what most of the people in Rome called him."

"I'll ride up front," Francois announced to the guards. The tone of his voice and the look in his eyes left no doubt in anyone's mind that he had just reclaimed his position as the head of the Vatican's legendary security force.

Crawling in behind Leo and Evita, Morelli wiped the sweat from his brow and squeezed in next to Gwyneth Hastings. "I forgot how humid it is here in the summer."

Hastings fanned her face with her free hand. "I can't see how you people can stand wearing those stiff collars around your necks."

"It reminds us of who we serve, Ms. Hastings," Morelli said. As soon as the words were out of his mouth he looked down at the clothes Acerbi's people had given them at the hotel to replace the homespun clothing that had been taken from them and burned in the hotel incinerator the day they arrived.

His mind drifted back to Julian Wehling and the Cathars who had shielded them from Acerbi's forces at a very high cost to themselves. The simple clothing of the Cathars had probably been very similar to that worn by the first Christians when they had traveled to Rome in the first century, and in a chilling historical replay, many of them had just suffered the same fate delivered by a creature who had tried to set himself up as the world's new emperor.

Spurred by his memories, Morelli suddenly remembered the other plane. "What about the cargo plane, Ms. Hastings. Did they make it OK?"

Gwyneth's fingers hovered above the virtual keyboard of her smart phone as she looked up from one of her constant texts. "Their plane landed almost an hour ago at that abandoned air base in Spain."

"But there's nothing there except for empty buildings," Morelli said.

"They'll be receiving some additional supplies along with a detachment of British soldiers later today. As I explained to the cardinal, it's the safest place for them to be right now. Keep in mind that we're still in a transitional period, and we're still not sure how some of the Acerbi loyalists are reacting to the news that there's a new sheriff in town. We need to keep them out of sight until things settle down, because none of us wants another repeat of what happened at the castle."

The piercing whine of jet engines drowned out all further conversation, causing them all to turn their heads just in time to see Samantha Jennings waving from the cockpit as she pushed the throttles forward and began taxiing to the main runway. A few minutes later, the jet carrying their Israeli and Spanish friends could be seen climbing out over the city in a southern arc that would take them home to the Holy Land.

As the jet faded into a dot on the horizon, the three SUVs pulled out of the parking lot and headed for Vatican City. The blur of traffic on the freeway made it seem as if nothing had changed, and in the distance, the dome of Saint Peter's beckoned.

Ahead of them the wind caught a billowy piece of gray material and carried it across the roadway, followed by another. The gray material seemed to be everywhere, and after they exited the freeway into the hodgepodge of narrow streets in the ancient section of the city, they saw smoke rising from a burning pile of the same gray material as an old woman clapped her hands with a mad gleam in her eyes.

"More uniforms," the driver said. "They're everywhere."

"Uniforms? Where are they coming from?" Morelli asked.

"Acerbi's forces, sir. They're throwing away their uniforms and deserting in droves. From what we've heard this type of thing is happening all over the world. The borders between countries are already beginning to reappear as their leaders take charge again. Turns out people didn't much like outsiders telling them what to do. I guess all the people who were so excited about the new world order didn't count on having their unique cultures being erased, and in the last few hours some pretty horrific pictures of atrocities committed by Acerbi's forces have begun turning up on the internet. People are enraged, and Acerbi's soldiers are trying to distance themselves from him as fast as they can."

"Looks like your bluff worked, Cardinal," Hastings said, looking out the window.

Leo nodded silently as they passed a cobblestoned *piazza* filled with smiling people who had gathered at outdoor tables to toast the sunshine with a glass of wine.

"What are you thinking, my love?" Evita whispered in his ear. "Aren't you happy to be back?"

Leo's expression remained dark. "Yes ... of course." Leo hesitated, not wanting to spoil their return to Rome, but he felt compelled to speak his mind. "I only hope all of this isn't just a brief intermission. Satan is a great deceiver, and I can't see him giving up this easily. On the surface it looks like everything is returning to normal, but in reality, this may be the most dangerous time of all. Adrian has left the world swirling in an undercurrent of mistrust. The entire world felt the shock of his sudden arrival, and there will be aftershocks left in the wake of his departure. We're entering uncharted waters, and there's no telling how people will react if things begin to crumble and another so-called savior appears on the scene. They're going to want answers, Evita, and I'm not sure we can provide them with any just yet."

Lost in thought, the two glanced up just as the vehicles approached Vatican City and sped through the *Via de Porta Angelica* before coming to an abrupt stop in front of the Apostolic Palace.

Stepping from the SUV, Evita looked at the church through Bernini's columns. "What about the chapel?"

"The chapel?"

"The one under the Vatican. Maybe there's something there that can help you figure all of this out."

Stunned with a sudden realization, Leo stared back at her. "The fourth wall!"

Evita's expression was blank. "The what?"

"The fourth wall. It's the only wall of the chapel that we never got around to excavating."

Listening in on their conversation, Morelli stumbled from the vehicle. "My God, Leo! Why didn't we think of that sooner? The exterior wall behind the altar is still buried under the ancient debris of the catacombs. There's no telling what we'll find there."

"I'm putting you in charge of the excavation, Anthony," Leo said, grabbing his friend by the shoulder. "We must start work right away, because I have a strong feeling that something's coming … and we have to be ready when it arrives."

CHAPTER 39

TWO WEEKS LATER

The sun's warmth reflected off the cobblestones in Saint Peter's Square, sending shimmering waves of rising heat into the air that distorted the view of photographers who were trying to snap a picture of the basilica from a distance. In the San Damaso Courtyard, dozens of black limos were parked in a line in front of the Apostolic Palace. Over the past week the Vatican had been flooded with cardinals from all over the world. They had come to elect a new pope—a real pope to replace the one who had been appointed by Acerbi, and in the marble corridors of power names had been whispered back and forth, like feathers drifting on the wind.

Across the street, behind the weathered Victorian façade of the Hotel Amalfi, Leo had taken up residence on the third floor in the same room he usually stayed in whenever he was in Rome. He had been coming here since the 1970's, and over the years, he and the owner, Arnolfo Bignoti, had become close friends.

After a creaky descent to the ground floor in the hotel's ancient, cage-like elevator, Leo crossed the black and white terrazzo tiles that covered the lobby and stopped at the front desk polished over time to a high sheen by the thousands of arms that had leaned against it. "*Buon giorno*, Arnolfo."

Arnolfo's head popped up over the counter. "Ah … *buon giorno*, Cardinal. How was your sleep?"

"I tossed and turned all night. Are there any messages for me?"

"Only one, Cardinal. Ms. Vargas left the hotel early this morning. She wanted you to know she had some shopping to do."

"I'll have to catch up with her later. Right now, I'm late for my meeting with the other cardinals."

"Then maybe you should drink this." Arnolfo removed a small porcelain cup and filled it from a dented copper espresso machine.

"When does the conclave start?" he asked, handing the cup across the counter.

"Tomorrow." Leo downed the steaming dark liquid in a single gulp and handed the empty cup back to Arnolfo before rushing outside. A sudden gust of wind caught his long black cassock as he crossed the street to the Vatican and threaded his way toward the Apostolic Palace through the growing crowds that had gathered to await the announcement of a new pope. Looking over his head, he saw a line of thin white clouds flowing in over the city, their wispy swirls aligning in pairs that reminded him of angel's wings.

He uttered a quick prayer while he walked, asking for their guidance before he entered the palace. The hallways were filled with other red-capped cardinals, all dressed in their traditional long black cassocks and huddled together in small conversation groups. Leo could only guess at what they were discussing as they glanced in his direction before he descended a narrow stairway to a cavernous meeting room that had been constructed beneath the palace for high-level church meetings before Pope Michael's death.

Rows of plush, cushioned seats filled a space that sloped down to a small podium below a large screen, and most were already filled as Leo made his way down the aisle. Sitting five rows from the front, he spotted Cardinal Ian McCulley, the hulking ex-cop from New York City who had traded in his badge to become a Jesuit priest thirty years earlier, and seated next to him was Father Leonardo Vespa, the young priest who had resumed his previous position as the Vatican's camerlengo.

"Ah, Leo." McCulley waved Leo to an empty seat beside them. "It's good to see you again. Rumor has it that you are the one who is responsible for our return to the Vatican."

"I'm but a small cog in a very big wheel, Ian. Many paid the ultimate price for our return to the Holy City."

Vespa stood to shake Leo's hand. "Have you heard any news about Adrian Acerbi … on where he is now?"

"Strangely, no. We haven't heard a word from him after he stepped down, and despite some discrete inquiries, he seems to have disappeared."

"That does seem strange."

"Ominous might be a better term, but his avoidance of the limelight was not totally unexpected, especially considering the circumstances of his departure. The past two weeks have been a whirlwind of diplomatic activity around the world, and I think people are trying to shove Adrian to the back of their minds right now. To the relief of many, the former U.S. president is now back in the White House, as are most of the leaders of the other countries that are digging their way out of the bureaucratic debris left in the wake of Acerbi's failed takeover."

McCulley glanced at his watch. "Does anyone know what this meeting is about?"

"I would imagine Cardinal Tucci will be going over the rules of the conclave," Leo said.

"As if we don't know them already," Vespa responded. "Not to sound rude, but Tucci tends to be a little long-winded. One can only hope he keeps this short. Acerbi's people made a mess of the Vatican library looking for something, and it seems that I've been tasked with putting it all back together again. I don't have time for these endless meetings."

Leo smiled with memories of his own youthful impatience; when he had first come to the Vatican as a newly-ordained Jesuit priest. "Things will sort themselves out in time, Father, We just have to …"

"Excuse me, Cardinal."

Leo looked up into the pleasant eyes of an elderly nun standing in the aisle.

"There's a woman in the courtyard outside the palace, and she insists on speaking with you."

"I'm sorry, but I'm afraid I can't leave right now. Maybe I can speak with her some other …"

"She said to tell you her name is Colette Acerbi, and there is another woman with her."

"Colette!" Leo literally jumped from his seat. "Please tell her I'll be right there."

McCulley's eyes grew wide. "Did she just say the woman waiting for you is named Acerbi?"

"Yes. Colette Acerbi. She's Eduardo Acerbi's widow. I thought she was killed in the attack on the castle in France. I'm afraid you'll have to excuse me."

"Go, Cardinal," McCulley said. "We'll keep you posted on events here."

Without replying, Leo hurried up the aisle and out into the courtyard. Immediately he spotted Colette standing behind two large Swiss Guards with a much younger woman. Rushing forward, Leo gently wrapped his arms around her frail body. "You don't know how relieved I am to see you. We all thought you were dead!"

Colette smiled up at him with the same kind of smile usually reserved for mothers who had just spotted a child who had been away from home too long. "As you can see, Leo, I'm very much alive. I was picking berries in the forest below the castle when it was attacked. I returned to Foix and have taken up residence in the old farmhouse."

Leo exhaled. "Why didn't you contact me sooner to let me know you were alive?"

"I believe that's what I'm doing now," she said, watching Leo's green eyes react. "But as happy as I am to see you, Cardinal, I'm afraid my journey here was motivated by other concerns." Her warm smile faded as she stepped back and nodded toward a young woman standing beside her. "I want you to meet Alexis … Alexis Velde. We need to speak with you … in private."

"Of course." Leo glanced over at a group of cardinals looking in their direction. "Why don't we take a little walk around the basilica to the Vatican gardens?"

Taking Colette gently by the arm, he guided the two women through Bernini's columns to a narrow walkway that led into a walled-off area that protected an oasis of splendid greenery from the curious eyes of wandering tourists. The woman with Colette was wearing sunglasses, and she had hair that was so blonde it almost matched her white blouse. Standing mute in the lush surroundings, she seemed uncomfortable in the bright sunlight.

"Are you sure you wouldn't rather go to a small café and have lunch? I have a favorite nearby. My treat."

"No, thank you, Cardinal," Colette answered. "That won't be necessary. We ate on the train and we must hurry. We're returning to France tonight."

Leo could feel the tension building in the air. "What's the rush? There's a lovely hotel across the street, and …"

"Alexis claims to be Adrian's real mother, Cardinal … his birth mother. She's the one who left him on my doorstep years ago, and she has something to tell you."

For a second Leo felt as if his mind had suddenly been jolted from his body, as if it was floating free, looking down on the physical world around him with a strange sense of detachment.

Adrian's birth mother?

The two women waited as Leo struggled to comprehend.

"I'm sorry, Cardinal," Colette continued, "but I couldn't think of an easy way to tell you. I felt the same way when she showed up in Foix two days ago."

"Does she speak?" Leo finally asked, staring at his own reflection in the woman's large sunglasses.

"Yes, Cardinal … I can speak." The woman's accent was tinged with a hint of Scandinavia.

"I don't mean to offend you, Ms. Velde, but if you are really Adrian Acerbi's birth mother why have you waited so long to come forward?"

"I think the answer to that question should be obvious to you, Cardinal, especially after people started calling my son the Antichrist. I've come here to tell you that, although Adrian might be a lot of things, he's definitely not the Antichrist. It's an impossibility."

"An impossibility, you say. And what makes you so sure?"

"Well, for one thing, Cardinal, I'm no jackal … and Steig Lundahl is the boy's biological father."

Once again Leo could feel his mind detaching from his body.

CHAPTER 40

A fine, chalky dust drifted through the catacombs, making it hard to breathe as Leo climbed up onto the spindly wooden catwalk that encircled the ancient Christian chapel in the catacombs beneath the basilica. The excavation of the fourth wall was well underway, and as Morelli worked with his assistants to expose the exterior surface, he was so covered in dust that there was no discernible difference between the color of his hair and his skin, making him look like one of those spray-painted, monochromatic human statues entertaining people on street corners all over the world with their robotic-like movements.

"Ah, Leo. Where have you been? We should be finished here by midnight."

Leo grabbed Morelli by the elbow and led him away from the others. "I just received some news you might find interesting, Bishop. Colette is still alive, and she just showed up with Adrian Acerbi's birth mother."

"Acerbi's birth mother?!"

"Yes, and there's more. Maybe you should be sitting down."

"Just tell me."

"She says the father is Pope Michael's brother, Steig Lundahl."

"What! You've got to be kidding. How can that be?"

"I have no idea, but the fact that she claims to be Acerbi's real mother has certainly muddied the waters. Colette wanted to return to France with her tonight, but I talked them into staying. They're checking into the Hotel Amalfi right now, and I asked Francois to have his men keep an eye on them. Her story defies reason, especially now, coming on the heels of Adrian's removal from power. We need to keep her close until we can find some proof that she's really who she says she is."

"What about the code in the Bible? We must be missing something."

"Lev and Daniel are working on it. I've also been talking to the Jesuit astronomers who've been keeping an eye on the dark star that approached the earth the day Adrian underwent his transformation in Turkey last year. According to them, it's been hovering in the same spot at the edge of our solar system."

"Which means it's still watching over him for some reason," Morelli said. "If you want my opinion, it's not a star at all. I believe its evil incarnate … a repository for something of great power that wants to remain hidden … who knows."

Leo stared off into space. "Whatever it is, it's not good, and now this woman shows up out of the blue and claims to be his birth mother. It's too much to process right now."

"I think that's the point, don't you, Leo?"

"Yes, I do. Things aren't what they appear to be. I believe Satan has played a masterful hand of poker, and his stack of chips grows larger by the minute. He's kept us so far off balance that we have no idea who or what's coming at us next, and as far as I can tell he's holding all the aces."

Morelli reached up and scratched his head, releasing a puff of dust that cascaded down over his shoulders. "And the conclave of cardinals … is that still on for tomorrow?"

"Yes. The Church needs a real leader now more than ever. We're proceeding as if nothing has changed."

"Bishop!" The excited voice of a young female archaeologist called out from the far end of the wall. "I think you need to see this."

The Pavlovian-like trigger of potential discovery caused Leo and Morelli to sprint past a row of industrial-type lights on yellow tripods that illuminated the entire exterior wall of the mysterious chapel they had discovered after following a series of clues from an equally mysterious code in the Bible.

It was also here that they had been threatened by *Agaliarept*, Satan's grand general over hell, and where seven archangels had come to their aid, chasing the demon from the chapel and turning it from a place of fear into a place of miracles.

Although the chapel's origin was still clouded in mystery, they had discovered messages from the past on its walls; messages that had lain dormant for two thousand years, waiting to be revealed at this exact point in history when mankind was being threatened by an evil force that none of them really understood. Now, through the swirling dust painted orange by the halogen lights, the fourth and final exterior wall was about to be revealed to them.

210

As soon as they arrived at the far end of the newly excavated space, the young female archaeologist pointed to the wall. Leo and Morelli squinted through the haze but could see nothing.

"What is it?" Morelli asked. "What are you looking at?"

"It's not painted like the previous images you found on the other walls, Bishop," the young woman replied. "It's engraved." She walked to the wall and began brushing another layer of dust away from the carved surface, enabling the two men to see the emerging outline of several letters.

Stepping closer, Leo ran his fingers over the etched stone as the woman continued to brush, until finally the entire inscription was revealed. It was in Latin.

Defensoris Agro Daemonum—Defender of the field of demons.

Standing to the side, Leo waited for her to finish brushing the dirt from the second inscription below the first.

Venit Ab Aquilone—She comes from the north.

Leo backed away from the wall to study both inscriptions.

"What do you think it means, Leo?" Morelli asked.

"I'm not sure." Leo repeated the words out loud in English. "*Defender of the field of demons—she comes from the north.* This is like nothing else we've found here before." For a long time he continued to stare at the wall, thinking. "Something about this reminds me of a place Lundahl described to me when I was in Norway."

"What kind of place?"

"He was talking about a place where a great evil had occurred … a rocky field in the Norwegian forest that contained a ring of stone monoliths like the one we found in Turkey, only the one in Norway was standing in a field near a village that had suffered some kind of demonic event back in the 1800's. The village was abandoned on the advice of a Jesuit priest who turned out to be one of Lundahl's distant ancestors. The priest told the villagers that the entire area was under the influence of a demonic force that flowed from the stone ring. Steig told me that Marcus had been fascinated by the story … that he had actually traveled alone to the site when he was only fifteen years old. Apparently, the experience so affected him that he decided to become a priest like his distant ancestor."

For several minutes, the two men stood in silence as the bright lights behind them projected their elongated shadows against the chapel's ancient walls.

"Does anyone know Norwegian?" Leo finally said.

"The inscriptions are in Latin, Leo," Morelli answered.

"I know a little Norwegian," the girl said. "I spent my first summer after college in Norway."

"What about names … Norwegian names. Did you ever learn any of their meanings?"

"You mean their historical origins?"

"Yes, exactly."

"No, but I have a laptop." She turned and scrambled over a mound of dirt to a wooden worktable and flipped the cover up on her computer. "What would you like to know?"

"Enter the name, *Velde*."

She typed in the name and opened a screen. "It's an old Norse name, Cardinal … from the word, *vollr*."

"What does that mean?"

"It's a word that means *field* … or *meadow*."

"What about the name, *Alexis*?"

The girl typed again. "That name has Latin roots. The name *Alexis* comes from the Latin, *Alexius*, meaning *defender,* or *guardian.*

"Oh, my God!" Leo turned and began jogging toward the exit.

"Leo! Stop!" Morelli shouted. "Where are you going?"

Leo spun around. "The woman with Colette … the one who claims to be Adrian's birth mother! Her first name means *defender*, and her last name, *Velde*, means *field*."

"And she comes from the *north*!" Morelli exclaimed.

"Exactly. *The defender of the field that comes from the north.*"

Morelli's face turned ashen. "What are you going to do?"

"I don't know yet. Call Francois and make sure they don't let her out of their sight!"

CHAPTER 41

Leo was running. The wispy white clouds he had seen moving over the city earlier had turned dark as he turned onto the *Via Germanico* and saw a line of black cars with flashing blue lights parked in front of the hotel. His stomach tightened as he continued to run, crossing the street and bounding up the stairs into the lobby.

"Leo!" Francois blocked his way. "They're gone."

"Colette gave me her word they wouldn't leave."

"Colette is still here."

"What are you talking about? You said *they*."

"Apparently, Evita left the hotel with the woman who came here with Colette."

"Evita … with Alexis? Did they say where they were going?"

"No, they didn't speak to anyone. I'm sorry, Cardinal, but my men said the woman was sitting in the lobby when Evita returned from her shopping trip. They talked for a few minutes, then got up and walked down the hallway to the small kitchen at the back of the hotel. My officers didn't want to follow them right away for fear of exposing our surveillance, so they waited in the lobby thinking the two women were just getting something to eat. When they didn't return my men got suspicious and discovered the kitchen was deserted. We've searched the entire hotel. They must have gone out through the back door."

Leo spun around, half expecting to see Evita standing behind him, but all he saw were Vatican security men swarming through the tall Victorian doors.

Francois searched Leo's face. "Who was that woman, Cardinal?"

"I'm not sure yet, Francois, but I think Evita may be in danger. Have you notified the police at the airport?"

213

"We sent out a general alert to every police station in Italy, as well as the airports and train stations."

An officer in a dark suit walked up behind Francois. "Excuse me, Commander, but we may have found something on one of the security cameras."

"Let's see it."

The man produced a small laptop and laid it on the front desk. "Is that Ms. Vargas?"

Peering at the screen, Leo saw Evita's long black hair blowing back from her face as she and Alexis were getting into the back seat of a Mercedes sedan. "That's them. What is she doing? She's a trained intelligence officer, and she just got into a car with a complete stranger and drove away without telling anyone where she was going."

"Maybe she was forced." The security officer enlarged the picture. The image of a large man standing on the sidewalk behind her came into view, and as they focused back on Evita in the next frame, they could see that she had glanced up at the security camera before getting into the vehicle. "We couldn't make out the face of the driver, but we have the license plate number, and every police officer in Rome has this same picture popping up on their cell phones."

"This doesn't make any sense," Leo said. "What could that woman possibly want with Evita?"

The cell phone in Leo's pocket began to vibrate. "Evita?"

"No, Cardinal. This is Adrian Acerbi."

"Where's Evita?!"

"I can assure you that your girlfriend is quite safe … for the moment. Please try to keep the shock on your face to a minimum, because we wouldn't want to alarm the police standing next to you. I think it's time you and I had that little chat I've been looking so forward to. The time has come for me to make a few demands of my own, Cardinal. I'm in Norway, and Evita will soon be joining me. Come alone."

"Where will I find you?"

"I think you know where we'll be."

The line went dead as Leo dropped the phone on the desk and stared through the hotel's tall windows at a cold rain that had begun to fall over the eternal city.

CHAPTER 42

Francois was livid as he stared out at the rain and paced the carpet in Leo's hotel room. "You're not going to Norway alone, Cardinal, and that's final! We've already lost one person today, and I'm not about to lose another."

The look in Leo's eyes telegraphed the overwhelming sense of helplessness he was feeling to the Swiss Guard commander. "You know I have to go, Francois. This latest move by Acerbi tells us he still has eyes everywhere, and if I don't follow his instructions to the letter we could lose the only chance we have of saving Evita."

"I admire your chivalrous intentions, my friend, but his request for you to go alone sounds like a line we've all heard in a thousand movies." Francois was working hard to keep his voice calm. "Evita will be in even more danger if you go alone. You know as well as I do that you can't play by Acerbi's rules, because if you do you'll lose. He wants you out of the picture for what you did to him, and he's smart enough to know that the only way he can lure you out into an obvious trap is through Evita. Do you really think he's going to let her go when he's done with you?"

"What do you suggest?"

"First, I think we should contact Lev Wasserman and Danny Zamir. The Israelis have ways of crossing international borders without drawing any unwanted attention, and we could use their expertise. They're your friends, Cardinal … we all are, and we're not about to let you face this thing alone."

Francois paused, searching Leo's eyes before he asked his next question. "Have you spoken to Colette yet?"

"Yes. She had no idea what that woman was up to."

"Are you sure about that?"

215

"I'm positive. She's nothing more than an innocent victim in all of this."

"You're probably right. It makes perfect sense when you think about it. Acerbi used someone you trusted to walk that woman right through our circle of security. Do you think she's really Adrian's birth mother?"

"I have no idea, and those inscriptions on the chapel wall that Morelli and his team just uncovered only added to the confusion. I'm surprised she even gave us her real name."

The French doors leading to the balcony outside rattled with the increasing wind as it swirled through the darkness.

"Maybe that was part of the plan," Francois said. "She could just be a pawn like everyone else on Acerbi's human chessboard. You know, in all my years on the job I've never been caught off guard like this before. I only wish we knew what Acerbi's end-game is. If we had the answer to that it might help shed some light on his next move. Even though he told you to come alone, I'd bet my pension he knows you'll be coming at him with everything you've got. I only hope we're not playing right into his hands again."

"I think his end game goes beyond anything we can imagine, Francois. Remember, we're not dealing with a man. We're dealing with an evil entity that's hiding its true intentions, but something tells me there's an even greater evil out there somewhere … I can feel it. It's hiding in the shadows … waiting and watching, and whatever it has in store for us will probably pale in comparison to anything we've seen in the past."

Francois stared straight ahead, his jaw tightening as he ran his hands through his short, gray-tipped hair. Filling two glasses with dark red wine, he handed one to Leo. "Acerbi won't do anything to Evita until you're directly in his crosshairs. She's his trump card, and that should give us the time we need to run through all our options and come up with a solid plan to rescue her."

Looking at the visible pain on Leo's face, Francois finished his wine and stood. "Get some rest, Cardinal. I have men posted outside your door and all around the hotel, but I'd feel a whole lot better if you spent the night inside the walls of Vatican City."

"I'll be fine here, Francois."

"Of course, that's your call, sir, but since you've got your mind set on staying here tonight, I'll take the room across the hall. I'll wake you in the morning before the sun comes up. Don't answer the door for anyone but me."

Francois closed the door behind him, leaving Leo alone with his thoughts as he sat on the edge of his bed and punched in some numbers on his cell phone. After two short rings, Leo heard Lev's distinct Israeli accent on the other end of the line.

"Leo ... I thought you would be calling soon. Any word yet on Evita?"

"No, Francois and I were just sitting here trying to formulate a plan."

"I know ... he just called to tell me he believes Acerbi has her in Norway somewhere. How can I help?"

"I need to get there as soon as possible. How long will it take you and the others to get here from Israel?"

"We're not in Israel."

"Not in Israel? But ..."

"We're in Spain, Leo ... on board the Carmela."

"The entire team?"

"Yes. We wanted to retrieve the yacht as soon as possible. Acerbi's men pretty much trashed the furnishings, but thankfully they left the engine room and communications center fully intact. We were planning on returning to Israel this evening until Francois called a few minutes ago. I'm very sorry, my friend, but we'll get her back. Are you speaking on an encrypted phone?"

"Yes. Did Francois tell you about the inscriptions we found on the fourth wall of the chapel?"

"We've already begun a computer search of the Bible code."

Leo could feel a surge of adrenalin as he contemplated his next move. "I should fly to Barcelona tonight and join you. Acerbi has taken Evita to the site of the old village Lundahl told me about. There's a lot I haven't had a chance to tell you yet, but beyond the burned remains of the village there's a circle of stone like the one we discovered in Turkey. It's surrounded by a rocky field where the villagers used to bury their dead. That's where Adrian will be waiting for me ... inside the circle of stone. Have you spoken to the others yet?"

"Yes ... hang on a moment, Leo." On the other end of the line Leo could hear voices until Lev returned. "It seems that Daniel has already uncovered something in the code. From what I'm seeing, it looks like our access to the circle of stone will be limited once we arrive. It appears that only the *chosen ones* will be safe traveling with you inland to the edge of the field, but only one person will be safe entering the actual circle."

"What did the passages say, Lev ... the exact wording."

Another prolonged silence ensued before Lev finally answered. *"Only the chosen will be protected when they walk with the Shepherd of the Church to the field of the demons."*

"Shepherd of the Church? Are you sure that's what it said?"

"Positive."

"What about the other passage?"

"The shepherd must walk alone into the circle of stone."

"That doesn't make any sense," Leo shot back. "The Church has no shepherd right now. The Conclave of Cardinal's won't even begin their deliberations until tomorrow, which means we are still without a spiritual leader."

"I believe it's referring to you, Leo. You're the Vatican's Secretary of State, which means you're in charge until a new pope is elected. You must be the one the code is pointing to."

"I don't think you understand, Lev. Only a sitting pope can be called the Shepherd of the Church. The Holy Father is Christ's Vicar here on earth … not the Secretary of State. The Vatican isn't exactly a democracy, and the curia has been pretty clear when it comes to the subject of papal succession. Once again Adrian seems to have struck when the Church is at its most vulnerable spiritually … when we are without a pope."

"If you're not the shepherd, then who, Leo? Acerbi is obviously afraid of you for some reason, and he's gone to great lengths to lure you to a place where he can deal with you on his terms. Why else would he be so fixated on you if you aren't the shepherd?"

"I have no idea, but at this point it doesn't really matter." Leo could hear his voice beginning to rise. "I'm still going after Evita regardless of my title. All I can do at this point is ask for your support. Adrian will be keeping her close to him in case he senses danger, which means he's holding all the cards right now. I have to go … shepherd or no shepherd."

"You know you have our support, Leo, but we have to tell the others that there's a line they can't cross once we reach that field." Lev paused, thinking. "As much as I'd like send for Team 5 I'm afraid we'd only be putting their lives at risk. We'd be exposing them to something they have no defense against, because it appears that the battle that's coming will be spiritual, but I honestly don't know how anyone will be able to restrain Alon from following you into that circle of stone if he senses that something is about to happen to you."

A dark picture swam into Leo's mind. "I'll talk to him before we fly to Norway."

"I don't think flying is a good idea, Leo."

"What?"

"Flying will be too risky."

"What are you talking about, Lev! We all flew out of England together. What's changed?" Leo's heart was pounding in his ears. "Evita may be safe for now, but Adrian's clock is already counting down. He won't wait forever. We have to fly!"

Lev's Israeli accent thickened. "Acerbi knows you won't be coming alone despite the fact that he told you to, and we know that there are people who are loyal to him still embedded within the military. Now that the radar coverage over Europe has been restored, they will be watching the skies over Norway for our arrival, and we both know he seems to have a penchant for bringing down planes full of people. He might have been blinded before, but having us all together on board a single aircraft again could be the golden opportunity he's been waiting for. I have a better plan, but I'm afraid we'll have to discuss it in person. For now we must keep our discussion short. Danny Zamir believes Acerbi may have another quantum computer hidden somewhere that hasn't been taken offline, which means all of our encryption software is good for only a few minutes before it's decoded. I'll see you soon, my friend. Get here as fast as you can."

A click on the other end of the line signaled their conversation was over. Standing, Leo felt drained. His emotions were numb as he walked to the French doors and peered out at the outline of the basilica. Through the droplets of water left from the rain on the wavering glass, the lighted dome glistened in the distance. It seemed to be speaking to him, warning him to stay away from the deep shadows that lay just out of sight along the path he was about to take.

Was it really just a feeling, or was something reaching out to him?

Suddenly, it felt as though all of the air had been sucked from the room. With a growing sense of dread, Leo pushed against the doors and stepped outside to breathe in the rain-scented air. The downpour had turned to a slight drizzle, and as he turned his face to the sky, the falling mist clouded his vision, blurring the twinkling lights that winked back at him from the seven hills of Rome.

Something was coming!

CHAPTER 43

The small motorboat cleaved its way through the gentle Mediterranean swells before it slowed and edged up alongside the huge blue and white yacht anchored in the Spanish harbor *of El Port De La Selva*. After climbing the teakwood boarding stairs, Leo and Morelli were greeted on the main deck by Lev and the others.

Circling the group with his eyes, Leo could see that everyone was there. To his right, Alon and Nava were squeezed between Daniel and Sarah and John and Ariella, and standing beside them, Javier Mendoza and Dr. Raul Diaz were talking quietly with Moshe, the former Israeli general who was in charge of security on the yacht. The only one missing from their group was the person on everyone's mind—Evita Vargas, and they had all made a silent vow to themselves that they wouldn't be returning from Norway without her.

"Welcome back aboard the *Carmela*, gentlemen," Lev said, puffing on a cigar while the others took turns greeting the two new arrivals. "We'll be getting underway in a few minutes. We just finished reprovisoning the boat and the cooks are preparing lunch. Hope you're hungry."

"Not really," Morelli said. "Commander Jennings evaded radar all the way to Spain by flying her little white jet a few feet above the water. I could swear I felt the bottom of the plane hit a wave. What I need right now is a drink."

Lev smiled. "Follow me."

Moving into the main salon, Leo and Morelli noticed that the grand piano was missing and that several crewmembers were busy repairing scratched woodwork and scrubbing the stains from some of the yacht's elegant furnishings. It was a stark reminder that Acerbi's men had treated the yacht harshly when they had moved aboard after Lev and the others had been forced to abandon her in their escape across the Pyrenees to the safe haven of the Cathar castle.

"It doesn't look too bad, Lev," Leo said, "I was expecting much worse."

"This boat will have to be hauled into dry dock and totally refitted when we return home," Lev grumbled as they climbed the interior stairway to the less formal salon above. "There's a year's worth of marine growth below the waterline, which means our transit time will be slowed considerably and we'll be forced to use more fuel."

Topping the stairs, a young crewmember behind the bar spotted Lev's sour expression and placed three glasses on the black granite countertop.

"Just some ice water for me," Lev said, leaning against the bar. "But I think my two friends here might like something a little stronger."

"We can take care of that. What can I get for you gentlemen?"

"A glass of Cabernet Sauvignon sounds good to me," Morelli said.

"And for you, Cardinal?"

"A cold beer will do."

"Domestic or imported?"

Leo gave the man a blank look as Lev's dour expression turned playful. "Since he's an American on an Israeli yacht anchored in a Spanish harbor, he probably doesn't know how to answer that question. Give him a cold San Miguel. I've never seen him turn down one of those. Why don't we grab a seat out on the back deck?"

Glasses in hand, the three men walked through the sliding glass doors onto a curved teakwood deck that overlooked the larger main deck below. Settling into a cushioned deck chair, Leo could feel himself begin to relax in the comfortable familiarity of being with close friends as he looked to the distant mountains rising up behind the coast. "Any news yet on how the Cathars are faring at the abandoned air base?"

"Apparently, no one could restrain Gael and some of his men from going to the castle," Lev said. "He called last night from Foix to tell me that they found Julian's body in the ruins. They laid him to rest in that little grassy area next to the waterfall. It's very peaceful there. I think Julian would have approved."

"Gael must have been devastated," Leo said. "The last time we talked he was still holding out hope that his brother was alive and hiding somewhere in the mountains."

Morelli set his glass on the table and leaned back in his chair. "You forget the teachings of our Cathar brothers and sisters, Leo. They've always looked on their earthly life as a mere transition point on the journey to

222

their final destination. They still believe the world we live in is ruled by an evil entity … a dark mirror image of the God of light. For a Cathar, leaving the earth plane is a cause for celebration, especially for someone like Julian who had reached the pinnacle of his faith."

Leo nodded in agreement. "Still, I will miss the many philosophic discussions we used to have after dinner. The world has been robbed of too many good people lately. I suppose it's always been that way, but I don't plan on letting Evita become one of them. How long do you think it will take us to reach Norway, Lev?"

"I'd say at least half a day to round the Strait of Gibraltar, then another day and a half up the English Channel and into the North Sea. Alex and I have been going over some Norwegian coastal charts, and he believes our best bet is to sail up the fjord closest to the point where you'll be heading inland."

"Alex is a fine captain, and I trust his judgment, but the crew will have to be warned to remain on board. In fact, it might be wise for the rest of you to stay behind as well. We're still not sure about those passages Daniel found in the code that refer to the Shepherd of the Church. My presence could offer no protection at all, and anyone who follows me to that field could be making a fatal mistake."

"Then we might as well leave Alon behind here in Spain," Lev said, "because I'd have to shoot him with a tranquilizer dart if he saw you walking away from the yacht by yourself."

"What new passages?" Morelli snorted, looking back and forth between Leo and Lev.

Leo glanced at Lev before standing and walking to the railing. "I wanted to tell you this sooner, Anthony, but I knew what your reaction would be. It appears that Daniel has uncovered some new passages encoded within the text of Leviticus, and they were pretty specific about who should enter the circle of stone where Acerbi will be waiting."

"Yes, Cardinal … I think a little heads-up would have been most considerate of you." Morelli downed the rest of his wine and folded his arms across his chest. "What new information did these passages contain?"

Leo leaned against the railing and took a deep breath. *The Shepherd of the Church must walk alone into the circle of stone.* Leo said it quickly, spitting out the words as though the mere act of saying them quickly would somehow lessen the effect they would have on his Jesuit friend.

Morelli was incredulous. "You can't be serious, Leo. The word shepherd is obviously referring to a pope, which means you can't go anywhere near that stone circle."

223

"It's more complicated than that, Anthony."

"There's nothing complicated about it, Leo. The Church is in a period of *Sede Vacante* right now. The throne of Saint Peter is vacant. The Church is without a shepherd until a new pope is elected."

"But Leo is the Secretary of State," Lev said. "Doesn't that count for something?"

"Yes, it does," Morelli said, "and Camerlengo Vespa is working with the College of Cardinals to run the day-to-day administrative affairs of the Church, which also makes him a leader of sorts, but only a pope can lay claim to the title of Shepherd of the Church."

Morelli's face had turned the same color as his bright red hair, and his withering stare made it obvious that he didn't like the fact that Leo hadn't filled him in on all the details. "Technically, Leo, you lost your job as the Vatican's Secretary of State the day Pope Michael died. After you returned and exposed the fact that Cardinal Acone had been chosen in a sham election orchestrated by Acerbi to gain control of the Church, the other cardinals naturally looked to you as our temporary leader, but the true Shepherd of the Church can only be a pope. In other words, my friend, if the encoded passages are correct, you're walking into a trap."

Finishing off his wine, Morelli continued. "You know as well as I do, Leo, that Adrian is counting on your love for Evita to manipulate you into following his instructions. You're a soldier of the Cross, and soldiers don't follow the commands of their enemies. I hate to keep saying this, but none of us really knows what the end-game of all of this is. It could simply be an act of revenge for the times you've repeatedly outwitted him in the past, but I'm not buying that scenario. I believe his real goal is gaining access to your soul."

Lev's eyes grew wide. "I never thought of that. Anthony has a point, Leo. Think about it for a minute. We're caught up in a war between heaven and hell, and by agreeing to meet with him in a place of his choosing you'll be laying yourself open to a demonic assault the likes of which you've never experienced before, and the code says nothing about this so-called *shepherd* surviving. He will use false information and alternately cajole and threaten you ... all in an effort to draw you in and make you lower your defenses."

Leo faced the other two men with a look of grim determination. "I know I don't have to tell either of you that demons are very powerful creatures, and if Agaliarept is the one who's looking back at me from behind Adrian's human eyes, then I'm walking into a meeting with one of the most powerful demons of them all. I realize that the passage in the code stated that only the Shepherd of the Church would have any chance at all of coming away from that meeting unscathed, but if you ask me we've become lost in a battle of semantics. The title of shepherd may be reserved for the pope, Anthony, but sometimes we have to look at the figurative meaning behind the messages we receive. Besides, what other option do I have? Right now I'm Evita's only hope."

Lev fished a cigar from his shirt pocket and lit it with a match. "Maybe we have become lost in a battle of semantics. In the absence of another, Leo is a shepherd to his flock in every sense of the word. No one else in the church comes close, and we're running out of time."

"You're right, Lev," Morelli said quietly. "Leo is a shepherd in every sense of the word except for the one that counts. We're not talking about the pastoral work of one cardinal over their own diocese. We're talking about someone who's been chosen to be the shepherd of the entire Church, and he must be chosen by a group of men whose decisions are inspired by God … the College of Cardinals. There's no way around it. No matter how you try to paint it, if we allow Leo to go against the demon alone we're sending him to his physical death as well as his spiritual death. Have you considered the consequences of that action?"

"What consequence could be worse than doing nothing at all?" Lev asked.

Morelli signaled the crewmember behind the bar for another glass of wine, giving Leo a chance to study his old friend. His easy-going manner had always had a way of disguising one of the sharpest intellects in the Church. Even in his youthful days back in seminary, his intellectual capacity to sift through centuries-old dogma to zero in on a theological problem with laser-like intensity had impressed his professors, not to mention his fellow seminarians.

Leaning back in his chair, Morelli sipped from his refilled glass. "If you ask me, it's not just Leo who's in danger. Whatever is waiting for him in Norway is after control of the entire Church, and one very good way to achieve that goal is by gaining control of a much beloved cardinal … a cardinal like our good friend Leo here … a cardinal who has a good chance of becoming the next pope. We're dealing with a master of deceit, and when we send Leo in there to face him alone there's a very good chance that the Leo who is with us now won't be the same Leo who returns to us. Think about it for a moment. What better way to regain control of the Church than by placing a respected cardinal on Saint Peter's throne after the dark one has claimed him as his own?"

The three men stared silently at one another as a muted rumble shook the deck beneath their feet, announcing that Captain Alex Pappas had just started the engines. Moments later, he was guiding the large yacht out of the harbor and into the building waves of the Mediterranean Sea. They were on their way to Norway for a meeting with whatever was waiting for them in a dark and ancient forest.

CHAPTER 44

Evita Vargas was mad. She was mad at herself. Why had she allowed herself to be maneuvered away from the safety of a well-guarded hotel lobby by a woman who was a complete stranger? She had been a trained Spanish intelligence officer, and in a single momentary lapse of judgment she had just made one of the biggest rookie mistakes of her life.

Rule number one. Don't trust friendly-looking strangers. In Evita's defense, Alexis had been cleared into the hotel by Vatican security, and her offhand suggestion that they grab something to eat in the hotel kitchen had seemed innocent enough—until she had pulled a gun from her purse and forced Evita through the back door of the hotel, where a very large man had ushered her into the back of an idling Mercedes parked behind the building. At least she had thought to glance up at the security camera before getting in the car.

Surprisingly, her captors had treated her more like a special guest than a kidnap victim. They had left her unrestrained and had even allowed her to walk freely to the private jet at the airport in Rome, and after the jet had landed at an isolated windswept field, no handcuffs or duct tape had appeared when they took her to a cozy warm cabin with small windows and no metal bars to block the view of a snow-covered field and the forest that lay beyond.

Now, an hour after she had arrived, she heard new voices outside followed by the sound of the front door opening. Rising from her chair in front of the fireplace she saw the chilling image of Adrian Acerbi standing in the doorway.

"Good afternoon, Ms. Vargas. I hope these accommodations are to your liking."

"They would be better if they came with a view of Rome. Where am I … Norway?"

"What gave it away, Ms. Vargas? Was it the cabin … the forest … or maybe the snow-capped mountains all around us?"

"I've heard you have a very sarcastic wit, Mr. Acerbi."

"Please, call me Adrian. I apologize if I come off sounding superior. It's probably because I am. How long do you think it will take your friend the cardinal to get here?"

"Who knows? He could be standing right behind you."

Acerbi blinked hard but resisted the urge to spin around to see if Leo was really there.

"An interesting man … the cardinal," Acerbi continued, "but then again, look who I'm talking to. It seems that you also find him interesting. Why is that, Ms. Vargas? He's at least twenty years older than you are. Could it be that you are one of those women who are drawn to powerful male religious figures?"

Evita remained silent, her brown eyes searching Adrian's expression for any hint of the person he had once been before the demon had robbed him of his humanity. She almost felt … *what? Sorrow— pity?* Was that what she was feeling for the thing standing in front of her now?

"That's quite alright, Ms. Vargas. I really didn't expect you to answer that. I'm sure the cardinal will be along shortly. Until then, please enjoy your stay. We'll try to make you as comfortable as possible."

Adrian turned, the ends of his heavy, knee-length fur coat billowing behind him as he strode from the cabin past the building snow drifts to the warmth of a waiting SUV.

As soon as he drove away, Evita heard the solid click of the front door being locked from the outside, followed by the muted silence that surrounded her idyllic prison. Collapsing onto a long, overstuffed couch, she pulled a blanket up to her shoulders and leaned back to listen to the crackle of the fire licking around the logs in the rock fireplace.

What was Leo doing?

Wherever he was she hoped he would find her soon, because she had also begun to feel the creeping sensation that something worse than anything they had faced before was coming, and only Leo could stop it. The clatter of china made her turn her head. Entering the room from the kitchen, Alexis Velde set a silver tray down on the coffee table. "Would you like some tea, Evita?"

CHAPTER 45

The yacht's engines strained as the Carmela's bow rose into the air before crashing back down onto the backside of one of the heavy blue waves marching across the frigid waters of the North Sea. Peering through the large, angled windows on the bridge, Leo held on as Captain Alex Pappas leaned with the roll of the boat and braced himself for the next blue giant already heading their way.

"I've never enjoyed piloting boats through the waters in this part of the world," Pappas said to Leo. "The waves are even higher along the Norwegian coast, but once we enter the fjord the water will become as smooth as glass."

Grabbing onto a stainless-steel railing, Leo pulled himself next to the captain. "How much longer till we get there?"

"If it wasn't so cloudy you could already see the mountains from here. I'd say at least another hour until we pass the first marker and make our turn for the coast. It's still early, so we'll have to anchor somewhere until it gets dark. With no moon out tonight, the yacht will be almost impossible to spot when it enters the fjord. Once we turn off all the lights on board, we'll be nothing more than a big dark shadow on the water."

Leo was feeling the first pangs of seasickness as another wave crashed over the bow, sending a frothing mass of swirling whitewater cascading over the deck and draining back out though the scuppers. "I think I'll go down to the communications room. Maybe I'll feel better down there."

"By all means, Cardinal. The bridge probably isn't the best place to be when we're in seas like this. You can really feel the roll of the boat this high up." Alex watched Leo's complexion drain. "It looks like you should go now, sir. The com room sits right in the boat's center of gravity, so you won't feel the movement as much down there."

Leo just nodded as Alex grabbed a barf bag and shoved it into his hands. "Here … just in case you need it while you're making your way downstairs. The good news is we're only a few hours away from calmer water."

"Thanks," Leo mumbled as he lurched from one hand hold to another, working his way to the back of the bridge and down a short set of stairs that led down a stainless-steel hallway to the Carmela's state of the art communications center.

Inside, the glow from a wall of flat screens provided the only light in an otherwise darkened room as a group of men and women stared into their computer screens. On loan from the Israeli Navy, these specialists had joined the yacht when she had stopped at Gibraltar to refuel before heading north. They had been sent by Danny Zamir to back up Lev's crew and monitor the threat environment around the yacht, and each were experts in computer systems, satellite communications, and radar surveillance.

Zamir had even thought to send a sonar operator who had wheeled some classified equipment aboard to scan the depths below the yacht when she made her way through Norway's inland maze of waterways—a time when she would be at her most vulnerable due to her inability to maneuver within the tight confines of the narrow fjord they were heading to.

Closing the steel door behind him, Leo could sense that the rolling motion of the boat had lessened as he felt the cool air blowing from a vent above his head, drying the beads of sweat on his forehead. Alex had been right. This was a much better place to be in rough weather, and already Leo could feel the creep of nausea begin to subside as he took a seat next to Lev. "Any problems so far?"

"No," Lev replied. "We're just picking up the usual navigation chatter. Gwyneth Hastings used her connections at MI6 to clear our entry into the country with the Norwegian authorities, but not before two of their fighter planes took a quick peek at us."

"What about the people in their military still under Adrian's control?"

"Hastings told us that the Norwegians have been pretty good at finding Acerbi loyalists within their ranks, and only their most trusted people are manning their radar screens, but there have been sporadic outbreaks of violence within the militaries of other countries. A battalion of his soldiers tried to reclaim their hold on the Turkish government, but after a short skirmish with the Turkish army they surrendered. It's going to take time for the individual governments to eliminate the rogue elements attempting to take advantage of an unstable situation while they make the transition back to the way things were before."

Lev paused to light a cigar. "Any idea what you're going to do once we arrive?"

"To tell you the truth I have no idea what I'm going to do until I finally come face to face with Acerbi. We're dealing with a demon who dwells in the shadows and cloaks his outward appearance to conceal his true identity. It's not Adrian we're after, but the thing inside him. Adrian Acerbi is nothing more than an innocent victim who has a soul and his whole life ahead of him. The demon has total control over him now, but he's still in there somewhere … trying to reach out for our help. I can feel it."

"Are you still convinced that you're facing the same demon we encountered in the Negev Desert and the secret chapel under the Vatican?"

"I'm certain of it," Leo said. "Only Satan's darkest angel would have the power to pull off something like this."

Lev sunk in his chair as he stared straight ahead at a blank computer screen. "It seems we've come full circle, my friend. Remember when we were sitting in that tent in the desert a couple of years ago, watching the sun go down while we were waiting to enter that cavern beneath the sands of the desert?"

"How could I forget a moment like that? It was the first time we ever mentioned the demon's name."

"Yes, and do you remember what we said about him? There's a reason the Assyrians and Babylonians looked upon him as one of the most malevolent forces in the Middle East. He was known as the dark angel of the fatal winds, and he's the most feared of all of the demonic entities … a messenger of the Beast and the most ruthlessly destructive demon of them all. He possesses the power to discover all secrets and represents the destruction of human life itself."

"Yes, that's all true, Lev, but we've faced him before, and I have no doubt that God is still watching over us."

"I think you've missed my point, Cardinal. Let me repeat myself. The thing you're about to face represents the destruction of human life itself."

"What are you getting at?"

"Well, to begin with, we still have no idea what his ultimate goal is." Lev watched the thick bluish smoke curl from the end of his cigar. "If he isn't the Antichrist, then what's he up to? Satan doesn't want to destroy humanity, he wants to control it. He wants to rob God of our love for him,

231

but his most trusted demon seems to be seeking our destruction instead. It doesn't make sense. Satan wants us for his own, for without us his well of souls will wither on the vine and die. I'm afraid that something else is going on, and you're standing in his way."

"That's right. I am standing in his way, Lev. Not only am I standing in his way, but I'm going after him, and when the dust settles we'll see just who is left standing."

Lev's looks hardened. "The area you're going to has been specifically linked to demonic activity. That's some very dangerous ground you're about to cross, my friend. From the story Steig Lundahl told you, it sounds like there's something there that we haven't anticipated yet, and I believe Jonas Lundahl might have caught a glimpse of it when he traveled to that village alone. Whatever is out there must have been there for a very long time, and to this day the area remains a cold, desolate place. The fact that Jonas ordered the villagers to burn their houses and never come back tells me that his attempts to rid the area of the evil he encountered failed. That means it's still out there, and that's where Adrian Acerbi will be waiting for you."

Lev pulled a folded piece of paper from his pocket and handed it to Leo. "You may want to read this before you go."

"What is it?"

"Morelli just received a message from his assistant working under the basilica. They've found something else on that fourth wall."

Leo patted his flat shirt pocket. "I seem to have forgotten my glasses. What does it say?"

Lev unfolded the paper and squinted at the small text. "Apparently, the archaeological team working below the basilica finally uncovered the last section of the wall, and they discovered some additional text engraved in Latin. *Qui immutabuntur fortis init*—the warrior who enters will be transformed."

"Transformed?" Leo repeated, staring back at Lev. "I've heard that term before in conjunction with the same stone circle, but I have no idea what kind of transformation it's referring to."

"Neither do I, Leo, but it doesn't sound good. There's something else. Daniel found three additional passages encoded in Leviticus last night, and except for one they seem to coincide with what we were just discussing."

Leo blinked back without answering.

"There are three lines of text that intersect on a single page," Lev continued. "The first runs horizontally across the center of the page. There are just four words ... *Satan watches from afar*. The second passage crosses the horizontal line of text vertically. It reads: *The demon in the north will resist his master.*"

"What about the third line?"

Lev exhaled. "That's the most puzzling passage of them all. *The father will take the place of the son.*"

Leo gripped the arms of the chair as the room began to spin. "We have to go to Bergen."

"Bergen?" Lev reached over and tapped his computer keyboard, bringing up a multi-colored map of Norway on the large screen at the front of the room. "Bergen is over a hundred miles from the site of the stone ruin. Stopping there will only delay our trip up the fjord."

"We're missing something, Lev, and I believe the answer is in Bergen. Jonas Lundahl compiled a written record of what happened in that village after he returned to Bergen over a hundred years ago. Steig showed me a bound leather book that contained some of the priest's notes, but the narrative ended abruptly on the last page. There has to be more, but after he died, the rest of his papers were locked away in a room beneath the only Catholic Church that existed in Bergen at the time. We've got to go to that church and see what's in those notes, because I have a feeling we're only looking at part of the picture."

Lev stared at the map on the screen for a full minute before finally picking up the intercom phone and calling the bridge.

Leaning sideways against the roll of the boat, Alex Pappas reached for the phone. "Bridge. This is the captain speaking."

"Alex, this is Lev. Change of plans. Instead of anchoring in the channel waiting for it to get dark, we'll be making a stop in Bergen before we head up the fjord."

233

CHAPTER 46

The Carmela's bow emerged from the salty mist of the North Sea and entered the inland waterway through a narrow opening in the breakwater before turning left and sailing past rows of multi-colored houses to the port town of Bergen. Situated between the coastal towns of Stavanger and Kristiansund, Bergen lay on a thin strip of land known as the Vestlandet that ran along the western coast of Norway. This was the land of the fjords, where the sea reached inland, cutting through the mountains with fingers of deep blue water that had provided ancient mariners with shelter for thousands of years.

Keeping his eyes on the fast-moving current that swirled around the rocky barrier islands on the port side of the yacht, Alex Pappas kept the Carmela in the center of the channel until the city dock came into view. Parking a two-hundred-and-thirty-foot yacht in calm water was a challenge all by itself. But maneuvering a boat of that size in fast-moving water full of rocky outcroppings took an extra measure of skill.

With eyes that had been focused on the sea for most of his life, Alex picked a spot and shoved the throttles into neutral before using the bow and stern thrusters to guide the big boat to a gentle kiss against the protective tires hanging from an industrial concrete dock. As soon as the boat was secure, Pappas picked up the intercom phone and called Lev's stateroom.

"Yes?"

"We've docked in Bergen, sir. Any new orders?"

"No, thank you, Alex," Lev yawned. "Just keep the engines warm. I'm hoping we won't be here long."

"Will do, sir." Alex walked from the bridge and lit a cigarette as he looked out over a city that looked like it had been scrubbed clean every morning. Next to Oslo, Bergen was the second largest city in Norway. It was a good jumping off point for those who wanted to explore places like the *Lysefjorden*, a spectacular fjord made famous by *Pulpit Rock*, a massive granite cliff that rose vertically five hundred feet above the water, or the *Sunnfjord* and *Nordfjord*—the *enchanted fjords* that wowed visitors with their impressive glaciers, tall waterfalls, and secluded beaches.

Tossing his lit cigarette overboard, Alex saw Leo talking with John and Ariella on the dock below as Lev and Alon ambled down the gangplank.

"Where do you think we should go first?" John asked.

"The fish market." Leo pointed across the street to a line of trucks backed up to an immense wooden building.

Ariella crinkled her nose. "The fish market?" Lifting her camera in an effort to look as touristy as possible, she peered at the building through the viewfinder. "Why the fish market?"

"I read somewhere that it's a big tourist draw here in Bergen, and since we're trying to blend in, I thought we should start there. Alon and Lev will be following along behind looking for anyone who might be showing any unusual interest in our arrival."

While Alon and Lev waited on the dock, a break in the traffic allowed the trio to sprint across the street to a weathered building that smelled surprisingly fresh, like the sea. The Norwegians had inherited a proud fishing heritage, and only the freshest seafood was offered for sale by rubber-booted fishmongers who displayed the catch of the day on dripping, ice-filled tables that covered acres of wet concrete.

Ariella watched John's face break into a grin, but when he opened his mouth to talk she held up her hand.

"Don't even go there, John."

"What?"

"I know you too well. You were getting ready to say that you think there's something fishy going on around here."

John's shoulders slumped. "Alright, Ariella … I'll try to hold off on the corny jokes, but I don't like the way that monkfish is looking at me. Where do we go from here?"

"Jonas' body is buried behind Saint Paul's church at the top of the hill," Leo said. "If I'm right, the papers we're looking for are stored in the basement below the main church building. Alex said there's a trolley stop in the square behind this building. We can probably catch one to the church."

Passing through the creosote-scented maze of thick wooden pilings used to separate the local fish mongers' stands, Leo glanced over his shoulder. Alon and Lev were maintaining a safe distance behind as the group flowed through the building and exited the opposite side between stacks of water-logged crates. Looking out over the busy town square, they crossed the street and scrambled up into one of the local green and white trolleys.

Inching across a wood-slatted seat, Ariella felt the trolley lurch as she gazed out the window and listened to the metal wheels clicking over the rails through the older, cobblestoned section of town before beginning its climb up the steep hill that led to the church.

She saw street signs with names like Lungegardsvann and Nygardshoyden. Compared to Israel, it seemed that Norway was the most alien-like of all the places she had visited, and when she inhaled the aroma of sea air tinged with the scent of pine blowing down from the surrounding forest, she felt the thrill of adventure take hold again. She hadn't felt this way in almost a year, and the exhilaration of living back out in a world full of new discoveries had thrown her senses into overdrive.

Topping the hill, Leo nodded toward the door and the three stepped off the trolley onto a steeply sloping sidewalk. Across the street, Saint Paul's Catholic Church stood at an angle that jutted from the hillside. Built in the late 19th century, the imposing gray structure had a pitched roofline and a large, round stained-glass window over the main entrance, and toward the back of the church, a seven-story bell tower looked down on the rectory behind the church where Jonas Lundahl had spent the last days of his life.

Ariella aimed her camera and snapped a few pictures before the trio climbed the steep sidewalk and crossed the street to the church, where they waited for the next trolley to deposit Lev and Alon on the street corner below. As soon as they arrived, Leo nodded to John and Ariella and the three mounted the steps in front of the church and quickly entered through the massive wooden doors.

"Now what?" John whispered.

Leo glanced toward the back of the church. "We start looking for a door to the basement."

"What's our excuse if someone catches us down there?"

"Then I'll just have to play my cardinal card."

Slowly, the trio made their way down the main aisle, brushing against wooden pews polished by age as they passed through dusty shafts of light that changed color as they swirled beneath the stained-glass windows above. At the back of the church, they entered an area beneath the choir loft and stopped in front of a wooden door set back into a squared stone wall. As soon as Leo opened it he saw right away that they were standing directly below the bell tower. On one side of the bare space, a curved wooden staircase ascended to the floor above, while on the opposite side of the cold stone room, another stairway disappeared through the floor into the basement below.

Exchanging glances, the three made their way down the stairs that led below, ending up at the end of a lighted hallway with doors that ran along both sides.

"It looks like people come down here all the time," Ariella said. "This place is spotless."

"Can I help you?"

The trio spun around to see a young priest standing behind them at the base of the stairs.

"You're welcome to explore our church," the priest smiled, "but this is a storage area and there's really not much to see down here. You might want to check out the bell tower instead. The view from the top is magnificent."

Leo stepped forward and extended his hand. "Please excuse us. We didn't see anyone, and …"

The priest's eyes widened. "Cardinal Amodeo?!"

Leo smiled as the two men shook hands. "I'm afraid you've found me out. These are my friends, John and Ariella, and we're on urgent Church business."

The priest continued to stare open-mouthed at the three. "I'm Father Kees. It's a pleasure to meet you, Your Eminence. What can I do to help you?"

"We're looking for the church archives, Father … specifically for some papers that might have been left behind by a former priest who once served at this church."

"Of course, Cardinal. The archives are down at the end of this hall."

Kees immediately set off down the hall and opened the last door on the right. "All of the old church papers are in here," he said, switching on the light to reveal a long room lined with rows of metal shelves filled with cardboard boxes. "Everything is filed alphabetically," Kees said. "Whose papers are you looking for?"

"Jonas Lundahl's," Leo said.

The color in Kees' face drained for a moment before returning to normal. "Lundahl?"

238

"Yes, Father Jonas Lundahl."

"I know who you're referring to, Cardinal, but his papers aren't here."

"Not here?" Once again, Leo was seized by the familiar feeling that something was working against them. "What do you mean they're not here? What happened to them?"

"I mean they're not in the archives, Cardinal. They're in the tomb."

"The tomb? What tomb?"

"Father Lundahl's tomb," Kees responded. "It's in the garden outside … below his statue."

"You mean all of his papers were buried with him?"

"Not all. Some of his books and other personal effects were sent to his family after his death, but all of his private papers were placed in the tomb … it was one of his last requests before he died."

"Well, I guess that's it," John said. "We can't exactly go digging up one of Pope Michael's ancestors."

"Dig him up?!" A look of horror crossed the young priest's face. "I'm afraid you've misunderstood me. Father Lundahl's body was laid to rest in an underground mausoleum below his statue. The papers you're looking for are sealed inside the chamber next to his casket."

"Can we go down there?" Leo asked.

"Of course, Cardinal. You can go anywhere you want on church grounds. There's an iron door at the base of the statue that leads to a stairway, but it hasn't been opened for over a hundred and forty years."

"Well, maybe it's time someone took a look at what's down there. Don't you agree, Father?"

The look of excitement on the young priest's face told the others that he had been seized by the spirit of discovery as he led them back upstairs and grabbed a flashlight. "I've always wanted to go down there," he said, continuing on through the back door that opened out into the small garden separating the church from the rectory.

Approaching the base of the statue, he cast a sheepish look back at Leo before producing a ring of keys. "They make me carry all the keys because of my name. It makes it easier for everyone to remember that Father *Kees* always has the church *keys*."

The others smiled patiently as the excited priest fumbled through at least two dozen keys of all shapes and sizes, until finally he held out a large brass key that was obviously very old. "I think this is the one." With a single twist, the rusty lock clicked open and the priest pulled the iron edge of the door away from the crumbling wooden frame. Angling down from the doorway, a dizzying set of steep stone steps descended into the darkness.

A sudden gust stirred the musty air drifting from the open doorway, making them all stand back as the fresh air from above mixed with the dank air below. Stepping through the doorway, Kees switched on his flashlight and began brushing aside cobwebs as they groped their way down the narrow steps chiseled from solid rock.

At the bottom of the steps a rotting wooden door opened up into a low space that had evidently been hollowed out from solid stone just like the steps, and in the center of the chamber, a simple wooden casket with a cross carved into the top rested on a hand-laid stone base.

For a full minute everyone stared at the casket in silence. The body of the man inside represented an enigma to them. He had devoted his life to the service of his God and had battled evil wherever he had found it, but something had happened to him in his last encounter with darkness. From all accounts, he had returned from the village beyond the mountains a changed man. He had withdrawn from his pastoral duties and retired to the rectory, where he spent the remainder of his short life in seclusion hiding from the world or something he feared had just entered it.

"I believe his papers are in there," Kees said, breaking the spell when he pointed to a dust-covered trunk lying next to the base below the casket.

After laying his hands-on top of the casket and reciting a brief prayer for a man he had never known but had come to admire, Leo knelt down and examined the large iron lock. "Do you have a key for this too?"

"No, I was told that it was sent to the Lundahl family years ago and eventually ended up at the Vatican after Cardinal Lundahl became Pope Michael."

Without a word, Leo jerked the lock off the rusting clasp and opened the top. It was filled with papers, but Leo was looking for something in particular. With help from the others he began carefully removing brittle stacks of yellowed paper until he spied a single bound book that resembled the one belonging to Steig Lundahl. Placing his fingers around the edges, Leo lifted the small tattered book from the faded cloth that lined the bottom of the trunk.

While the young priest eagerly shined his light over the cardinal's shoulder, Leo carefully opened the book to the first delicate vellum page and began to read. Right away he could tell that the handwriting was the same as that found in the book Steig Lundahl had shown him in the lodge, and the narrative that had ended so abruptly in the first book seemed to continue on where the other had left off.

With the others looking on, Leo's shoulders suddenly shook with an involuntary shiver as his eyes froze halfway down the first page. Looking up, he closed the book and shoved it under his coat. "We have to go … now!"

The priest recoiled. "But Father Lundahl left strict instructions that this trunk and everything in it was to remain in his tomb for all eternity!"

Leo's green eyes bored in on the young priest. "I've learned over the years that our concept of eternity is relative at best. I think I can safely say that Father Jonas won't mind if we borrow this for a while. I believe he left it behind for those of us who would follow in his footsteps someday."

The priest silently searched the eyes of the three people looking back at him. "This has something to do with that village Father Jonas traveled to before he died, doesn't it?"

"Yes," Leo answered. "Yes, it does. And if anyone else approaches you about Father Lundahl's papers, you're to tell them you know nothing about them."

Nodding his head, Kees slowly closed the trunk before the group made their way back up into the garden and waited for him to lock the thick iron door. At the end of the path that led to the rectory, Leo spotted Alon and Lev trying to look inconspicuous as they stood gazing down at a row of rosebushes.

Glancing in their direction, Kees spoke to Leo in a quiet voice. "I wouldn't worry too much about them, Cardinal. I don't think they're looking for old notes. We have some rare species of roses in the garden, and they seem to have captured the attention of some members of the local horticultural community who are helping us extend our garden."

Leo smiled when he saw Alon and Lev looking in their direction. "Thank you for your help, Father. I promise to return the book when I'm through with it." A chilled breeze swept down from the mountains, prompting Leo to turn the collar up on his coat before he shook hands with the priest and led John and Ariella out to the street and down the hill.

As soon as they were away from the church, Alon caught up with Leo. "What did that priest say to you when he spotted us in the garden?"

Leo winked at Ariella and John. "Oh, he just said that he was glad to see a couple of big, strong, flower-loving men like you and Lev admiring their roses."

Narrowing their eyes, Alon and Lev glared back at Leo and a giggling Ariella as the group crossed the street to the trolley stop for their return trip back to the waterfront and the safety of the Carmela.

242

CHAPTER 47

Standing alone by the Carmela's stern railing, Leo looked up from the main deck of the yacht at a jagged opening south of the green mountains rising behind the town of Bergen. He was looking at the entrance to one of the many fjords along this section of Norwegian coastline, but this particular fjord would be the one they would be entering after the sun dipped below the horizon.

"There you are, Cardinal."

Leo turned to see Lev Wasserman standing by the doors that led into the main salon. Pulling a cigar from his shirt pocket, he lit it with a match and let the bluish smoke drift overhead. "Everyone is waiting for you in the dining room."

Gazing back out at the purple haze of dusk settling over the town, Leo turned and followed Lev through the main salon to a small paneled dining room. Seated around a long, Koa wood table, the members of the Bible Code Team waited patiently, sniffing at the aroma of freshly grilled fish stuffed with lemon and garlic that wafted from the kitchen.

Across from Alon and Nava, John and Ariella were engaged in some muted chatter with Daniel and Sarah, while beside them, Javier Mendoza and Dr. Raul Diaz sat quietly drinking their wine as Lev joined Leo and Morelli seated at the opposite end of the table.

Never one to let diplomacy interfere with whatever was on his mind at the moment, Dr. Diaz rubbed the two-day-old stubble on his chin as his Spanish eyes drifted to Leo. "So, what did you find on your little expedition today, Cardinal?"

Shaking out his napkin, Leo returned the doctor's gaze. "I'm afraid we would have been making a terrible mistake by pressing ahead without reading Father Lundahl's notes."

243

A murmur of voices shot up around the table as Leo reached for a bottle of red wine and filled his glass. "At first I couldn't understand why Steig Lundahl didn't have all of Jonas' notes. Then I remembered something the church priest told me. He said that some of Jonas' books and personal effects were sent to his family after his death, but that he wanted the other books and papers in his trunk to be sealed in his tomb with his body. I believe that's how the first book of notes ended up in Steig Lundahl's possession. The first book was returned to the family, but the second book has remained locked away next to the body of Jonas Lundahl for all of these years."

"But why separate the two?" Mendoza asked.

"So that only we would find it."

The others exchanged puzzled glances.

"According to his notes, Jonas knew he had failed," Leo continued. "The evil he faced alone was too strong. His only option was to flee from the field before he himself became possessed, and he urged the villagers to do the same. He ordered them to burn their homes to prevent them from returning to the area, but he knew that one day others would return to face the same evil. In his notes he called them the *chosen ones*. In other words, the second book was left for us … the chosen ones, and somehow he knew that only we would find it."

Ariella gasped. "But how is that possible? I mean, even we didn't know we had been chosen for anything until we saw it spelled out in the code and started having the same dreams out in the Negev Desert."

"I think sometimes we forget that we're being led by a force greater than ourselves, which means we'll never have all the answers to our questions." Leo paused to gauge the effect his words were having on the others. "It's been that way for thousands of years. Some have been chosen to receive God's word while others haven't, and I believe Jonas Lundahl was one of the chosen. In other words, he was one of us, but he was forced to work alone. I can't even begin to imagine how difficult that must have been for him."

"So where do we go from here, Cardinal?" Nava asked, twirling her long black ponytail.

"We're still going to that field. Make no mistake about that." A vision of Evita's smiling face flashed through Leo's mind as he opened the book of handwritten notes and gently laid it on the table. "After Jonas left the village he camped along the fjord before returning to the area two days later. The villagers had burned their homes as he had instructed, but one house remained. When he went to check, he found a young couple living alone in the house."

"Who were they?" Ariella asked.

"They were the last remaining villagers. The couple told Jonas that they believed someone had to remain behind to warn others to stay away from the area. Despite his pleas they refused to leave, so he blessed their house and gave them the cross he wore around his neck to keep them safe."

"So, the couple stayed?"

"Yes, but before Jonas left, they told him that they felt that it was their duty as Christians to make sure their descendents also stayed to let others know that a great evil stalked the forest beyond their house. Jonas wrote that he felt as though he had failed them somehow, and it weighed heavily on him. His last entry talked about returning to the village to check on them, but sadly he died before he had the chance. If I'm right, that house is still there, and Alexis may be descended from that couple. She's the *defender of the field,* but instead of being a defender of evil like we first thought, she's standing guard against it by warning others away. In Latin, the words defender and guardian are the same."

"Then why would she claim to be Adrian's birth mother and kidnap Evita?" Nava wondered out loud.

"That's something we'll have to find out on our own," Leo said. "Jonas only had knowledge of events happening then, but somehow he knew we would follow, and he wanted us to know that the person watching over the field might be an ally instead of an enemy."

Lev chomped down on an unlit cigar as he squinted across the table at Leo. "And this girl … this Alexis … she's just living in a little house in the forest all alone, warning people to stay away from an evil stone circle?"

"Sounds like a fairy tale," Diaz quipped.

"Think what you will," Leo exhaled, "but I'm afraid that's all we have to go on for now. These notes are over a hundred and forty years old, and there's no telling what happened to the couple that chose to remain behind … or if they even had any children for that matter. All I know for certain is that Adrian is waiting for us and he has Evita … and we're going after her."

Alex Pappas poked his head into the room. "There's a man on the dock who says he has to speak to you, Cardinal."

"Did he give a name?"

"Yes. His name is Gunnar Neilson, and he said you two know each other."

CHAPTER 48

Standing in the lengthening shadow of the harbormaster's office, Gunnar smiled when he saw Leo walking down the gangplank. "It looks like I'm your one-man welcoming committee to Norway again, Cardinal."

Leo extended his hand. "It's good to see you, Gunnar. We were just sitting down to dinner. Would you like to come aboard and join us?"

"I'm afraid I don't have time, Cardinal, and neither do you."

"Why? What's happened?"

"Nothing yet. That's why I'm here. Mr. Lundahl sent me to warn you that some Acerbi loyalists know the yacht is here in Bergen, and they've set a trap. They're waiting along the tops of the cliffs in the fjord with heavy weapons … weapons that will surely sink the yacht when she passes below on the way to your destination."

"Then I take it you know where we're headed."

"Of course." Gunnar winked. "And there's something else. We've pinpointed the area where Acerbi is keeping Ms. Vargas."

Leo grabbed Gunnar by both shoulders. "You know where Evita is?! Tell me!"

"Somewhere in the vicinity of the old village that burned."

"How do you know all of this?"

"Believe me, Cardinal; nothing happens in this country without Mr. Lundahl's knowledge."

Leo stepped away and glanced back at the looming shape of the yacht. "We have to leave right away!"

"We kind of figured you'd say that. We have a plan that involves the yacht, but you and your friends won't be on it. There are two SUVs parked around the side of the building across the street. Now that it's dark we want your people to begin leaving the boat one or two at a time and walk

247

straight to the vehicles. After your group is ashore, we want the yacht to move into the fjord as planned. As soon as the boat is out of sight of Bergen, the captain will stop. Under no circumstances should he take the boat any farther up the fjord. This will serve as a diversion while we take you and your friends to the site of the village on the other side of the mountains. It's the only way, Cardinal. We're ready when you are. I'll be waiting in one of the vehicles."

"OK. I'll tell the others … and Gunnar, thank you." Leo looked around and made his way back up the gangplank to the deck of the Carmela as if a thousand eyes were on him. Moving into the main salon, everyone started asking questions all at once about the man on the dock.

Leo held up a hand and waited for the din of competing voices to die down. "The man on the dock works for Mr. Lundahl. They know where Evita is, but he said some of Adrian's men have set a trap for the yacht in the fjord, which means we'll have to travel overland to the site."

"Are you sure you can trust him, Leo?" Lev asked.

"Yes. His name is Gunnar. He was the one who was responsible for keeping me alive when I was in Norway before, and he risked his life helping me escape. They have some vehicles parked around the side of the building across the street, and we have to move quickly."

Morelli stood, his face a mask of concentration. "I realize the urgency of the situation, Leo, but we need to think this through before we all go running off with someone the rest of us know very little about. I mean, Adrian's real target is you. Evita is just the bait. He wants you alive so you can enter the circle of stone for some reason, and if we place ourselves into the hands of someone else, then we lose contol of the situation. Whatever happens after that is up to them. Remember the passages we discovered in the code? *Only the chosen will walk with the Shepherd of the Church to the field of the demon,* and *the shepherd must walk alone into the circle of stone?* According to the code, we're all destined to make this journey together, and this sudden offer to take us overland could be a trap laid by someone else … someone who doesn't want us to go to the field for some reason."

"That's all true, Anthony," Leo said. "But frankly, some of the passages we've discovered in the code so far have only served to cloud our thinking. As you pointed out before, I'm not the *Shepherd of the Church.* That title only applies to a sitting pope, so we're kind of back to square one on that issue."

"What about the other passages, Leo?" Daniel asked. "They're just as confusing. Think of the wording for a moment. *Satan watches from afar; the demon in the north will resist his master,* and then there's the most confusing one of all: *The father will take the place of the son.* I've been giving a lot of thought to this, and if you ask me we're about to step right square in the middle of a spiritual battle we know nothing about. Bishop Morelli is right. This could be a trap, and the best traps are laid by people you trust."

Leo stood in the doorway facing his friends with a look of grim determination. "Right now, my first goal is to rescue Evita. We'll sort everything else out once she's safe. Anyone who doesn't want to come with me is welcome to stay here in Bergen, but I'm leaving with Gunnar right now."

Trading glances, the others stood and hefted their backpacks over their shoulders.

"Lead the way, Cardinal," Lev said, lighting a cigar with a match as he scanned the other faces in the room with pride. "Alon and Moshe will go first and scout the area around the vehicles. I'll have some of the crewmembers start walking back and forth from the boat to the dock to confuse anyone who might be watching while I call Alex and have him start making preparations to move the yacht out of the harbor." Lev reached for the intercom phone on the wall and paused. "Oh … and one more thing. Once the boat has left the dock we've lost our safe haven, so keep your eyes and ears open."

CHAPTER 49

Darkness came late to the far reaches of the northern hemisphere in summer, locking the two SUVs carrying Leo and the others in a claustrophobic embrace as they raced from the city through a narrow valley between the mountains. Looking through their windows, they watched the bright headlights paint the trees along the sides of the road with eerie, dancing shapes that seemed to be enticing them onward—pulling them toward the ancient circle of stone that had been waiting patiently for this moment for over a thousand years.

At the dock in Bergen, Alex Pappas looked down from the bridge and listened to the yacht's engines rumble to life. As soon as the deckhands released the lines, the captain edged the big boat out into the middle of the harbor and shoved the throttles forward. The bow rose higher, parting the reflections from the city lights on the dark water as it sliced its way around a jutting peninsula and slowly faded from view between the towering walls of a deep fjord.

As the yacht departed, those who had worked late at their jobs in Bergen were hurrying home past brightly-lit shop windows to the warm glow of their fireplaces, but a single window in a tiny loft above the fish market remained cloaked in darkness. Inside the darkened room, a man who had chosen to remain in the shadows punched a number into his cell phone and waited.

"Yes?" The voice that answered sounded course but pleasant.

"The yacht just pulled out of the harbor, sir."

"What about the vehicles?"

"They left thirty minutes ago, Mr. Lundahl, but they have their phones turned off as you requested."

"Good. It won't be long now."

251

                                    * * *

Speeding toward the site of the old village, the SUVs followed a twisting road through flat farmland that had been carved from the forest hundreds of years before. With the dawn only a few hours away, most of the team members napped, their heads rolling from side to side on the backs of their seats as the vehicles leaned through a series of seemingly endless curves.

Peering at his watch, Leo found sleep impossible. "How long until we reach the site of the old village?"

"About another couple of hours, Cardinal," Gunnar replied. "Now that it's summer the sun will be coming up again soon. Why don't you try to get some rest while it's still dark outside?"

Looking out at the lights of farmhouses dotting the rolling pastureland, Leo leaned back in his seat and closed his eyes. A hundred different scenarios ran through his mind. He thought about Jonas Lundahl and how difficult his overland trek on foot must have been a hundred and forty years before. Even if he had managed to skirt the mountain range by following the trails that ran along the fjord, it must have taken him days to reach the village.

The image of the lonely figure of the priest crossing the rugged terrain in darkness to a place caught in the grip of an unseen evil haunted his thoughts. He could feel the chill and picture the torchlight that had probably greeted the exhausted priest when he finally reached the village. The images came in flashes, like those that appeared through the gossamer filters of our dreams.

"Cardinal." Leo felt a hand shaking his shoulder and opened his eyes to see Gunnar peering over the back of the seat at him. "We're here."

Looking outside, Leo saw the vehicles had stopped with their headlights painting a dirt road that led between a stand of pine trees to an open area that lay beyond.

"Are you sure you don't want us to come with you, Cardinal?"

"No. I'm afraid this is as far as you go."

"But I …"

"Thank you for bringing us this far, my friend, but if you're thinking of following us you should put that thought out of your mind right now. It's time for you and your men to go."

                                    252

In the silence that accompanied the approaching dawn, only the ticking of the cooling engines could be heard. Through his window, Gunnar looked out at the humped shapes of the surrounding mountains blotting the stars from the sky along the horizon and handed Leo a satellite phone. "I know you all have your own sat phones, Cardinal, but this one is special. It's pre-programmed with our number, so if you need us just hit *send*. We'll be waiting for you in the next town ten miles up this highway."

In the darkness, the cardinal's eyes were hollow pools as he and Gunnar exchanged a silent look of understanding before he motioned to the others, and a few minutes later the chosen ones had disappeared into the darkness.

CHAPTER 50

The dirt road leading to the site of the old village angled off away from the main highway, twisting through overgrown, long-forgotten fields that had once been tenderly nurtured by weathered hands in a seasonal grab for the life-giving grain that had sprung from the rich loamy soil.

Leading the group, Alon peered ahead at a barely perceptible glow on the eastern horizon, and in the distance, they all saw a thin column of smoke rising from a clay chimney protruding from the shingled roof of a small white house.

Pausing for a moment to listen, they continued on, walking toward the house in silence, their eyes straining in the faint light as they looked through the trees running along the sides of the road for signs that they were being watched. Rounding a slight curve, the faded road disappeared beneath an overgrowth of grass and weeds, and as they kept walking, they could hear a crunching sound beneath their feet when they stumbled over scattered bits of debris in the tall grass.

Shining her light down at the ground, Ariella was the first to see the charred remains of burned timbers worn down over time by the alternating heat and cold that came with the changing of the seasons. All around them, as the others shined their lights at the ground, the outline of the burned remains of the old village began to emerge, and beyond the littered remains of those who had left the world long ago, the little white house beckoned to them with an invitation that drifted on the wind like the smoke from the chimney, calling out for them to enter.

"Should we keep going?" John asked.

"Yes," Leo said, his eyes glued to the outline of the house. "According to Steig Lundahl, the stone circle lies in a field beyond those trees in the distance, but we need to see who's in that house before we go any farther."

By now the sky had turned a shade lighter, but the sun remained hidden behind the mountains as Leo tromped through the tall grass to a brick walkway that led through a picket fence and crossed a neatly-trimmed yard to a blue door at the front of the house. He knocked, but no one answered. As the others gathered behind him, he knocked again and tried the door, but it was locked.

Stepping off the walkway, he moved along the front of the house, brushing against the smooth chalky walls until he came to a small window fogged from the warmth inside and peered through the glass. There, sitting in a rocking chair facing the fireplace, he saw Evita Vargas, rocking back and forth, staring at the glowing embers of a dying fire.

"Evita!" Leo shouted. He pounded on the window pane, but she continued to rock, staring straight ahead. Running to the door, Leo slammed his body against the thick wood, ripping it from its hinges before it fell inward to the floor with a loud crash. Rushing to Evita's side, he grabbed her by the shoulders and lifted her up, but her unmoving eyes continued to stare into space with a trance-like intensity, as though Leo was invisible, and she was looking right through him. "Evita … it's me … Leo! Talk to me!"

Suddenly she blinked. "Leo?"

"Yes, my love. I'm here!"

"I can assure you she's quite alright, Cardinal," a familiar voice called out behind them.

Leo and the others spun around to see Steig Lundahl standing at the bottom of a wooden staircase.

"Steig!?"

Lundahl took a few steps forward but stopped when he saw the look in Alon's eyes. "This might be a good time to tell everyone we're on the same side, Cardinal."

"What are you doing here, Steig?" Leo could feel Evita beginning to sag in his arms. "What have you done to her?"

"She was like that when I arrived. I believe what we're seeing is a physical reaction of one who has come into contact with a powerful demon that has revealed itself."

Leo lifted Evita in his arms and gently lowered her down onto a long sofa. Glancing back at Lundahl, his eyes betrayed the pent-up rage that had been building inside him. "Where's the woman who brought her here?"

"I'm afraid Alexis had no choice in the matter, Cardinal. In fact, she did Evita a great favor."

"A favor!" Alon stepped closer to Lundahl, his body trembling with anger.

"Yes, a favor. She talked Acerbi into allowing her to bring Evita here herself instead of letting him send some of his goons after her. She wanted to be close to her in case they tried to harm her." Lundahl paused as he and Alon stared across the room at each other. "I know of your reputation, Mr. Lavi, but if you want to hear what I have to say I suggest you hold your emotions in check until I have a chance to explain my. Demons are masterful deceivers, and it was Adrian's plan to take Evita to the circle of stone and make her one of his own before using her against the cardinal."

"How do you know this?" Leo demanded.

"Alexis told me. I was here when Adrian arrived and took her away, but I was forced to hide upstairs until they were gone. As much as I wanted to intervene, I wouldn't be standing here talking to you right now if I had done so. I knew you were coming, and I had to be here to tell you what was happening."

"Where are they now?"

"Waiting for you in the circle of stone."

Collapsing down onto the sofa next to Evita, Leo stroked her long black hair as she continued to look back at him with a blank expression. "Once again you have me at a loss for words, Mr. Lundahl. If what you say is true, why would Adrian leave Evita here and take Alexis with him instead? He knew that keeping her close to him would draw me in."

"And he has drawn you in, Cardinal, but Alexis prevented him from taking Evita at the last minute, so he took her instead. He knew you would still come after him."

"I'm afraid I don't understand. What could prevent him from carrying out his plan to take Evita with him?"

Lundahl pointed to a crude silver cross hanging on a chain around Evita's neck. "He was prevented by that. It's the cross that Father Jonas gave to the family that remained behind in this house to protect them against the evil in the forest. As you've probably guessed, Alexis is a descendent of that family, and as the sole remaining daughter of the last couple who lived here, she decided to sacrifice everything and remain here alone, living a life of solitude out of a sense of duty to her Christian faith."

Unable to control herself any longer, Ariella stepped into the fray. "And this is the same woman who claims to be Adrian's birth mother … who told us you're his father?"

Lundahl hung his head and peered out at the distant forest through the open doorway. "Yes … all of that is true."

257

John eyed the enigma standing before them and shook his head in disbelief. "Wow! It doesn't get much stranger than this."

"No … no it doesn't, my young friend," Lundahl said. "And I'm afraid there's more. However, since time is a luxury we can ill afford to waste, I'll keep my story short. As I told you before, my brother's fascination with this area brought him here when he was still just a teenager, but he had been warned to stay away from the circle of stone by the couple who lived in this house.

A little over twenty years ago, before Marcus became a cardinal, he returned home for one of his annual visits to our parents' home. Before he left, he told me he had been thinking of that couple and asked me to check in on them from time to time to see if they needed anything. Naturally, because of what had happened here in the past, I felt obliged to do so.

When I arrived for my first visit, I met Alexis and learned that both her parents had died the year before. At the time she was still very young … only twenty-seven … and she was living here all alone.

I tried to talk her into leaving, but she refused. She told me it was her Christian duty to warn others of the evil that lived in the forest, and when I told her that she herself could be in danger, she showed me the silver cross around her neck and told me that it would protect her. She was really quite beautiful, and despite our obvious age difference, I found myself falling in love with her on my subsequent visits."

"So that's how you ended up becoming Adrian's birth father," Ariella said.

"Yes. I make no excuses as to my actions, or hers, but our mistake went even deeper. The day Adrian was conceived, we were walking near the field by the stone circle when our passion for one another blossomed. After the child was born, Alexis changed. She became despondent, pacing back and forth in the yard in front of the house for hours at a time, staring out into the forest. She had become convinced that the child had been conceived on tainted ground … that one day the evil in the forest would lay claim to him as it did to those whose bodies disappeared from their graves over a hundred years ago, and there was nothing I could say or do to convince her otherwise.

"On my first visit after the child was born I discovered she had taken the baby and left, and when she returned a week later our child was gone. She told me that she had been guided by dreams to a house in France, where she had left the boy with an older couple. She was convinced that as long as he remained away from the tainted ground he had been conceived on he would be safe. But it was a horrible mistake, because once the child had been separated from his mother it left him open to the very evil she had tried to protect him against."

"Did you ever make contact with him, Mr. Lundahl?" Ariella asked.

"I made several trips to France. I was surprised when I saw that Eduardo Acerbi had been the man who had adopted him. I mean, everyone thought he was dead at that time, so I maintained my distance. I used to sit and watch Adrian playing in the yard of his house from my car on the highway. On all of my visits he appeared perfectly normal, but when he came to power his mother and I both realized that there was something different about him; that the evil we had feared had manifested itself despite our efforts. But there was also something else … something Alexis made me swear not to share with another living soul … not even my brother. Despite the many rumors to the contrary, we both knew that Adrian couldn't be the prophesied Antichrist many were calling him, because we were his parents … and his birth had been natural."

Leo looked at all the bewildered faces around the tiny room listening with rapt attention to Lundahl's fascinating story. "Why didn't you tell me any of this before, Mr. Lundahl?"

"I tried to, Cardinal, but I couldn't bring myself to reveal my involvement in bringing Adrian into the world. You might believe confession is good for the soul, but Lundahls prefer to keep their dirty laundry tucked away from public scrutiny, especially when one of them was the pope. As I said before, ours is a very private family."

"So your involvement with Alexis was the reason Marcus remained distant from the family?" Leo asked.

"No." Lundahl managed a weak smile. "The reason for that was much simpler. As you noticed from the pictures on the wall during your visit to the lodge we are a family of hunters, but Marcus hated hunting with a passion. He was a great animal lover, and he and my father had many heated arguments on the subject on more than one occasion. Rather than alienate himself from the family, he decided to limit his contact with us until we changed our ways."

Standing by the fire, Lev lit his last cigar and peered out through a kitchen window. "I think it might be a good idea to move away from here until we see what Acerbi is up to. Your man Gunnar told us that some Acerbi loyalists were planning to attack the Carmela after she entered the fjord, and there could be others close by."

"There are no men waiting to attack the yacht, Professor. I'm afraid that was a little white lie on my part to get all of you here sooner. Crossing overland from the only place in the fjord where a yacht the size of the Carmela could have docked would have added an extra day to your travel time … time we couldn't afford to lose. When Alexis put the cross around Evita's neck to protect her from Adrian, he became enraged. Neither of us ever dreamed he would take his own mother instead and flee into the forest."

Tears began to stream down the elder Lundahl's face. "Alexis sacrificed herself to protect Evita from her own son, Cardinal, and life without her would be unbearable to me, so I beg you … stop him from whatever he plans to do before it's too late."

By now the line of pale light running along the tops of the eastern mountains had grown brighter. Gently, Leo rested Evita's head on a pillow and rose from the sofa just as the satellite phone Lev was carrying began to beep.

"Hello." Lev nodded his head before thrusting the phone toward Leo. "It's for you, Cardinal."

"Who is it?"

"It's the astrophysicist you visited at the Vatican observatory last year. He says he has some urgent news for you."

Leo grabbed the phone and listened, and as the others waited, they saw the color draining from his face. A few moments later the ground around the house began to shake, sending flocks of birds screeching from the trees. The shaking stopped as suddenly as it had begun. Handing the phone back to Lev, Leo walked outside and stared up into the sky.

Something was coming!

CHAPTER 51

Flowing through a pair of towering doors into the Sistine Chapel, a sea of red marked the procession of over a hundred cardinals; their long cassocks brushing the floor beneath Michelangelo's magnificent ceiling as they made their way to their seats along facing rows of linen-covered tables.

Standing next to the entrance, Francois Leander and Father Vespa noticed Cardinal Ian McCulley motioning to them from the far end of the chapel. Hurrying behind the line of tables, Vespa leaned in close to the cardinal. "Did you need something, Your Eminence?"

"I was wondering if anyone has heard from Cardinal Leo or Bishop Morelli. The conclave is about to begin, and once the doors have been sealed and the voting begins they'll be barred from the proceedings."

"I'm afraid not, sir," Vespa whispered. "The last message we received from Bishop Morelli stated only that they were leaving Spain on important church business, but we haven't heard back from them for several days now. To tell you the truth, Cardinal, I'm starting to become a little concerned about them, and so is Francois. It's not like either of them to break contact like this, especially now that the conclave is about to begin. It's very strange."

"Yes … very strange indeed." McCulley glanced at the Swiss Guards standing by the door. "It looks like they're preparing to seal the doors. Have you tried calling them again today?"

"Yes. Their cell phones go to voice mail."

* * *

The breaking dawn revealed a low gray mist hugging the ground as Leo and the others gathered outside and peered across the clearing between the little white house and the line of trees in the distance.

"Who was that who just called?" Morelli asked Leo.

"One of the Jesuit astronomers from the observatory. It seems our learned brethren have noticed some movement in the dark star."

"Movement?"

"Yes. Apparently, it moved from its stationary orbit at the edge of the solar system this morning and they've lost sight of it. They're busy making some calculations, but they thought we should know about it right away."

"Should we tell the others?"

"No. The tension here is high enough already, so let's keep that little bit of news to ourselves for now." Leo turned back to the group and held up a hand. "I think everyone here knows me well enough by now to know that I don't go around issuing orders unless there's a reason, so here it is. Some new information has just come to light, and I've decided that Bishop Morelli will be the only one who will accompany me to the field."

"Just the two of you!" Lev shouted. "But what about the passage we discovered in the code? It specifically stated that the rest of us would be safe as long as we didn't enter the circle of stone itself. Please, Leo, at least let us …"

Leo interrupted him with another wave of the hand. "The field around the stone circle is tainted ground, Lev. One of the most active areas of demonic activity in the world lies just beyond the trees on the other side of that clearing, and we don't know how far the influence of the stone circle extends out into the field around it. In other words, you may all be safe up to a certain point, but we don't know what that point is. I'm afraid my decision is final. There's no reason to put anyone else at risk, so I'll have to ask the rest of you to remain here until we return."

"You mean *if* you return, Cardinal," Alon said. "I don't like it. We're as much a part of this as you are. Who called you on the sat phone?"

"Someone who just saw something that tells me the rules may have just changed." Leo rested a hand on the big man's shoulder. "I need you here watching over Evita while I'm gone, Alon. I'm leaving her life in your hands, so please … will you do this for me?"

Alon's hulking frame hovered over the cardinal. "No harm will come to her, Cardinal. That I can promise you."

Walking up next to Alon, Nava took him by the hand. "We'll be waiting for you, Leo." She glanced over at a solemn-looking Morelli. "Hurry back … both of you."

With a quick look back at the others, Leo stuffed a small leather case in his waistband and turned up the collar on his black nylon jacket. Motioning to Morelli, the two men turned away from their friends and headed off across the clearing toward the murky outline of the tall trees in the distance. A few minutes later, they had disappeared into the world of shadows that lay beyond.

CHAPTER 52

Pushing their way through the thick underbrush to a faded path that trailed off through the forest, Leo and Morelli caught fleeting glimpses of ancient, lichen-covered Viking burial mounds nestled among the trees, and there was a strange hum in the air, as if the area they were walking through had suddenly become electrified by their presence. Moving deeper into the forest, the feeling grew stronger. It made the hair rise on the backs of their necks and sent shivers of unreasoning fear down their spines. Every broken twig that cracked beneath their feet sounded like a gunshot warning of their approach, but they continued on with the knowledge that whatever was waiting for them already knew that they were there.

Leo thought back to the time when they had descended into the black tunnels beneath the Negev Desert, but the feeling there had been different. In the electrified atmosphere that crackled around them now, it felt like they were walking toward a large power station that buzzed with the invisible energy of a deadly charged force—a force that was barely contained from leaping out and bringing sudden death to those who had failed to notice the signs warning of the danger that lay beyond.

By now, thin shafts of light were streaming through the treetops, illuminating their path through the forest as they emerged from a pine-scented world full of life and stopped at the edge of a world that screamed death. Standing in the distance, a dark structure made from a ring of gigantic stone monoliths rose from the center of a barren field covered with toppled headstones.

With the sun's light reflecting off the large gold pectoral cross hanging from Leo's neck, he pulled the leather pouch from his waistband and removed a small glass bottle. Opening the top, he began to sprinkle holy water, but a sudden gust of hot wind blew from the circle of stone across the field, catching the tiny droplets and carrying them back toward the forest before they could touch the ground.

Leo and Morelli exchanged glances. Whatever lay within the stone circle had just shown them that it possessed the power to summon the wind in an effort to protect itself from the two dark-clothed men who had just entered its territory.

The devil's breath.

Immediately the ground beneath their feet began to shake, and without waiting, both men began to pray out loud. *"In the name of the Father, and of the Son, and of the Holy Ghost. Amen."* They recited the age-old prayer in unison. *"Defend us against the rulers of the world of darkness …"*

The earth began to shake even more violently than it had before, but they continued to pray, sweat dripping from their foreheads as the hot wind increased, pushing the chilled morning air from the field. Glancing up toward the circle of stone, Leo froze. Standing silently between a pair of massive stone columns, Adrian Acerbi was just standing there, watching silently. After a moment that seemed more like an hour, he raised his hand and motioned to Leo before turning away and disappearing into the shadows.

Slowly, Leo took a dreamlike step forward.

"Leo … stop!" Morelli moved to block his path. "You can't go in there. Only the Shepherd …"

"It's too late for that now, Anthony. All I ask is that you pray for me. Shepherd or no shepherd, we'll know soon enough, because this ends here today … one way or the other."

"Can't you see you're being taunted by a master deceiver to your own destruction? Please, Leo. Let's think this over for a moment."

"There's no time, Anthony. Something is happening, and it's happening now."

"The demon is playing tricks with your mind, Leo. You're being pulled into his world."

"I know. I've been feeling his tug for quite some time now, but there's something else waiting for me across this field. I was meant to be here now, at this exact time in history, and Alexis is in there. She saved Evita by trading places with her, and I'm going in there after her."

Gazing back at the towering columns, Morelli's thin red hair flattened against his head as he leaned into the wind and tried to steady himself, and for a second he thought he saw the structure pulsate before the wind suddenly calmed. Turning his head, he saw Leo standing perfectly still with his eyes closed.

"Leo!"

Slowly, Leo opened his eyes and began walking across the field.

"Leo!" Morelli shouted again. But his shouts went unanswered as Leo stumbled across the unholy ground, making his way to the dark circle as if an invisible force was pulling him to it. By now the field was flooded with sunlight, but the ancient structure remained dark, rejecting the light in favor of the darkness that surrounded it beneath a veil of evil.

As Morelli clutched his rosary and watched from the edge of the forest, Leo continued his solitary walk across the field, stopping every now and then to look down at the depressions dotting the ground around the rows of blackened headstones before looking back up and continuing on. Like the ancient monolithic temple they had discovered in Turkey, this one also sat upon a raised stone platform, and when Leo reached the base, he climbed a short set of steps and passed through the time-ravaged pillars without looking back. Once inside, he looked out over a seemingly empty, open space, but Adrian was nowhere to be seen. His entrance had been met by an eerie silence.

There were no chirping insects, no birds flying overhead, no sound of any kind. Even the breeze Leo had felt when he was making his way across the field was now absent. It was as though he had entered a dead zone, where all life within the circle had been extinguished, leaving nothing behind to remind him that any other world existed other than the one he had just entered.

A maniacal laugh echoed behind him, making Leo spin around, but again his gaze was met by nothing but empty space. He started to pray, but when he tried to mouth the words, he found that his thinking had become cloudy, making it hard to concentrate. He took a step forward but stumbled. Along with his ability to think, it seemed as if his physical body was also beginning to fail him. A generalized weakness had seized his muscles, making even the simple act of walking seem more like struggling against a strong current, until finally he stopped, frozen in place on a cold stone floor as an overwhelming feeling of abandonment and loneliness crept into his soul.

Why couldn't he pray? Where was his God!?

Morelli had been right. He wasn't the Shepherd of the Church. He had ignored the warnings, and he had just entered an area reserved for abandoned souls—an area where even his prayers had been trapped in a black void of hopelessness.

Was this how it was going to end for him? He wondered. *Was he about to disappear into the abyss without even a whisper from above?*

267

A flutter of wings made him glance upward.

Were the angels here to protect him?

But the wings he saw were black, not white, and the thing that landed beside him made him cringe with terror. He was staring into the blood-red eyes of *Agaliarept*, Satan's grand general over hell, and off to the side, he saw the figure of a much younger-looking Adrian Acerbi, clinging to Alexis at the base of one of the gigantic pillars of stone.

What was happening here?

Leo fought to control his emotions.

God help me!

Agaliarept drew closer, his monstrous head coming within inches of Leo's face; his foul breath filling the air with the unbearable stench of death as he spread his leathery, red-veined wings and extended his lizard-like body to its full height.

"Your God cannot help you now, Cardinal!" The demon's words echoed off the weathered stone. "He's abandoned you and all of your kind. The war between heaven and hell has reached a stalemate, and even Lucifer has backed away. They've given up on you. Humanity has been left to its own fate, but I'm still here. In fact, I rather like it here. It's just you and me now, Cardinal, so why don't we put our petty differences aside and join forces? Together the world could be ours. I've been looking forward to this day for a very long time now, and I ask only that you listen to what I have to say."

Leo suddenly felt his physical body released from the grip of the demon, and as Satan's general folded his wings and settled in beside him, he could feel his thoughts begin to clear.

"What's the matter, Cardinal?" The demon's voice had become soothing, and the scene had begun to take on the surreal quality of a meeting between two old friends who had just sat down for coffee. "Does my appearance offend you?" The demon shifted its gaze to Adrian. "Would you feel more comfortable if I re-entered the body of that whimpering soul over there?"

Like a man who had suddenly found himself trapped in a room with a venomous snake that blocked the only visible exit, Leo worked to control his breathing as he looked up into an empty sky.

"Stop that, Cardinal!" the demon hissed. Somehow it had sensed that Leo was trying to pray. "You forget that I can read minds. As I said before, your God is of no use to you now."

Leo remained silent, for he knew that to engage a demon that had revealed itself could lead him further into a cunning trap of circular dialogue.

"I can see that you are fearful of a trap." The demon paused, searching Leo's face. "Despite the warnings from your friends, you came to me of your own free will, so whatever happens to you from this moment on is up to me."

Leo exhaled with the knowledge that he had just taken a seat at a cosmic poker table with a lethal opponent that knew it held the high cards. "What do you want?"

The demon's laughter filled the spaces between the tall pillars. "Your soul of course."

"Of course," Leo said. He glanced back over his shoulder at the huddled figures of Adrian and Alexis, and it was obvious from the glazed look in their eyes that they had no idea where they were or what was happening around them. "What about them?"

"Pawns, Cardinal, but you already knew that. It is you I came for, and it will be you who will serve me well when I return to the world stage."

Leo tried to keep his mind a blank as he fought the paralyzing fear rising inside him, but when he gathered the courage to look into the demon's probing eyes, he caught a flash that indicated it was having trouble reading his thoughts as a shadow passed over them. Something was happening. The sun was fading, and when Leo looked up, he saw that the sky was streaked with red.

"I can tell that you want to ask me something, Cardinal," the demon said, casting a glance above. "We will soon have an eternity together for questions, but go ahead, ask away."

The demon's words made Leo's blood run cold, and as the sky grew darker, he caught a brief glimpse of hundreds of tiny black dots swirling high overhead.

"You want to know why we are here in Norway instead of my master's temple in Turkey where Adrian underwent his transition, don't you?"

"Yes," Leo answered, stalling for time.

"Because this is my house, Cardinal! There are several gateways from the world of darkness into the world of light. The one in Turkey was the first, but it belonged to Lucifer."

"Belonged?"

"Yes, Cardinal ... as in the past tense. He's grown weary of your world ... a world that has sunk to such great depths of depravity on its own that it no longer holds any challenge for him. But he has failed to see that there

269

are still many who struggle against the inevitable darkness that is to come. The time is right to make it my own, so I have parted ways with my master and have sealed off his entranceway into a world that now belongs to me. What was once his is now mine. In the last century I have delivered more souls through the gates of hell than Lucifer did in the preceding thousand years. That was my work, Cardinal, not his, and I am taking what rightfully belongs to me. You might say that this is my coming out party, and you're the guest of honor. Together we can harvest the rest of the crop and create our own army of dark angels."

Leo could feel the sweat drenching his shirt. *This demon had gone rogue.* He was rebelling against Satan. This was evil without a master—the kind of evil that could run unchecked and flash through the human race like a forest fire gone out of control with no one left to extinguish its flames.

Where was God? Where were the archangels that had come to his aid against this demon before?

Leo looked to the heavens again. Compared to Lucifer, this demon was a mere speck on the face of the universe, like a fly on a screen that he could swat at his leisure.

The demon continued to probe Leo's thoughts. "Why do you continue to wonder about the gateway in Turkey, Cardinal? Are you wondering about Adrian's transition?" The demon laughed again. "Did you really believe he was the Antichrist? No, Cardinal, he was mine all along. You and your friends misinterpreted the signs. Adrian was never born in Turkey. He was born here, on ground that was given to me. The two snakes you saw painted on that ancient scroll represented the dark seeds of hate and mistrust that were planted at the site of the Turkish ruin thousands of years ago by my predecessor. They were sent to grow within the human race, and grow they did, but I was the one who delivered Satan's evil crop to him. I deserve the credit. I've created my own army of dark angels, and soon I will reap my reward and grow even more powerful."

A thunderous roar rumbled across a red-streaked sky that was becoming progressively darker, and as Leo stole an upward glance, he saw the unbelievable sight of hundreds of misshapen figures circling a gigantic black orb that was blotting out the sun as it descended toward the earth.

What was this?!

Whatever it was, Leo decided the time had come. He would rather die right now with God's name on his lips rather than risk being taken by the demon. Clutching his crucifix, he reached inside his jacket and pulled out the vial of holy water, throwing the contents into the face of the demon.

Shrieking in agony, the demon recoiled as an invisible force sent Leo's body flying through the air against one of the stone pillars. "Have it your way, Cardinal. You could have lived an eternity in luxury, but now all I can promise you is a very painful death as you plead with a God that has abandoned you!"

In an instant the floor around Leo erupted in blue flame that turned orange as it spread up his body, enveloping him in a roaring inferno, but as the demon's laughter echoed through the air, Leo stepped from the fire, miraculously unharmed. Suddenly the demon stopped laughing. His blood-red eyes widened as he glanced nervously up at the approaching dark orb and began to back away.

"Impossible!" he shouted. "You're not the Shepherd! You have no protection here!"

By now, the misshapen figures circling above were filling the sky, and as Leo squinted up into a red mist that had begun to form, he realized that he was looking at a swarming army of dark angels, their numbers so great they blotted out the sun. Beneath his feet he could feel the base of the structure begin to shake. The shaking gained in strength, making it impossible for him to stand as the massive pillars began toppling around him, turning to dust when they hit the stone floor.

Something was coming!

The demon shrank back, growing physically smaller as hundreds of winged demons began landing all around him, their red and yellow eyes glowing with anticipation and their leathery black wings touching as they moved closer. The panic-stricken demon looked to Leo before focusing its attention on Adrian. The demon scuttled forward in an effort to escape back into the safety of the human form he had inhabited for the past year. He was inches away from Adrian when something caught his eye and made him stop. A tall cloaked figure emerged from the red mist and pulled back the black hood covering his head, revealing the unmistakable face of Steig Lundahl. Unfazed by the hideous apparition standing over his son, he stepped closer and placed himself between the demon and Adrian.

"No more!" he shouted. "Take me instead."

Instantly the demon leapt, but an unseen force blocked him just as the black orb touched the earth, enveloping everything in total darkness.

Flattening himself against the stone floor, Leo prayed for deliverance for the four souls now trapped in the demon's world. He had never felt this kind of fear before. Something else had just arrived in the darkness surrounding him, and Leo could hear the terrified demon screeching for mercy as it tried to flee.

Time seemed to slow, and as the fog of confusion began to clear, Leo suddenly realized why the demon was so terrified.

Satan himself was present!

He had come for his rebellious general, and through the swirling mist, he could see the demon pleading with an unseen presence hovering above him. Against the rustle of hundreds of black wings, the demon's pitiful cries for forgiveness rose into an unforgiving sky, but it was too late. A dark shape reflected in its eyes. The creature seemed dazed, unable to comprehend what was happening, and then, in the blink of an eye, he was flung up into the darkness, his screams echoing across the heavens before they faded from existence forever.

Looking up from the stone floor, Leo watched in amazement as the dark orb began to move away. It had taken on the appearance of a gigantic black nest swarming with angry insects, and as the light from the sun reflected against it, Leo could see that it was crawling with thousands of pairs of moving black wings—the wings of an army of demons that were clinging to its surface as it retreated from the earth, leaving a ghostly black trail in its wake that drifted in the eerie stillness.

Slowly, the chilled breeze returned, filling Leo's lungs with the pine-scented aroma of the forest as the black orb departed. The ancient structure was now gone, converted to a grayish dust, and lying a few feet away, Adrian Acerbi was curled in a defensive ball next to Alexis, peering out at a world he scarcely remembered. To him it seemed as if he had just awakened from a long nightmare, and lying next to them, the body of Steig Lundahl lay stretched out on the ground, his unblinking eyes staring up at a clear blue sky.

"Leo!"

Looking up, Leo saw Morelli standing over him.

"What happened?"

Trying to clear his mind, Leo shook his head and sat up. "Didn't you see it?"

"You mean the light?"

Leo pointed to the sky. "The star … the dark star!"

"No. All I saw was a flash of bright light that blinded me for a few seconds, and when I was finally able to see again, the stone structure was gone. You were just lying here on the ground." Morelli lifted a bottle of water to Leo's parched lips and tried to make him drink.

"I think they need it more than I do." Leo nodded to the huddled figures lying a few feet away.

272

Following Leo's gaze, Morelli almost dropped the water when he saw the body of Steig Lundahl lying next to Adrian and Alexis.

"His eyes," Morelli said, looking at Adrian. "They're no longer black! Is he still …"

"No, he's free from the demon's grip now."

"What about Steig?"

"I believe his direct confrontation with the demon was too much for his aged heart. In the end he did what any father would do. He tried to sacrifice himself for his son, but the demon was jerked away by something before it could take his soul.

"The father will take the place of the son!" Morelli repeated out loud. "So that's what that passage in the code was referring to."

"I believe many of our questions have been answered today, Anthony. Steig was right. There was no Antichrist. Satan had a rebellious demon on his hands. I spoke to him."

"You spoke to him!?" Morelli unconsciously backed away. "To speak to a demon that has revealed itself to you is to invite him into your soul."

Leo touched the gold cross hanging from his neck. "I wouldn't worry too much about him anymore. He's been banished from the earth plane forever. I saw it happen with my own eyes. You might say that, in a strange way, Satan was just forced to save the world from one of his own. Just like the time when he was expelled from heaven after he tried to seize God's throne for himself, Lucifer was also forced to expel one of his most trusted dark angels. It seems that even the devil has to watch his back."

"But I was standing right here, Leo." Morelli gazed up into the sky. "There wasn't any dark star. There was only a flash of bright light. I don't understand."

"I think your vision from outside the circle was much different from what I observed inside, Anthony, but I believe we both witnessed the hand of God at work." Leo slowly lifted himself to his feet and both men walked over to Adrian and Alexis. Together, they lifted them from the ground and said a prayer over Steig Lundahl's body before leading them from the field. Behind them, the circle of stone had completely disappeared, and after taking a few steps, they stopped, stunned by what they saw in front of them.

The depressions in the earth that had dotted a field full of blackened headstones were now gone, and instead of the moss-covered mounds of churned black soil, the field was now covered with spring wildflowers that undulated across a green meadow filled with upright headstones that looked like they had just been scrubbed clean.

273

"It appears that the souls that were taken from this field by the demon have been released back into God's hands, Leo," Morelli said, taking in a breath of fresh air. "I have no doubt that Jonas Lundahl is looking down on us right now, and Marcus and Steig are with him. You finally finished what Jonas tried to accomplish over a hundred and forty years ago."

Voices in the trees caused Leo to look toward the edge of the field just as the others emerged from the forest. Now fully recovered, Evita ran to Leo, but as the others approached they stopped dead in their tracks when they saw the bewildered-looking figure of Adrian Acerbi standing next to Alexis.

Alon took a menacing step forward. "Is that who I think it is?"

Leo held out a hand and blocked his advance. "Yes, and he's no longer a danger to anyone. He's been released from the demon's grip and he's under my protection until we can get him to a safe place."

"What happened to the big circle of stone that was supposed to be here?" Alon asked, his attention diverted from Adrian to the empty field.

"It's gone," Leo whispered back hoarsely. "We're all safe now."

Alon instinctively kept his distance as John stepped forward "We know we weren't supposed to come this far, Leo, but we had to tell you. Something's happened in Rome."

Leo recoiled. "What?"

"Relax, Leo," Evita said, seeing the fear return to his eyes. "We have good news for a change, and we thought Lev should be the one to tell you since he received the call."

Standing on shaking legs, Leo was still breathing heavily from his encounter with the demon when Lev walked over to him with the satellite phone in his hand. "I just had a very interesting discussion with Cardinal McCulley, Your Holiness."

Leo shook his head, wondering if his hearing had been affected. "What did you just call me?"

"Your Holiness," Lev repeated. "The conclave just voted for you in absentia. You're the new pope, Leo!"

The Shepherd of the Church!" Morelli shouted. "I should have known! You became the Shepherd of the Church when you were facing the demon inside the circle of stone!"

Leo felt the blood rushing from his head as the others crowded around to congratulate him. Still dazed by events, he could barely comprehend what was happening. He felt someone squeezing his hand, and as he looked to his side, he found himself gazing into a pair of liquid brown eyes blinking back at him.

"Do you know what name you'll choose?" Evita asked.

Taking her in his arms, Leo closed his eyes and held her close. He felt as though his legs were about to fail him as he struggled to smile.

"That's OK, Leo," Lev said. "You've had quite a day. There will be plenty of time to deal with those kinds of questions after you've had time to rest."

"I haven't even decided if I'll accept yet," Leo said weakly.

Evita pushed a strand of hair from his forehead. "But you will, my love ... you will. The Church needs you now ... and I'll be right by your side."

EPILOGUE

With summer's warmth returning to the streets of Rome, pods of tourists sat clustered together in elevated groups on the Spanish Steps, soaking up the sun, reading, or just slurping gelato as they went about the time-honored tradition of people watching.

On the street below, a little red motor scooter sped by, the white robes of its rider flowing out behind him as he swooped around a corner and came to a stop. Instantly the people on the steps were on their feet. Globs of gelato splattered on the ground, books were dropped, and the flash of cameras filled the air as people rushed to catch a glimpse of the new pope stopping at one of his favorite stands to buy flowers before heading across the piazza to have lunch with a woman who had become so famous that she was known to everyone by her first name alone—Evita.

Arriving on the heels of the pope, a phalanx of Swiss Guards jumped from their black SUVs and tried to form a barrier between their impulsive charge and the hundreds of admirers who were swarming around him, shoving their children to the front of the line for a quick blessing while reaching out to touch him as he passed.

Francois Leander was the first to reach the new pope, his eyes wide as he scanned the crowd for potential threats. "You can't keep jumping on your little motorbike and taking off like this without your security escort, Your Holiness."

"I can't change who I am, Francois," Leo said. "I won't be locked away in the jeweled box of the Vatican. This is where the Shepherd of the Church belongs ... out here among the people."

"And I agree with you, sir, but please, all we ask is that you notify us before you go speeding off into Rome on that ... thing!"

Leo smiled back at his ruffled protector and winked. "I'll try, Francois … I promise. I have no desire to make your job any more difficult than it already is."

"We'll see, Your Holiness … we'll see, but ever since you've become the new pope I keep discovering new gray hairs when I look in the mirror every morning."

"I believe mine's also turned a shade lighter," Leo said, running a hand through his hair as they approached a sidewalk café surrounded by Vatican security men. "It looks like Evita has arrived."

"Yes, sir. Five minutes ago." Francois scowled at the growing crowd. "At least she lets us know when she's going somewhere."

Walking over to her table, Leo held out the flowers and kissed her on the cheek, eliciting cheers and applause from the parade of people following in his wake.

As soon as he was seated, Leo shook out his napkin and smiled across the table. "There's nothing quite as enjoyable as a quiet romantic lunch together all alone."

Evita waved to the crowd before turning her attention back to Leo. "The Carmela just arrived in port, so we have only a few minutes to enjoy a little espresso. Lev and the others are expecting us on board the yacht for lunch, and I thought it would be a nice way to reconnect with our friends without the frenzy of activity that follows you wherever you go."

"Sounds wonderful … especially if Hadar is doing the cooking. By the way, are you enjoying our little house in the country?"

"If you're talking about the palazzo Morelli gave us as a wedding gift, then yes, of course … it's beautiful. I love the gardens. I only wish you were home more often, but I understand the constraints of your position." Evita lifted her small cup. "*Todo el que quiera military para Dios* … to whoever desires to serve as the soldier of God."

The two touched their tiny white cups together and gazed into each other's eyes.

"I'm glad you chose the name Ignatius for your papal name," Evita said. "Pope Ignatius … it has a nice Spanish ring to it, but more than that it reminds people of who you are."

"And what would that be, my dear?"

"A soldier, of course. I think most people are aware of the fact that Ignatius of Loyola was a soldier before he founded the Jesuit order, and by taking his name you have let the people know you are here to fight for them. I think he would be very proud that the second Jesuit pope in Church history has adopted his name."

"Papa … Papa!" The shouts of endearment from the Italian crowd were growing louder as Francois herded Leo and Evita into the back of an SUV and sped away though the crowded piazza into the narrow streets of the city. Thirty minutes later, the arrival of the papal entourage was announced in a blaze of flashing lights from a line of motorcycles and escort vehicles that entered the Puerto Romano harbor and stopped on the dock below the yacht.

"I see His Holiness has arrived," Alon said, peering through the smoke wafting from the Bar BQ grill on the top deck as he flipped an unrecognizable piece of charred meat.

"I hope you're not thinking of offering that to the pope," Nava scolded. "What are you doing?"

"They told me Leo was coming for lunch. I just thought …"

"Close the lid on that thing and change your shirt. Hadar has been busy all morning preparing a special lunch."

As a chastened Alon scurried away like a mad crab, Nava looked over the railing just as Leo and Evita stepped from the boarding stairs onto the main deck and looked out over all the linen-covered tables set up under a blue and white awning. A cool breeze was blowing from the water, lifting the corners of the tablecloths as everyone found their seats and tried to keep from staring at Leo in his new white cassock.

Rising from his chair next to Leo, Lev tapped his glass. "I'd like to welcome everyone back aboard the Carmela. You'll be glad to know she's been totally refurbished since we returned from Norway, and we've added a special papal suite now that our friend Leo here has become Pope Ignatius."

Leo could feel the color rising in his cheeks. Yes, it was true; he was now the pope, and he was hoping that his friends wouldn't treat him any differently.

"I'd also like to congratulate our good friend Anthony Morelli on becoming a Prince of the Church," Lev continued. "Although his modesty would force him to disagree with me, I think his promotion to Cardinal has been long overdue."

Dr. Diaz, swaying in his chair at the next table from too many pre-lunch cocktails, tried to focus on the pope's table. "I couldn't help but notice that Morelli became a cardinal right after he gave Leo his country house."

His remark cast a sudden pall over the proceedings until Leo burst out laughing. "Thank you, Dr. Diaz. I was just sitting here wondering if any of you were going to start treating me any differently."

"I don't think there's any chance of that, my friend," Lev said. "We all know you too well."

Through the doors leading from the main salon, crewmembers began flowing out onto the covered deck with trays of appetizers, and for the next hour the food continued to arrive until everyone finally surrendered to Hadar's culinary onslaught.

Throughout lunch, the chosen ones had made a point of passing Leo's table to pay their respects to the new pontiff. Daniel and Sarah, John and Ariella, Alon and Nava, Moshe and Hadar … all except for Javier Mendoza, who was busy trying to convince his well-oiled friend Diaz that he should go below to his stateroom for a much-needed nap.

The cool breeze continued to wash over the deck as Lev stood and invited Leo to join him for a stroll along the deck to the bow of the yacht. Reaching into his pocket, he produced a cigar and lit it with a match as the two old friends stood looking out over the harbor.

"You know, Leo, this time last year I never thought I would see this sight again."

"I also had my doubts."

"You, Leo?"

"Yes. Most people never realized it, but I spent the entire year living in fear … fear of the unknown. I could feel something coming, but I didn't know what it was until that day in Norway when I entered that circle of stone."

"What did you see, Leo?"

"It's not so much what I saw as what I felt. There was something else there … I could feel its dark presence all around me, and it was stronger than the evil I sensed coming from the demon. There's no doubt in my mind that Satan himself was present that day. Satan's grand general had rebelled against him … a fatal mistake when you're dealing with mankind's oldest enemy. If the demon *Agaliarept* hadn't rebelled against his master, he'd still be out there somewhere, threatening our very existence. He may be gone forever, but others will take his place, and they could be even worse."

"What do you think happened to him?"

"That's a question I continually ask myself. We know what happened to Lucifer when he was cast from heaven by God, but what happens to a rogue demon when he is banished from his world of darkness is a theological question I can't even begin to answer. The cultural desolation now spreading around the world in the absence of moral criticism has given Satan even greater power, and as a result, I believe some within his legions have begun to grow envious. There are other ancient relics out there that serve as doorways for evil, and those who deny God and choose to ignore the presence of evil have been rendered incapable of resisting the creatures that will inevitably use them to enter our world. Every day more and more people are filled with aimless self-interest, giving little thought to the harm their selfish actions have on others, and someday soon the real Antichrist will arrive and step out onto the fertile ground they've created."

Lev gazed back into the green eyes of his longtime friend. "It doesn't sound like you're holding out much hope for the future, Leo. If what you say is true, it sounds like the battle is already lost."

"Not all is lost, my friend. I also felt the angels around me in the field that day. They were watching … waiting to see what Satan would do, and they are still around us. They nurture the greater nature of our species, and as the pope, it is my job to call upon them to bring a spiritual cleansing to the world. There is still hope. God hasn't abandoned us yet as the Evil One would have us believe. That is my message to the faithful, and as a soldier of the cross, it is my duty to spread that message until the day I draw my final breath."

Lev leaned out over the railing and watched the tiny fish swimming around the bow of the yacht in the greenish water below. He was standing next to a man who had just been called upon to follow the same path of others who had been called the *fishers of men* by Christ. If anyone could stem the tide of apathy toward God now spreading across the world, it was Pope Ignatius.

"Have you heard from Colette lately?" Lev asked.

"Yes, she called the other day to tell me Adrian's youthful appearance has returned, and he's readjusting to normal life as the boy he once was. According to him, it all seemed like a bad dream. He barely remembers any of it, but he still shies away from leaving the farmhouse in Foix. He prefers to spend his days reading in Eduardo's upstairs library. I'm afraid only time will tell if he was left scarred by the experience."

"And Alexis?"

"She's no longer condemned to a life of loneliness in that little white house. She inherited the bulk of Steig Lundahl's estate and lives in his mountain lodge now, but according to Gunnar she also rarely ventures out except for occasional visits with Colette and Adrian. He told me she refuses to discuss what happened. I also heard from Gael. Our Cathar friends have returned to their beloved mountains and are rebuilding their castle. He said he saw the two pilots who flew you back from Norway."

"They're living in France?"

"No, Barcelona. They live there with their girlfriends now and have given up flying. One is an artist and the other opened a tapas bar."

Lev smiled as he tapped the ash from his cigar. "Gael also told me that the joy has returned to the simple lives of his people. Most have taken up farming and tend to the vineyards in the valley, but others are rebuilding the castle in preparation for the day when the real Antichrist arrives.

"I hate to say it, Leo ... I mean, Your Holiness, but they are a strange group of people. I mean, don't get me wrong, they're our friends and I will always hold a special place in my heart for them, but they seem to have a penchant for oversimplifying life. They shake off the bad and welcome the good. It's like they're living in two different worlds."

"Maybe that's why they're all so happy most of the time, Lev. They seem to have struck that magical balance in life the rest of us are always trying so hard to find. They embrace all that is good and reject that which they know to be evil. I've noticed those same qualities in Evita, and I strive every day to become more like her. She's helping me to create an ecumenical council made up of different religions from all over the globe to help bring about the spiritual healing it so desperately needs. We have our first meeting next week. Maybe you and the others can be a part of it."

"You know we're always here for you, Your Holiness."

Leo nodded his head and stared up into a cloudless sky. "I don't think I'll ever get used to being called that."

Lev took a last puff from his cigar and let the bluish smoke drift off with the fresh sea breeze. "It seems to me that I remember you making a similar statement when you became a cardinal. With great power comes great responsibility, and I can't think of a better man for the job. You'll be a great pope, Leo ... the kind of pope the world needed to follow in the footsteps of Pope Michael."

"Thank you for saying that, Lev, because every day I ask myself what he would have done in a certain situation. If ever a man burned so brightly with the fire of genius, it was Marcus Lundahl. He left behind some very big shoes to fill."

Lev smiled as he turned to look back toward the city. "I think you'll find they are a very good fit for you, Your Holiness."

"You're a good friend, Lev Wasserman." Leo grinned. "Too bad you're not a Catholic. I was wondering. Do you ever go back to that fountain in Jerusalem ... the one with all the lion statues?"

Lev flicked the remainder of his cigar overboard and leaned against the rail. "Funny you should mention that. I go there often. It's a very peaceful place, and it reminds me of all of us … the chosen ones. We will always be God's Lions, Your Holiness, and I think Satan just heard us roar.

OTHER BOOKS BY JOHN LYMAN

GOD'S LIONS – THE SECRET CHAPEL

GOD'S LIONS – RISE OF THE BEAST

GOD'S LIONS – THE DARK RUIN

THE DEEP GREEN

JEKYLL ISLAND

Made in the USA
Monee, IL
18 November 2019

16998883R00167